THE TRIGGERMAN

by

Matt Schafer

For
Shelly, Ronan, Alia, Brody
and
Mom

THURSDAY

Chapter 1

It's amazing what a man in a suit can get away with in this town.

That thought passed through Blake Sergeant's mind as he walked through a hotel lobby on his way to kill a man. This victim wasn't his first and wouldn't be his last. Tonight, he was in the lobby of a nondescript hotel chain in Times Square with marble floors and glass chandeliers.

Blake was a hair over six feet tall with black hair, cut short, and built like a lineman on a football team. He made sure his suit wouldn't get him noticed in New York. Years ago, he read an article about a tailor who ran a business selling suits to Wall Street investors. He didn't have a store. He carried around a booklet of fabrics and the high rollers would pick the color of their suits. Custom fit. Custom made. His cheapest suits started at a couple grand a piece.

Blake's suit was bought on clearance at a retail chain in a Saint Paul suburb. When he bought the suit he was currently wearing, he received a gray suit for free. The franchise owner guaranteed he was going to like the way he looked. He was right. He did. Neither suit would stand out in a crowd.

Sergeant glided unseen through the lobby. Past the bellhop who was busy checking out a blonde walking to the hotel bar. Past the security guard who was distracted by an unruly customer at the front desk. In his peripheral vision, Blake saw the guard standing attentively, facing the angry customer. The customer had a southern accent and a yellow button up shirt. He noticed a man with short black hair sitting in the hotel lobby, pretending to read a newspaper. The guy's hair was dyed black and he looked like he was in his mid-thirties. Premature graying?

Sergeant caught an empty elevator and rode to the seventeenth floor. He stood in the back and stared at his mobile device, scrolling through articles on the web, appearing oblivious to the surveillance camera above him. He exited and took the stairs to the thirtieth floor as he rehearsed two weeks before.

***

Nicolay Belov poured two glasses of wine and anxiously checked his watch. He was in a hotel room across town his suite at the Waldorf Astoria and his security detail, minus one man in the lobby and another wandering the hotel. This room was registered under the name John Heinz, which happened to be the same name on his fake driver's license and credit card. It took months to create Mr. Heinz's identification but the time spent was worth the effort to preserve Belov's reputation and business interests.

A 16-year-old by the name of Jenny Camarillo was on her way up to Mr. Heinz's room for a very lucrative night of sex and booze. While Belov's little secret would most certainly bring shame upon his family, business interests and his country, the truth was he didn't need to jump through these hoops for a piece of ass. He enjoyed the thrill of the chase. Americans were narrow minded when it came to their young girls, and plucking a piece of the forbidden fruit as he was doing business with their country was simply too decadent to resist. That's what made nights like these so exhilarating.

He took a sip of his wine and rechecked the notes he scribbled on his notepad. Jenny was supposed to jump on the subway after school. That would put her in the hotel at around 5:15. A missed train here or a long wait there could cost her a few minutes. It was rush hour in the city that never sleeps.

He heard a knock on the door and walked toward the main entrance of his suite.

"Is that you Jenny?" he said with a thick Russian accent.

No answer.

"Come on in Jenny, the door is unlocked."

***

Sergeant pulled on a pair of leather gloves and fastened a silencer to his nine-millimeter pistol. He carried a similar sidearm for eight years as a cop. He bought this particular weapon at a gun show outside of Indianapolis. He checked his watch. 5:15. Showtime.

He walked through the hallway of the thirtieth floor as if he owned the place, straight to the suites. Clearly his target paid top dollar for the accommodations. Sergeant peered into the eyehole and knocked on the door.

"Is that you, Jenny?"

The target came into view. Sergeant looked at the photograph in his jacket pocket and back through the peep hole. Target verified.

"Come on in Jenny, the door is unlocked."

***

Belov took a breath and tried to remember his pseudonym as the door opened. He was John, today. He loved the moment when he finally got to see someone he met online in person. Would she look the same way she did in her photos?

The knob turned and door opened swiftly. Too swiftly. Instead of a teenage girl Belov was staring into the expressionless eyes of a grown man. He froze. He had feared something like this happening but told himself that fear was misguided paranoia.

The man raised his gloved hand and fired once. Twice. Belov never felt the bullet shattering the cartilage that made up the bridge of his nose. He only saw a brilliant flash of light as he fell backward.

***

Sergeant fired once and blasted a hole in his latest victim's face. The second shot ripped through his throat as his head was snapping back. The third, fourth and fifth shots ripped through the victim's chest creating new stains in his hotel bathrobe.

Belov's lifeless body hit the floor with a crash, splashing merlot across the room. The first shot knocked him out and the next four ensured he wouldn't wake up. Sergeant walked up to his lifeless body and fired four more rounds.

He turned, walked out the way he came in and moved to the stairwell. He unscrewed his silencer and stuck it back into his laptop bag, which also held the holster for his nine-millimeter. His gloves went in next. He made his way down the stairwell back to the seventeenth floor. There was no reason for the number, only ensuring it was nowhere near the floor where he killed a man.

He entered the elevator and quickly retrieved his phone. He stared at the screen like a zombie, barely acknowledging the older couple he shared the ride with. The husband had a Boston accent and they were looking forward to dinner and a play. In three minutes, he was outside the lobby and climbing into a cab. In 10 minutes, he was on a ferry to Hoboken, New Jersey. He threw Belov's picture in the trash can at the ferry station. He tossed the silencer in a waste basket on the way to his vehicle. The key to a great escape was pretending that you had nothing to run from. That was his trademark.

He tossed his suit jacket and tie into the back of his Escape and climbed in the front. He unbuttoned the top buttons of his shirt and started the vehicle. An old Bouncing Souls song filled the air with noise as Sergeant pulled out of the parking lot and patiently waited to get onto I-95. Stuck in traffic. Inching along. Getting away with murder.

Belov's security director would find his body at 7:30, when he was instructed to check in. By then, Sergeant was south of Newark gliding along with the window rolled down and "Milk Lizard" by The Dillinger Escape Plan blaring on the CD player.

Sergeant left pieces of his weapon in several trashcans along the turnpike. Firearms were easy to come by. In three years as a professional killer, Sergeant had purchased different varieties of weapons from pawn shops, gun shows and pretty much any venue that wasn't going to bother him with a background check. He was always prepared with a hard luck story involving overzealous cops and an ex-wife. Gun salesmen always had ex-wives.

He pulled into a motel parking lot in Alexandria, Virginia two rush hour commutes later. The motel was a few miles south on Route 1 not too far from the Woodrow Wilson Bridge. Just a few short years earlier he patrolled these streets in a black and white squad car but he knew nobody was going to recognize him. He had no reservation but they had an extra room. He paid cash and the motel cashier asked no questions.

Once settled in his room, he set a pen and pad next to his bed and set an alarm on his phone. He laid in bed waiting for his adrenaline to die down. He listened to the soft buzz of traffic passing by his room from the nearby highway and was asleep ten minutes later.

If asked by the one other human being who knew of his occupation why he did what he did, Blake would say the answer was simple. He killed for money. That wasn't the truth. The truth was he was killing to remember the worst night of his life.

Blake suffered a debilitating injury nearly four years ago, and like an old car, his mind wasn't what it used to be. Most of the lights were on and someone was home. The problem was some of the rooms remained darkened and he hadn't yet figured out how to light them. That was the case for the room that contained all the memories from when his family died.

The only time he could remember that night was when he killed. He couldn't explain it. He wished there was another way, yet here he was, hours removed from snuffing out Nicolay Belov, hoping for a chance to dream about a memory.

The dream began the way it always did. Sergeant was still a highway patrolman nestled away in Alexandria in the parking lot for the Metro station off Eisenhower Avenue. A small hill from the adjacent parking lot helped conceal his vehicle from anyone coming from Old Town after a few drinks, taking a back road to avoid cops. The perch also provided a good vantage point to ensure the working people leaving the train station could retreat to their cars in peace. He waited like a sentry for his next drunk driver or a possible call. Whichever came first.

His cell phone vibrated and he looked at the caller-ID. It was Cade Stuckley. He didn't answer the call. He was on duty and would call back later. Then came the call on the radio. House fire off Huntington. They called out the address and it was his home.

He remembered cranking the sirens and flying at breakneck speed to his home. He rushed inside past the flames, noticing that he probably wouldn't be able to exit through the front door. He found his wife Nicole and daughter Annabelle – Anni for short – both in Anni's room. Both had gunshot wounds to the chest. Nicole had two more bullet holes in the middle of her baby bump. Their son was due in two months. They knew he was a boy, but hadn't decided upon a name.

Sergeant felt the urge to panic and resisted. He carried Anni out first, rushing her down to the basement and out the back door, whispering into her ear that everything was going to be okay. She muttered something, but "Daddy" was all he heard. He looked at the blood from her exit wound on his hand and it looked black, not crimson. That wasn't good.

He rushed back up and grabbed Nicole and carried her down. She was almost lifeless though he told himself he heard a pulse. He wondered if he should have carried her first.

As he was laying Nicole on the grass next to Anni, he felt a bullet graze his left shoulder and it flipped him on his back. He took cover behind a large oak in their back yard. He spotted the shooter. 5'7 maybe 5'8, knit cap, about two hundred pounds, Middle Eastern descent, mustache. Portly. Two more shots fired. Sergeant took cover and drew his weapon.

He radioed for backup and heard sirens in the background. The shooter was nestled behind a makeshift garden in their back yard. They bought the smaller house in part because of the relatively large yard. The shooter fired another shot Sergeant's way and took cover.

"Drop your weapon!" Blake yelled, but they both knew that wasn't happening. He fired another round, trying to draw the shooter out. The shooter responded by firing a shot at Nicole's body.

Blake screamed in response and fired two more shots charging out into the open to defend his family. He was exposed. The shooter fired twice and the first shot missed. The second blasted through a tree branch and hit Blake in the head.

He was onto the part of the dream that never made sense.

There was a flash of light, then an image.

He was laying in a hospital bed.

In his dream, he closed his eyes and open them again.

He's in his squad car running the license plate on a Prius, calling it into his radio, "Virginia YLC 68 . . ." He can't get a good look at the last number.

He squinted to make out the last number and another flash of brilliant light flashed before his eyes as if he were staring at the sun.

He's standing outside a vehicle of a man he just pulled over. Looking at his driver's license. He looks at the driver. African American. 25-years-old. *Something isn't adding up.*

Another flash of light.

He's in uniform, walking toward the desk sergeant. He has something to tell him, and he's trying to find the right words to say.

Another flash.

He's sitting in a conference room in the police station. Not an interrogation room, but one of the rooms they use for team meetings. He's in uniform. Detective Bob Hamilton is sitting with him. Hamilton was investigating Nicole, Anni and his unborn son's murders. Hamilton places Blake's hand on his knee and says something, but his voice sounds distant.

"You're a damned good cop, Blake," he says.

Another flash.

Darkness.

"Anni!" Blake yelled as he shot up, out of the motel bed. He dove to the left side, taking cover while reaching for a sidearm. All he felt was a pair of boxer briefs. His dream was over. He scanned the room for an unseen memory and sat back down. He took a breath, grabbed his note pad and pen, and began scribbling notes. Everything he could remember about the dream.

Sights. Smells. It didn't matter. He wrote things he had witnessed before in vivid detail, hoping perhaps he caught a glimpse of something he hadn't seen before.

After this routine, he would take a handful of melatonin, and drift back to sleep, into another dream.

He heard a song in the distance, but not just any song. It was one of the most irritating song written in the mid-nineties. *Wake Up Boo* by The Boo Radleys.

"Turn it off," he said aloud.

The song continued.

"Turn it off, I'm awake."

The catchy jingle rang on with horns in the background.

"You know you love it," Nicole said as she walked into his room wearing her red bathrobe. Her hair was still wet from the shower. She glided across the room and kissed him on the lips. He kissed her back. He could smell the fresh scent of the shampoo she used. Something she bought where she got her hair done. It was expensive, but she liked it.

"No, I don't," he said. "It's a terrible song."

"It's so uplifting," she cooed as she pulled open the curtain in their room revealing a fresh ray of sunlight.

"Did you know the guitar player wrote this song the morning after an acid trip?"

"And your point?"

She pounced on the bed and kissed him on the cheek.

"I love it," she snuggled against him and he wrapped his arms around her. "It reminds me of a better time, more innocent. College. Before 9/11. Before working in the ER."

"Before the night shift," he added. He hated to admit she was right.

They heard Anni stirring in the other room.

"I have to get ready," Nicole said, and slid off the bed.

"Better hurry up if you want a shower."

He relaxed and rested his eyes for another moment.

"Wake up, Boo," he heard her call out.

He opened his eyes again, and the song continued to play. It was his alarm. He had slept another five hours in a shitty motel.

Anni wasn't stirring. Nicole wasn't getting ready in the other room. They weren't in their bedroom. Anni and Nicole were dead. His bedroom burned down years ago. All that was left was the song she used to torment him with and he didn't hate it anymore. He clung to every last note and the innocence it symbolized.

He shut off the song, sat up and read his notes from his nightmare.

"Nothing new," he exclaimed to an empty motel room where the only other activity was the wheezing and percolating of a cheap coffee maker.

He closed his eyes and concentrated again, trying to remember any other details from his dream. A few moments passed and he scribbled a few more notes into the note pad. He studied his own thoughts on the paper and resolved that they might make more sense when he was back in St. Paul.

FRIDAY

Chapter 2

Jake Cavalera stared into the mirror and marveled at the man he saw looking back. He wore a black suit with an FBI issued nine-millimeter holstered under his jacket. His black hair was cropped short like a Marine out of boot camp. Emerging from the neckline of his dress shirt was a jagged edge of ink from a prison tattoo from a 10-month stint in San Quentin. For the better part of the past three years, he was Solomon Ortiz, a drug dealer turned smuggler for the Saavedra cartel which was now defunct with most of its officers warming beds in federal prisons across the country. A military style haircut replaced a bald head and a suit and tie replaced his usual attire of jeans and a wife beater.

Now he was back to being Special Agent Cavalera, fresh from his last court appearance that ultimately spelled the end of one of the largest crystal meth operations in San Diego. He had flown back to D.C. from LAX the night before. His undercover stint was originally supposed to last a few weeks during an investigation into the murder of three FBI agents in Tijuana. When he serendipitously worked his way into the inner circle of a cartel that the DEA had been trying to penetrate, three weeks turned into three years.

He had spent the last two months in his new unit in Washington, D.C. and the previous four months in Quantico under intense protection. His work was on its way to becoming legendary within the bureau, but that notoriety also meant his career as an undercover agent was effectively over. It would be a long time before he would ever be able to safely walk the streets in California. He could care less.

He grew up in Texas outside Austin. His dad was a high school teacher and baseball coach and his mom taught chemistry. He initially wanted to play baseball but joined the FBI when it was clear he would never make it out of the minors. Life as an undercover agent was nearly all he knew, and he was ready for that life to be over.

His new assignment was with a special Washington-based team that focused most of its time on investigating serial killers whose exploits crossed multiple state lines. He had limited relevant experience on paper but in his mind, investigations were investigations.

He walked across the hall to his new desk and had poured his first cup of coffee when he when he heard his name. Special Agent in Charge Denise Towe stood outside the door of her office summoning him for an impromptu meeting.

He knocked on the door of Towe's office and caught a brief glimpse of her office view of the hotel across the street as she invited him in. Towe had been in the FBI for twenty-nine years and had slowly made her way up the ranks, starting at a time when female agents were not a common sight. Standing just over five feet tall, she gained a reputation for an unparalleled aptitude for cracking cold cases. She had built a career on opening old files and finding details that her male counterparts missed. She heard the words "bitch" mumbled under agents' breaths more than once and loved every moment that vindication brought along.

For the last ten years, she had largely been out of the field and responsible for budgets, inter-agency coordination and managing special agents. Cavalera and Towe hit it off immediately during his screening process as she saw a ton of potential in him as an investigator.

"Have a seat Cavalera."

He followed her cue and stole another look out her office window.

"Are you glad to be back in D.C.?"

"I'm glad to be out of San Diego."

"Three years undercover," she mused, "How does it feel to finally close that book?"

"Weird," he responded. "For years, I was Solomon Ortiz. It was like I knew this whole other guy and spent every day with him for three years. It's a trip."

"You gonna miss him?"

"No ma'am," he smiled, "I never liked the son of a bitch."

They shared a laugh.

"You're gonna fit in here," she said, as she topped off her cup of coffee. She offered to do the same for Cavalera and he politely declined. "Speaking of which, you're going to have a new partner."

"So I've heard."

"Have you had a chance to meet Agent Gable?"

"Briefly," he said, "I was on my way out to San Diego and I think he was just in from Afghanistan. I only know what I've heard."

"And what have you heard?"

"Tough guy. Real good investigator. He's spent a lot of time overseas."

"Try ten of the last fifteen years. His wife divorced him right before this last deployment. The last couple of weeks were the first time he's seen his kids since."

He shook his head solemnly. "This job is hard enough on a family, but to add the Marine Corps to the mix? That's a lot. And why so many deployments?"

"Good question," she responded. "Word on the street is that this tour he just finished might be his last one for a while."

"And he's coming back on a Friday?"

"It's how he likes to operate. His first day back from deployment is usually the last day of the workweek. It gives him a chance to get reacclimated."

"Unless there's a Friday afternoon shit show."

"In any case," she took a sip of her coffee, "Steve Gable has been through a lot. I worry about him. I'd appreciate it if you kept an eye on him. Let me know if you see any signs that maybe he could benefit from a little more time with the family."

"Are you saying what I think you're saying, ma'am?"

"What I'm saying is I've seen a lot of agents who spent less time in the desert and they came home with demons. I don't want to poison the well with a new partner and I hate that I need to ask this of you. But, his last partner retired last year. Just keep an eye on him. Can you do that, Agent Cavalera?"

"Yes ma'am."

"Thank you," Towe returned to her seat behind her desk. "Gable will be here in a couple hours and I'm sure I will have a new assignment for the both of you."

Cavalera left the office and made his way back to his desk. Across from his relatively clean workstation was another desk that looked like it hadn't been occupied in nearly a year. A Marine Corps coffee mug sat next to a label that read "Stephen Gable."

Unbeknownst to him, the killer he would spend the weekend investigating was sleeping just across the Potomac River.

Chapter 3

Blake Sergeant's hotel had a makeshift gym which featured a treadmill that probably hadn't been used in six months. He christened it with a five-mile jog. He generally preferred the outdoors but was keeping a low profile.

While his theory of acting like a man with nothing to hide might have allowed him a little sunshine, something about this last job left him feeling uneasy. Everything went as planned. He was in and out unnoticed. The application he launched before walking into the hotel lobby in New York City released a virus that scrambled the hotel's computer network that included its surveillance system.

Instead of watching Sergeant's exploits, security guards watched a thirty minute loop from the previous hour. The data from his crime was long gone. Unrecorded. Intuitively, he knew that, but the uneasiness remained.

After his workout, Blake made his way to a restaurant located a few miles south of his motel.

Cade Stuckley walked into the diner and found Blake in a booth in the back drinking coffee and reading the paper. Blake and Stuckley had been best friends for nearly two decades, and had been business partners for the past three years. Though he would never say it aloud, Cade was pleased that Blake was already seated.

Through his adolescence, Cade was usually one of the smallest kids in the classroom. Even after his final growth spurt during his second year in the Marine Corps, he was still several inches shorter than his partner in crime. What he didn't have in stature, he made up for with an engineer's mind that allowed him to understand computers at a time when the world needed guys who understood computers. – smart guys like Cade Stuckley. Because he knew his way around a computer, he made a point to blatantly disregard dress codes by wearing trendy blazers over T-shirts and wearing sunglasses indoors. He grew a beard, but trimmed it to match the latest fashion trends. On this particular morning, a thin thread of brown facial hair made its way from his sideburn, across his jaw line to a goatee in the of his face. His hair was brown and spiky, with frosted tips.

At Blake's request, he opted for subtle attire on this particular morning, wearing dark khakis and a shiny, maroon button-up shirt and bright red dress shoes. Despite his flamboyant quirks and arrogant persona, Cade was as loyal of a friend to Blake as the day was long. He had his old buddy's back, which was one of the many reasons that Blake accepted his friend's eccentric tendencies.

The bullet that grazed Blake's head on the fateful night his family died left him in a coma for six weeks. When Blake woke up, he found a world that was nothing like the one he left just weeks before. His family was dead and buried. The doctors didn't think he would ever wake up, and Nicole's family decided to move forward with funeral plans. By the time he woke up, the only thing left of them were two headstones in Minnesota.

Everything he loved and worked for was gone, and his mind wasn't what it used to be. After months of rehabilitation, he eventually needed to acknowledge his days as a cop were over.

He got low. Real low. During those darkest days, it was Cade Stuckley who arrived at his doorstep with a twelve pack of beer and some bad ideas. He eventually persuaded Blake to join in on his venture and the rest was history. Cade handled the business end of their operation and Blake was the triggerman.

They agreed early on to share limited information about the victims to help preserve some level of plausible deniability, though Blake couldn't help but learn enough about the victims to piece together some obvious truths. They had cornered the market on snuffing out rapists and pedophiles. Most of the time, Blake's work was easy because he was sneaking up on people who unknowingly covered their tracks on the way to their own murder scenes. That dynamic complicated murder investigations. As for the victims, the market made sense. They were bad people. Nobody was going to miss them. Murder investigations were cursory at best, and half the time, investigators wouldn't have known whether to arrest the perpetrator, or give him a medal.

It was a Friday morning. Most Washingtonians were on their way to their respective jobs and this joint was off the beaten path.

The remaining group of patrons included a handful of regulars who worked in nearby offices, travelers passing through and retirees who were sticking doggedly to their routines. The smell of eggs and coffee filled the air as waitresses and busboys shuffled customers in and out of their seats.

Blake asked for a booth in the back, away from the modest bustle of the morning rush. Business was slow enough to give him his wish, and fast enough to have a coded conversation about murder that would go unnoticed.

Belov's murder made the New York Times but the details were vague. The report indicated that a body was found at a hotel with multiple gunshot wounds. The victim's name was not disclosed nor were there any specific details about his security detachment. The article also didn't mention that he was staying in a suite under a false name and had a perfectly adequate hotel room up the street.

"Good morning sunshine," Blake welcomed.

"How was your meeting?" Stuckley responded.

"It went well." Sergeant pushed the newspaper article toward Stuckley, who took a minute to read through the first few paragraphs. "This was the first time I met with a guy who had his own security escort," Blake said as his partner perused the article.

"How many?"

Sergeant paused and looked up at the waitress who had just approached their booth.

"You should try their coffee," Sergeant suggested. "Their omelets are pretty good too."

"What are you getting?"

"I already ordered. Coffee and eggs."

Cade placed his order and went back to the article.

"So his security detail was there?"

"Yup. Two men escorted him in. One big guy, one little guy. The big guy left and was probably patrolling the premises. The little guy stayed in the hotel lobby."

"Doesn't say much in the paper about him."

"Give them a couple of days. This one was risky."

"Yeah, but you pulled it off," Cade looked up and to the left,

"So how's your family?"

Their waitress returned with a fresh pot of coffee, and proceeded to fill their cups. Sergeant smiled politely and thanked her. She smiled back and moved on to the next table outside of earshot.

"They're still dead," Blake responded and sipped his coffee. "We probably shouldn't go back to New York anytime soon."

"Well, your next job is a little closer to home."

Cade slid his full backpack over to Blake under the table. Blake looked down long enough to see the zipper slightly ajar, and the shadow of cash inside. His usual fee fit comfortably in a bank deposit bag.

"What's this?"

"A down payment."

Cade slid a manila folder across the table and Blake quickly grabbed it. Blake recognized the photograph as soon as he opened the folder.

"Hey, this guy is a politician."

"Ex-politician."

"No," Blake read through the attached papers. "He's still a politician. His name's Peterson. I've seen him on TV. He was a congressman from Minnesota. Lives in D.C. now."

"Yeah, and now he's another talking head," Cade responded. "They're a dime a dozen in this town."

Blake thumbed through the documents. He saw a script, along with a signal. According to the document, Peterson was headed to his cabin in northern Minnesota. He was going to receive a surprise visit from an unnamed woman who was paying for Blake's time. If the visit went well, Blake would drive home without ever squeezing the trigger. Their down payment would become their entire fee. If it didn't, Peterson's next television appearance would be a murder mystery. The woman would provide Blake with another cash installment after the job was done.

"This isn't our usual customer, is it?"

Cade didn't respond.

"Is this from your family?"

"You should look at the timeline. It's kind of important." The meeting with Peterson was supposed to take place on Saturday night at 9:00 PM.

"Is it doable?" Cade asked. "Do you need to buy a plane ticket?"

"No. I know where this is," Blake responded. "It's not too far from what was supposed to be my alibi for yesterday."

"Can you do it?"

Blake read through the materials. There was information on the cabin's layout along with photographs. An additional write-up gave details about the neighbors' whereabouts. Whoever wanted this done provided very detailed intel.

"This is for your family, isn't it?" Blake asked again.

"I've got it under control. Do you need to look at your down payment again?"

Blake flipped through the papers, reading the details once more. Peterson's plane landed in Minneapolis at noon on Saturday, and he was expected to drive straight to the cabin. It was easily a six-hour drive, not counting any errands he might want to run.

Peterson would arrive in thirty-two hours. Blake could drive there in twenty-nine, if traffic was cooperative. Blake would have plenty of time to personally survey the area for a nice place to camp out and wait for his victim. With a little luck, he would be back in his motel room by midnight and in church on Sunday morning.

"How much is in there?"

"One hundred thousand. Not counting the 25K from this last job," Cade responded.

"You'll collect eight hundred thousand dollars in cash if this guy dies. With a payout like that, we can lay low for a while. I might spend a few weeks on an island in the Caribbean. You're welcome to tag along, or you can do whatever it is you do when you're not doing this."

The waitress arrived with their food. Blake stacked up the paperwork and set it aside. She provided him with a bottle of Tobasco sauce before he even needed to ask. Said he looked like a *Tobasco kind of guy.* Her sixth sense was going to win her a healthy tip.

He had a bad feeling about the job he completed the night before and wasn't feeling any better about this one. They were playing with fire, carrying out two jobs in less than a week and both targets were high profile. One had his own security detachment and this one was a television personality. They were begging for the shit to hit the fan.

Take the job, a voice said into Blake's ear. It was a woman. He looked over his shoulder and there was nobody sitting in the adjacent booth. *Did I just imagine that?* Blake thought to himself.

Take the job, she said again. This time Blake knew he was the only one who heard her, but couldn't explain why. He looked out the window adjacent to their booth at the passing traffic and tried to clear his mind.

"Everything okay?" Cade asked, watching him intently with a smirk.

"How do you like the eggs?" Blake asked. He felt it might be wise to forego bringing up the voice in his head to his business partner.

"Just as good as you said they would be. I might come back tomorrow."

Blake nodded and took another bite of his breakfast.

"I'll do it."

Cade nodded in approval.

"But, if anything goes wrong, I'm going to kill your whole family."

"I'll help."

Sergeant poured another generous helping of Tobasco over his eggs and stirred it together with the remaining potatoes.

"You still got my rifle in your storage shed?"

"No," Cade responded. "It's in the golf bag I'm gonna give you in the way out. I left a few other toys for you just in case."

Blake nodded.

"What happened to the gun you used last night?"

"Gone. It served its purpose."

Cade laughed and pointed his fork toward Sergeant. "So damned careful. That's what I get for working with a cop."

"I've seen guys busted with less evidence. Trust me."

A television screen behind Cade panned to a news report covering a crime scene. Sergeant paused mid thought and watched intently. Cade followed his gaze to the same piece. It was a local story involving a child's death. Blake strained to hear the details.

"Such a horrible story," the waitress said over Sergeant's shoulder as she topped off his mug.

"What happened?" Blake responded.

"You don't know?" she asked, surprised.

"I'm not from around here."

"A nine-year-old died," the waitress responded. "He was playing near a canal and fell in, hit his head and drowned. Every mother's nightmare. Except now, they think there's more to it. The police are investigating."

"What's there to investigate?" Cade asked.

"I don't know. The police didn't say. The news is reporting that it doesn't look like an accident. The parents are divorced and the father owed a lot of child support, but I just can't imagine . . ." her thought trailed off as tears began to fill her eyes. "I'm sorry. It's the mom in me. Can I get you anything else?"

"I completely understand," Blake responded. "I think we're fine with just the check."

The waitress left and Blake looked to Cade.

"So if they're opening the investigation, what's that mean?" Cade asked.

"It means it wasn't an accident," Sergeant responded. "Especially if they told the press. Back to our job. You should make sure your getaway plan is still ready to go. Two jobs in one weekend is a lot."

"They're in different parts of the country Blake," Cade pulled a billfold out of his pocket and dropped two twenties on the table.

"You need to relax."

Blake took one more swig of his coffee and stood.

"Just make sure you're ready. Always make sure you're ready."

They walked together to the parking lot where Cade handed Blake a set of golf clubs in a vinyl bag. Blake peered in the bag and saw a hidden compartment where the 2 and 3 irons should normally go.

"The rifle is broken down and freshly cleaned. I lubed it up this morning. Rounds and magazines are in the side compartment. If you unzip the larger compartment, you'll find a 9 millimeter in a holster. Loaded. I bought it at a gun show a few weeks ago, but there was no background check so be careful."

"Anything else I should know?"

"It's all in the file. Are you sure you can make it?"

"It's close, but doable."

"Okay, until next time."

Sergeant grabbed the clubs and shook Stuckley's hand. It was 10:30 AM.

He climbed into his Escape and fired up the engine. The gas tank was full, and he habitually typed the address into the GPS in his car. The truth was he knew where he was going. He thought a moment about the voice in his head.

He had heard voices before, but she was new.

"Maybe I'm losing my mind," he said to the steering wheel.

He put the car in drive and pulled out of the diner parking lot. He was in Pittsburgh by 2:00 and closing in on the Ohio-Indiana border by sunset.

Chapter 4

Steve Gable sat at his desk for the first time in nine months. He was checked back into the FBI and out of the Marine Corps. He was technically eligible for retirement, and considering hanging up his spurs. Having said that, he never made such a decision immediately after a deployment. He wanted to give himself a cooling off period.

For the next few weeks, he would have nightmares that he would never acknowledge publicly. Loud noises would prompt a quick jump to the prone position. Smells, sights, comments, touches and even thoughts would remind him of things he would rather forget and never think about again. His tactical level of awareness would be on overdrive, which wasn't the worst thing in the world as an FBI special agent.

Because his job in the Marines was nearly identical to his job in the FBI, the transition would be seamless. Just different criminals. He allowed the high and tight haircut he maintained to grow out to what the Marines called a low fade. His salt and pepper hair was still short by civilian standards, but he felt like a hippy. He celebrated his fortieth birthday before his last deployment, but military life had aged him prematurely.

The athletic physique he maintained religiously through hours in the gym was eventually giving way to a small paunch in his midsection. His eyes were surrounded by dried wrinkles from hours of squinting into the desert sun as the dry air beat down his skin. He looked like he was fifty. Getting old sucked.

He had completed most of his obligatory initial paperwork while on leave, which meant Friday could be his first day on the job.

Sitting on his desk was one lone document protector filled with several folders, paperwork and what looked like copies of incomplete police reports. His first case. He knew he was going to have a meeting in a half hour and appreciated having a little time to review. The first folder included a photograph of Nikolay Belov along with a police report from the previous night. He scanned the folder quickly, making a couple quick mental notes, knowing he would come back to the case for a deeper dive soon.

The second folder was slightly thicker. It was a cold case in Wisconsin. A priest named Joseph Duvall, shot twice in the back of the head at a rest stop in the middle of the night about a year ago. There were a couple old press clippings suggesting that he had been accused of sexually abusing younger parishioners in a church in Kansas along with some subtle accusations that the church shuffled him off to another church rather than allowing law enforcement to investigate sooner. His former victims had alibis that checked out.

Nobody was sad to see him dead.

The next folder involved a trucker named Tommy Montoya, a registered sex offender who did time for rape and was hauling crude oil in North Dakota. His body was found at a truck stop outside Minot with two bullets in the head. The murder took place this past winter and his corpse was nearly frozen solid when a good Samaritan found him. No weapon found. His former victim had an alibi. No real effort put into the investigation from what Gable could read.

The next victim was a guy by the name of Blaine Crockett. Former NFL player who never took a snap in the regular season, and had moved onto selling insurance. He was shot once in the face and four times in the chest at a playground two years ago. Recently found "not guilty" of an accusation of attempted rape in Baltimore. He was also accused of rape in during his senior year in high school in Wyoming. He had alibis in both investigations. There was a long list of names and alibis in this folder. The list included his victims and several cops from multiple cities. Another charmer.

There were four more folders with four more similar stories. Registered sex offender found dead in a motel room Tennessee. Accused child molester found dead outside a payphone near a motel in Dallas. One article covered a dead roughneck in North Dakota and another featured dead college professor in Montana. The cases were similar. Multiple gunshot wounds. Past sexual assault victims had alibis. Nobody was sad to see these men dead. Gable saw a serial killer and found himself feeling the same biases that every police investigator likely felt when looking at these murders.

Well aren't you the vigilante. He pulled out his steno pad and began noting similarities in deaths. The list slowly filled half a page as he thumbed from page to page of his dossier. In the corner of his eye, he saw Cavalera walk in and approach his cubicle. He wheeled back his chair and stood to meet him.

"Cavalera, right?"

"Yes sir," Cavalera extended his hand, "It's good to see you again."

Gable shook his hand.

"I hear we're going to be working together," he said.

"Same here," Cavalera looked at the open folder and notes on Gable's desk. "Is that our first assignment?"

"Yes it is. I hope you don't mind me taking an early look."

Cavalera shook his head, "Not at all, man." He walked around to his cubicle and saw a similar folder. "I'm guessing this is my copy."

Cavalera flipped open his copy and began leafing through an identical report.

"What do you know?"

Before Gable could answer, Towe emerged from her office.

"Cavalera, Gable," she called out, "can I have a moment with you gentlemen?"

She walked into her office, not waiting for a response as both agents grabbed their materials. Gable and Cavalera walked in to find Towe sitting behind her desk. It was a government issue desk made of a cheap plywood, dressed up to resemble oak. The only item on her desk was a briefing folder similar to the ones in her two agents' hands.

To the left of her desk sat Vernon Maxwell, who shifted and fidgeted nervously in his seat never quite finding comfort. Vernon worked for the bureau for nearly 30 years in computer forensics. He was a stout man, built like a mini-refrigerator with an awkwardly cropped bushel of grey hair that might resemble Moe from The Three Stooges when combed. A thick pair of coke bottle grasses rounded out his portly face which matched his body.

Maxwell suffered a severe nervous breakdown which led to a medical retirement about four years earlier.

He wanted to return to full duty. The truth was he never fully recovered from his breakdown, which was the result of a hostage situation. Gable and his old partner Flores were involved in that skirmish and Maxwell owed them his life for their troubles. Maxwell was a master sleuth when it came to scouring the internet for criminal activities bore uncanny similarities – an incredibly helpful trait when tracking serial killers. Some bureaucrats within the agency liked writing Maxwell off as a conspiracy theorist, but his ability to see trends where others saw random acts of violence made him an asset to Towe's unit.

Cavalera jumped at the unexpected sighting of Maxwell perched in the corner and Towe stifled a laugh. Gable had the benefit of seeing Cavalera's reaction and noticed the shadow of another figure in the office as they entered the doorway. He noticed that his new partner wasn't exercising tactical awareness in the workplace and made a mental note.

"Agent Gable," Maxwell cooed, "How are you?"

"I'm good Vernon, how are you?"

They shook hands and exchanged a nod, acknowledging an incident from years before that profoundly impacted Maxwell's life.

"How was Afghanistan?"

"It's still there," Gable said with a smile. He was known for giving very few details about his deployments around the office. His old partner was an old Army vet and they talked often. Others didn't get that kind of access.

"Well, thank you for your service."

"No problem, Vern. It's good to see you again," Gable extended his arm out to Cavalera, "and this is Agent Cavalera."

"Oh, your new partner," Maxwell stood and learned across the room to shake Cavalera's hand, "you're in good hands with this one."

"Well, Agent Cavalera has quite the resume as well," Towe interjected, giving Cavalera a nod.

"Oh yes, are you the former undercover agent?" he asked.

"I was," Cavalera confirmed, raising an eyebrow and looking at Towe and Gable for some sort of explanation for who the little old man was in his boss's office.

"Vernon Maxwell is a retired computer forensics investigator with the Bureau. We keep him on contract for special assignments like the one we are going to discuss today."

Maxwell returned to his seat as did the three agents, with their dossiers in hands.

"What do we know?" Towe asked, looking at Gable.

"I count eight murders with similarities. All victims died of multiple gunshot wounds. We would need to see the actual police files but they appear to be professional jobs. The crimes are spread out across the country and the victims have similar profiles. Some have been convicted of sex crimes. Others were accused. Their victims' alibis check out and none of the paperwork in these files document any significant monetary transactions that would indicate that the victims hired a professional. In my opinion, none of these murder victims are model citizens and I'm guessing nobody was sad to see them go. It doesn't look like great police work in some of these cases. In others, there doesn't seem to be a lot to work with. That suggests a professional job. Again, I would need to see the evidence and complete files before passing informed judgement."

Towe nodded.

"Is this a project Vernon has been working on?" Gable asked.

"Yes it is," Towe responded, "Vernon would you mind providing some details?"

"Yes," Maxwell nearly jumped out of his seat, "I've been scanning the internet for different trends and in the last couple years, there has been a real jump in crimes just like the ones you're looking at. I think there might be more but these are the articles I could find on the web along with public documents when those are available. The killings seem to have been taking place over the last three years but it has probably been going on longer. Most of the murders in your file took place in smaller towns and I'm guessing the police departments have smaller budgets. Plus, like Special Agent Gable said, the victims aren't good people."

"So why are we suddenly interested now?" Gable asked.

Maxwell flipped to Nikolay Belov's file, but Towe placed her hand across the desk to halt his momentum.

"I can take it from here," she said. "Last night, a Russian businessman with government ties was murdered in a hotel room up the street from the actual room registered in his name in Times

Square. The NYPD found some information on the hard drive of a tablet in his hotel room indicating that he had been exchanging messages with a 16-year-old girl who was supposed to meet him there. We found no evidence of his date ever attending."

"Great," Cavalera responded. "Does the NYPD still have the computer?"

"No," Towe responded. "This is where it gets complicated. Because Mr. Belov has a lot of political friends in high places both in his country and ours, the state department has possession of the computer. They're not real excited about anyone looking at that laptop anytime soon. The details could be embarrassing for his business associates, his country and a whole line of politicians he has been working closely with over the last 30 years. At least, that's what I'm told.

After our meeting, I'm flying up to New York for a meeting with the State Department, the Russian Ambassador and a bunch of other political types to figure this incident out. Mr. Belov's business associates want the killer brought to justice but they don't want to give us the computer. That's my Friday afternoon shit show." She and Cavalera exchanged knowing glances.

"Do we think this crime is related to the others in his file?" Cavalera asked, pointing at Maxwell.

"We don't know," Towe responded, "but this is a lead that we agreed to follow and see if there's anything there. And this one is being fast tracked, meaning you have unlimited resources for your investigation. I want the three of you to reopen these cases and pass along any additional information you can find to me. I'll share it with the command center in New York City and see if we are on to something. There are about ten other investigations related to this murder taking place now. We'll coordinate from the command center in New York. You see what you can dig up."

"Is there any additional information beyond what's in this folder that we can work from?" Cavalera asked, thumbing through the file.

"Not at this time," Towe responded.

"And our assignment is to give them more information via you, with no guaranteed additional intel as the investigation continues?"

"That is correct."

"Wow," Cavalera said under his breath as he scanned the Belov file.

"Wow is right," Towe added.

Gable quietly continued reading the files and making notes in his steno pad of similarities.

"It looks like the Cumberland Police Department investigated the case for," Gable flipped to the previous page he was looking at, "Blaine Crockett."

The other three quickly flipped to the file Gable was reading.

"I have a contact there. Maybe we can see if they have access to the football player's old computer. Plus, we can look at their police file and learn a little more about this case."

"Works for me," Towe responded.

"Okay," Gable responded. "I'll make the call. Is Maxwell coming with us? If they don't want us removing evidence from the premises, it might be good to have him around."

Vernon looked up from his folder with puppy dog eyes.

"If you believe it helps the investigation," Towe responded.

"Are you good traveling?" Gable asked Maxwell.

"I'm in," Vernon said with a nod.

"It sounds like we have a plan," Towe responded.

Within five minutes, the meeting was over. The agents returned to their cubicles as Maxwell made his way to a guest office. Towe left for the airport.

Chapter 5

Jim Peterson's plane landed in Minneapolis on Saturday at noon, and he was in a rental car heading for Northern Minnesota by 1:00. Rabbit Lake was nestled halfway between Bemidji and International Falls. Less than 200 people lived there, and most the residents made their living taking care of cabins scattered through the region, including the one Peterson was driving to.

Peterson spent the first forty years of his life in Minnesota. He started out as a journalist covering politics at the state capitol. After a few years, he returned to his home town about two hours west of Minneapolis and ran for office, serving for four terms as a state representative. He later served another four terms in congress before cashing out and becoming a lobbyist. He moonlighted as a talking head on the cable news networks which gave him a distinct advantage when shaping a narrative to benefit one of his clients.

Between his sources from holding public office and his journalistic chops, Peterson had become pretty adept at breaking the news on political scandals that would ultimately end careers and result in weeks upon weeks of salacious press. The secret to his success was sitting on every scandal he learned about like he did when he was in office, and waiting for the most appropriate time to break them. The appropriate time to break scandals generally correlated with his clients' business interests.

Sometimes he would sit on incriminating news to help his old friends with a necessary vote. Other times he simply waited until an election when most of the public would halfway give a shit. He wasn't the first to employ his style of lobbying and horse trading and he wouldn't be the last.

He was on the cusp of breaking a scandal that would end the career of a Democrat in Congress, unless she took a vote in favor of getting a major oil pipeline approved. The congresswoman declined his offer to trade and the scandal was going to break early the following week while Congress was in recess. Slow news week. Perfect timing.

That wasn't the reason for his trip out of town. A prospective client of his, Precision Energy, was about to get bought out by a much larger conglomerate. That was going to mean a very lucrative transaction for Jim and his firm. It would mean months, maybe years of steady work that was going to make him a rich man if he and his associates were ready to seize the moment. They were ready.

However, today was about spending a quiet weekend in a cabin nowhere near the beltway smoking cigars, drinking wine and resting. The next few months were going to be intense.

Chapter 6

Blake Sergeant pulled into the dilapidated driveway of an abandoned cabin off Rabbit Lake. He hiked a half mile to the adjacent cabin where Mr. Peterson would be arriving in a few short hours.

He looked instinctually one last time in the rearview mirror when he spotted something out of the ordinary. His reflection in the mirror was staring back at him, as if it were not a reflection at all. He caught his own glance and stared at himself for a moment when his reflection smiled and winked.

Sergeant shuddered and jumped back into his seat. He remained paralyzed for another moment before daring to peer at his reflection again. He looked once more and found himself staring back into his own reflection. Sergeant rubbed his eyes and tried to chalk it up to a long drive, but he knew that wasn't the case.

An hour later, Blake settled in between two jagged rocks about eighty meters from the back porch of the cabin Peterson planned to call home for the weekend. He had a clear shot and plenty of maneuvering space if needed. The woods were eerily quiet except for the occasional loon or autumn breeze. The weather was a balmy 70 degrees in October, though the forecast predicted rain in the coming days. He had five hours to listen to the hype surrounding one that would roll in by the end of the week. If it wasn't for the weather, newscasters in Minnesota wouldn't know what to talk about.

He read through his orders which looked more like a bullshit script from a crime drama than a job. He needed to wait for a dialogue, then wait for a signal. One flash of the headlights, no shot. Two flashes of the light, shoot Peterson in the midsection. She wanted to talk a little shit before he walked up and executed him.

Blake preferred working alone. He preferred killing his target on his terms without the theater. Waiting for Peterson gave him time to think. He thought about his growing hunch the end was near for he and Cade's business venture. He thought about the woman's voice from the café and his reflection in the mirror. Most of all, he thought about his family.

Chapter 7

Peterson arrived shortly before dusk and promptly slipped into his routine. He feasted on a plate of walleye at a small bar in the nearest town and brought home an extra dessert. George Strait crooned in the background as he fired up a cigar and popped open a three-hundred-dollar bottle of cabernet. If he was going to drink alone, he would do it in style.

In the unseen distance, Sergeant decided that the combination of cigar smoke and country music would give him an inappropriate level of joy in shooting Peterson.

As dusk turned to darkness, a pair of headlights bounced up and down a dirt road in making its way toward the cabin. Peterson had moved onto his second bottle of wine. He watched curiously as the car pulled into his driveway and wondered who found out where he was staying. There was no phone service in Rabbit Lake. Making an in-person visit the only way to reach him in case of emergency. He hoped under his breath that it wasn't either of his ex-wives. One was in Washington. The other was in St. Paul. This weekend, he was hoping they were both inside the beltway.

Congresswoman Patricia Lambert climbed out of the rented sedan and made her way over to the back porch, seemingly knowing exactly where to find him. She walked slightly hunched over, clearly exhausted from the drive and trying to stretch her hamstrings with every step.

She wore a powder blue business suit which was a departure from the cranberry power suits she was generally known for. She was currently serving her third term as a Democrat in a swing district where the deep blue-collar labor roots of the community helped deliver her victories on election day, offsetting millions of dollars spent on social issues. Every election, however, was a fight.

"Well good evening Congresswoman Lambert," Peterson cheered as he stood to greet her. "You're sure a long way from home. Welcome to Minnesota."

He stepped down clumsily fighting his wine-induced vertigo and shook her hand awkwardly.

"Can I offer you a glass of wine?" he asked cordially.

"Well thank you for your hospitality, but I think I might decline for the moment," she said with a subtle western twang. "I suppose we both know the reason why I'm here and I apologize for interrupting your weekend."

Peterson smiled knowingly, and walked back to his seat where he was perched before his arrival. He adjusted the volume on the boom box on his porch. George Strait had been replaced by a Brooks & Dunn album from the nineties that he particularly enjoyed. He kept the volume low enough to converse, but high enough to entertain him.

"I suppose your visit isn't a complete surprise though I'm a little intrigued by how you found me," he said with a smirk. "There were only a few people who knew where I was going."

Lambert ignored the passive-aggressive jab and looked up to make eye contact with him from her vantage point.

"I'd like to ask that you reconsider leaking the story about my son."

"Why whatever story are you referring to?" he responded. "Jim, please don't be coy with me. I might have worn my nice shoes to your cabin, but it certainly wasn't my intention to dance."

"Well frankly, I don't know what you're so worried about. The Pentagon has been very clear that it's perfectly acceptable for men and women to serve in the Armed Forces regardless of their taste in women, or in Kyle's case, men. Besides, he's a decorated war hero."

Lambert gritted her teeth and attempted to choose her words. "The rules might have changed, but there are and always will be politics within the military that no elected official will ever be able to change. This is a very personal matter and he should have a right to make the decision on when to come out on his terms. Not yours."

"Well, Congresswoman, I think we both know that our families lose a degree of privacy the day someone decides to go after an election certificate. I've certainly had to bear the brunt of public scrutiny."

"I appreciate that which is why I'm here today Jim. What is this about?"

"Well, I wish you wouldn't be coy with me. We both know there is a pipeline that a few of my friends would love to see built and you have been creating a lot of barriers."

"Do you mean the pipeline owned by a foreign oil company using Chinese steel? Yes, Jim, I do have some concern about the national security implications of your client's proposal."

"Careful now, Precision Energy is an American business. They're headquartered in Alaska. I could arrange a tour."

"Oh please Jim. We both know you're playing with fire. Don't you ever worry about it when we continue to write blank check after blank check to a bunch of people who don't like us very much?"

"My God," he laughed, "you sound just like John McCain. Are you sure you're a Democrat? You would fit in with our party."

"My son is a Sailor who has to fight the wars we cause. Yes, I probably do sound like Senator McCain."

"And that's why he will always be an outsider in my party. His paranoia trumps his commitment to the business community."

"I'm all for a good business climate, but I would prefer to do business with responsible American-owned companies. You and I both know that Precision Energy put service members' lives in danger so they could drill for oil in Iraq and I will continue to have a serious problem with them because of that."

"I noticed you also made a comment about Chinese steel, which I know has to be very popular among your constituents. But are you sure that's the real reason you came all the way out here to Minnesota? Because I think your visit has everything to do with your concern that your knuckle dragging steelworker buddies might leave you at the altar when they find out about your gay Sailor son."

"Mr. Peterson," Lambert said, taking a breath to control her anger, "I am trying to keep this civil and have a conversation with you. I would prefer that you show some respect when talking about my family. We are not going to see eye to eye on the energy proposal as drawn today for the reasons I have been very public about, but that doesn't mean I'm against domestic drilling. I'm here today as a mother, asking you to stop. Let's talk this through and work this issue out through compromise, not blackmail."

The liquor was hitting Peterson and he was feeling the courage. Normally he wouldn't be so cavalier, but she interrupted his vacation.

"Patricia, we have had this conversation, several times. You're not going to compromise on the issues where I want you to compromise, and you've done too good of a job of convincing the chairman to see this matter your way. I'm running out of options."

"So you attack my family?"

"I'm just a lowly lobbyist doing my job. The story will run next week."

Lambert took another deep breath and steadied herself.

"Is there anything I can do to make this stop?"

"You know what you need to do," he responded. "A change of heart would be a far more compelling news story than your gay son."

Lambert said nothing.

"Are you sure you don't want a drink?" Peterson asked, holding up his goblet.

Lambert quietly stepped back and began returning to her car.

"You have 48 hours Congresswoman," Peterson called out. "This can all go away."

***

Blake couldn't hear the dialogue but he didn't care. He kept his scope trained on his mark and waited for a signal. The woman began slowly walking back to her car with her head hung slightly. The guy called out to her from his stoop on the porch and Blake could see the change in her body language.

She gave a signal to the driver and the headlights flashed twice.

"Rock and Roll," Blake Sergeant said quietly. He flipped the weapon to semi, turned on his scope and settled back in on his target. He inhaled deeply and squeezed the trigger on the exhale.

***

Peterson watched with interest as Lambert walk away slowly. She flashed her hand to the driver of her vehicle and the headlights flashed twice.

A second later, a red laser came on and zeroed in on his midsection. The first round knocked the wind out of him. The second shot knocked him out of his seat. Peterson fell on his side with a thud, knocking over the small table that held his wine. He struggled to catch his breath, yet winced each time he tried to inhale. He tried to scream, but could only muster a wheeze. The pain sent shockwaves up and down his side.

Peterson's body tried helplessly to regain its normal breathing cycle. Another subconscious heave brought on a wave of dizziness. He saw his bottle of wine lying on the side of the porch. A crimson puddle formed at the lip of the overturned bottle. The music abruptly stopped as another bullet blasted through his cd player. He heard footsteps behind him.

He rolled over on his back and faced Lambert, who was now smiling with a gleam in her eye that he had never witnessed before.

"What a beautiful view," she said as she eyed the lake that backed up to his cabin, "even in the darkness you can tell this lake is something you could spend a lifetime gazing at."

She turned her gaze to Peterson who was still trying to control his breathing.

"Why Jim, you were so talkative just a moment ago. What changed?"

Lambert was joined by another man in his early thirties. He looked like a Capitol Hill staffer. Young, bespectacled, idealistic. Off in the distance, he could hear another set of footsteps.

"Just think," Lambert continued, "if you would have spent just a few hours practicing some real, legitimate journalism, you would have probably discovered my family's connections to a certain organized crime family in New Jersey. Now that could have ended my career. Instead, you fucked with my son."

Lambert squatted down and looked Peterson in the eye.

"Right now, a friend of mine is leaking some inconvenient truths from your past to the media. I think between that, your disappearance and murder mystery, there will be so much exciting news, nobody is going to remember little old me."

Lambert stood up. Peterson watched her smile at him one last time then step aside. Another man stepped in. His hair was cut short and he looked like an ex-football player. He looked up at Lambert and she gave him a nod.

Sergeant squeezed the trigger twice and watched the life leave Peterson's eyes as two bullets raced through the back of his skull.

Lambert's assistant looked nervously at Sergeant and shuffled his way, holding a large black gym bag. Sergeant looked at the bag then back at the assistant.

"Is that for me?"

"Uh yeah," the aide stammered nervously as he handed the bag to Blake.

"I really wish it wouldn't have come to this," Lambert said, "but he left me no choice. Please give your father my best."

Blake stared at her slightly perplexed, then politely nodded.

"You'll want to go back the way you came, dusting off your footprints. Don't touch anything," Blake responded.

The Congresswoman ignored him and wandered into Peterson's cabin. Blake looked at her aide, and he looked at his shoes. Lambert came out a moment later holding a bottle of wine.

"I think I am going to need a drink when I go to bed tonight," she responded. "You don't need to worry. We will show ourselves out, and won't touch much."

She turned her eye to her aide.

"Would you like a bottle for you and your wife, Don? He has quite the collection."

"Sure," her aide responded. "She'd love that."

"You should take a bottle, too," Lambert began to say, but her voice trailed off.

Blake Sergeant was gone into the darkness, walking quietly back to where his car was parked. She and her assistant strained their eyes for a moment peering into the darkness.

"Well that was rude," she finally said. "Let's go, Don. It's time to pick out that wine."

Chapter 8

Blake didn't want to waste another second in their presence. They were going to get caught. They didn't know who he was and the sooner he left, the less they would remember about him.

That wasn't the worst of it. As he stood there watching them pillage the man's home for wine, he wanted to puke. They were scavengers with nicer clothes. He enabled their greed, their self-preservation. He could feel a sense of entitlement oozing off the Congresswoman. Her demeanor challenged his own opinions about society's desensitization to violence.

He believed individuals didn't fully comprehend murder until they were front and center, watching someone take their last breath. That should have been a revelation or at the minimum a moral call to action. Instead, Peterson spent his last moments listening to a stump speech.

For the first time, Blake felt remorse for one of his crimes. When he was in the moment, the adrenaline kicked in and he was able to detach himself emotionally from the task at hand. Once the deed was done, it was easy to turn a blind eye to the brutality of murder. His victims' deaths usually meant they would never harm another individual, but this was different. Peterson was a guy unwinding after a long couple of months of work, and Blake took that away from him. Blake killed him so he could attempt again to dream about the night his family died, and that wasn't *as* selfish as stealing wine from a dead man's cellar. It was worse.

He hiked back to his car, drove two hours and several small towns to the west to solidify his alibi. He checked into another motel and paid in cash. Once he was in the room, he repeated his routine. There was a notebook on the desk across from the bed next to a pen and a bottle of melatonin on the nightstand.

SUNDAY

Chapter 9

Gable, Cavalera and Maxwell pulled their vehicle into a storage lot in Cumberland, Maryland. As they inched their car toward their chosen destination, they met a uniformed cop, a woman in her mid-thirties and a man in a black suit who looked like a tower.

The woman was Jackie Crockett. In a past life, she was the stereotypical suburban mom. She was the president of her school's local PTA, active in city politics and generally at a different neighbor's house sipping wine once or twice a week after the kids went to bed. Today she was a shadow of herself. She stood slightly hunched and her eyes were puffy as if the rush of long past bad memories rushed back to ruin her Sunday morning.

"Who's the giant?" Cavalera asked.

"Godward Akeredolu," Gable responded.

Akeredolu was six feet, six inches tall and weighed slightly under 300 pounds. His boots gave him an extra inch of height. He knew his way around the weight room, but his size was more so a product of a giant frame. He kept his head shaved and wore a pair of aviator sunglasses. His family immigrated to the United States from Nigeria when he was a toddler, and he spoke with a trace of an African accent. He carried himself with a studious demeanor that could quickly pivot to a cross-examination when questioning a suspect. He had no qualms with using his size as a source for intimidation.

"He's huge," Maxwell added. "Do they call him God for short?"

"Don't call him God," Gable responded. "He doesn't like it. Call him Detective A.K."

Both agents met the three in front of the lone open storage pod in the complex with Maxwell in tow. A cardboard box labeled "evidence" sat ominously in front of Jackie Crockett, still sealed presumably from her late husband's murder investigation. A.K. broke the silence.

"Welcome back Stephen Gable," he said with booming enthusiasm. The two men embraced briefly then returned to their regal postures, "It's good to see you back and in one piece."

"It's good to be back and congratulations on your retirement," Gable responded.

"Thank you kindly, I only have one job now."

"I'm sorry I didn't make your party."

"That's okay my friend, I knew you were out of town."

"Did you get my gift?"

"I did," he said with a widening grin, "we should talk more, later. I would like to introduce you to Ms. Jackie Crockett." A.K. then pointed to the uniformed officer, "and this is Officer Newsome."

Newsome nodded and kept his post, staring along the sea of storage sheds, looking for anything out of place. Jackie Crockett slowly stepped forward and Gable met her with a handshake.

"Ms. Crockett, my name is Special Agent Steve Gable. These are my colleagues Special Agent Cavalera and Vernon Maxwell, who helps us with computer forensics."

Jackie Crockett nodded and mustered a cordial, tortured smile.

"I'm very sorry about your husband," Gable offered.

"Ex-husband," she corrected, looking down and clenching her jaw. "We were separated when Blaine died. Our court date was scheduled. I was literally one signature from being finished with him and this happened. Now in the eyes of the law, I'm still considered his wife, and I still get calls like this."

She put her arm on Gable's arm, "please don't take offense. I don't mean to be rude to you."

Standing nearly six inches taller than her, Gable leaned down and lightly grasped her shoulder in empathy.

"I understand and am sorry that we have to bother you."

She nodded in response and regained her composure.

"His computer and some other belongings are in that police evidence box. I haven't opened it. We just put it in the storage unit, and to be honest, we don't need it back."

Gable nodded to Maxwell who scurried to the box like an eager rat. He carried the box back to the squad car and began going through its contents out of Crockett's line of sight.

"We're investigating a number of murder cases. There are a number of similarities between these cases and yours. That's why Mr. Maxwell would like to look at Mr. Crockett's computer, to see if he can find any additional leads."

"What kind of similarities?"

"Similar victims. Similar circumstances. Unfortunately, I can't get too specific."

"I don't know why Blaine was at a children's park in the middle of the night," she interrupted. "I've tried over and over to come up with something other than what I've always thought. He was probably there to meet a woman and met her husband instead, but that makes less and less sense as time goes on. Somebody would have confessed, or the cops would have found something if it were that simple.

"I think I'm probably the worst possible person for you to interview about Blaine. Who he was and who I thought he was were two totally different people. For years, I believed every word he said. Every explanation. Every excuse. Every lie. He was the all-star husband, a former NFL quarterback and I was perfectly content with being his homecoming queen."

"And everybody saw it except me. My father was a Marine like Detective A.K., and he saw right through Blaine from the moment they met. I didn't listen. I thought he was a typical dad who didn't want to lose his little girl. My mother thought the same thing but never said anything to me until we were separated and most of my friends waited until he was dead to tell me they didn't trust him either."

She shrugged her shoulders in helplessness.

"Now I feel like I don't know what I can and can't believe. I don't even know who I was married to and I wish I could just hate him for it for the rest of my life, but I can't. I have to see his face every day, every time I look into the eyes of my sons. I have to be able to look at my kids if I'm going to raise them."

Her remarks were thoughtful and prepared, and Gable learned from years of investigating cold cases to let her continue.

"They're both teenagers now and neither one wants to play football, ever, if that tells you anything. His death and his trial were very public and this isn't that big of a town. They both have went through just as much pain and suffering that I have and I'm trying to do everything I can to make sure they can somehow learn how to become better men than the one who was supposed to help me raise them. So, I haven't had time to think about what was true what wasn't. Whether he really raped both of those women or whether they were just horrible people who wanted to tarnish his pristine reputation. And honestly, I don't want to think about it anymore."

She burst into tears, turned and collapsed into A.K.'s arms. She sobbed tears onto his white dress shirt and blue tie as he calmly rubbed her back.

"I just want my boys to grow up to be nothing like him."

"You just keep those boys around that Marine as much as possible," A.K. said soothingly, "he will make them into men."

Officer Newsome broke his stance to offer her a tissue which she graciously accepted.

"I'm so sorry," she offered, "did you have any other questions Agent Gable?"

Gable waved her off.

"Not at this time Ms. Crockett," he responded, "I am sorry to have asked you to relive these memories."

"It's not you," she responded quickly, "I live these memories every day."

They exchanged goodbyes and Officer Newsome walked Jackie Crockett back to her car. Gable, Cavalera and A.K. watched them leave.

"People like Blaine Crockett never understand how much their actions affect others," A.K. finally said. "Does your computer guy have everything he needs?"

Maxwell gave a thumbs up as he rejoined their group.

"I have a place for you to do your work back at the station if you would like."

"What do you think, Vern?" Gable asked.

"I can work anywhere, guys," he responded. "I have everything I need."

"Then it is settled," A.K. declared with a smile. "I can't wait to allow you to sample the best police department coffee in all of Maryland. We brew Starbucks on Sundays."

Chapter 10

Blake Sergeant woke up in a cold sweat and dove for cover under the side of his bed. He reached for his sidearm, and only felt a pair of gym shorts. Aside from his shuffling, the room was silent, but in his mind, a barrage of gunshots rang out around him.

He peeked around the foot of the bed, straining to see his enemy, but only saw a motel room door. There was no smoke. No fire. No gunman.

There was just a little girl standing in the corner of the room, her brown hair falling over her shoulders. She hugged a stuffed rabbit tight in fear, and looked at him with empty, sad eyes.

Anni

He rushed across the room to embrace her, squeeze her and tell her everything was going to be all right. Instead, he grabbed empty air, then let his arms fall helplessly to the ground. Her little body was still buried six feet underground and a lifetime away from the false hopes created by the flashbacks that ravaged her father's fragile mind.

He remembered. He was back on Earth. He was alone. He was another day removed from his worst nightmare, and he had work to do.

Blake jumped to the desk and scribbled more notes into the pad. He then proceeded to begin sketching everything he could remember about the shooter from his dream. 5'7 maybe 5'8, knit cap, about 200 pounds, Middle Eastern descent, mustache. Portly. He drew and redrew the man's face, but he knew there was nothing new.

He wrote "YLC 68?, Green Prius."

Who is that?

The last number was seven. He knew green Prius had no connection to his family's murder. He found the car and owner years ago. Interrogated him. The guy's name was Abdul something. He worked at a pizza joint that also served gyros. It was open after hours and catered to drunk college kids after the bars closed. He was at work the night of the murders. He wasn't involved. *There is a connection. I can't find it.*

This was not new information. He had been over it several times over.

In a few hours, Blake would go to a church, not to worship, but to establish an alibi. He had to be seen pretending to pray. He needed to write a check that a pastor would remember. Then he needed to drive home, sleep a couple more hours, wake up, put on his rent-a-cop uniform and defend one nameless Minneapolis skyscraper from the other nameless Minneapolis skyscraper. Nicole and Anni were still dead. He was still a shadow of the man he was. His mind was still a house where only half the lights worked.

Blake chewed a handful of melatonin tablets and looked in the mirror. He examined his reflection closely, and again had the feeling he was looking at something deeper than his reflection. He reached his hand up to touch the mirror and hesitated. He made a fist and walked away.

It doesn't have to be this way.

It was the same voice he heard in the diner the previous morning. The woman.

You still have a chance.

"A chance for what?" he asked an empty room.

He heard nothing in return. He laid in his bed and quietly waited for sleep.

Chapter 11

Pastor Rick Sterling peered at his audience as he gave his sermon with the perceptive intensity of an infantryman on patrol. He paced around the stage, taking advantage of a new wireless microphone and sound system that the church invested in over Christmas. His pacing was occasionally accompanied by a minor limp from an old motorcycle accident, but he didn't let it slow him down.

He spoke from memory, looking for reaction, response or acknowledgement of his words. The church was filled with an eclectic mix of locals and Minnesotans from the Twin Cities visiting their cabins for the weekend. He always gathered a crowd as there were always more than a few Minnesotans who wanted to listen to the funny, charismatic veteran Lutheran pastor who rode a motorcycle to Sturgis each year, and sported a ponytail and an earring. The out of town numbers, however, were beginning to dwindle as summer gave way to fall and they would decrease more in the coming weeks when winter rolled in.

As the service ended, he wished parishioners well never losing sight of the lone man sitting near the back row, lost in thought, and seemingly unaware that the service had ended. Sterling smiled. Someone came to his church in need. Today was going to be a good day.

The bustle of church attendees rushing off to brunch gave way to a warm silence, and Sterling used the moment to approach the gentleman.

"Good morning," Sterling announced.

The man looked up at him and nodded in acknowledgement.

"Do you mind if I join you for a moment?" he asked quietly.

The man looked around and seemed to realize for the first time the rest of the pews were empty, and it was just the two of them remaining in the old chapel. His first instinct was to leave, but his body didn't seem to respond. He only nodded again, realizing that he had officially brought more attention to himself than what he originally intended.

Sterling politely sat next to him and peered at the cross displayed above the pulpit.

"It's always interesting, looking at the pulpit from this vantage point," he said. "In a couple months, I will celebrate my 28th anniversary of the first time I ever stood up there and bored people to sleep."

The man cracked a smile. Sterling nodded and continued.

"You know in that time; I've learned a couple things. For instance, I always try to begin every sermon with a joke. They always seem to loosen people up. The other thing I've learned is that if a man is still sitting in the pews ten minutes after the service ended, it either means he fell asleep, or he has a lot on his mind."

He looked over at the man once more.

"You weren't sleeping."

The man only nodded. He sat hunched over.

"I don't mean to intrude, but you look like you've been carrying a heavy burden on your shoulders for quite some time. And you look tired."

"You nailed it," the man agreed.

Sterling studied him for another moment.

"What branch did you serve in?"

The man looked at him with a puzzled expression. He instinctively looked to his left shoulder, noting his tattoo of an Eagle, Globe and Anchor was hidden under his sweater.

"The Marine Corps," he responded, "how did you . . ."

"We smell our own," Sterling smiled. "There aren't too many of us up here in Northern Minnesota, I was in the Army, '68 to '72."

"I'm sorry," the man responded. "Our country wasn't good to you, but thank you for your service."

Sterling smiled in response.

"No, it wasn't, but I've come to learn it wasn't me that our country was angry with," Sterling responded. "It's better now. People thank you for your service. They want to talk. They want to know what you went though and sometimes they want to apologize. I think your generation and maybe even the next generation might be finally undoing a lot of the damage my generation created, but it's going to take a long time. Guys like you and I will always feel like square pegs trying to fit in round holes."

The man nodded and Sterling continued.

"You see, when I was 18, my country called me to serve. I didn't think we had any business in Vietnam and I still think we had no business there. Don't think we had any business going to Iraq, but when our country called, guys like us responded and served."

"Vietnam was the first time it became okay for men to shirk their duty. They burned their draft cards, listened to Simon and Garfunkel, smoked a bunch of weed and were hailed as heroes. After it became okay to say no to your country, it became okay to say no to other things. It was easy to say no to fatherhood, marriage, turning to God. It became easy for men to say no to responsibility, and now we have an entire generation that doesn't value fathers, husbands or sons. We're depicted as idiots on TV. We're blamed for every problem under the sun, and when we are doing the right thing, we're mocked in pop culture. But I do think it's changing. I really do, little by little."

They sat quietly for a moment, before Sterling continued.

"I don't think the people who spat on me when I came home did it because of what I was. I think they spat on me because of what they weren't. I also think they know it too."

Sterling extended his hand, "I'm Rick Sterling."

The man shook his hand and responded, "Blake Sergeant."

"Pleasure to meet you Blake," he responded. "An absolute pleasure."

"Likewise," and Blake managed his first genuine smile in what felt like years.

Sterling and Sergeant spent the next five minutes talking about their respective times in uniform the way veterans do. They told inside jokes, and laughed about friends of yesteryear quickly forgetting they had only met moments before.

"What's troubling you Blake?"

The smile disappeared and was replaced with a helpless shrug and nod.

"You're right about my burden," he responded. "I've made a lot of mistakes. I'm not the man I used to be and I'm not the man I want to be."

He shrugged again helplessly and looked to his feet.

"You know," Sterling placed his hand on Blake's shoulder, "you don't have to carry that burden."

Sterling pointed to the cross hanging above the pulpit.

"He will carry your burden. All you have to do is lay it at his feet and ask."

Sergeant breathed deeply, but said nothing.

"Do you mind if I pray with you?" Sterling asked.

"I think so."

Sterling placed his hand back on Blake's shoulder.

"Lord, thank you for bringing Blake to worship today, and thank you for working your loving grace and allowing our paths to cross. Lord, please help Blake know that whatever he is going through, he is not going through it alone. Give him peace and comfort. Help free Blake from the pangs of regret that seem to be haunting him. Forgive us of our sins, and release us from the burdens that evil can bring. Please help Blake leave his burdens at your feet and lord, please let Blake know he is always welcome in your house. In the name of our father the holy spirit, Amen."

"Amen."

Sterling stood up.

"I have a couple of matters to attend to before I call it a day, but please feel free to sit here as long as you wish."

"Thank you," Blake responded. Sterling disappeared and reappeared a moment later.

"Before you go, I want to give you something." Sterling handed Sergeant a book entitled "Jesus Calling."

It was a daily devotional book. Blake thumbed through the pages. There was a page for every day of the year with what looked like a word of encouragement and a couple bible passages.

"It's pretty self-explanatory. This book has helped me when I go through dark times and passages always seem to help provide an answer for whatever I'm dealing with. If you need a bible, you're welcome to take one from the pew in front of you."

Blake pulled out his wallet, and Sterling held out his hand to proactively decline.

"No charge. Just come and see us again," he said.

He stood to walk out and paused again.

"I have to ask. Have you ever had the privilege of being called Sergeant Sergeant?"

Blake smiled and nodded, "a few times."

"And I'm sure you've never been asked that before."

"It's been a while."

Blake stood up and grabbed his jacket, which had been sitting next to him.

"I should get on the road while there's still some daylight."

"Minneapolis or St. Paul?"

"St. Paul."

"I knew there was something I liked about you."

They shook hands again.

"It was a pleasure meeting you Blake. Please stop by again,"

Blake thanked Pastor Sterling and headed to his car. He chastised himself for nearly confessing his murder to his would-be alibi and felt even worse for using the pastor. However, he also knew that nearly everything he said was true. As his Escape chewed up pavement on the way back to St. Paul, he wrestled with the conflict in his mind.

When he began killing for money, it was because the act helped unlock memories that were lodged in his mind. He saw pictures of the day a man killed his family, and with each homicide came another glimpse. The guys Cade was finding were not model citizens. Every one of them was expecting a confused teenager who was too young to be fooling around with a grown man. Every case was covered in the media and the focus would inevitably turn to his victim's past. Eventually, their alibis would check out and the public would decide the dirty preacher, the naughty trucker or the guy who beat two rape charges deserved to die.

His last guy was different. He was a politician. He was probably guilty of something and he was probably an inherently bad person. But did he deserve to die? That wasn't Blake's right to decide. It wasn't his right to decide the fate of any of his victims. Watching the congresswoman and her peckerhead assistant raid a dead man's wine stash was allowing him to acknowledge some truths he had been running from for too long. Blake did it for the addiction to the glimpses of a memory that had long since past. He had learned nothing new from the last five jobs. Perhaps there was nothing else to learn. Perhaps he wanted to quit, but would he? Deep down, Blake knew the answer to that question.

Chapter 12

Vernon Maxwell sat hunched over a tablet plugged into Blaine Crockett's computer, punching away at the keypad, occasionally stealing sips of his coffee. He occupied a makeshift cubicle that A.K. provided. A uniformed officer stood nearby finalizing reports from his shift and a desk sergeant sat a few yards away listening to the bells and hums of chatter over the radio. The chatter was minimal.

Gable and Cavalera sat across the room from Maxwell, giving him space to work. They each reviewed a copy of the murder investigation that A.K. provided along with a copy of the investigation of Blaine Crockett's rape allegations.

"These reports are so organized," Cavalera opined. "It's textbook."

"It's A.K.," Gable responded. "I've deployed with him a couple times. You won't find a more meticulous investigator."

A.K. walked into the room and dutifully refilled both of their coffee mugs, then topped off the mugs sitting next to Maxwell and the desk sergeant.

A.K. stepped behind Cavalera and Gable who continued to pore over the police files.

"You flew out to Wyoming?" Gable asked

"Marion, Wyoming," A.K. responded. "It's a little mountain town off I-80 just over the Utah border. Makes this place look like a metropolis. Part of the murder investigation. Crockett beat a rape charge when he was growing up there. His victim is a cop now."

"Really?" Cavalera responded.

"Really," A.K. said back. "It's all in the file."

"You said victim," Gable responded. "Do you think he did it?"

A.K.'s cordial demeanor gave way to an expression of disgust.

"I know he did it," he responded, "but it's not about what you know."

"It's what you can prove," A.K. and Gable said in unison. Cavalera looked around the room and nodded in acknowledgement.

Meticulous.

"He was the high school quarterback, homecoming king, going to play in the NFL," A.K. continued. "She lived in a trailer. Raised by a single mother. Who's going to believe her?"

"Did she report it?" Cavalera asked.

"She reported it that night. He said it was consensual. His church paid for a fancy lawyer and they went after the victim. Local cops didn't want to make their golden boy look bad so they fudged the investigation. He walked."

"And she's now on the force with them?" Cavalera added.

"I kid you not," A.K. responded. "Fifteen years no less. Her mom ended up marrying one of the cops after the investigation. He's now the deputy chief. The guy who led her investigation died ten years ago."

"Did she kill him?" Gable asked.

"Car accident. No evidence of wrongdoing. She even pulled the file for me," A.K. finished that sentence with a smirk. "Told me a story about a local ghost who probably killed him."

Both agents looked up from their reports inquisitively.

"It's in the report," A.K. said, pointing his coffee mug toward the records in their hands. "Outside of town, just over the Utah border, there's a little ghost town but it used to be a settlement. The locals claim an ex-civil war soldier went on a killing spree out there in the 1800s. Townspeople killed him in self-defense, but his ghost still haunts the place."

"Do you believe her?" Gable asked.

"I think she believes herself," A.K. responded. "I have the feeling the old ghost soldier had some help."

"Is that why you flew out there?" Gable asked. "To find out about the other victim?"

"One of them. I wanted to learn more about Crockett."

"And what did you learn?"

"Confirmed what I already knew. He was a sick bastard. He raped that girl, and he raped the woman in Baltimore. They had enough evidence to go to court when he was in high school."

"What about Baltimore?" Gable asked.

"Not as good of a case," A.K. responded. "Victim didn't report it for a few days. By then there wasn't much they could prove in the investigation. There were issues with the initial processing of evidence. Not the best police work. He hired a good lawyer again who was able to spot the gaps in their reporting."

"You know what I need to ask next," Gable responded.

"Ask away my friend," A.K. responded. "You're doing your job."

"Do you think any corners were cut in your investigation, given the his history?"

"No," A.K. responded, "and you have my word on that. The officers processed the crime scene to the best of their ability. I personally conducted the subsequent investigation and talked to all suspects to ensure we could answer the question you are asking today. Checked alibis of all the cops in my department and Baltimore. Checked alibis for the victims and their families. Flew to Wyoming. Looked at bank information for all suspects as well."

"It was a professional job in my opinion. Possibly prior military. The suspect policed his or her brass, arranged to meet Crockett at a park near a freeway entrance. Shots were delivered at close range, possibly with the use of a silencer. No witnesses. About the only place where you might be able to find something we couldn't is on that computer," A.K. said, pointing at Maxwell.

"Who originally handled the computer forensics?" Maxwell asked.

"Gadget Technologies. We're a small force. Need to outsource that piece of the investigation. Are they considered a respectable contractor in your summation?"

"They're okay," Maxwell responded. "But I'm better."

A.K. exchanged glances and smiles with both agents.

"I assume your other victims have similar characteristics?" A.K. responded.

Gable nodded.

"Whoever did it knew the victim well enough to get him to that park after hours," Gable said. "If there's anything on that computer to tell us who he has been talking to, Maxwell will find it."

"How long do you think it will take, Maxwell?" Akeredolu asked.

"Five minutes. Five hours. Tough to say."

"Maybe we can crack open that bottle of scotch in a few," Akeredolu said with a smile.

"Wait!" Maxwell interrupted. "Found something."

Maxwell typed franticly, then pulled up a string of an old instant messenger conversation. Gable, Akeredolu and Cavalera joined him, and read the contents together.

Maxwell found a deleted email message. Crockett was having a very steamy conversation with a girl named Kylie, and they wanted to meet in person to live out some of the fantasies they had talked about. Kylie's parents were on a date and wouldn't be home for a few hours. She could sneak out and meet him, but they had to hurry. Her neighbors were nosy so they couldn't meet by her house. Crockett said he had problems of his own. They chose to meet at a park late at night.

"We know why he was at the park," Maxwell exclaimed.

"But who's Kylie?" Cavalera asked.

Maxwell punched in a few more keys and the monitor flashed with different images to match his key strokes. He pulled up an IP number, then typed it up on his tablet.

"I can't tell you who Kylie is," Maxwell said, "But I can tell you whose computer she used."

He typed a few more keys and a new name popped up.

"Cade Stuckley. He lives in Alexandria, Virginia."

"Address?" Gable said.

Maxwell grabbed a tablet and scribbled the information down on the first page. He tore off the sheet and handed it to Gable, who handed it to Cavalera.

"How much more time do you think you need?" Gable asked Maxwell.

"Maybe an hour, but if we can get this back to the headquarters, I can do everything else I need to do there."

"That's fine. Cavalera will brief the boss, and it will take at least an hour to get us a warrant." Gable looked at A.K. "Would you mind if we took Mr. Crockett's computer back to the lab?"

"Be my guest," A.K. responded.

An hour later, Gable, Cavalera, Maxwell and Akeredolu walked out of the station to Gable's car. As the agents pulled out of the police station, Akeredolu held his coffee mug in one hand and waved with the other.

"So I've gotta ask you a question," Cavalera spoke.

Gable didn't respond.

"Your buddy, Detective A.K. told us a ghost story."

Gable nodded.

"He then proceeded to tell us he wrote the ghost story in his police report."

Gable nodded again.

"And you didn't bat an eye."

Gable nodded, flicked his turn signal and watched for traffic.

"Am I missing something?"

Gable looked back at A.K. through his rear-view mirror and cracked a smile.

"Detective A.K. had a number of experiences during his last deployment that forever changed how he approaches his police work."

"Are you going to tell me a ghost story too?"

"You should make sure someone meets us on site with a signed warrant," Gable responded.

Chapter 13

Cade Stuckley sat in his home office reading the letter he had written one last time. He scanned for grammar and content, then signed his name. As he folded the message and stuffed it into an envelope, he hoped the words would never see the light of day.

He received word earlier that morning that Peterson was dead and the cash was in Blake's possession. Once he acquired the gym bag from Blake, he would work with his hired middleman, who would exchange the dirty cash for clean cash. From there, Cade would deposit half the money into his account as business income.

He would then have his middle man transfer a large sum of money to an offshore account. His operation had become too lucrative for his web business to pass muster as a believable front without his family's help. He didn't want his family's help.

He kept enough cash on hand to pay for an escape plan to get him to the Cayman Islands. From there, he could access the rest of his resources. It was a good plan, and Peterson's death gave him enough money that he could give Blake Sergeant the signal to lay low for a while. Sergeant worried too much from Stuckley's perspective, but he was willing to tolerate it. He owed Blake that much.

He leaned back into his chair and gazed out the window of the sliding glass door in his apartment when the flicker of outside movement caught his eye. When he looked closer, he spotted what he hoped he would never see. He spotted one white male wearing a bulletproof vest creeping up to his door. Cade pulled a drawer open on his desk and drew a Beretta M9 pistol. The man stopped and took a knee. It appeared as if he was waiting for further instructions.

Cade swerved in his chair to face a series of computer monitors, then typed quickly on his keyboard. Footage from three surveillance videos popped up on the monitors. He spotted two more men tiptoeing slowly to his front door with weapons holstered under their suit jackets. They weren't cops. One was white and the other was probably Latino. They weren't from his family, but they were definitely coming for him.

Cade slid across the room to his kitchen and opened a lower cabinet next to the stove. He quietly pulled out the floor panel within the cabinet, exposing his gas line. He opened the adjacent bottom cabinet which included a series of accessories designed to aid in triggering his escape plan. The process was designed to take 30 seconds and he was hoping everything would work as planned.

He pulled out a knife and sliced a series of incisions in his gas line. He then pulled a charcoal igniter molded to wrap around his gas line out of a box and soaked it with lighter fluid. He attached a homemade fuse that was wrapped in a spool to the igniter. He carefully lifted the fuse spool out of the cabinet and rolled it across his dining room floor near the glass door where he spotted the first gunman.

The gunman was still posted, waiting final orders.

Cade turned on the gas.

The other two were walking up the stairs to Cade's apartment.

Cade turned his attention to a small router inside the cabinet and plugged it into the outlet. He pushed the configuration button and grabbed a remote detonator that lay next to the router. If plan A didn't work, plan B would. The router hummed and the lights flickered, sending messages to several smaller computers attached to blocks of c4 strategically hidden around his apartment. The lights blinkedx back and forth to each other, acknowledging life and awaiting further orders.

Cade peeked at his security screens. The men were at his door and drawing their weapons. The man by his sliding door nodded his head and held his weapon at the ready. Cade saw the cord from an earpiece stringing out from the third man's ear, then flowing under his shirt collar.

Cade rolled to his desk, popped his laptop out of its docking station and stuffed it into a backpack next to his desk. He shoved the sealed letter into the backpack as well, and slung it over his shoulder.

The first gunman tried the door. It was locked.

Cade crept back to the dining room, and ignited the fuse. The flame crackled with life and methodically began its journey to the gas line, leaving a trail of ash.

Cade ran to his bedroom, shut the door and slid open his window. He quietly slid himself out onto the ledge behind the third gunman and drew his pistol.

The first two men kicked the door open.

Cade jumped and fired his weapon at the third gunman. The first two rounds missed, but the third one caught him square in the back. The gunman fell forward, gasping for air.

The first two gunmen ran through the bedroom door.

Cade clicked the detonator, and dove behind a cable box near the apartment. He caught a glimpse of the other two men rushing to the window when the gas line exploded, followed by the c4. The explosions were deafening, setting off every car alarm in the parking lot. The first two men were dead.

The blast sprayed rock, glass and momentum toward Cade and the third gunman. Cade felt something graze over his back and assumed it was a projectile from the blast.

He staggered to the third gunman, who was still breathing. He grabbed the man's wallet and rushed for the wooded area behind the apartment complex. Behind him, the third gunman crawled through the rubble of the explosion and drew his sidearm. He trained his eye on Cade and fired.

Cade heard a pop and felt a sharp pain in his shoulder blade but never broke stride. He heard three more shots and heard a bullet whiz past his right ear. He ran faster, knowing he could find cover in the wooded area behind his home. Two more rounds fired. One missed and the other blasted through his backpack, exiting out the side and somehow missing him altogether. Cade wondered if the bullet hit his laptop. Cade disappeared into the wooded area.

The gunman tried to stand and winced. The bullet hit his vest and probably broke the skin. Pieces of wreckage from the explosion landed on him. A shard of glass was sticking out of his left hip. He pulled it out and watched as blood poured like a stream down his pant leg. He couldn't put much pressure on his left leg. He was injured and bleeding. He needed to escape before authorities arrived.

He stood, peered into the window and saw the charred remains of his team members splattered all over the walls of what used to be Cade's bedroom. He looked back to the wooded area where his target was likely hiding. There wasn't time to finish the pursuit. Tenants were already exiting their apartments to inspect the damage.

He limped away quietly and disappeared around the other side of the building adjacent to Cade's unit. A young boy in the window of the adjacent unit spotted him, but his getaway was otherwise clean. In five minutes, he was back in a silver Nissan pathfinder they rode to the apartment in.

Cade dove into the woods and crawled in the long grass. The wooded area gave way to a small decline behind trees and shrubbery that led to a creek. Cade knew it well and slid down the hill quietly. He crossed the creek and felt the first few raindrops of an oncoming storm as he crawled up the other side of the creek bed. He smiled knowingly. Nothing messed up a crime scene like rain. Thunder crashed above him and a hard rain followed.

Cade climbed out of the wooded area, and ran to a set of storage units on the other side of the stream. He sprinted to the unit he rented monthly, and unlocked his padlock. Inside sat his getaway vehicle, a Ford Mustang that was registered with the state in his father's name. The fact that his father had been dead for twenty years seemed to evade the state's records, but the tags were up to date. Hacking the DMV's website was a hobby of Cade Stuckley's that felt uncomfortably simple.

Cade tossed his backpack in the car and grabbed a blanket from the back of the shed. He didn't know how bad he was hurt, but he didn't want to bleed on the leather seats. He loaded a handful of items in the trunk, then crept outside his storage unit to survey the premises outside of his line of sight before escaping.

The surviving gunman, a young mercenary named Kevin Wisnewski, made one call on his burner phone.

Anthony Byrd answered on the first ring.

"Speak"

"Target is hit but still moving," Wisnewski responded, "Two men down and I'm hit. I can pursue the target by vehicle."

"Were you made?"

"No."

"Can you pursue?"
"By vehicle."
"Do that," Byrd concluded, "then report to home base."

Wisnewski's ears were still ringing from the blast and the dizzy spells he experienced when he staggered back to his vehicle hadn't subsided. He put the vehicle in drive and creeped to the exit of the apartment complex to Edsall Road. A flurry of police sirens rang in the distance as a crowd gathered around the remnants of Cade Stuckley's home and Wisnewski's partners.

He took Edsall to Van Dorn, turned right and spotted a storage lot off the highway. The wooded area his target ran into backed up to the storage lot. Wisnewski deducted that his target was either hiding in a narrow tree line, or was renting a storage unit as part of an escape plan. That's what he would have done if he were in the same position.

The rain paused.

The employees of the storage unit were out of their office and staring into the wooded area trying to catch a glimpse of an explosion they heard in the distance. Wisnewski drove behind them avoiding any attention. He drew his pistol and drove slowly through the aisles of the lot.

The sky opened, sending another volley of rain onto the lot and the employees back inside. Wisnewski kept his window down and weapon at the ready with his right hand as he drove with his left.

Cade spotted the vehicle pulling into the lot just as he was about to exit. He pulled the door of his storage unit shut and listened to intermittent raindrops.

He heard the low hum of a vehicle creep through his aisle outside the door. The shooter would have four more rows of storage units to patrol before circling back. That would probably take about 60 seconds in Cade's summation. The vehicle grew silent. Cade listened intently for any sign of life. He began to count.

One.

Cade quietly slid the garage door open, careful not to make a sound. The process took eleven seconds.

Twelve.

Cade started his engine and put the vehicle in drive, careful not to press the gas.

Sixteen.

Cade pulled out of his shed and pointed his vehicle toward the exit. He jumped out of the vehicle and ran to the shed drawer, pulling it down quietly and listening for the idle of Wisnewski's engine two rows away.

Twenty-four.

As the other vehicle's idle grew more distant, Cade pulled out of his row and turned right, timing his movement with the other car's declining line of sight.

Thirty-four.

Cade pulled out to the exit and waited for a van to pass before he turned onto Van Dorn. He stayed under the speed limit and patiently stopped at a red light. He spent most of the next minute staring in his rear-view mirror. The light turned green and Cade turned onto the freeway. He knew the last gunman wasn't on his tail anymore. The gunman would likely take another lap around the storage unit and maybe cruise past the tree line looking for his target. In another five minutes, he would decide the crime scene was getting too hot, and leave.

Cade drove north on 495, heading toward the Woodrow Wilson Bridge. He heard sirens and caught a glance at a police car on the other side of the freeway. The gas in the car was almost two months old. He made a point to fire up the engine every few weeks and hoped the ritual would pay off.

He would hit traffic on the Maryland side of the bridge, but not enough to cause any real anxiety. He and Blake had rehearsed the escape plan several times over, and Cade struggled to adhere to his partner's sage wisdom from his law enforcement days.

A man on the run looks like a man on the run. Don't panic. Use your turn signals. Drive the speed limit. Remain alert, but be subtle about it. Stay cool.

Cade did everything he could to hide his anxiety and hide it well. Phase one of the escape was a success. He knew what he needed to do next.

Chapter 14

Gable and Cavalera walked through the ash covered crime scene that used to be Cade Stuckley's home. The burnt carpet beneath them squeaked as each agent took a step, full of water used to extinguish the flames from Cade's trap.

Forensic agents from the FBI and the local police department worked alongside each other methodically gathering evidence, knowing the building they were in was no longer structurally sound.

The investigation team spent an hour waiting for the fire department to put out the fire and inspect the building. It was a three-story unit and Cade lived on the second level. The fire marshal declared the units above and below his apartment unsafe to reside in. That was going to displace several tenants.

Outside the complex, rain showers washed away critical evidence. Police investigators tried to gather whatever they could, which was minimal.

Most of the units were rentals, but a small number of residents including Cade exercised a narrow opportunity to buy their condos a few years back. Some residents restored their homes and put them on the market a couple years later. Cade lined his walls with explosives and installed surveillance cameras around the premises.

Massive holes in the sheetrock exposed damaged studs and clear evidence of explosions from bombs strategically placed around the house. Gable imagined Cade Stuckley sitting at his desk eating a bowl of cereal, staring at the footage from his surveillance cameras with bombs strapped to the walls of his apartment. Were they concealed under decorative baskets or possibly a fake dear's head? Or were they displayed like blatant symbols of destruction?

There was no kitchen table and only one bed. There was one couch, one workspace and one big box television set with a DVD hooked to it. Gable imagined he spent most of his time in his office that served as the dining room in other units.

The smell of singed hair hung in the air serving as a morbid reminder of the two bodies in the main bedroom, both of whom were splattered on the walls and cindering on the floor. Neither body appeared to have ID, though a DNA search might bring some clues. Their skulls were surprisingly intact, which raised the odds of a dental match.

"This could have been us," Cavalera remarked and Gable nodded in response.

"Do you think someone tipped him off?" Gable asked. Cavalera didn't immediately respond. The rainstorm slowed down to a handful of sprinkles. Both agents walked outside.

"We'll have to visit the wife first," Cavalera finally said.

"And the cops," Gable added. They stared out toward the wooded area behind the complex, watching the D.C. Metrorail train line travel off in the distance, presumably to the Van Dorn station.

Cavalera surveyed a growing crowd on the other side of Cade's office looking to see if any of the spectators looked out of place. He was familiar with far too many stories of suspects visiting the scene of a crime they committed to never taking anything for granted. Two uniformed cops urged spectators to step back. As a third officer strung a fresh line of police tape, expanding the scope of the crime scene. They were going to need more tape.

"Witnesses said they heard a blast, followed by a couple small blasts," Cavalera spoke again. "Could have been gunfire or thunder."

Gable kneeled and removed a pen from his jacket simultaneously. He pointed to a shell casing located directly beneath Cade's apartment.

"Gunfire," Gable responded.

Cavalera flagged down a nearby forensic agent, and waved him over.

"Bring your friend with the camera," he called out.

The photographer took a picture of the casing in the grass. The forensic agent waited for the photographer, then began processing the casing as both agents surveyed the area around them. Gable had already found one other casing.

He rose and extended his thumb and index finger in the shape of a makeshift pistol like most children did on playgrounds across America. He pointed to the balcony off Cade's apartment.

"Bang?" he asked.

Cavalera followed his lead, but allowed his index finger to survey the apartment behind them. It was a terrible place tactically to take a shot. He pointed to Cade's bedroom window, which was about eight feet from the ground. Maybe higher. The ground apartment units were basement units. Residents needed to walk down a couple of stairs to get to their back patios. Seemed like a bad design in a flood zone, but here they were. Available to the lowest bidder.

Cavalera scanned down from the apartment window, and found two damp and fading footprints under the window.

"No," he responded. He retraced his finger-scan down from the apartment to the footprints.

"Jump," he pointed to the footprints, "and boom." He raised his fingers back up to the window.

They began inspecting the debris behind the apartment and near the casings. Cavalera pointed toward the wooded area across from his apartment.

"He ran that way," he said.

Gable knelt down and pointed his finger-gun.

"Bang! Bang! Bang!"

"We only have two casings."

"Yeah," Gable responded, "but our boy blew up his apartment after he had unexpected guests."

"Our boy jumps out the window and runs that way." Cavalera pointed to the wooded area.

"Shooter didn't see that coming. Blast knocks him on his ass. Our boy runs past him. Shooter gets a couple shots off. Either he hit something or he missed a couple when he was policing his brass."

"You know what's over there?" Cavalera asked, still looking at the wooded area. "Storage units. I saw them on the way in."

"Fuck." Gable stood from his kneel and groaned quietly. Both agents scanned the wooded area, then looked back at the smoldering apartment. “Surveillance cameras. Apartment hardwired to detonate. This guy lived with an escape plan.”

“Like I said,” Cavalera said as he watched the forensic agent collecting the two shell casings, “this could have been us.”

Both agents began walking toward the wooded area behind Cade’s apartment

“Gentlemen,” Towe called as she walked over to Cavalera and Gable.

“Ma’am?” Gable responded. “I thought you were in New York.”

“We have a problem,” she said, cutting niceties. “We’ve got a mole.”

Cavalera and Gable both nodded in agreement.

“Not on your end,” she added quickly. “We got a whole command center in New York working this Belov case. More suits than you wanna know about. Cade Stuckley was the closest thing we had to a lead. Not thirty minutes after I briefed the group, we get a call from our informant with the Carbone family.”

“Who?” Cavalera asked.

“Organized crime,” Towe responded. “Gable can fill you in later. Do you know who your boy is?”

“We didn’t know he existed four hours ago,” Gable responded.

“Angelo Carbone’s grandson.”

Gable shook his head and was about to speak.

“This is not on you Gable,” Towe exclaimed, “this is bigger. Our informant tells me Carbone got a courtesy call from the Russians saying they were going to be paying Cade Stuckley a visit. Our guy only knew him by legend. Sounds like he was never too close to the family.”

“When you say the Russians,” Gable asked.

“I don’t know what that means,” Towe responded, cutting him off impatiently. “Government. Mafia. Both.”

“With this president, I thought we were all Russians,” Gable responded.

“Don’t get me started,” Towe said, “I already need a drink. The Russians, whatever that means, were gonna take this boy out and they aren’t waiting for us. I need you to find out everything you know about Cade Stuckley. That is all you are working on. You report directly to me. You follow this lead wherever it goes."

"Right now, it looks like our lead went that way," Cavalera said, pointing toward the wooded area behind the apartments.

"What are we waiting for?" Towe asked. As if on cue, a small entourage of forensic agents and uniformed cops led by an Alexandria homicide investigator walked up behind their conversation. Gable pointed them out.

"This is Detective Bob Hamilton," Gable began, and introduced the detective to Towe, Cavalera and Maxwell. An African American man in his fifties with a bald head and a tan overcoat, Hamilton nodded in response to the niceties.

"I got your text," he said.

"The breadcrumbs lead this way," Gable responded.

"Watch your steps," Hamilton growled to the group, "don't want you fuckin' up my crime scene."

Their group slowly walked toward the wooded area, looking for signs of a struggle.

As they approached the tree line, Cavalera pointed out a fresh tear in the bark of a tree that looked like it could have been caused by a bullet.

Hamilton pointed out fresh tracks followed by commotion on the ground where Cade slid to the ground to dodge Wisnewski's gunfire.

Forensic agents met each discovery with a routine of shooting pictures and marking off the spots of interest.

The group deliberately stepped away from identified evidence while watching intently for clues. They found additional footprints where Cade climbed up the creek bed and ran to the rear boundary of the storage lot.

As they were scanning the pavement looking for a sign of evidence, an employee from the storage service called to them from a distance.

"Well that's one hell of a response time," she said as he approached the group of investigators. "Don't you guys usually have cars?"

Hamilton stepped in front of the group, flashed his badge and briefly introduced the group.

"I know," the employee responded, "I just got off the phone with y'all a minute ago. Come on, I'll show you what we found."

The employee, a grandmotherly type who had seen everything there was to see in the storage business and then some, walked the group back to the front entrance of their facility. During the trip, she shared her narrative. She and a colleague stepped out of their office to catch a glimpse of the explosion and gunshots behind their storage units.

The rain quickly ended their pilgrimage, and they ran back to cover. When they returned, they found that neither surveillance cameras were working. One of her employees looked at the camera and found that someone had installed a small device behind the outlet plugging the camera to its power source that they had never seen before. Her employee immediately stopped tinkering with the device and called the police.

Gable waved Maxwell over, who took one look at the device and solved their mystery.

"It's an adapter that would allow someone to shut off your camera using a remote control," he said. "From what I can tell, they used the same technology used to install a garage door opener or an automatic car starter."

"Or an EOD," Gable added.

"Whoever installed this knew what they were doing," Maxwell concluded.

The group retreated into the storage company's main office to view the footage. Maxwell dropped back from the crowd and lightly grabbed Towe's elbow.

"Didn't they have problems with the security camera with the Russian?" he asked.

"They did," Towe responded.

"Did they check their hotel server for a similar adapter?"

"I don't know," she exclaimed, "but we're going to now."

A review of the footage allowed them to watch Kevin Wisnewski's pathfinder pull into the lot, but cut off before any additional footage was available. Hamilton called the dispatch office to run the plates. The agents and officers listened intently to his conversation as they rewound and played back the camera footage hoping for another clue. A third officer entered the office inconspicuously and stood amongst the crowd of law enforcement.

"Today?" Hamilton asked. "Seriously?"

He pulled a note pad out of his coat pocket and held the phone to his ear with his shoulder as he wrote.

"That Pathfinder has stolen plates," he announced. "The plates belong to a Chrysler owned by an 80-year-old man in an assisted living complex."

"I took that call this morning," added the officer who snuck in the back door.

"You sure?" asked one of the other officers sitting in the room.

"Well yeah, unless there's two 80-year-old men who had their plates boosted off their Chryslers," the cop added. "I can run back to my squad and pull the . . ."

"That's not necessary right now Officer," Hamilton interrupted. "It's Harris, right?"

"Yes sir," Officer Harris responded. "First call this morning. It's gotta be the same guy. If it is the same guy, I can't tell you when his plates were stolen. He hadn't driven his car in a week. No surveillance footage."

"Professional," Cavalera added.

The agents and officers shook their heads in disgust, cursing under their breath.

"Can you tell me if Cade Stuckley rents one of your storage units," Gable asked, trying to read the employee's nametag, "Mabel?"

"Already working on it," Mabel responded. "I just needed a name."

The agents and officers waited intently for a response.

"Pod 182," she spoke up. "That's one of our bigger units. Customers usually use them to store automobiles."

"Do you have a key?" Hamilton asked. "He might still be in there."

Mabel handed him a set of bolt cutters and a map of their complex.

"Tenants are responsible for locking their pods," she said, "The map will show you how to get there."

The combination of officers and agents found Cade's pod shut, but no padlock. They entered in tactical fashion and found an empty shed. There was a stack of boxes piled up against the rear wall and a handful of expensive power tools hanging up a plywood board on the side panel. In the middle of the room was an empty space large enough to fit a sedan. Tire marks graced the concrete floor and the smell of exhaust hung in the air from the time Cade sat with the car running.

"Our guy was here," Hamilton said.

"And he's now on the run," Gable added. "Whatever he was driving was smaller than a Pathfinder and he likely added the remote detonated kill switch to the security cameras."

"He did it in time to make sure nobody saw him come or go," Hamilton added as he walked around the shed trying to piece together Cade's steps. All three agents along with Hamilton scanned the ground and surrounding area looking for any other clues that would give a sign of where Cade was going. There were what appeared to be smudges from a slow oil leak, but nothing clear at first glance.

"He had this planned out for a while," Cavalera added.

"He was gonna be running from something," Towe responded.

"But where's he going?" Hamilton asked.

The agents and officers stood in silence taking in the crime scene.

"Detective Hamilton," Harris said, finally breaking the silence, "I didn't come here to tell you about the stolen license plates. I might have some information pertinent to this investigation."

"I'm listening," Hamilton responded, still scanning the perimeter.

"The owner of the apartment," Harris asked, "Cade Stuckley?"

"Yeah," Gable, Cavalera and Towe answered in unison.

"You know who that is, right?" Harris said, looking at the other uniformed officers. Nobody responded. "He was that computer guy that Blake Sergeant used to hang out with."

Nobody respond immediately. The mention of Blake Sergeant brought forth an unspoken deference of his story, his past and what his fate represented. Cavalera caught the nuance in the room and asked respectfully who Sergeant was, invoking his status as a new guy.

"Blake Sergeant was an officer with the Alexandria Police Department," Harris responded. "One of our best for a while." The uniformed officers nodded in silent agreement.

"Nobody, and I mean nobody could spot a drunk driver better than him," Harris continued. "About four years ago, he got an award from the city for all the drunk drivers he arrested over the last year. It made the news. One of the offenders, a lawyer on K street, saw the story and got pissed off. She got some halfwit journalist to write this bullshit story saying he was racially profiling. Wasn't true. We were fighting it, and we were gonna win, but it caused a lot of controversy. A few days later, Sergeant was on patrol. He gets the call, shots fired, his house is on fire. He's the first one on the scene. Found his pregnant wife and daughter in the nursery, all shot up. He carried them both to safety. Radioed it in. Administered first aid. Shooter is back there too. Starts shooting at Blake. A bullet ricochets off a tree in their yard and hits him in the head. When he woke up six weeks later, his house was burnt down and his family was dead."

"He tried to come back onto the force for a while but needed to opt for a medical retirement," Hamilton added. "The newspaper company that wrote the article about him gave Blake a pretty big libel settlement. The lawyer's firm kicked in some money too. Enough to live on for a while. The lawyer and journalist were both fired. The journalist committed suicide last year and the lawyer is still in town working for someone else. But we would take Sergeant back on the force if he came here tomorrow and was able to perform his duties."

"Because of the bullet that hit his head, Sergeant couldn't remember the guy's face," Harris continued. "Thought he was of middle eastern descent, but that was it. We ran through every mugshot of every arrest he ever made, but nothing ever rang a bell."

Everyone stood in silence. The police officers knew the story by heart but it felt like the shooter's bullets were hitting them every time the words were uttered out loud. Blake was a brother to them, and he lived every officer's worst nightmare.

"I remember when it happened," Towe finally spoke. "I am so sorry."

"Anyway, Cade Stuckley was Blake's friend," Harris added. "He was the short dude. Dressed like a hipster. They served together in the Marines and Blake brought him around the guys a couple times. A couple of us thought Cade was bad news and shared that with Sergeant. Blake didn't see it. He was loyal. Sometimes too loyal. Whatever this Stuckley guy is in to, I can't imagine Sergeant is a part of it. But they are friends. Sergeant might know where he is or where he might be going."

"Where is he now?" Gable asked.

"Minnesota," Hamilton and Harris said in unison.

The agents didn't respond. Towe only nodded at Gable and Calavera.

"We can go up there and talk to him," Cavalera said. "I'm sure we could bring one of you along if you think that's helpful."

Towe nodded in approval.

"That won't be necessary," Hamilton responded. "We have a lot of evidence to process and a couple crime scenes to investigate. We'll put out a BOLO for the Pathfinder with stolen plates. We will get you an address for Officer Sergeant. You'll share whatever you learn from the investigation?"

Nobody corrected Hamilton's slip-up regarding Blake's job title. Nobody wanted to.

"Absolutely," Towe responded.

"Got some more evidence here for you," Gable said.

The group turned around to find him squatted down near the floor pointing to a drop of blood next to one of the tire tracks.

"There's another drop of blood back here," a uniformed officer yelled out, now that everyone was looking at the ground.

Two more crimson droplets were found on the ground of the storage area, painting a picture of a man quickly executing his getaway. It also showed sign of a vulnerability.

"Our guy is hit," Gable said.

Chapter 15

Angelo Carbone hung up his phone and stared at three glasses of scotch sitting on his desk. Next to the sniffers laid his reading glasses, an unwelcome reminder that the old crime boss was pushing 78 years of age. His weathered face bore a few scars from youthful indiscretions, but they were now largely hidden by age. Although he continued to have his hair dyed jet black out of habit, even he knew he should have hung up his cleats long ago.

For the first time in his career, he felt in over his head and the world felt crazier than ever. Given his family's history, that was saying something.

"You can come back in."

Billy Carbone and Frank Silvera entered the room. Billy was Angelo's youngest son, the youngest of four kids. He wasn't heir to the throne due to a lack of business acumen, but he was a trusted hand when cleaning messes. He was a spitting image of his father forty years removed with fewer scars on his face, and more soreness in his knuckles. The first shades of grey were threatening to surface on his sideburns, and he gladly followed his father's steps with the hair dye.

Frank was Angelo's son-in-law, married to his oldest daughter. If Frank were Angelo's biological son, he would be taking over the family business. Frank didn't dye his hair. He was a broad shouldered man with graying brown hair, weathered skin and a gravelly voice from decades of smoking.

He fell in love with and eventually married Angelo's oldest daughter Elizabeth, or Bette, and essentially became her caregiver as well as her husband. She battled a series of drug addictions, alcoholism, bipolar disorder and the consequences of a whole host of other poor life decisions. Frank kept coming back despite knowing that she would always love another man. The truth was he probably stopped loving her two nervous breakdowns ago, but the marriage had since become a means for keeping him inside the Carbone's inner circle.

Both men sat in the guest chairs in Angelo's home office.

"That was the Russians," Angelo spoke. "He got away."

Frank and Billy nodded their heads in amazement.

"Killed two of their guys, injured another," Angelo continued. "Blew up his damn apartment."

"He killed two Russians?" Billy asked in surprise.

"No, no," Angelo said, waving his hands in front of him to add emphasis, "Americans. Mercenaries. They've used them before for overseas shit that I don't want to know about. Bad people."

"Do they want our help, now?" Frank asked.

Angelo didn't respond. He only sipped his scotch and stared the pictures on his desk.

"We knew it was dangerous to work with them," he exclaimed to nobody in general, "and I don't think they know about Cade's other job, yet."

"We should have just stuck to drugs," Billy said.

"I agree," Angelo responded, then sighed. "I agree."

"How much does Cade know?" Frank asked.

"He doesn't know what he knows," Angelo responded. "The asshole didn't know who Belov was until it was too late."

"He knows enough," Billy added. "If he talks about some of his other jobs, a good cop could put some pieces together that we don't want them to see."

"He'll talk if the cops catch him," Frank said.

"He'll talk if the Russians get him," Billy added.

"The Russians don't want him alive," Angelo responded tersely, then considered Billy's point. "But if he did talk, that would be a big problem."

The men sat in silence, pondering their options.

"We've got eyes and ears in the investigation and so do the Russians," Angelo said after a moment, breaking the silence. "I think you both know what needs to happen."

Both men nodded.

"So what's the next move, boss?" Billy asked. Angelo looked at Frank.

"We pay Cade's Marine buddy a visit," Frank responded. "We start there and box him in."

"That wasn't my first guess. What makes you think he'll go there?" Angelo asked.

"He needs protection," Frank responded, "and he thinks his buddy can offer that."

"You know what to do," Angelo responded.

Chapter 16

Blake Sergeant stepped out the French doors of a chateau and into the sunlight of a summer afternoon. A warm breeze met him at the entrance along with the faint smell of perfume. Ahead of him was a picturesque view of a massive river flowing between two bluffs, the remnants of a glacier dragging across a prairie millions of years ago to create a tributary to the ocean. A riverboat moved slowly in the distance dragging two pallets of wooden shipping containers.

He walked to a lone table with two seats, one of which was empty. In the other seat was a woman holding a glass of red wine. She wore a white dress with a shawl draped over it, and dark sunglasses. She had brown hair with a prominent streak of white permeating over her bangs, which she wore long and styled over the right side of her face. She looked to be in her fifties, but something told Blake she was much older.

He had never seen her before but he knew who she was. He had heard her voice. He felt her presence sitting in the back seat the previous night, and a part of him knew she had been present in every dream he had over the past three years every time he killed.

He told himself she was an illusion from too many hours on the road and a mind working on overdrive for too long. He reasoned that was he saw wasn't real, but there she sat. He wasn't sure whether she was a ghost or a mother figure long forgotten, but he knew she had been watching him for a while, and he wasn't afraid.

"Hello there Blake," she finally spoke.

Blake didn't respond. It was the same voice he heard in the diner with Cade and in the motel, the night before.

"Don't be a stranger, have a seat," she spoke again, "We've been making eyes at each other long enough. It's time we talked,"

Blake sat down, still trying to assess his surroundings.

"Where am I?"

"You're at a vineyard in southern Minnesota. That's the Mississippi River in front of us and it's a beautiful summer day. We don't have a care in the world."

Blake felt disoriented.

"Do you like red wine?"

"I used to," he responded. That was a secret that he and his wife kept from the rest of the force. They once spent a weekend visiting vineyards in southern Minnesota and went to their share while living in Virginia. Their getaways like felt like they happened in another life.

"Join me for a glass," she said, pouring wine into his empty glass. "I don't like drinking alone. I hope you like sweet reds." He swirled the wine, took a sip and puckered as the taste sent shivers down his spine. It had been a while.

"What do you think?"

"It's definitely sweet," he responded, getting a little more comfortable in his seat.

"The name of the grape used to make this particular bottle is called the King of the North," she said. "It has one hell of a story that I will have to tell you sometime. One of my favorites."

Blake took another sip and allowed himself to enjoy it.

"I'll bet you have questions for me," she said.

"I don't even know who you are," he responded, "but it feels like I should."

"You can call me a Harvester for now, because that's what I am," she said.

"Like a farmer?"

"No," she responded, "like a Harvester. Our universe and our very existence are part of the same balance. Gravity keeps us all glued to the ground and the stars in the sky. Balance creates the gravity that keeps the moon orbiting the earth and the ocean tides from crashing into our homes. Balance keeps this planet rotating around sun just like millions of other planets in other solar systems.

Balance keeps this world and parallel worlds from bleeding into one another. There's a balance between good and evil as well that's just as important as gravity keeping the wine in our glasses. It's my job to help manage that balance, and lately there's been a lot more evil than good in this world."

Blake nodded and took another sip of his wine. *Take that, gravity.*

"Why do you kill?"

"For money," he responded.

"That's not true," she said curtly. "Please pretend that we don't both already know the answer."

"If we already know the answer, why do you want me to say it?"

"Because I want to hear you it from you."

He took another gulp of his wine, nearly finishing the glass.

"I kill because I want to know who killed my family. The only time I ever get a glimpse of that night is on evenings when I commit murder."

"And why do you want to remember?"

He paused and thought about the question.

"Retribution. I want to see his face. I want to know who he is and I want to end him."

"And then what?"

"Don't know. Maybe I'll take a vacation. That is probably why we are talking."

"And why is that?"

"Because you just said there is a lot of evil in the world. Right now, I'm the most evil son of a bitch out there."

"But your victims are presumably not very good people. Aren't they usually about to do something they shouldn't be doing when they meet you?"

"Doesn't matter," Blake responded. He thought this one over during the long drives across the country and was feeling the effects of one glass of wine. "Most of them are usually waiting to have a consensual sexual encounter with a minor. So, yeah, in the eyes of our society, they are bad people. I had no right to judge them."

"But you aren't the judge. You're the triggerman."

"Every bullet I fire is a judgement. I can't keep asking other people to die for my selfish reasons. I have become the source of evil that I took an oath to protect people from, and I'm ready to be done."

"It's good that pastor gave you a book to help you reflect," she said knowingly, "because you're not done killing. You're just getting started."

"Is that why you're here?" he asked.

"Blake," the Harvester said as she refilled his glass, "that sense of impending doom you've been feeling is not unfounded. I was just like you. I wanted justice and didn't get it from a system I believed in. A man-made system. So I did some things I'm not proud of and here I am. I'm a harvester. I collect souls that have been overcome by evil to atone for my sins."

"Is that why I'm here? Atonement?"

"Let's enjoy our wine," she said. "There will be plenty of time for me to answer all your questions."

They stared at the majestic view and each took intermittent sips from their wine glasses. Blake closed his eyes and felt the warmth on his face as the tingle of intoxication danced on his skin. When he opened his eyes, he was laying in his bed, awake two minutes before his alarm was supposed to ring. He realized that he didn't know how he got home. He didn't remember the drive. He didn't remember crawling into bed and he was still wearing the clothes he wore to church.

His phone rang. He looked at the caller ID and saw a 234 area code. He stared at the number for a moment and answered.

"Do you remember that thing we talked about on seven?" Cade Stuckley said distantly.

"No," Blake responded. "I don't remember much these days. I'll need twelve cups of coffee to get my head on straight."

Cade's line was their mutually agreed upon emergency code, and Blake's response was a notification that they would talk in twelve minutes.

Blake hung up the phone, put on his uniform and headed out the front door.

Chapter 17

Melody Slater took a drag of her Camel Light and watched the sunrise outside her apartment. She didn't like smoking indoors and needed time to decompress from her shift.

"You're up early," she called out to her neighbor as he hurried out his front door.

"So are you," Blake replied turning to face her. She was wearing a Vikings shirt that was three sizes too big and a loose pair of flannel shorts. Blake could still make out the curves of her body beneath the fabric, and Melody enjoyed watching him look her up and down. She knew that look, and liked seeing him have that look. She thought about inviting him back to her apartment.

"I saw you pull in earlier, but you seemed distracted," she finally said.

"Did I?"

"Yeah, you just looked out of it. I think you were talking to yourself," she said with a raised eyebrow. "Should I be concerned?"

"What were you doing home?" Blake asked, ignoring her comment.

"Watching a video. I tried to talk to you, but you looked . . ."

"Out of it," he let the comment drift. She waited for him to finish the sentence and smiled uncomfortably.

"You just walked into your apartment. I thought you might have been drinking but that's unlike you. Are you okay?"

"I'm fine," he finally said, and tried to forget the conversation. He started walking toward the green line on University.

"I have to work tonight, and need to take care of a couple of things," he said while walking, "it's good to see you."

Blake walked calmly around the corner to University Avenue, then headed west to the Hamline college campus. He pulled a roll of quarters out of his pocket and called the phone number that Cade called him from.

"Is this what I think it is?"

"Phase one is complete."

"How you doing?"

"Not good," Cade replied, "but I'll manage."

"ETA?"

"Thirteen hours."

"Remember the rendezvous point?"

"10-4."

"Out."

Sergeant hung up the phone and walked to the Green Line station on the way to his day job, working the graveyard shift as a security guard in downtown Minneapolis. As he walked in darkness, he thought about his friend and business partner.

Blake first met Cade Stuckley on Okinawa. They arrived on base around the same time, and lived in the same barracks. Cade worked on computers and Blake was an MP. They didn't travel in the same circles, but living in the same building gave them opportunities to interact.

Field days, company formations and the occasional encounter in the chow hall made up the extent of their encounters for the first six months of their year-long stint on the rock. They eventually learned that they grew up in the same part of the country. That's occasionally where service members form some common bonds outside their occupational social circles.

Both Marines were Denver Broncos fans. They both drank copious amounts of celebratory beer as they watched John Elway lead their team to an upset victory over media darling Brett Favre and the Green Bay Packers. Since Japan was on the other side of the planet, they watched the Super Bowl live on Monday morning. They went back to work drunk, made it through their respective days and went out for more beer later that night to compare notes.

It was that night both men learned they lost their fathers shortly before joining the Marines. Both of their fathers died violent deaths. Both men put their deceased fathers on pedestals, forgetting any imperfections. Everyone has imperfections.

A few months later, both Marines received orders to Headquarters Marine Corps, located in the shadow of the Pentagon. There weren't a lot of enlisted guys at their new unit, and there certainly weren't a lot of "fleet Marines" who had served overseas.

By the time the Denver Broncos returned to the Super Bowl to throttle the Atlanta Falcons, they were both corporals. They were also both smart enough to take leave that subsequent Monday. They drank all night after the victory and managed to alienate every single Atlanta native in the bar that night.

Blake and Cade became best friends under these circumstances, and in some ways, Washington, D.C., was just as much of a foreign country to them as Okinawa. Cade might have come to live with his mother's family in New Jersey after his father's death, but he was only there for six months. As soon as he finished high school, he was on a drill field in Parris Island.

They were two boys from the west who grew up in a culture where boys were expected to work, schoolkids said the pledge of allegiance in the morning and serving one's country was still seen as a noble endeavor.

Small towns had their cliques and imperfections, and those imperfections were precisely why neither man would ever return to rural life. However, city life was still a different culture. Diversity wasn't as big of a deal. The military was diverse. They had grown used to living in a world that wasn't mostly white and Hispanic. There were other differences.

It was the nineties. Most the college kids they encountered in town viewed service members as thugs, punks and losers who were too stupid for college. *That* was different.

When Blake once told a group of young professionals he joined the Marines to serve our country, they referred to him as a gullible loser. He broke four noses that night, none of which were his.

Cade helped his hot-tempered friend escape. Together they concocted an alibi and avoided arrest. Cade was a smart guy. He knew he could make a lot of money in the private sector with the skills he was learning in the Marines and he was planning on doing so.

Blake liked being an MP, but he didn't want to be a beat cop the rest of his life. He wanted to be an investigator. He needed to go to college for that.

Both Marines left active duty and enrolled in community college at the same time. They moved in together.

Cade found a job where he made more in a month than what the Marine Corps would have paid him in a year. He grew out and dyed his hair, re-pierced his ear and began investing in a flamboyant wardrobe. That was his way of cutting all ties with the military.

Blake took a job working as a campus security officer and didn't mind seeing cute college girls all day instead other Marines. Eventually, Blake met Nicole and Cade met a girl named Melissa.

They finished their degrees and married their girlfriends, and that's when they began to drift like most friends do. There was the occasional happy hour, but between work and family, those reunions were infrequent.

Cade was a casualty of the dot com recession. He found work quickly, but he wasn't making as much money. He started his own business designing websites, but eventually needed to sell the house he and Melissa never should have bought. They sold the cars they never should have bought as well. They were divorced within a year and Blake never heard from Melissa again.

The nurse in Nicole suspected that Cade had gotten physical with his wife and the cop in Blake didn't disagree. They saw a few telltale signs, but never brought it up to Cade. Nicole only asked that Blake refrain from bringing Cade around the house.

As Cade went through his struggles, Blake dutifully finished his bachelor's degree, applied for and completed training at a local police academy. He became an Alexandria cop. He and Nicole had a daughter, bought a house they could afford on a cop and nurse's salary and drove used cars with loans they probably shouldn't have taken out.

As time went on, their happy hours went from infrequent to virtually nonexistent. It wasn't until after Nicole, Anni and their son were gone that Cade reappeared on the doorstep of Blake's St. Paul apartment with a twelve-pack of beer and some bad ideas.

Three years later, Cade was on his way back to that same apartment. The consequences of those bad ideas were not too far behind.

Chapter 18

First Sergeant Anthony Byrd entered the newly-painted office of his boss and mentor Colonel Doug Gayton. After a decade of purgatory, it felt good for Gayton Security to have an office on a military base again. Sure, the accommodations weren't ideal, but Boling Air Force Base was in the heart of Washington, D.C. Their new home was situated in a nondescript office building on the outskirts of the main action that would have been otherwise mothballed.

Nonetheless, Gayton, who was never a colonel, and Byrd, who left the Army with a general discharge at the rank of sergeant, had the means to pay for the space and the connections to get their operations back within the perceived good graces of the United States military.

Gayton looked the part of a retired officer who had found a way to continue making the military career after his days in uniform were over. He had a full head of white hair cropped short, tanned skin from years in the field and a regal demeanor. He was used to people calling him "sir." His mercenaries occasionally remarked that he looked like he "came from money," and they were right.

In the wake of multiple scandals involving defense contractors in the Middle East, the Bush administration began the process of cleaning house. President Obama's administration continued the cleanup process, and specifically made a point to ensure Gayton Securities would not be doing any business with the United States at the request of a young veteran turned Congressman from Illinois.

Kevin Wisnewski stood at parade's rest in Gayton's office. He had stitches over his left eye and a bandage over his right shoulder where debris from Cade's apartment struck him. Another bandage covered up the better part of his left leg, and he struggled to hide the limp.

"Wisnewski was just debriefing regarding his after-action report," Gayton explained.

"Is that right?" Byrd responded as he stood in Wisnewski's personal space, looking up to make eye contact.

Wisnewski stared forward and fought to hide the fear in his eyes. He was losing that fight.

Byrd wasn't a large man in stature, but he didn't need to be. He walked with the hard wired swagger of a drill sergeant. When it came to corn-fed white boys like Wisnewski, a swagger and a dirty look was all an African American badass needed to invoke discomfort.

"Did anybody see you?"

Wisnewski thought about the kid from the apartment complex.

"No, sir," he responded.

"They found the brass you didn't police," Byrd growled.

"Where's that gonna lead?"

"Nowhere, sir," Wisnewski responded. "I procured the weapon overseas years ago. First time it has been fired in the United States."

Byrd didn't respond. He only stood in Wisnewski's space, scowling. Wisnewski wanted to bust Byrd's skull wide open but refrained out of fear.

"It's on me, sir," Wisnewski admitted. "I take full responsibility."

"And the vehicle?" Byrd asked.

"It's in the motor pool," Gayton responded. "He entered through the rear entrance with no sentries. No cameras."

"I called in a couple favors," Byrd said. "Do I need to worry about you fucking up again?"

Wisnewski clenched his jaw.

"No sir."

"Dismissed," Gayton said.

"Get the fuck out of here and stand by," Byrd added. "We need all hands."

Wisnewski promptly left the office as ordered. Byrd stepped in and took a seat.

"We underestimated this guy," Gayton said. "Went in with limited intel and he was ready for us."

"We've had tougher missions," Byrd responded. "With less information."

"Either way, he was ready for us," Gayton said calmly. He leaned back in his chair and spun it around. "I've informed our employer that we would appreciate better intel and more lead time. Finding our guys' bodies is a mess I will need to call in a favor to clean up."

"I thought they could handle that."

"They probably can," Gayton said, "but there are a lot of eyes on this case."

"They have a lead in Minnesota. I'll have an address for you by morning."

"Very well. Take a fire team. Leave Wisnewski here. I want him to clean a few more toilets for me," Gayton responded. "When you know something, I want to know something."

"10-4," Byrd said. He exited the room and walked to his team's squad bay.

MONDAY

Chapter 19

Cade Stuckley pulled up to a garage sized storage shed similar to the facility he had just left. He had been behind the wheel for roughly twenty-four hours bleeding slowly into a poorly applied bandage he wrapped around his shoulder shortly after he called Blake from a rest stop in Ohio. His jacket was caked with blood and the car seat bared streaks of crimson embedded upon its leather exterior.

Blake Sergeant opened the storage unit as soon as Cade arrived. The storage space was larger than the space in Alexandria with a wall of weapons to the right.

Stuckley pulled in slowly and parked in the garage unit. He had been running on adrenaline and gas station coffee for 24 hours, taking advantage of oblivious and overtired cashiers in the middle of the night. He opened the door to step out of the car and collapsed toward the concrete floor.

Sergeant caught him before he made impact and eased him to the ground. Sergeant surveyed the blood-stained car and Cade's pale complexion. He admired his friend's tenacity.

"I'm all right," Cade insisted repeatedly.

Blake rested him on the concrete, ran back to his car and offered his friend a bottle of water. Stuckley sat up and winced at the pain.

"Hell of a getaway," Blake exclaimed.

"There were three of them," Cade said between exasperated gulps. "Two were caught in the blast. The third guy was knocked out, or at least I thought he was."

"Any idea who they were?"

"Professionals, I think. They weren't cops. They weren't there to arrest me. They had their guns drawn and didn't announce themselves." Cade fished Kevin Wisnewski's business card out of his pocket. "I grabbed this. Ever heard of Gayton Security?"

"Not until now," Blake glanced at the business card from behind Cade, but he was more concerned with his partner's back.

"Do you mind?" Blake asked as he tilted his head toward Cade's wound. Cade only nodded.

Blake peeled off Cade's jacket to expose a blood caked t-shirt that used to be blue covering a poorly applied bandage. Sergeant raised his shirt and took a peek under the bandage. The cut didn't look like a bullet hole. It was a gash, like getting hit with shrapnel or broken glass. There was a deep bruise on Cade's left shoulder blade coincidently near the actual cut. He pressed on the point of impact and heard Cade groan. He wanted to clean it up to get a better look.

Cade stared at Blake's wall of weapons, taking in this arsenal of assets.

"Is that a rocket launcher?" he said, staring straight ahead.

"It's an AT4," Blake responded, not looking up. "You probably fired one on active duty. The military had a surplus."

"How'd you get it?"

Blake smiled.

"We live in America, my man, land of opportunity."

"I'm sorry. I fucked up."

"Don't worry, you did good," Blake said as he inspected the wound. He could have been upset. He always had a hunch his partner would be the one to slip up, but he was surprised and impressed that Cade made it to Minnesota. In his mind, Blake never thought his friend would succeed on his end of the getaway plan. Blake always imagined Cade waking up passed out from a bender to find Alexandria's finest kicking down his door. He imagined Cade getting caught up in a sting operation or possibly snuffed out by his family.

"Fuck, Cade, it looks like you were shot, but the round didn't break your skin," he said. "And your cut doesn't look like a bullet hole."

"Something hit me when I blew the apartment," Cade replied. "It was probably glass or a splinter from my window frame."

"I saw the pics online," Blake responded. "Looked like you used a lot of C4."

"I wasn't discreet."

Blake surveyed the garage.

"We can't do this here. Let's get you back to my house. I'll clean this up later."

He lifted Cade and guided him back to his Ford Escape. He took a moment to scrub the seat of Cade's car briefly with some cleaning supplies in his storage unit. He made a decent dent, but it was going to take a little more time and attention before the vehicle was ready.

Melody Slater was playing on her phone when Blake pulled up. He was happy to see her out front.

"I need to break a rule on our getaway plan," he said.

"Does it involve her?" Cade asked, checking Melody out as she surveyed his Escape. "Please tell me it involves her."

"You need a professional to look at your back, and you need rest."

"Can she look at my back? Does she have one of those skimpy nurse suits?"

Blake let the comments pass.

"She knows someone who can, and will understand our need for discretion."

"How do you know she'll help?"

"She owes me a favor."

"Does she owe you two favors? I only need six minutes."

"That's five more than I would have guessed, smart guy. Stay put."

Melody watched in shock as Blake helped a hobbled Cade Stuckley out of the car. Stuckley winced and grunted as Sergeant moved him forward.

"I need a favor," Blake said as he helped Cade to the front porch of their duplex.

"Uh, sure," she replied as she put out her smoke and hustled down the steps to help Cade up.

"I'm Melody."

"I'm Cade," he replied, "are you a nurse?"

“Only if you ask nice and pay in cash,” she said with a smile and a wink.

“This just keeps getting better,” Cade said back to Blake.

They made it into Blake’s apartment and laid Cade down on his stomach. Blake pulled Blake’s shirt up and explained the extent of the wounds to Melody.

“Do you still have that doctor friend?” he asked.

“Yeah, but he’s gonna be pissed about this one.”

“We have the money,” Blake responded.

“Fuck,” Cade interjected, “we make all this cash and I’m still paying for health care?”

“Shut up,” Blake responded wanting Cade to refrain from sharing any pertinent information.

“I blame Obamacare.”

“You should have ducked,” Blake shot back.

Blake ran back to his bathroom and returned with rubbing alcohol and fresh bandages.

“I can dress the wound, but he needs a doctor,” Blake continued, talking to Melody. “And discretion is necessary.”

She nodded and stood to head for the door.

“I’ll call in sick today if you need me.”

“I might,” Blake responded, “thank you.”

“No problem,” she responded. “I knew you had secrets, Blake.”

“We’ve all got secrets on the east side,” he responded.

She laughed and disappeared.

Blake poured rubbing alcohol on Cade’s back and listened to him scream as he tended to his wound.

“This might hurt a little,” Blake said in response.

“Your bedside manor fucking sucks,” Cade shot back.

Blake used a rag to lightly clean Cade’s wounds and get a sense of the damage.

“So you remember all the discretion you asked for regarding our business?”

“Yeah man,” Cade responded.

“It needs to end now. We are in escape mode.”

“Sure you wanna do that?”

"We're here, man. We are officially on your leg of the getaway and you're injured. I need to know where we are going and who we have been working for."

"You're gonna be pissed," Cade warned.

"That doesn't matter now." Blake finished cleaning the wound and dressed it. "Besides, I know enough to have a general idea."

"How much you wanna know?"

"Everything."

Cade sighed and took a breath. Blake put a blanket over him and gave him his water.

"Got anything stronger?"

"Not before we see the doctor."

Cade took another swig of his water.

"We've been running an online death pool, taking bets on pedophiles and rapists."

Blake didn't respond. He felt his stomach turning as Cade continued.

"It didn't start out that way. You remember Corporal Martinez? From admin?"

"Yeah," Blake managed to say while throwing away Cade's clothes and blood-stained bandage. He tried to keep himself busy.

"Well he's a cop now, over in New Mexico. He was in town a few years back during a conference, and he's telling me about this piece of shit they got for raping a 14-year-old girl. Anyway, this guy gets off with a three-year sentence and Martinez is convinced it's because the victim was Native American. He serves one year, and the state gives him an ankle bracelet. The dude's a trucker, so he's driving around the state free as hell, and this victim and her family? Their lives are ruined. She is going through all sorts of therapy and scared shitless this guy is gonna come back and find her. The cops have been driving past her home on routine patrols and one cop even drives her to school on the days she doesn't dare to leave the house."

"Where's this clown? Driving his truck. Listening to country music. Doing God knows what until one day he just disappears. They think he's in North Dakota hauling oil. They don't have the money to go looking for him. The North Dakota cops didn't have time to go looking for him because of the oil boom. They had a whole state full of roughnecks doing all kinds of shit. You remember those guys, from when we were kids?"

"My uncle was one of those guys. He was all right, but yeah, I remember."

"Anyway, he says half his department, this small-town police department has like $20,000 in meth money in their evidence locker, and it's off the books. I don't know how they did that."

"It's not impossible."

"They're planning to take some leave and go looking for him, but these guys got families. Responsibilities. And they're cops."

Cade paused for effect.

"And?" Blake responded.

"That guy was Tommy Montoya."

"I remember him."

"We killed the motherfucker. Anyway, there was almost no investigation. One detective flew in from North Dakota for two days. After he interviewed that poor girl Montoya raped, Martinez said he knew the guy didn't give a shit if he never caught us. He had to leave early because some guy back home died in a bar fight. That was it. That's when I knew this idea would work. A few weeks later, Martinez called me with a similar job and I set the wheels into motion. And you were game. You came back ready for blood, man." Blake remembered. He specifically remembered his dreams from that night.

"Is Martinez in on this?"

"Not anymore. He just bets like everyone else these days."

"And who is everyone else," Blake called out from the other room. He was looking for an extra change of clothing that he bought for Cade in case they ever reached the moment they were presently living in.

"Victims, family members of victims, law enforcement, people that our justice system has failed. Guys like the ones we've taken out don't deserve to live. That's what most Americans believe. That's why we're able to get away with this for so long."

"Until now," Blake responded, setting down a pile of folded clothes next to Cade. There was a blue button-up shirt and a pair of jeans that still had the department store tags on them.

"These should fit you. Might be a little big."

Cade examined the conservative attire which beared no resemblance to his sense of fashion.

"Did you buy these at K-Mart?" Cade asked.

"No, Target," Blake responded. "We're in Minnesota."

Cade shook his head and smiled, knowing his old friend was messing with him.

"Thank you," he managed.

Blake nodded in return, enjoying the moment of unspoken levity his subtle joke delivered.

"When did your family get involved?" Blake asked again.

"Last year. They knew I had an operation and approached me with a business offer. They get a cut of the proceeds, but we have a much bigger revenue source. There's plenty of cash to pay out the winners and pay for the overhead – you and me."

"And you're still running all the money through your business."

"What business? I haven't done any IT work in six months. This is my full-time job."

Blake was strangely serene. He couldn't will himself to get angry. It felt as if the Harvester was keeping him lucid. He thought Cade's logic was flawed, but he didn't want to waste time and energy on a debate. Cade needed to heal. Blake had heard enough.

"What's our getaway plan after this?"

"We got a flight out of country, but we'll need to take a road trip to get there."

"Where are we going?"

Cade paused.

"Marion, Wyoming."

"Fuck, Cade!" Blake responded. Now he was pissed. "What the fuck?"

Marion was the closest city to the small town where Blake lived during his teenage years. He left when he was nineteen, shortly after his father's funeral. That was almost twenty years ago.

"I'm sorry man, that's where our best option is," Cade responded.

"Martinez can't help?"

"No," Cade responded. "Remember Blaine Crockett?"

"I know who he was."

"Yeah, well the girl he raped is a cop. Her stepdad's the assistant chief. They owe us and more importantly, they're more loyal to me than they are my family."

"You're sure about that?"

"I have to be."

Blake paused, thinking through the options.

"We don't have another option, Blake," Cade said. "This plan will work. People want to help us. We'll fly to Canada, then take a ship due south. Everything is off the books. We'll be in the Caribbean by this time next week."

Blake shook his head. He had the feeling the walls were about to come down, and here they were. It was a stupid plan.

"You know we were doing a good thing, right?" Cade asked.

"I know we had a good business model," Blake responded. "We went after guys nobody was going to miss. We made a lot of money, and if there was a betting pool, it was there because our society is desensitized to violence. We would still be doing it, but the two guys we killed this weekend were different. One had money and the other had power. Your doctor will be here soon, but I want to know who the hell," Blake paused and read the business card Cade gave him, "Gayton Security is."

"Well if you're so fucking high and mighty, why the hell did you stick around so long?"

"Easy," Blake said still staring at the business card, "it's what I'm good at."

Chapter 20

Scott Warner followed Melody Slater to her apartment with a backpack on his shoulder and a pensive expression on his face. Warner was an emergency room doctor at Regions Hospital. He was used to spending the better part of his life with people who lived in neighborhoods like Frogtown.

He wasn't an imposing figure, standing at five foot six, and having the distinction of looking about ten years younger than his actual age. Over time, that was changing as he spent more and more time at Slater's place of employment. He had been working in the ER for just over eight years because he liked the rush of never knowing what type of wound or ailment he was going to face next. He never wanted to be the kind of doctor who treated runny noses or operated on the same knee joint every day. He wanted to see people and help them at their worst possible moment in life. He wanted to save lives. That was why he went to medical school.

Over time, this decision cost him countless dollars as his colleagues took jobs in the suburbs where life was a little more routine and lucrative. It also cost him his marriage when it was clear his wife was more interested in marrying a rich doctor and not an ER doc working in a public hospital.

He took the news hard, and became more and more disenchanted. The fact that he would periodically see patients arriving to his emergency room via taxi from a hospital in Dakota County began to piss him off. He grew tired of the fact that a cadre of ethnocentric politicians were spewing paranoid rhetoric that did little more than scare immigrants away from coming to the emergency room because they were worried about getting deported.

After his wife left him for a realtor in Minnetonka, Scott started making house calls. He would go to the homes of families who probably weren't in America legally, and visit their sick kids. He would treat their earaches before they had to come to the emergency room. He resolved what he could with house calls and over the counter drugs. When the kids needed treatment in a medical facility, he drove them to a community clinic. In these cases, the parents were more comfortable as they had the chance to pay for the services he was delivering. After all, these people worked and earned money, too. The Hispanics in particular had a lot of pride, he observed.

The unfortunate byproduct of gaining the reputation he had was that he occasionally had to see people like Melody Slater's friends. He knew this was a shady deal, but in the end, he wasn't a cop. He was a doctor.

Melody knocked on the door and Blake answered. He nodded and invited them in.

"Are you the doctor?" Blake asked,

"Yes, Scott Warner," he responded, and held out his hand. Blake shook his hand and led him in the dusty apartment.

"This is Cade, and he had an accident," Blake explained. Cade looked Warner over and turned his back to face him. Scott took in the wound. It was infected, and clearly happened a while ago. It wasn't as bad as he was anticipating, but the man needed stitches and possibly some down time. That would be a little challenging given the lapse of time, but certainly possible.

The deep bruise was another matter. Scott asked Cade to rotate his shoulder, which Cade was able to do with ample pain. It was unclear where the irritation was from the wound or the bruise as they were both on the same shoulder. Scott smiled.

The maximum range of a handgun was impressive on paper, one thousand meters for a nine-millimeter, but those metrics assumed a shot was fired in ideal weather conditions by a trained marksman. The range also assumed the target wasn't running or jumping for cover. It also assumed the target wasn't wearing a jacket or backpack. Cade was wearing both. Scott had seen deep bruises like this one before and knew immediately what it was. Lucky shot. Unlucky target. A realistic example of the effective range of a handgun in imperfect conditions. An x-ray would show a deeply bruised shoulder blade. Maybe even a hairline fracture. Cade's mobility suggested there wasn't anything terribly wrong and Scott quickly went to work.

"Do you need any help?" Blake asked.

"No, this shouldn't be too difficult," Warner replied, and with that, Blake disappeared into the bathroom. Seconds later, he heard the shower. Cade and Melody gave each other a confused look as Scott pretended not to notice.

This was a shady situation, Scott thought to himself. Blake Sergeant didn't look like the kind of guy who lived in a dingy apartment like this and that usually meant one thing. He was hiding. *Focus on the cut, Scott.*

Within twenty minutes, Scott was finished, and Sergeant was out of the shower in his security uniform. From a distance, the uniform looked like that of a street cop, but up close, one could read the embroidered patches from a local rent-a-cop shop. Scott acknowledged his presence, and cleaned up his mess.

Son of a bitch, my name is Mudd. Scott thought as the Primus song written about the poor physician who unknowingly provided medical treatment to John Wilkes Boothe after he had shot President Abraham Lincoln. Mudd was eventually prosecuted as an accomplice. Warner had no idea whether the uniform was real or not, but he wanted to leave before he saw enough to land him in a courtroom.

The cut was deeper than he anticipated and there were early signs of infection. Scott decided to leave behind some antibiotics and a few sample packets of Tylenol for the pain. This guy looked like a wounded animal ready to get back out into the wild, but his body was clearly sending him a different signal. He put the drugs on the table next to Cade.

"So here is the deal," Scott started, "I'll start with the bruise. It looks deep, and your mobility is limited. You're experiencing a lot of pain. It's unclear whether that's from the laceration, which we will get to, or the bruise itself. I honestly wouldn't be able to tell you more without an x-ray. Second, you were cut pretty deep. I stitched it up, or at least as good as I can get it. Your skin is swollen and there are some early signs that it could get infected if you leave it alone. I want you to clean it regularly, and apply an ointment. Neosporin will do the trick. Take these antibiotics for the swelling.

You should take two with each meal until they are all gone. I am also giving you some Tylenol 3 for the pain . . ."

"Say what?" Cade finally asked.

"I'm sorry?" Scott responded, clearly confused.

"You're giving me Tylenol?"

"Yes, but you shouldn't take more than . . ."

"What the fuck?" Cade said, raising his voice. "Do I look like a fucking 4-year-old? Are you out of Flintstone pills?"

Blake started to step in, and Scott put his hand out to hold Blake back.

"I assume you want something stronger?"

"Fuck yeah," Cade responded.

"Are you in an uncomfortable amount of pain?"

"You're goddamned right I am!"

"Then I would suggest that you consider paying a visit to Regions hospital or HCMC."

Scott looked at Blake, "If you want an opioid, you will have to see me at my practice."

Cade mulled it over, and Scott finished cleaning his equipment up. This doctor had balls.

Cade pulled his Beretta out from under the couch he was laying on and stuck the barrel of the pistol in Warner's face. Warner stopped what he was doing and only stared at the weapon. Tears welled up in his eyes as a lump grew in his throat. His ex-wife used to tell him his mouth was one day going to get him in trouble. He cringed at the thought of her being right.

"You've got a smart mouth on you," Cade said with a snide undertone. "Should we splatter it on my friend's kitchen floor?" Cade stroked the trigger with his index finger, and flipped the weapon off safe with his other hand. Warner only nodded in the negative.

"Cade!" Melody shrieked, "What the hell?"

"Zip it or you're next," Stuckley growled.

Melody stared at Stuckley with his gun in Scott's face, frozen in her shoes.

"You don't know how much I want to kill you," Cade snarled with a dark smile.

Cade touched the barrel of the pistol on Warner's forehead to let him feel the cold steel. At first, he just wanted to scare the guy, but it felt good to have this kind of power. He wanted to squeeze the trigger and add to his list of bodies. Why not? He was already a fugitive.

"Put it down, Cade," Blake finally said, never raising his voice. "You've made your point."

"Have I?"

"Yes," Blake said using the same cerebral monotone delivery. Warner looked at Blake and was surprised at his calm demeanor. He wondered if the guy's heart rate even went up. Cade cracked a smile at Warner and slowly raised his pistol. It felt good watching a man who only thirty seconds ago was giving him the kind of condescending attitude that too many people put up with these days. Now this doctor was within seconds of losing his life.

"You're lucky my friend is a nice guy," he said. "I would have loved putting a round in your grape."

The fear in Warner's eyes gave Cade an adrenaline rush. Now he knew what it was like to stick a gun in a man's face and watch him squirm.

"Get the fuck out of my face," Cade growled.

Scott Warner obligingly grabbed his bag and shuffled for the door. Sergeant followed him firing a glare at his partner.

"Why don't you thank the good doctor?"

"Thank you, good doctor," Stuckley growled back.

Melody quickly followed Blake and Scott to the door, only to have Blake wave her off.

"The doctor and I need to talk for a moment, then he's all yours," Blake said calmly. "I made coffee. You should have a cup."

Warner's hands were shaking as Blake let him out of the house.

"I apologize for my friend's temper," Blake said calmly. "He has had a long weekend."

Warner looked at Blake and got the distinct sense that as intimidating his ex-patient was, this was the guy he didn't want to mess with. He grabbed his hands, trying to keep them from shaking. Blake noticed.

"It's a good thing he didn't put a gun in your face before you did the stitches." Warner laughed uncomfortably.

"Your friend has lost a lot of blood," Scott finally said. "I don't know what your situation is, but he should really try to take it easy for a few days. And consider going to a hospital if his cut gets infected."

"Duly noted," Blake responded. Blake handed Warner a wad of cash.

"This is for taking care of my friend, and thank you for your discretion."

"You know," Scott said uncomfortably, "That really isn't necessary. I mean, I don't know if I would feel comfortable, you know . . . taking money given the circumstances." He let his voice trail off as he searched in his mind for an excuse.

"I get it," Blake said. "It would make me more comfortable if you did take some money for your troubles. You took time to care for my friend, and he wasn't appreciative of the risks you took coming here. I would like to pay you for the service."

"It's just, uh, I, I could get into a lot of trouble for taking money from you in this situation for ethical reasons," Warner's responded, but beginning to take an interest in the wad of cash. He did have a gun stuck in his face.

"Look," Sergeant responded, "I understand you're a little rattled, but I want you to take this money. Give it to charity for all I care, but you're taking this money." Scott took the cash.

"I don't think I need to tell you this, but the less you say about this situation, the better," Blake said.

"I would get in just as much trouble as you would, mister,"

"Smith. John Smith," Blake Sergeant said with a smile, "and maybe not as much trouble as me."

They shook hands, and Blake knew Dr. Warner wouldn't say a thing about his house call.

Blake walked in, and Melody walked out to drive the doctor home.

When Scott Warner returned to his home, he promptly threw up and cried for a while, thanking God he was alive. All he could think about was the look in Cade's eye. That man wanted to pull the trigger. Scott Warner would go to church for the first time in almost two years that next Sunday, and made a promise to himself to avoid the gentlemen's club for a while.

Sergeant walked past Stuckley without making eye contact.
"Please don't lecture me," Cade growled.

"I wasn't going to," Blake replied as he returned from his bathroom and placed two full bottles of prescription drugs on his table next to Cade.

"The first one contains enough Vicadin to kill a horse, and the other one is Ambien, to help you sleep. Stuckley read the bottles as Blake spoke.

"These are three years old," he responded. "Is it even safe for me to take these?"

"We'll find out," Blake replied as he set a glass of water on the table. "After he finished shitting his pants, the doctor said you should get some rest."

Blake grabbed his jacket and walked to the door.

"You're really going to work?" Cade called out behind him.

"Yeah. We need to figure out who Nicolay Belov is because chances are they'll be following us. I think he is the connection to Gayton Security."

"Don't you think that's a little risky?"

"Walking into a hotel room in New York City and putting five rounds in a guy's skull is risky."

"Yeah, but you know we have a lot of people looking for me."

"That's why you aren't going to leave this house. Do you have your cell phone?"

"No. I blew it up."

"Good. Get some sleep."

Sergeant walked out to University just in time to catch the green line to downtown Minneapolis.

He sat on the train staring at the business card.

You know, the authorities are hot on his trail. They're probably waiting for you now.

"I'm counting on it," he replied softly.

So what is this? Is this how you stop killing? Turn yourself in?

"You heard the doctor. Cade needs rest. Besides, don't you want to know who's after us?"

What is your real motivation? Where is all of the moral conflict you've been wrestling with over the last twenty-four hours?

"My moral conflict has never dissipated and it has been there way longer than twenty-four hours. Besides, if you're so damned powerful, why are you so worried about my choices?"

Only you control your freewill. You can't change what you are.

"I never said I could."

Blake looked up and saw another passenger watching him nervously as he carried on the conversation with himself. He shifted his gaze to the window. *Great,* he thought, *I'm the crazy guy on a train.*

His train reached its stop and he picked up dinner on the way to the downtown building he was going to spend the next eight hours guarding.

As he walked through the front doors, he saw his supervisor, Tyrell Marcus, sitting in the front lobby with two guys in black suits. They all stood a little too eagerly to come across as smooth. They were FBI agents, and Blake was expecting them.

I love it when things work out, he thought.

Be careful, the Harvester responded.

I'm only getting started.

Chapter 21

Gable and Cavalera sat in the lobby of the ING building in downtown Minneapolis. Known as the "building on stilts" to anyone trying to draw a distinction between it and the other nondescript skyscrapers in the area, the centerpiece of the lobby was a giant chandelier hanging above the front information desk.

They identified Capstone Security as Blake Sergeant's employer from his tax records, and decided to meet him at the beginning of his graveyard shift. It was planned. They would ask him a few questions. If he knew anything, he would have to spend the next eight hours sweating. Their hope was that he would surf the net and give them a couple of hints. Once his shift was over, Vernon Maxwell would check the memory on the computer at the security desk.

Maxwell was in his Downtown Minneapolis hotel room drinking coffee and scouring the web looking for anything he could find on Cade Stuckley. He was making progress. Using Cade's IP address and records from the internet dating site where he established contact with Blaine Crockett, Maxwell was able to isolate times when someone using Cade's computer was chatting on one of their online forums.

The lawyers representing the dating site were engrossed with a fight with the Bureau's lawyers regarding the procurement of specific details surrounding Cade's conversation, but Vern had his own way of looking for whatever information he could preemptively find. A timeline for Cade's activity was worth its weight in gold.

If Cade Stuckley was on his way to Minnesota, Gable and Cavalera would be near enough to apprehend. If Blake was not a fruitful lead, there were other leads in the area they could pursue.

Gable looked at the office directory.

"I recognize the name of this firm," he said, pointing at a law firm with several Norwegian last names stitched together.

"Yeah?" Cavalera responded.

"Yeah," Gable said with a chuckle, "I think a guy I served with works here. He was PAO. Long time ago. Heard he's a lobbyist at their state Capitol."

Cavalera made a note to ask him later on what "PAO" meant.

"Do you know someone in every town we go to?"

"Probably," Gable said, marveling at the directory, "but I haven't thought about this guy in years."

"If we're here long enough, maybe you can pay him a visit."

"Nah," Gable responded, waving his hand, "the guy was a fucking asshole."

Sergeant walked through the building's security entrance 15 minutes early just as his supervisor, Tyrell Marcus, said he would. He had a gym bag in one hand and a sack from Chipotle in the other. All three men stood a little too abruptly to meet him.

"Good evening Mr. Marcus," Blake said.

"Sergeant," Marcus said in a mock authoritative growl in return, "These gentlemen are from the FBI. They would like to have a word with you."

Sergeant watched Cavalera visibly wince behind Tyrell while Gable sized him up. The door opened behind them, and in walked a business man who headed for the elevator, barely acknowledging their presence. Tyrell rolled his shoulders back and gave the man an authoritative stare that he would have noticed had he not been fiddling with his cell phone. Sergeant turned his attention to his guests.

"The FBI, huh," Sergeant responded. "Well, what brings you to the quietest building in Downtown Minneapolis?"

"Blake Sergeant," Cavalera finally said. "I'm Special Agent Cavalera and this is my colleague Special Agent Gable. Is there somewhere we can talk?"

"Sure," Blake responded. "There's a small conference room downstairs that I doubt anyone is using. Does that work?" Sergeant looked over at Tyrell whose stoic gaze turned into an expression of confusion as he processed the question. Tyrell looked at Cavalera and Gable.

"Would that work for you gentlemen?"

"Yes," Gable responded, looking at Blake. It was subtle, but Sergeant was controlling what he could about the environment under which he was going to be questioned. Both agents noticed.

The three of them went to the conference room, stopping only for coffee at a nearby break room. They sat down across from each other as Blake sipped his coffee. Cavalera pulled a tape recorder out of his briefcase and proceeded to set it up. Blake only hummed in response. *Cool as a Cucumber,* the voice in Blake's head said in its eerily soothing tone.

"Is something wrong?" Gable asked.

"No," Blake responded. "What can I do for the FBI today?"

"We'd like to ask you a few questions about Cade Stuckley," Cavalera said. "Have you ever heard of him?"

Stay cool, Blake.

"Yeah, I know Cade," Blake responded.

"How well do you know each other?" Cavalera continued.

"We served together in the Marine Corps, and have been friends ever since."

"Would you call him a good friend?" Cavalera asked.

"I would call him one of my only living friends. Is he all right?"

"Why do you ask?" Cavalera responded. Gable grimaced behind him but Blake didn't acknowledge it.

"Well, I am sitting across from two FBI agents on a Monday night, and they are asking me questions about Cade," Blake said. "That can't be good."

Cavalera and Gable looked at each other and Gable spoke.

"There was an explosion in Cade's apartment on Friday afternoon, and he hasn't been seen since. When was the last time you talked to him?"

Blake let his eyes widen, and acted surprised. "What do you mean by explosion? Was it a gas leak? Arson?"

"We're still trying to figure that one out," Gable said. "There are a lot of unanswered questions. Right now we're trying to see if we can find your friend and make sure he's okay."

"Or see what the fuck he got himself into," Sergeant said shaking his head. It was a little too easy expressing frustration toward his partner in crime. *How much C4 did you use, anyway, Stuckley?*

"Do you know if he's still in D.C.? He has family in Idaho." *That's right. Act concerned, Blake. Don't give them anything to work with. They got nothing.*

"That's what we're trying to find out now," Gable said, taking note of Blake's seemingly innocuous questions. "When was the last time you talked to Cade?"

"Last week," Blake responded. Blake looked at the closed conference room door and did what he could to muster up the expression of a concerned employee. "I have been thinking about moving back to Virginia, and I was there this past weekend. Haven't told the boss about my plans yet, so it would be good if the two of you didn't share that with him." Both agents nodded and Sergeant continued, "Cade and I had lunch."

"What did you guys talk about?"

"We talked about me moving back. I assume you guys know about my family."

Gable and Cavalera nodded awkwardly.

"Yes," Cavalera finally responded, but sensing an opportunity to get this guy to talk. "I didn't live here – or – I didn't live in Washington at the time, but a lot of my colleagues did. They remember reading about it in the news."

"I wish people would forget," Blake said, looking intently at the conference room in front of him.

"It's every agent's worst nightmare," Gable responded, seeing the opportunity, yet stating the obvious. "There is no way to forget it. We know every day we go to work, that is a risk we take. That is a risk we ask our families take."

"Yeah," Blake responded and exhaled. He rubbed his eyes. "I never thought about it. I spent five years on the force pulling over drunks, speeders and other traffic violators. I would sometimes see guys or women in the grocery store who I pulled over at one time or another. Usually, they were trying to avoid *me."*

"So you and Cade had lunch and talked about you moving back?" Gable said.

"Yeah," Sergeant responded while eyeballing his dinner. "You guys mind if I eat?"

"No, suit yourself," Gable responded.

"Thanks," Blake said, "We're not supposed to eat dinner on duty and I need to clock in as soon as we're finished."
The agents nodded in response. Blake pulled a burrito bowl out of his take out bag from Chipotle. He unwrapped the chicken and black bean surprise as he talked, filling the room with its aroma.

"When I left Alexandria, the chief said I would always have a job waiting for me if I wanted it. I tried to come right back to the force after my family died but I wasn't ready. I had to leave. I was finally starting to feel like it's time to come back. I wanted to get situated before I contacted anyone, and that was what Cade and I spoke about."

"Did you talk about what Cade was up to, at all?" Gable asked.

"Yeah, we did," Sergeant said in between bites of his dinner. The smell of the burrito filled the room, leaving both agents feeling a little hungry. "He said work was a little slow, but he was close to finishing a deal with a new client. It didn't seem like he was in any trouble. We talked about me crashing at his place for a while. Guess that isn't going to happen. Do you think someone tried to break into his place?"

"Like I said," Gable responded, "we're very early into our investigation."

They sat in silence for a moment then Blake spoke again.

"If Cade is in trouble, I would suggest that you take a real close at his mom's family. Stuckley is a good guy. He has his demons. We all do, and he's doing the best he can. That family of his is nothing but trouble. He tried his whole life to get away from them, but I would say that whenever trouble finds Cade, they're involved."

"What can you tell us about his family?" Gable asked.

"The Carbones are bottom-feeders. Nothing but a pack of assholes and degenerates. They pull in a lot of money and my guess is they're into drug trafficking. His mother's psychotic and his dad – who raised him – died when he was a teenager. They live up in Jersey somewhere. I'm sure your organized crime unit up there has a file on them."

"We're looking into it," Cavalera responded.

"Good. That whole family belongs in jail. Or in a nuthouse. I guarantee you if Cade is in trouble, they're involved."

Gable felt like Sergeant knew more. He was also hoping they didn't just fly all the way out to Minnesota to find an old Marine buddy who was looking out for his friend.

"So why did you move to Minnesota?" Cavalera asked. He had a feeling there was something else there, and wanted to see what else he could learn.

"I like lakes," Blake responded facetiously

"Come on, man," Cavalera responded. "I lived here for three years and hated every second of it."

"Where did you live?"

"Rochester."

"Well, there's your problem," Blake responded. "Rochester sucks."

The walls echoed with Cavalera and Sergeant's laughter as Cavalera shook his head in agreement. "Not a lot to do on your free time."

They both laughed some more and even Gable managed a smile. *This guy has potential.* Gable thought of Cavalera. Rapport was built.

"I hear they're doing a bunch of construction down there, but haven't been around to see it. This is a decent place," Sergeant said, clearing tears from hid eyes. "Good place to raise a family. Nice suburbs."

"Why would you want to live in Minnesota?" Cavalera said with a smile.

Blake exhaled and thought about the answer.

"My wife and kids are buried here," he responded. "It's where Nicole grew up. When we lived in Virginia, her family was always trying to get us to move here. I would never have it. I was stationed in D.C.. I went to college in Virginia. It was my home. Plus, Nicole loved it. We had a nice house. We had good jobs. Why would we want to move somewhere where it's winter nine months out of the year? They were always concerned about her safety, and I thought that was stupid. D.C. is a violent city, I'll give you that, but so is Minneapolis. So is St. Paul. So is any other city in this country. There are bad people in every town. You know that. When my wife and kids died, I missed everything about them. Now days, the closest I can come to seeing them is sitting next to a couple slabs of marble, knowing they're buried beneath me."

"Do you ever see her family?" Gable asked.

"We went to dinner a couple times. They were trying to be cordial, but you can tell they blame me. They're right."

"So why do you want to come back to D.C.?" Cavalera asked.

"I think it's time for me to rejoin the living."

They talked for another five to ten minutes, and Blake told them everything he wanted them to know. He and Cade were close. He thinks Cade's family is involved. Blake scribbled his information on a pad and asked them to call him if they had more questions. Please let him know if his buddy was okay. In the end, the agents had little reason to believe Sergeant knew anything. Sergeant finished his burrito and walked out the room to find Tyrell in the hallway.

"Sergeant," Tyrell growled.

Blake walked slowly to him.

"Anything I need to be aware of?"

"A friend of mine from the Marines is in some trouble," Blake responded. "They wanted to know if I knew anything."

"They flew here from Washington for that?"

"Your tax dollars at work."

Tyrell tried to stare Sergeant down, but it's difficult to intimidate a man when you're four inches shorter than him. Sergeant only smiled, knowing he could put his fat little boss through a wall anytime he wanted to.

"Carry on," Tyrell finally growled.

Sergeant walked off hiding a growl. He hated it when civilians who never spent a second in uniform tried to talk military. It only made Marcus sound like an asshole. He watched Marcus walk in to kiss the agents' asses a little more and walked off to his post. He had work to do.

Gable and Cavalera watched Sergeant walk out of the isolated conference room. Cavalera stopped the recorder.

"Are you thinking what I'm thinking?" Gable said.

"He knows something," Cavalera responded. Gable nodded.

"We'll see if the Minneapolis field office can have a couple of guys tail him for a while. We'll track his phone records as well."

Chapter 22

Blake Sergeant waited for his boss and the agents to leave and volunteered to walk the building. There were 22 floors, consisting mostly of office space. A law firm took up most of the 20th floor. The firm was named after three Swedish partners and provided steady competition to their Norwegian counterparts in the same building. One of the older partners had all the passwords for his computer written on a post-it note sticking on the monitor. Some of the security guards knew of this little breach and would occasionally surf porn on his computer. Their indiscretions were difficult to trace as the lawyer shared the same fetishes.

Blake had other plans. He entered in the password and started using the Internet to find out everything there was to know about Gayton Security and Nicolay Belov. He knew the agents probably had a plan for snagging the CPU after his shift to view the site history and that was okay. They could spend some quality time figuring out who this group was if they didn't know already.

Belov was a Russian businessman who worked for an investment company with a lot of activity in energy and defense contracting. There were pictures of him with local politicians and leaders from several other nations including the President. His business had a couple of write-ups in English revealing a few details but nothing substantial. If Blake could read Russian, he could have probably learned a lot more. Either way, the guy had money.

Gayton didn't have an official website. Sergeant didn't expect them to, but a few conspiracy theorist blogs mentioned the group in passing. There were allegations of their group conducting illegal activities in Iraq.

The Washington Chronicle had a long write up about several contractors conducting illegal and unethical activities. A freshman

Congressman from Illinois singled out Gayton and seemed to be going out of his way to ensure they wouldn't be getting any business from the United States. That was in 2007. Another article the following year referenced the contractors in question again, and noted their line items in the defense budget that year had disappeared.

Sergeant took out the card that Cade snagged off his would-be assassin. He looked around the empty building lobby he was guarding, then focused on the card.

He closed his eyes, and let his mind leave the office with a view of the Minneapolis skyline. The darkness gave way to several visions that flashed in and out like snapshots on an old film projector. He had a vision of an older man, possibly retired military, taking a blowtorch to the head of another man. The next vision was of soldiers running through an obstacle course. The course gave way to a vision of service members was combat in the desert, followed by a vision of a handful of mercenaries escorting a 5-ton through a jungle. The next image was Cade's apartment exploding, followed by a plane landing on an isolated airstrip with the city of St. Paul in the background. The last images were in his own apartment. Sergeant saw enough. It was time to move.

For the first time in a career of security, military service and law enforcement, Sergeant left his post early. He called a cab that arrived shortly before 4:00 AM and dropped him off at the storage shed that held Cade's Mustang. Sergeant slid open the door and walked past the car to a small craftsman toolbox in the back.

He pulled some cleaning supplies out from a shelf adjacent to the toolbox and finished his original job of wiping down the Mustang's driver's seat, cleaning as much blood as he could scoop up.

Blake proceeded to his wall of weapons and selected a 9-millimeter Smith and Wesson semiautomatic pistol and a silencer that lay next to it. He bought the pistol years ago at a gun show in West Virginia, and kept it as his backup in a location away from home in case of emergency. This was an emergency. He also pulled out an old combat knife that he bought as an 18-year-old PFC in the Marines. The knife had a blade on one end and a serrated blade on the other designed for the wielding pleasure of young high-and-tights who were vying to be the next John Rambo.

While on active duty, he more frequently used the knife for more practical matters such as cutting 550 cord or any other menial task that gave him the opportunity to show it off. He also made a habit of sharpening it during long nights on duty. Now it was going to be used again.

Blake put the knife in a sheath and threaded it onto his belt. Returning to the car, Sergeant popped the trunk and took a peek in back. The trunk light shined on three black gym bags which were each zipped up. Sergeant slid the storage room door shut and allowed for the trunk light to illuminate the room. He unzipped each bag. The first bag was full of clothing. Winter clothing. Blake remembered Cade telling him to pack a similar bag as part of their getaway plan. He went back to the toolbox and grabbed his gym bag packed with winter clothing per his partner's advice.

Cade's other two bags were filled with cash, organized in billfolds. There were 100s, 50s and 20s. Mostly 20s. Blake stared into Andrew Jackson's eyes and shook his head, but not in surprise.

"You were holding out on me, Cade," he said aloud to the nighttime air. "I wonder what other secrets you've been keeping."

There would be plenty of time to ask those questions, but Sergeant's mind returned to the task at hand. He slid out of the storage shed and disappeared into the night, headed toward his house just a few blocks away.

Chapter 23

Melody heard them first. For years, she had been an insomniac, never able to get more than four or five hours of sleep at night. She tried over the counter and later prescription meds, but the treatment plan went by the wayside when she realized what an advantage her insomnia gave her as a dancer. The problem was she was still unable to sleep on her nights off and this was no exception.

She heard the truck pull up and didn't recognize the engine idle. She lay in bed thinking about that unfamiliar idle when she heard feet shuffling outside her bedroom window. She rolled out of bed and onto the floor hoping they didn't see her.

Cade popped three Vicadin tablets and chased them with half a bottle of old tequila he found after Sergeant left. He was sure this was not the appropriate dosage or means for consumption, but at the time, he was keyed up and needed rest. His painkiller cocktail knocked him out, which wasn't a difficult achievement when considering he had spent the last 26 hours driving across the country.

Melody pulled him off the bed and onto the floor. Cade tried to mutter something about being left alone, but was only able to slur his speech.

"Cade," she said, "Cade. Come on. We gotta go."

Cade shuddered, wiped his groggy eyes and looked around. Still half asleep, he shivered again trying to wake up.

"Cade!" Melody said in a whispered shriek. Her measured tone from seconds earlier was becoming less stable. She struggled to drag him out of Blake's bedroom to the living room. From there, she would drag him to a seldom used door that connected her and Blake's apartments, which neither of them used until that night. They were halfway across the room when she could hear the wooden floor panels outside her front door creaking and the knob on her front door rattling. Somebody was at the door.

Unaware of the sound, Cade tried to stand up, but the dizziness from the pills landed him back on his side. He couldn't concentrate. Melody's hands trembled as she tried to hold him steady. She didn't know what to do.

She looked through the living room, to the sliding glass door that led to Blake's patio. On the other side of the door stood a large man. The moonlight prevented her from making out any distinctive features, but she could see that he was smiling as he slid open the unlocked door.

Melody tripped over Cade and tumbled fell backwards. The growing lump in her throat left her breathless as her chest grew tight with fear. She was paralyzed. He held one finger to his mouth, then reached into a holster on his left side to pull something out. A shadow seemed to move behind him as the headlights from a passing car off in the distance bounced off the back of their house. She saw the leather straps to a holster and didn't have to guess what he was pulling out. The man opened his mouth to speak as he drew his weapon, but never got a word out.

Chapter 24

Blake didn't bother trying to slit the man's throat. That task always looks as simple as cutting butter in the movies. The truth was that skin can be difficult to penetrate and you need time to catch another man's throat at just the right angle. Plus, this was a big guy who looked like he had spent his share of time in a weight room. Blake wasn't looking for a fight.

He simply reached over the man's shoulder and stabbed him in the windpipe. The man's entire body froze as Blake pumped the knife up and down. Sergeant ripped the knife out, and stabbed the man again in the throat before he could react. This time, Blake pulled the man's hair to the left as he yanked the knife to the right, trying to cut through the meaty part of his neck.

The man fell to the ground bleeding and gurgling. Blood shot out onto the kitchen floor and into his windpipe. He clutched helplessly at an open wound over his windpipe, trying to stop the bleeding.

Blake stabbed him in the throat again from behind, this time from the other side and ripped the knife back, nearly severing his head. As Blake ripped the knife through the right side of the man's neck, completely severing his jugular vein, the man gagged and trembled. He clutched his own throat and stop the bleeding, but his hands betrayed him. He felt tingling in his fingers as his body grew cold. Blood filled his lungs but he no longer had the capacity to cough.

The man doubled over, gripping helplessly at his throat to stop the bleeding. Crimson streams of blood ran across his fingers, but appeared black in the darkness. Blake punched the man in the back of the head sending him face first to the ground with a thud.

Blake kneeled on the man's back and pulled his hair up fully exposing the two open gashes in his neck, both of which were now leaking blood onto the hardwood floor. With the threat of resistance gone, Blake slit the man's throat one last time from ear to ear, widening the second wound he created while putting all of his strength into finishing the job. He let go of the man's hair and let his face hit the ground.

Blake crouched to the side of the man listening to his moist, guttural dying heaves and watching him twitch.

The clicking of the front door in Melody's apartment stole Blake's attention, and he listened intently as the man's partners attempted to break into the wrong residence. Blake pounced through the door that connected the two apartments and into the darkness with his weapon drawn.

Melody watched in amazement as her neighbor disappeared from the room. She never heard him hop the fence or sneak up on the intruder. She saw the knife before she saw Blake and wondered if her eyes were playing tricks on her for Blake's face looked more animated than she had ever seen him before. His eyes were lit up like a child at a carnival and his white teeth glistened in the moonlight as a grin made itself at home on his face. She realized that was the first time she ever saw him happy. And then he was gone.

Sergeant positioned himself adjacent to the wall beside the front door. The door would give him some cover as the intruders entered, unless they had the situational awareness to clear the room. He crouched, raised his pistol and waited. The deadbolt slid open and Blake took a moment to admire their lock picking skills. If he didn't know any better, he would have guessed they had a key.

They walked into the room as if they owned the place. They didn't duck. They didn't crouch. They made no effort to cover each other. They walked in with the expectation that all residents would be sleeping quietly. These guys weren't mercenaries. Blake figured that much out. The man in front was easily fifty pounds overweight, but he looked like a fit fat guy who could knock a few heads together under the right circumstances. He was a thug and his gun was drawn.

The second guy was small and wiry. He looked like he aspired to be a lightweight boxer. He would be the faster of the two when the time came to take cover. The big guy scanned the room, allowing his eyes to get used to the darkness. The little guy closed the door behind him, twisting the knob as if to make minimal sound. It wasn't until the door was nearly shut that he realized he was staring down the barrel of a silencer less than two feet away from his chest.

Sergeant squeezed the trigger twice. Both rounds ripped through the man, flinging his body into the door he was attempting to shut. Blake didn't waste time watching his handy work. He aimed in at the big guy and squeezed the trigger again. The first round caught the back of his neck and exited through his face. The second round was slightly lower, blasting through his spine, between his shoulder blades. Pieces of his face shot across the room and splattered against the opposite wall in the living room. He fell like a rock. A big rock.

The little guy managed to open the door and stumble to the front porch. He steadied himself against a post and stared at the front porch willing himself to make it down the stairs. He tried to take a breath and step down, no longer thinking coherently. He heard a footstep behind him, but it was already too late. Sergeant stabbed the meaty part of his neck, just inside the collarbone and ripped the knife back.

The little guy fell to one knee on the porch and grabbed at the new open wound on his throat. Blood streamed through his shaking fingers like water leaking through a dam, and he could fill the blood bubbling in his lungs, causing him to choke. He was going to die this morning, but not without a fight. He twisted himself around and saw Blake Sergeant walking back into the apartment presumably to finish killing his partner.

The little guy kept his left hand clutched tightly around his throat and raised his pistol with his right hand. He aimed at Blake's back and put his finger on the trigger. He held his breath, because he knew an instinctive gasp for air would only fill his lungs with blood. He had one shot, and he intended to take it. Before he could fire, a single bullet ripped through the little man's forehead thus ending his kamikaze mission.

Blake looked up to see Melody standing in her living room with Cade's gun pointed at his would-be killer. The weapon shook in her trembling hands. He looked back at the body, then turned to face Melody. He took the gun out of her hand and whispered in her ear,

"Thank you."

She nodded in response, still in shock.

"Now go back in my room and sit down," Sergeant said softly. "Keep an eye on Cade. Make him drink some water if he's conscious."

With that, Blake spun around and dragged the smaller man's body into the house and stood over the bodies, thinking. He breathed in and out. Rubbed his forehead. He looked at the bodies, and said to nobody, "We'll take their car."

He rifled through the pockets of the bodies until he found a set of keys and disappeared out the back of his sliding door into the ally behind his apartment, gun in hand. He approached the vehicle slowly, scanned the area, and drove the car into the ally he had just come from.

Melody remained sitting next to Cade who was still showing little signs of consciousness, much less sobriety. As Blake walked past, he noticed the hard liquor and stale narcotics on his kitchen table and wondered briefly whether Cade's vices might necessitate a trip to the emergency room. Didn't matter. That wasn't in the cards.

Blake opened the locked door to the second bedroom of his apartment which nobody other than him had ever seen until that moment. He pulled out two duffel bags full of cash including the one that was in his car the night before and ran back out the back door.

Melody wandered into the second bedroom still in a daze. She spent most her adult life around bad men who did bad things, but the way Blake killed three men without hesitation gave her chills.

There was a treadmill in one corner of the room and a set of weights in the opposite corner. A single picture of Blake's family hung across from the treadmill in a frame that looked like it was purchased on sale at Target.

The weight bench was relatively new, but the weights looked like they sustained some fire damage. Either way, it was clear he used them. Next to the weights was a resistant band and small desk with a laptop computer hooked to a printer. Hanging on the wall above the desk were 8x10 mug shots of men of Middle Eastern decent. Most of the faces had "X's" drawn across their faces.

On the wall next to the mugshots were the letters and numbers, "YLC 68?, Green Prius." There's a piece of notebook paper with a list of theories behind the car. “Stolen car? Accessory? What’s the connection?”

Next to the pictures are a handful of drawings of Middle Eastern men similar to the mugshots, but not the same.

“They were guys he arrested when he was in Virginia,” Cade slurred drunkenly from behind her. He was standing behind her in the doorway leaning against the frame. He looked at the pictures with a little more focus. “He’s still trying to solve his wife and daughter’s murder.”

“How does he know the killer was black?” Melody asked.

“I saw him,” Blake said from behind, “and he was from the Middle East. Probably Morocco. Can’t remember his face. He killed my son, too.”

Blake walked in the room and stared again at the pictures. He then took the portrait of his family down and grabbed another gym bag from the closet.

“Can one of you grab my laptop?”

Cade and Melody snapped out of their awkward silence. They were caught staring at the skeletons of a killer’s closet. Melody began packing the laptop into a bag as Cade stared on.

“He’s much worse than I ever imagined,” Cade said. “He lives for revenge.”

Cade trudged back out of the room in silence and met Blake as he was coming back in from outside.

“We have about four minutes to get out of here,” Blake said to Cade before turning to face Melody. “You need to come with us. Grab your purse and pack a bag with a few changes of clothes. At least enough for a couple days. We’re not going to hurt you, but the guys who are on their way here now will.”

Melody nodded, still in shock, then walked slowly back to her bedroom.

“Are you healthy enough to help me move three bodies?” Blake asked as he turned back to face Cade.

Cade felt nauseous, but wasn’t about to admit it. They grabbed the body of the big guy Blake nearly decapitated, and carried him out.

“Do you know these guys?” Blake asked as the loaded the first guy up.

"I don't know the two big guys," Cade responded. "The little guy was Frank's nephew. He drove truck for Frank. Half his rig was full of auto parts. The hidden compartment inside his trailer was where he hid drugs."

"What kind?" Melody asked from behind, holding her purse. Blake was impressed with how fast she packed.

"Coke, H, bath salts and synthetics, LSD. Usually meth."

"No weed?" she asked.

"Sometimes, if they could get their hands on something profitable. But with all the states legalizing it, there's more supply than demand. Easier to break the law."

Blake unlocked the trunk with his free hand as Cade continued.

"Frank can still make a lot of money off moving high risk product."

"Well now she *has to* come with us, Cade," Blake responded.

Cade stared into the back of the Explorer and saw two new shovels with the Home Depot tags still attached. Blake immediately read his mind.

"They would have done the same thing to us," Blake said.

"My family didn't come after me in D.C.," Cade said.

"I know. The guys who came after you are much more dangerous, and they're still after us. Let's go."

They loaded the second body into the car and walked up to the little guy – Frank Silvera's nephew. Cade finally started to sway and turned his head.

"If you need to puke, do it in the toilet and flush twice," Blake advised.

Cade breathed deeply, nodded and headed for the bathroom. Blake grabbed Tony's body by himself and carried it to the Explorer. As he walked past Melody, he told her to get in the front seat. She wasn't about to argue with a man with a corpse hanging over his shoulder like a sack of potatoes. Blake returned to the front porch to wipe up any blood he could see using a bleach disinfectant. It was a hasty job meant to get rid of larger puddles and splatters. He didn't have time for a detailed cleaning.

He found Cade in the bathroom next to a toilet full of vomit. He was dizzy and nauseous again, from the combination of old opioids and hard liquor. Blake helped him up and drug him to the car. Melody followed them both with a second, larger bag that probably contained more clothing than she was going to need.

Cade got into the back seat of the car and laid down. Blake locked the doors to his apartment, grabbed his trusty booklet of CDs and got into the car. There were probably witnesses, but the best thing about bad parts of town was the general mistrust of law enforcement. Fear would keep the neighbors quiet for a little while.

Blake, Cade and Melody pulled out of the ally, and drove toward the storage shed where Cade's getaway vehicle was hidden. Behind them, a man named Jerry Campanella hid behind a car watching their every move. He was the would-be fourth gunman but he knew what fate awaited him if he intervened. Once they were out of site, Jerry called Frank Silvera to let him know his nephew and other employees were dead, and there was a GPS device on Cade and Blake's getaway car.

Meanwhile, Blake, Cade and Melody transferred their bags from the Explorer to the Mustang. Blake intended to hide the three gunmen and their vehicle in his storage unit, and drive the Mustang. Thanks to Cade's hacking skills, it would be another two days before the cops knew what they were driving. Maybe longer.

Cade laid down in the back of the Mustang and went back to sleep while Melody sat in the front seat. Blake changed his clothes in the alley and placed his bloody security uniform in a garbage bag which also went in the Mustang. He would ditch the clothes at a rest stop later that night. Blake took a breath of the October Minnesota air and welcomed the autumn season. It was cool enough to keep the stench of the decomposing bodies from discovering them for at least a few days. With a little luck, perhaps a thunderstorm or a dusting of snow would buy them enough time to make their escape. At the core of his external optimism, Blake knew there were dark days ahead.

He hopped in the driver seat, popped in Temple of the Dog and turned right on University Avenue. They drove for 200 feet before stopping at a red light and stopped at another light about 500 meters later. Blake sang along softly as Chris Cornell crooned his way through *Reach Down*, paying homage to Andrew Wood. The laid-back tempo of the song helped calm Sergeant's nerves. He would listen to music until he was on the freeway during which he could switch to the news. This was the moment he had been anticipating for years, and right now he needed to stay cool.

Cade was inebriated in the back seat and he had his stripper neighbor riding shotgun, who was never part of the plan. It was better to bring her along for now, and use the sluggish commute as an opportunity to ponder her fate. Melody stared at Blake in amazement. His demeanor appeared serene as if they were heading out to the cabin for a weekend by the lake.

Remind me never to doubt you again, The Harvester whispered into his mind.

Blake only smiled. He was getting used to the voice in his head. Remorse would sink in eventually, but for now, he basked in his adrenaline rush. He was good at this shit.

Blake hung a left on Snelling and turned into the gas station adjacent to the entrance onto I-94. He paid for his gas in cash and came out with three cups of coffee. If Cade didn't wake up soon enough, Blake would drink two. As he prepared to turn back onto Snelling, he glanced at his watch. It was 6:30 in the morning.

"Can I talk to you?" Melody finally asked.

"Sure, talk," Blake replied as he took a sip of his coffee.

A police cruiser pulled up next to their car as they sat at yet another red light.

"You just killed three men," she replied.

"It was them or us."

"You're acting like you're happy about that."

"I am. They fucked with the wrong guy."

Melody's facial expression grew more perplexed.

"Do you think you will kill more?"

"Yup," he said.

"And what about me?"

Blake paused and pondered the question.

"I haven't figured that out yet. The people who were after us will now be after you. When those assholes broke into the wrong apartment, they effectively issued you a death sentence. There is a far more dangerous group of people following us and they would find you, no matter where you went. We'll cut you loose eventually, and give you enough money to compensate for your troubles, but for now, it's safer for you to travel with us. Keep in mind, you killed one of those guys."

"I did that to save you," she said, her voice rising.

"Keep your voice down. We don't want to give the policemen next to us any reason to give us extra attention." Melody looked down and fumbled with her hands instinctively. The light turned green and Blake continued south. He had lived in the Twin Cities long enough to know that even at this hour, there was potential for traffic in Minneapolis to be a mess. It was smarter to stay in St. Paul.

"The best way to flee the scene of a murder is to pretend like you've got nothing to hide."

As traffic into the cities began to accumulate, Blake, Cade and Melody traveled quietly from Snelling to Selby. The opening chords of *Hunger Strike* filled the Mustang as Blake turned right on Ayd Mill Road and traversed slowly to the freeway. By the time a trooper left the comfort of his squad car to find found droplets of blood on Blake's front porch, Sergeant and company were already driving south on I-35E, crossing the Minnesota River.

Blake took 35E to I-494 south, and would follow a sluggish stream of traffic to the exit onto Highway 212. It would eventually be safer to travel on highways versus the interstate. As they approached the Eden Prairie city limits, Blake turned on Minnesota Public Radio to hear a news report that local law enforcement discovered the body of former Congressman and cable news television personality Jim Peterson.

There were no details on the condition of the body, but Blake was sure such information would surface in the coming hours. Blake peeked into his rearview mirror to ensure Cade was still sleeping off his pills and booze, and glanced over at Melody who was equally oblivious. Peterson's body was found sooner than Blake anticipated, but that was irrelevant. They were already on the run. More importantly, there was no mention of a shooting in St. Paul yet.

Meanwhile, Campanella followed the signal of his GPS tracking device to Blake's storage unit, and was the first to unearth the bodies of the three men with whom he flew to Minnesota the night before. His plan for tracking the man he was supposed to kill had been effectively diffused.

Frank Silvera expected Cade, or at the minimum his partner to ditch the rental, and made a note to himself to quit underestimating his stepson's group of misfits. Cade wasn't smart enough to come up with this plan, he thought, but his partner was. Nevertheless, Frank had a couple backup plans.

He quickly fired out a digital photo of Cade to his network of smugglers and dealers across the West and promised a $50,000 finder's fee to bring him back alive.

Chapter 25

Kevin Taylor parked on the Sherburne Avenue in a run down late '90s model Pontiac that looked right at home in Frogtown. On most days he wore a suit and tie to work. Today, the newly minted FBI agent was wearing jeans and a faded T-shirt and an old black leather jacket he bought more than a decade ago.

While most of their field office was on the way to Rabbit Lake to investigate the murder of a "somebody" in politics, Taylor had the envious task of sitting on his ass on a makeshift stakeout per instruction from Washington. He had two photographs, and was asked to call two D.C. agents if he saw anything out of the ordinary. One was a photo of Blake Sergeant from his days on the force in Virginia, and another was of Cade Stuckley from the website he maintained for his business. Taylor was supposed to keep an eye on Sergeant, and call immediately if he saw Stuckley.

It was a quarter to seven and Taylor surmised that this part of the city wouldn't show much sign of life for at least another hour or two. He pulled out a thermos and used it to fill a mug with the first of what would be many cups of black coffee. It was a rookie mistake. The fact that the Minneapolis field office sent a rookie alone demonstrated that Washington's request wasn't seen as a priority.

As he sipped his first mug, Taylor noticed a black and white squad car circling the block slowly. Two minutes later, another car followed. One squad car parked up the street and Taylor watched as a female officer slipped out of her squad car and walked around the back of the same house Taylor was charged with watching. Two more officers, both male, with the second squad car parked closer to the house and walked up the front steps. As they reached the doorway, Taylor watched both officers, look down and draw their pistols.

The third officer joined them, pistol drawn as well, as the second officer spoke on his radio. The first officer knocked on Sergeant's neighbor's front door. He heard the cop bellowing the obligatory warning that there were police who had an interest in entering the building. Seconds later, the officers kicked opened the door and ran in with their weapons drawn.

This would qualify as out of the ordinary, Taylor thought as he set down his coffee and reported the activity. He exited his vehicle and approached the house with his badge drawn. Hopefully these overeager troopers wouldn't shoot him. He gave them time to clear the building, and heard a siren in the distance. Two of the cops walked back out of the front door and congregated around the trunk of the squad car parked in front of the house. Both officers looked about the same age as Taylor. One was possibly of Indian decent and the other was the female who originally snuck around the rear of the house. Both officers looked up to see Taylor approaching with his badge in plain view.

"FBI," Taylor announced.

"Did you see anything?" the female officer asked in lieu of pleasantries.

"No, I just pulled in."

"What brings the FBI here?" the Indian officer asked as he strained to read Taylor's badge.

Before Taylor could say anything, the third officer emerged from the front door. This one was a sergeant. Although the rank conveyed his superiority, it wasn't necessary. His commanding stride and the other two cops' nonverbal deference made it clear he was in charge.

The sergeant looked up at Taylor.

"Who's he?" He asked the female officer.

"FBI," the female officer answered.

"Really?" the sergeant said with surprise but without reverence. The female cop nodded. The sergeant read Taylor's badge momentarily, then looked to his fellow cops.

"All right," the sergeant said, "It looks like there was a shootout, both houses involved, and the bodies were drug out the back. Gupta, I want you to watch the back of the building."

The Indian officer ran around the back side of the building.

"Maloney, go back to your squad car, and grab a roll of yellow tape. I want the entire front yard and the back alley taped off. Don't touch anything."

The female officer disappeared.

The sergeant was the epitome of a blue-collar man who clearly had written his share of speeding tickets. He was husky, but fit, and carried himself like a man who knew his role in setting up a crime scene.

"Why is the FBI here?" he finally asked Taylor.

"The neighbor of your crime scene is a person of interest for an ongoing investigation," Taylor responded.

"Well, your person just got a lot more interesting," the sergeant responded. "There was a shootout here, and the residents of both apartments were involved. No bodies, but two puddles of blood. It looks like the bodies were dragged out the back of your person of interest's house."

Taylor nodded.

"Please don't take this the wrong way, but are you new to the FBI? I haven't seen you before," he said with a thick northern accent.

"Yes," Taylor responded. He was a state trooper in Nebraska before he joined the Feds and planned to make a priority of always cooperating, "no offense taken."

"All right, I'm Sergeant Beckett. We already radioed in our homicide unit who should be here shortly. As I'm sure you're aware, we need to investigate this like any other shooting that takes place in St. Paul. Do you mind calling your field office and getting someone down here we can coordinate with? We always work well with the FBI here."

"On it," Taylor responded.

"Good to go," Beckett responded. "Now if you'll excuse me, I need to get this crime scene taped off."

***

Gable, Maxwell and Cavalera were still in Minneapolis looking at the computer at Blake's place of employment when Taylor's call came in. Gable spent the first five minutes cursing himself because he *knew* that Blake Sergeant was withholding information.

"You know," Gable growled, "the whole time we were talking to him, I thought, what's wrong with this picture? Then I realized, he was pumping us for information."

"You're right," Cavalera agreed. "At first, I kept thinking it was his old police instincts kicking in, you know, trying to see if there was a way he could offer us some clues."

"And we walked right fucking into it."

"He has to know something."

"He's involved. For all we know, he might be the one shooting these guys."

"Like a partner?"

"Yeah. Stuckley lures these guys into the trap, and Sergeant takes 'em out."

"It makes sense, but something's missing," Cavalera responded. "Where's the motive? I could see Sergeant helping his buddy out, but something just isn't right."

"A partnership does make sense, though," Maxwell chimed in. Both agents halfway forgot he was sitting next to them.

"Why's that?" Gable asked.

"Well, there have been a few problems with our new timeline for when some of these guys were killed. Having an accomplice would help answer those questions."

"Example?" Cavalera asked.

"Belov was murdered in a New York City hotel on a Friday night. Cade Stuckley was on his computer two hours later. He could have been at a Starbucks in New Jersey, but the timing doesn't make sense."

"Why not?" Gable asked.

"He was fleeing the scene of a murder," Maxwell responded. "I don't know this for sure, but if I was fleeing the scene of a murder, I would at least wait until I was back at home."

"If he is the guy," Gable posed, "don't you think he might intentionally log in to throw us off our tracks?"

"And chat for two hours?" Maxwell asked. "The guy would have to have balls of steel."

"I wouldn't rule that out," Gable said, "I'm not ruling anything out."

***

Billy Kim was the first one to hear the call regarding shots fired on the police scanner. Thirty minutes later, Byrd's team was awake, ready and listening to the scanner. Byrd had already yelled at his FBI contact twice that morning.

After stewing in their cheap motel room for a half hour, the group decided to pay a visit to the crime scene.

Kim and his mercenary sidekick Antrell Love were selected to pose as onlookers primarily because of their races. Byrd was never going to go in undercover unless necessary because the odds of him getting recognized were too high with the FBI involved.

Kim and Love ambled in separately, dressed in blue collar rags to watch the investigation among a growing crowd. Kim loved undercover work of any kind. He loved the adrenaline rush that came from blending in with a crowd. Love was less enthusiastic, but had the better observation skills of the two.

The key to being a good observer was to only hang out while there was a critical mass of people. Once the crowd dissipated, they would each walk around the block in separate directions trying to pick up any additional details.

***

Gable, Cavalera and Maxwell arrived shortly after 8:30. They found Taylor first, who issued an apology on behalf of their field office for not being at the house sooner. They ignored the comments and simply asked that he introduce them to the St. Paul homicide investigator, a guy by the name of James McEvers – Jimmy to his friends.

McEvers stood just under six feet, and had clearly seen the inside of a weight room three or four times a week for the last two decades. He wore a thinning light brown crewcut and wire rimmed sunglasses.

McEvers exchanged niceties with the agents but otherwise skipped the small talk.

"What brings the FBI to St. Paul?" McEvers asked.

"The neighbor of your crime scene is a person of interest for an ongoing investigation," Gable responded.

"Well, your person just became a lot more interesting," McEvers responded.

Taylor cringed at the redundant conversation behind the two D.C. agents and frumpy tagalong who were visibly less than pleased that nobody had arrived from the FBI prior to the shootout.

"We responded to a call reporting gunshots. There was a struggle here, shots fired. No bodies, but a lot of blood in both apartments, "McEvers said. "Our forensic team is analyzing the scene right now, but I can give you the cook's tour."

"Sounds good," Cavalera responded. "I didn't have a chance to grab breakfast."

McEvers grinned, Maxwell groaned and Taylor cringed again.

"I know I don't need to say this, but please don't touch anything," McEvers said as they walked up the steps.

"Understood," Gable responded.

McEvers walked both agents through Melody Slater's front door, showing them the blood splatter on the front porch. They stood in Slater's living room next to the door that connected she and Blake's apartments. Two forensic agents scoured the house, filling evidence baggies with hairs, probable prints and anything else that looked like a clue.

"Now we just got here, but by my guess, there were at least three people killed or injured this morning. Two individuals entered the front door either without force or by picking the lock. I don't see any signs of forced entry, but our lock guy will be here to confirm that shortly. They were likely shot as they entered the house."

"I assume our shooter was behind the door. Shot both victims from behind," McEvers squatted and held his palms together, index fingers extended and lower fingers folded to resemble a pistol. He fired his imaginary gun for effect. "The first victim fell forward right here," McEvers said as stood up and drew imaginary circles around a blood puddle in the middle of the living room with his finger. He then pointed to the opposite wall decorated with blood, pieces of the big guy's face and a bullet hole.

"The second victim fell backwards or tried to escape out the front door," McEvers said as he pointed at one crimson stain that stretched intermittently across the living room and into Blake's apartment. He stepped back out of the front door and pointed at the front entrance where the front porch looked marginally cleaner than the rest of the porch. "Take a look at this," McEvers continued.

Blake Sergeant had wiped up some of the blood on the front porch, but the stains on Melody Slater's carpet were a dead giveaway for the third body. McEvers led the agents through the doorway that separated Slater and Sergeant's respective apartments where they were greeted by a much larger puddle of blood on the living room floor.

"Victim number three was right here," he said solemnly. "Given the large volume of blood, this one spent some time on the ground bleeding out. Forensics hasn't been through here yet, but I don't think this one was a gunshot wound. Too much blood in one spot."

"My money's on a slit throat," Gable added.

"Does your person of interest have a history of playing with knives?"

"Not sure," Gable responded, "but it looks like the victim was laying face down in a pile of his or her own blood. Hell of a way to go."

"By the way, but we are now in your guy's house," McEvers responded. "It looks like the bodies were dragged or carried out through his back porch."

"So we have two victims who came in through our guy's neighbor's apartment? Where's the neighbor?" Cavalera asked.

"Like I said," McEvers responded, "we just got here. Her name is Melody Slater. That's all we know so far. It looks like guy number three came in through your boy's back sliding door. Melody Slater's backdoor is shut, locked and untampered with."
He gestured to Melody's untouched sliding glass door.

"This is one strange crime scene," Cavalera said. Gable nodded in agreement trying to take it all in.

"It gets better," McEvers said as he led the agents into Sergeant's spare bedroom where they were immediately drawn to the mugshots on the wall. Black markers crossed out the faces of most of the men while others were left untouched. Beneath the marked photos were notes indicating alibis that checked out or other details which contributed to their elimination from consideration. There were only two remaining photos without lines crossing out their faces.

Cavalera and Gable only stared in disbelief.

"Remember what he said last night?" Cavalera asked.

"He said he looked in the eye of the man who killed his family, but couldn't remember his face," Gable responded.

"He's trying to remember," Cavalera said to the room.

"I'm sorry to spoil the moment, but can one of you gentlemen fill me in on what you're discussing?" McEvers asked.

"Blake Sergeant was a patrolman in Virginia," Cavalera responded. "Three years ago, an intruder broke into his home, murdered his wife and daughter and set the house on fire. The gunman shot him in the head. Sergeant spent the next few weeks in a coma. When he woke up, his family was dead. His house was gone. Memory loss prevented him from being able to provide any meaningful information to solve the murder. It looks to me like he has been trying to remember the killer."

"Fuck me," McEvers said, responding empathetically to Blake's story. "And he thinks it's one of these guys?" McEvers asked, pointing at the mug shots.

"That's what it looks like," Cavalera responded.

"So what's he doing here?"

"His wife and kids are buried here," Cavalera responded.

"Do you have kids, detective?" Gable asked McEvers.

"Two daughters," McEvers responded.

"What would you do if you were in his situation?"

"I'd find the sonofabitch who did it and kill him," McEvers responded without hesitation.

"Me too," Gable added as he surveyed the room. He stared at a bookcase adjacent to the desk, which held several notebooks. They were the kind one could find at a department store for a dollar, and were each labeled with dates. The book in front was listed, 7/15-6/16. Cavalera looked back at the detective.

"Do you mind if we look at this?" Cavalera asked, pointing to the steno pad.

"Be my guest," McEvers responded.

***

Kim stood in street clothes behind a Hmong family typing notes into his cell phone. Each text message sent different nuggets of information to Byrd. 'No bodies,' 'shots fired,' 'FBI is here.'

The last message drew a response from Byrd – 'Call me.'

Kim hopped on the phone and walked away from the crowd to continue the discussion. He would tell Byrd that there was one FBI agent on the scene who he didn't recognize, but it sounded like more were on the way. When he returned to the scene, there was an extra rental car parked on Sherburne that he wouldn't notice.

Love walked around the back of the house to watch a forensic investigator stare at, take photos of and gather samples from crimson streaks and droplets of blood that speckled the concrete walkway from the back porch to the alley. If he would have pulled up a seat and impersonated a homeless man, he would have probably been less conspicuous. Instead, he chose to squat down behind a wastebasket.

As the investigator worked away, Love also sent text messages to Byrd's cell phone.

Sitting in a black rented Explorer just a few short blocks south on Aurora and Victoria, Byrd and two other mercenaries waited patiently, reading the text messages as they appeared.

***

Cavalera thumbed through the notebooks with interest. On the first page was a series of incomplete sentences with descriptions of Sergeant's home, his wife, his daughter and the man who killed him. The words looked as if they were scribbled frantically.

Some of the sentences such as 'black skull cap,' 'male – middle eastern – NOT BLACK,' were vivid descriptions. Others like, 'I smelled Anni's hair tonight,' left Cavalera feeling like he was watching a man's sanity get eaten away by grief and obsession. The next page featured a chart with each observation from the previous page listed. In a column to the right, each observation was categorized as "dream," "memory" or simply "?". The subsequent pages included drawings done presumably by Sergeant. Some were of the inside of his home, the structure of the basement, stairways and kitchen. Others laid out what looked like a back yard, and the scene of a shootout. The shooters were drawn in as silhouettes, and fields of fire were added to indicate where bullets were theoretically fired.

Most of the pictures were Sergeant's attempt to remember the face of his would-be killer. One page was nothing but very attentive sketches of eyes, eyebrows, eyelashes, with and without glasses. Another page was several sketches of round faces, each of which with slight double chins. Some portraits had a thin mustache, others didn't. More importantly, every page and photo was dated.

Cavalera scrolled back and started looking at the dates as Gable and McEvers examined the mug shots. Finally, one date jumped out at Cavalera.

"Hey, why does January 19th, 2016 sound familiar?"
Gable and Cavalera made eye contact, and without a word, realized they may have found the lead they flew out to Minnesota to search for.

"Where's Maxwell," they both asked as they walked out the front of the door.

***

Kim hung up the phone and walked back to the crowd when he saw both agents from D.C. walking out of the front door of Sergeant's house. He immediately recognized both agents, one was white and the other Latino, standing on the lawn with0 a mousy looking little man who might have been with them in D.C. The mousy guy was nursing a cup of coffee decorated with the logo of a local hotel chain and holding a thick binder under his arm.

Both agents were walking with a purpose when the Latino agent glanced briefly at the crowd. They made eye contact for just one second before the agent looked away.

***

Cavalera's most educational day working undercover came outside San Diego, when he was tagging along with the heavy for a cartel he was infiltrating. He was supposed to be the getaway driver, but the enforcer, Padilla, asked him to pull around the corner so he could change his clothes. Cavalera then stood awkwardly for thirty minutes next to Padilla, who spent every moment relishing the experience of watching the man he just shot carried out of a deserted home full of junkies and drifters. Cavalera watched Padilla's every move and studied everything he could about it that day. He planned to use that knowledge at every crime scene he was on for the rest of his career.

He didn't quite recognize the short Asian man with his first glance, but a small voice in the back of his head urged him to look again. They made eye contact, and Cavalera knew he had seen the man before. His original focus was on Maxwell and the binder, but he had just stumbled upon a new lead from hell.

Gable, McEvers and Cavalera crowded around Maxwell and before anyone could speak, Cavalera took control of the crowd.

"Don't look, but we have a crime scene spectator who was at Stuckley's apartment two days ago."

"Are you sure?" Gable asked.

"Was Stuckley's apartment another crime scene?" McEvers asked.

"Yeah," Maxwell responded.

Gable backed away, pretended to check an e-mail message on his Blackberry, and scanned the crowd as well. He recognized the man too. Thought he seemed out of place in Alexandria, and knew he seemed out of place now. The man was wearing a Yankees ballcap. They were in Twins country.

"All right," Gable added. "I'm going to walk back through the house and out the back. Give me one minute. Detective McEvers, can you help us out?"

"Absolutely. We'll approach from the right and rear," McEvers looked at Cavalera, "do you want to approach from the front?"

"Check," he responded.

"Okay. Wait for my signal."

Gable and McEvers walked into the house. As they passed through the doorway, McEvers radioed Sgt. Beckett and relayed the plan.

***

Kim froze in his steps upon making eye contact with Cavalera. He stared straight ahead at the crime scene, trying to watch their discussion from the periphery. When the white agent and St. Paul cop started walking into the house, Kim acknowledged that sick feeling in the pit of his stomach.

He called Byrd.

"I've been compromised," he said when Byrd answered.

"You know what to do," Byrd responded. "Go to LZ Alpha Grotto."

"Check."

A uniformed officer approached Cavalera holding a radio, and they exchanged niceties.

Kim slowly backed away from the crowd, keeping his eyes straight ahead. A uniformed officer started to approach him from the Southeast, but he was a good 20 meters away. He looked like a corn-fed white boy who wasn't going to win a footrace. Cavalera, on the other hand, looked fast, and Kim knew he would need a solid head start.

The cop spoke in the radio, and Cavalera immediately looked up at Kim. This was it. Compromise was official. Kim's cautious backpeddling gave way to a dead sprint across the street and through the lawn of a neighboring rambler. Two onlookers on the front porch flinched as Kim zoomed past them, hurdling the stairs and running around the side of one house through the back yard.

Cavalera immediately busted into a sprint behind him, yelling "FBI" as he pursued Kim. The proclamation inspired the crowd to part ways clumsily as Cavalera busted through in pursuit of Kim. Sergeant Beckett was at his side, shouting into his radio to Maloney to grab the squad car.

***

Gable and McEvers were walking out the back of the house when they heard Beckett announce over the radio that their eavesdropper was sprinting toward University Avenue. They quickly ran around the side of the yard when something caught the corner of Gable's eye.

Fifty feet across the alley behind the house was an African American male squatting behind a parked car, speaking into a cell phone. At first glance, the man could have been just another spectator. At second glance, Gable noticed the familiar handle of a Glock holstered under the man's unbuttoned jacet.

Gable grabbed McEvers's shoulder and pointed to the man.

"Is he one of yours?" Gable whispered.

"No," McEvers responded.

"Beckett," McEvers said into the radio, "Request backup for your pursuit of the Asian male. We have another person of interest back here."

***

Love picked up Byrd's call on the first ring.

"Kim's been compromised. Anything going on where you're at?"

"Nothing in back," Love turkey-peaked around the side of the house, "Kim is sprinting South toward University. I see three officers in pursuit including one of the Washington agents."

"Which one?"

"The Mexican."

Love turned back around to see the white agent and a uniformed officer checking him out, and knew it was his turn to run.

"I'm compromised. Going to LZ West Charlie Grotto."

"Negative. Go to St. Albans and Fuller. ETA three minutes."

"Check."

Love hung up the phone and broke into a dead sprint West, then crossed through the yard of a house between Avon and Grotto.

***

"We've got a runner," McEvers observed.

Gable smiled. He loved being the hunter.

"Radio for backup," he said, "Let's do this."

They both broke into a sprint to the front of Sergeant's house, and turned left on Charles.

Love turned to see their change in course, and darted back into the alley where he had been hiding to run west. This would take a while. Gable saw Love's move and quickly returned to the alley with McEvers not far behind.

Love darted across Avon and sprinted through the middle of the block as soon as he saw a yard without a fence. He had a good 20 yards on Gable and McEvers, and he needed to keep it that way.

Gable rolled back his shoulders to give his lungs more room to breathe and swung his arms in tandem with his gallop. He was a big guy, but he could run four to five eight-minute miles. His person of interest was running fast, but he would grow tired. They always did. McEvers ran not too far behind, losing some ground while trying to direct squad cars toward Love.

Love crossed Charles Ave. and ran through another yard onto Sherburne, then right. There would be a squad car in pursuit soon enough. Gable followed him through the yard, keeping his distance. University was a busy street with train tracks in the middle. Gable would gain some ground there and they both knew it.

Love hung a right on Grotto and darted across University like a jackrabbit. He hopped the rails separating the Green Line from traffic effortlessly as a train roared his way from a distance, railing on its horn.

A sedan squealed its breaks and fishtailed to miss him, only to clip another motorist in the other lane. The impact sent the sedan across its lane into an illegally parked car on the side of the street.

Love paid the cars no mind as he sprinted South on Grotto toward Aurora.

Gable dodged the car wreck and hurdled the Green Line's rails and dividers, knowing the train would cut off most of his backup.

A semi approached from the opposite side of the street, but Gable had time. McEvers didn't and wasn't about to cause another wreck.

The train and truck each moved past in opposite directions, and McEvers watched angrily while requesting backup to address the wreck that Love caused. He would continue to follow the foot chase, knowing it was unlikely he would be part of an apprehension.

***

Kim smiled as he sprinted across University Avenue. There were no cars from the left and two from the right that he could outrun. The agents would need to stop. The Green line train was off in the distance, but it wouldn't affect his stride.

Back in his Army days, senior officials believed Kim never took the military, or anything in life for that matter, seriously. He had a habit of laughing nervously at the inappropriate times leaving most officers and senior enlisted personnel pegging him as a soldier with a lack of military bearing – one of the worst insults that could be placed on anyone in uniform.

What made Kim appealing to Gayton was his fervor in combat and lack of compassion. He followed any order he was given. He killed when necessary and sometimes when unnecessary. He was merciless and the uglier war became, the more Kim giggled. This was unsettling in the eyes of the Army. When he signed his discharge papers, some speculated it would only be a matter of time before he was wearing an orange jumpsuit or a straightjacket.

He was a specialist at getting information out of prisoners of war, and was not above the most brutal of torture tactics. There was one story of Kim taking a blowtorch to a prisoner of war handed to Gayton by the Army. That pretty much gave him a job for life as a mercenary.

As he reached the other side of University, Kim darted into a Vietnamese restaurant. There was no reason for the change in course, other than it added a little flavor to the chase.

Cavalera, Beckett and Gupta followed Kim, with Cavalera leading the way. Kim shot past a hostess who was about to welcome him, and shoved a cashier into a plant as he made his way into the kitchen. He grabbed a rack of pans and fry trays and pulled it down behind him as he darted for an exit to the alley he spotted.

A cook who was feeling brave tried to step in his path and Kim punched the man in the face with a swift right hook. As the cook flew back momentarily stunned, Kim shoved his body toward a burner. The cook stuck his hand out to steady himself only to find the business end of a pot of boiling oil.

Kim was out the door in a flash as he heard the screams of the man he had just assaulted.

The back of the kitchen landed him in an alley and he ran South. He knew that if he headed South, he would end up at his rendezvous point. Kim was terrible at remembering street names, but he had a good enough sense of direction to get from point A to point B. That was why Byrd gave him the easier meet up point.

Cavalera followed Kim into the restaurant. He managed to bump into a waitress, spill a tray of green curry on a patron and sprint past a female cashier who was struggling to climb out from under the flowerpot she had been thrown into. Cavalera knew he had at least two cops behind him. They could help the woman. He jumped over a tipped rack of pans and ran past a man who was waving his hand frantically in the air screaming in pain.

Cavalera turned to a sink to his left, turned on the cold water and pushed the man to the sink, shoving his hand under the water. Another cook grabbed his friend from behind to help with the effort, knowing his friend was too distracted from the pain to slow down the burning of the oil.

"The cops will be here soon," Cavalera yelled as he ran to the door.

"Who the fuck are you?" one of the cooks asked.

"FBI!" Cavalera yelled back as he sprinted after the person of interest who would now have an assault charge to contend with.

Beckett hurdled the rack of pans behind the cooks and saw the other cooks holding the man's hand under the faucet as he screamed in pain. The man was in bad shape, and they needed to help him. Beckett grabbed the cook with the burning hand and helped his friends keep the man's hand under the cold water. He looked over at Gupta who was climbing over the shelf.

"Can you help this guy?"

Gupta nodded and grabbed the cook where Beckett was standing. Beckett saw the man's hand long enough to see blisters forming.

"Call an ambulance and then let Maloney know I'm pursuing on foot!"

With that, Gupta helped treat the cook while speaking into the radio and relaying the message Beckett gave him.

The skirmish in the kitchen turned out to be a pleasantly surprising distraction that left one agent chasing him and one cop in the distance. Kim sprinted down Victoria, finally remembered the name of the street he needed to find and turned south on Aurora.

***

St. Albans St. was a steady incline making it difficult for Gable to see anything beyond the block ahead of him. He made note of the Aurora-St. Albans intersection as he passed it, then looked forward to see Love slowing down.

The incline turned into a steep hill as they made their way up the next block. Love slowed down more, looked back at Gable and darted off to the right on Fuller. *He slowed down intentionally,* Gable thought to himself.

As Gable made his way up, he looked for a street sign and anything out of the ordinary. He had the distinct impression that his suspect was trying to lead him to an ambush. As he made it to the corner of Fuller and St. Albans, Gable saw a black Ford Explorer idling on the corner of Fuller facing west. Tinted windows. The passenger window was rolling down automatically. The muzzle of a semi-automatic emerged as the window continued to roll down.

Gable turned and dove behind a rusted Oldsmobile he had just run past. Bullets rattled across the hood of the vehicle and the concrete where he stood less than a second before. Gable rolled to the other side of the car while drawing his .44 Automag and fired two retaliatory shots in return. The passenger fired back, but only briefly. Gable tried to get a look at the shooter, but couldn't make out any substantial details. African American male. That was it.

Love ran to the Explorer and Gable knew he had one chance to turn this into a real gunfight. He aimed the Automag at Love's leg and squeezed the trigger. Byrd sent another barrage of bullets Gable's way, causing him to jerk as he got the shot off. The shot was from about 50 yards from the prone position. The round ripped through Love's hip as he tried to cross St. Albans, sending him spiraling to the ground in the middle of the street, screaming and reaching for his own weapon. Byrd fired more rounds toward the rear passenger tire of the Oldsmobile where Gable took cover. Gable brought his knees to his chest and waited for the shots to stop. Byrd yelled to the driver to pull forward and grab Love.

The brief pause in fire gave Gable his moment. He crawled to the driver's side of the Oldsmobile and squeezed another round off Love's at good leg. He couldn't tell for sure, but it looked like the round hit his inner thigh, just above the knee. This would make a footrace a little less likely.

Byrd returned suppressing fire as the Explorer pulled up to Love who was now screaming in pain and grabbing his left leg. He was caught in the middle of a horrific game of cat and mouse.

"FBI!" Gable growled as he crept around the passenger side of the bullet riddled Oldsmobile. Byrd leaned his frame out of the passenger window and let out a war cry as he blasted another volley of rounds down range. Gable dove back to his initial spot behind the vehicle. He felt a hot pain streak across his forehead and took cover.

"Aw fuck!" he yelled as he leaned down behind the vehicle, trying to make himself invisible. Byrd took the opportunity to pull Love into the explorer.

Gable gripped at his face trying ascertain how badly he was hit as Byrd peered back out of the passenger door. He opened the car door, stepped out, aimed low and knew he had a shot. Gable saw the weapon and knew he had nowhere to go. He drew his pistol up and sighted in on Byrd, but could feel blood flowing freely into his left eye. A chunk of broken plastic from the taillight sliced open his forehead, and he was losing blood fast.

"Let's do this cowboy," Byrd growled.

Two more shots rang out, breaking Byrd's focus. The first round hit the Explorer. The second one hit Byrd on his right side with a thud. Byrd jumped as he fired, sending his round of bullets a foot higher than their intended target. McEvers leaped out from behind the house on the corner of St. Albans and Fuller and ran out into the open with no fear. He took two more shots at Byrd before diving behind a retaining wall adjacent to house's front porch. A tree on the corner gave him some extra cover.

Gable rose up and fired a round directly into the passenger window as Byrd hopped back into his vehicle and pulled the door shut. The round zoomed past Byrd's face and struck the front windshield at the bottom corner of the driver's side. They were on the move again with Love crying in the back.

"Drive!" Byrd yelled. The Explorer hit the gas and sped South on St. Albans as Gable and McEvers fired their weapons, shattering its back windows. The cop and agent ran after the vehicle reloading their weapons.

"You okay?" McEvers yelled.

"I'm fine," Gable yelled back, "let's get these bastards!"

Gable chambered a new round and sprinted behind the vehicle as McEvers kept pace with him, while yelling into his radio. The Explorer turned East on W. Central and sped out of sight.

Gable and McEvers stopped on the corner and scanned the premises, breathing heavily. Sirens howled in the background and Gable tried to get his bearings.

"Dale Street is the next block, which leads to a freeway entrance," McEvers grunted.

"No," Gable said while staring at the crossroads which faced them both. "No, that's not right."

There was still one of their guys on the loose, who was probably a half mile west of them.

"Where is the next freeway exit going west?" Gable asked.

"Lexington," McEvers responded. "A mile from here, but that doesn't make any . . ."

McEvers' voice trailed off as they both instinctively looked down St. Albans just in time to see the bullet riddled Explorer creeping across St. Anthony Avenue off in the distance.

The Explorer slowed down to a crawl. Gable looked into Byrd's eyes from 100 feet away. Still too far away to hold up in court, but close enough for them to both know who they were dealing with.

"Oh boy," McEvers observed.

"I see four vehicles that we can use for cover," Gable growled. McEvers only nodded.

They both broke into a sprint toward the vehicle, this time with McEvers leading.

***

Cavalera heard the gunshots and instinctively looked East. It sounded like World War III was erupting a few short blocks away. Kim heard it too, and giggled nervously has he darted to the corner of Avon and Grotto. He zig-zagged the blocks effortlessly, occasionally losing track of where he was, but knowing that as long as he headed Southeast, he would reach his objective.

Cavalera drew his weapon, and struggled to keep up. Kim was fast, but Cavalera was gaining ground. He could hear sirens in the background, but wondered how much help they would be. Gupta was with the cook in the restaurant. Beckett was a good half block behind them giving the block by block layout on his radio.

Cavalera knew the freeway was not too far south of them. Kim turned right on Grotto and accelerated. Cavalera turned the corner as well and could see a dead end off in the distance. Kim broke into a sprint, putting some distance between him and the agent. Cavalera picked up his pace as well, while surveying the twelve-foot-high chain link fence. *Dead end*, he thought to himself. At the end of the block, he watched Kim dart across the next block and hop onto a pedestrian bridge across the freeway. The chase was far from over. Cavalera continued to pursue.

***

Byrd peeled back his shirt to see if McEvers' bullet penetrated his bulletproof vest. No hole. Just a welt that would become a bruise.

"Oh fuck, man," Love cried from the backseat. "I'm bleeding bad, man. I'm bleeding bad!"

Love struggled to hold his hand over a gaping hole located on his inner thigh. He trembled and convulsed as he watched crimson life pump intermittently out of his jeans, forming a small sea between his legs. Byrd looked over his shoulder at the wound.

"I think it hit his femoral artery," Byrd said to the mercenary driving the Explorer, who only nodded.

"What?" Love asked. "What did it hit?" His eyes filled with tears.

"It's all right," Byrd said, "our next stop is the doctor."

The Gayton mercenaries turned right on Dale and right on St. Anthony, then crept slowly down the street. Byrd stared out the window and reloaded his weapon. They slowed down to a crawl as the vehicle crossed St. Albans and Byrd made eye contact with the agent and cop they traded gunfire with just seconds before. They stared each other down in recognition and Byrd didn't flinch as he watched both men run toward their Explorer.

The driver put his foot on the gas.

***

Cavalera saw a black vehicle slowly making its way down St. Anthony out of the corner of his eye. He made a quick determination that he could make it to the bridge before the truck made it to him and stuck his hand out, signaling for the vehicle to stop. He heard the driver accelerate, and something in his mind clicked.

He looked up and raised his weapon, but it was too late. He felt the bullets before he heard them. He felt his feet leave the ground and the pavement slap his back. He felt the air leave his chest and the strength leave his body.

The Explorer stopped.

"Byrd, Byrd," he heard a man yell in a boyish voice, heavy Korean accent. "I'm over here!"

"Byrd," Cavalera gasped.

He heard more gunshots coming from behind him. Then more gunshots from the Explorer. More sirens. The sounds didn't concern him. He couldn't breathe.

***

McEvers and Gable made it to St. Anthony just in time to watch Byrd empty half a magazine into Cavalera's midsection. Gable yelled, sprinted toward the vehicle until he was less than fifty feet away. He raised his cannon and began firing at the Explorer.

The Asian man who fled the scene jumped into the back seat of the Explorer and took cover as Byrd traded fire with the other patrolman whose name Gable didn't catch. Gable took one more shot at Byrd and missed. McEvers was aiming for the empty spot where a rear window used to be and watched his first round shatter what was left of Explorer's front windshield. He then took aim at the tires and fired.

The Explorer sped off as McEvers and Gable followed. Gable dove to Cavalera's side as he fought for each breath of air.

Gable applied pressure to a hole in Cavalera's chest that seemed to be causing the most trouble. In the periphery, he could see Beckett limping over, gripping his side. Beckett fell to one knee. Maloney arrived in a squad car and stopped next to the scene.

Gable tore off his jacket and placed it over Cavalera while trying to keep his chest from bleeding.

"Go after them!" Gable yelled. "Call an ambulance! I've got this!"

McEvers nodded. He hated to do it, but he had to leave two men down and pursue the Explorer.

Gable pressed down on Cavalera's chest as he heard Beckett crawling over to help. The poor bastard took two or three bullets of his own, but all he could think about was helping the agent.

"Byrd," Cavalera wheezed.

"Just take it easy, Cav," Gable responded. "You did good."

"His name is Byrd," Cavalera wheezed louder this time. Gable stopped.

"Are you fucking positive?"

"His name is Byrd," Cavalera responded.

Gable reapplied pressure.

"I heard it too," Beckett added. "His name is Byrd."

Gable's face contorted into an expression of pure hatred. "I know," he growled in response.

The paramedics arrived in record time and tended to Cavalera and Beckett as Gable backed off. Gable started to feel dizzy, and felt one of the paramedics sit him down on the curb. He handed Gable a bandage to press on his forehead and raced back to Cavalera.

Another ambulance rolled in from the distance, as an army of squad cars began converging on St. Anthony Avenue. Within minutes, Gable had a ride of his own to the hospital as paramedics began working on Beckett's wounds. Gable didn't say another word. Cavalera said it all in four short words. *His name is Byrd.*

***

"What the fuck happened to you?" Kim asked, then giggled.

"What the fuck do you think?" Love growled back.

"Put pressure on his inner thigh. We need to slow the bleeding," Byrd growled.

Kim did as ordered; using his flannel shirt as a bandage.

"This is bad, dude," he said solemnly.

Love looked up and closed his eyes.

The team had already lost two men in the last 48 hours and a third was fading fast.

They drove West on St. Anthony, hung a right on Milton and pulled up on the yard of an old rambler, and behind the shed out of public view.

They listened intently to sirens as two squad cars drove west on St. Anthony and turn presumably on Lexington. Kim hefted Love's leg up on his lap so he could use his belt as a tourniquet.

"Hey Love," Kim said. Love only fluttered his eyes in response.

"Remember that strip bar in Texas? That one in the middle of nowhere?"

"Yeah," Love smiled broadly, "country girls work hard for the money."

They laughed uneasily with Kim's high-pitched giggle drowning out the Love's low, tired snicker.

"Keep it down," Byrd counseled as he and his driver scanned the perimeter planning their next move. Their Explorer was riddled with bullet holes. Traveling inconspicuously wasn't an option.

The driver elbowed Byrd and pointed to their right. A repair van for the local cable company was parked on Melton, and the driver was in the driver's seat, engrossed in watching his cell phone. He had a set of ear buds in and was in a trance playing a video game less than a mile away from a shootout and car chase. Police sirens were still howling in the distance.

"Only in America," Byrd said in amazement. He signaled Kim and pointed out the van.

Five minutes later, the driver was on his stomach on the side of the road with his hands and feet bound together with cable ties they found in his repair truck. Byrd and company were headed toward a charter jet waiting on an air strip in South Saint Paul.

Love was unconscious, and he was dead by the time they reached their destination. The team would ultimately choose to leave his body in the van, parked up the street.

They were in their plane in a half hour, still processing the events of the shootout.

Byrd looked at his cell phone and made a call. Gayton picked up on the third ring.

"We've got a problem."

Chapter 26

Steve Gable opened his eyes, and immediately felt dizzy. He closed his eyes, took a couple deep breaths, then opened them again. The sterile glow of florescent lights shined on his face as he surveyed his surroundings. There was an IV hooked to his arm. A floodlight and other metal appendages from a hospital bed were hanging over him, and small flat screen television set across from him, hanging over an assortment of drawers and shelves holding medical equipment. His dress shirt was gone and his undershirt was cut down the middle.

Small suction cups were stuck to his chest with cords leading to an EKG machine. The digital monitor told him he was still alive.

It wasn't his first time waking up from a firefight in the hospital, but it was the first time in a while. His mouth felt dry with a metallic aftertaste and he was slightly dizzy. He could feel an overly medicated dull throb across his forehead that felt like the preamble to a hangover after an all-night bender. The pain meds made it hard for him to concentrate. He hated anesthetics. They took pain away and replaced it with nausea and a foggy mind. He would rather take some ibuprofen and deal with any residual pain.

He attempted to sit up in the hospital bed and was immediately interrupted by the nurse on duty. She was friendly enough, but quickly used a remote control to adjust the hospital bed to match his upper body.

"My partner was shot," he stated. "His name is Jacob Cavalera. Is he here?"

"You'll get answers soon enough, but right now I need to take your vitals."

"Can you tell me if he's alive?"

"He's still in surgery."

Gable could tell he was testing her patience.

"How long have I been unconscious?" he asked.

"About three hours," she responded. "Much of that was due to anesthesia."

"Why did you give me anesthesia?"

"You were unconscious when you arrived and the medic thought you were shot in the head," she said. "It turns out you have a deep cut that required stitches and probably a concussion, which is why I'm here."

"What does probably mean?"

She began taking his vitals and he patiently went through the motions, opening his mouth when prompted and fighting the urge to jump off the bed and find his partner. He used the time to control his breathing. He needed to stay cool and get back to observing all of his surroundings. He had a long list of people to call and things to do.

"Are you anxious?" she asked while taking his blood pressure.

"Yes."

"We are almost done, and the doctor is on his way. But you have small line of important people waiting in line to talk to you." The nurse finished up and walked out.

Seconds later, his room was filled with three senior police officers, one of whom was likely the chief and Detective McEvers. The officers were clearly giving the chief deference. He was slender with a long, weathered face and blue eyes, with graying hair that might have been brown once upon a time.

"How are you feeling?" he asked, though the pleasantry wasn't sincere. His tone was one of a man who was ready for a brawl. He quickly introduced the other police officers in the room, closing with McEvers, with a snide, "you've met."

"I'll be brief," he continued. "My name is Kieran Casey and I'm the chief of police in this fine city. I have a busboy in the burn unit whose hand looks like hamburger. I have a mayor and a room of reporters who want to know why my city was a shooting gallery this morning. I have your partner in another room, probably still in surgery. Last but not least, I have mother with two small children in the hospital lobby."

He paused, but it wasn't for effect. A lump grew in his throat and he took a moment.

"Two little boys. I cancelled a meeting with the Governor today because I'm going back to the lobby to play cars with them when you and I are finished. It feels like the least I can do because there's a pretty good chance their dad is going to die today. His name is Sergeant Justin Beckett and he's my only concern. Your boss and a bunch of muckety mucks are flying here now and they should land in the next hour. I spoke to her on the phone and wasn't impressed. It is my sincere hope that you do everything that is humanly possible to coordinate with my colleagues standing before you, and shine some light on what the fuck just happened in my city."

The room fell silent. Gable waited in deference to the officers in the room.

"Who is Byrd?" McEvers asked.

"Do we have an audio recording of your sergeant and my partner calling out his name?"

"That's why I'm asking you," McEvers responded.
Gable surveyed the officers standing in front of them.

"His name is Anthony Byrd," Gable responded. "Before I say anything else, do you have any way of recording this conversation?" The officers and mayor looked at each other as if they were perplexed by the question while McEvers produced a small handheld tape recorder. He pressed the record button and handed it to Gable.

"Everything I say from this point needs to be on record," Gable explained. "My name is Stephen Gable and the badge in my wallet identifies me as a special agent with the FBI. That is not the case. For the past twelve years, I have been a special agent with the Navy Criminal Investigative Service, working undercover investigating the FBI. I am breaking that cover now."

Gable went on to explain that as a Marine sergeant on his first deployment to Iraq, he was asked to investigate an incident where two Marines were accused of rape and murder of an Iraqi national. There was enough evidence to convict. A cursory review would have resulted in an open and shut case. Both men had brushes with Marine Corps authority in the past, but something was off.

One of the accused was married with a small child. He made mistakes in the past, but had all the makings of a reformed man. The other was a devout Christian who poured himself into the Scriptures as a way of coping with the stresses of war. The guys in their unit didn't buy the charges, and that's what stuck. In Gable's experience, Marines held high standards for themselves and others. That could occasionally translate into a "guilty until proven innocent" mentality where being investigated was akin to being a failure.

These two Marines had dirt under their fingernails from past transgressions. It wouldn't have been unreasonable for them to find themselves on the outside looking in, but they weren't. Their superiors didn't believe it. Their peers didn't believe it. Several officials up and down the chain of command within Marine detachment were openly questioning the judgment of authority in the combat zone. Something was off. Gable was asked to investigate.

What he found was a cover up. It was a defense contractor. At that time, defense contracts were given out like candy, and there were several private security firms and mercenaries flocking to the Middle East for odd jobs. In the movies, mercenaries were often portrayed as ramrod straight protagonists taking on an evil establishment.

In Gable's experience, mercenaries were usually undisciplined shitbags who couldn't handle active duty. They couldn't shoot. They couldn't patrol. They couldn't provide security well, but what they didn't have in talent, they made up for in political connections. Gable got the charges against the Marines dropped, and quickly identified two suspects. Both suspects were providing private security services to an American business drilling for oil. Gable detained both men from Gayton Security for questioning and managed to secure a recorded confession. His actions set off a political firestorm.

There was no way to prosecute either mercenary under international law and the military investigator was being told he wasn't even allowed to investigate a military contractor for any type of crime. If the two contractors were guilty of rape, that would be taken up through an arbitration process set up by their own employer. The two mercenaries walked and were out of the country within hours. When Gable transferred both mercenaries out of his custody, he turned them over to Anthony Byrd, who referred to himself as "First Sergeant."

This experience tipped Gable off that something far more sinister was taking place. He began revisiting other old investigations and found case after case after case where a service member was sitting behind bars for a crime that was likely committed by a private contractor. Each investigation read like a timid lackey taking the path of least resistance and gracelessly allowing an innocent man or woman to serve time for a crime they didn't commit.

Somebody was helping defense contractors avoid prosecution for crimes committed, and using service members as scapegoats when the crime demanded the need for one. Upon returning to Washington from deployment, he continued investigating. He wanted to know who the hell was behind what he now regarded as a fact.

As time went on, he found there was a ton of opposition to his scavenger hunt, and the defense contractors like Gayton had friends all over Capitol Hill. Gable's job was threatened. His desk was looted. His computer was hacked. He was given a threat that only someone within the FBI or CIA would have known was a vulnerability. When he still refused to back down, he found himself serving multiple consecutive deployments overseas. He still didn't give up. The Navy and Marine Corps quietly helped him, and eventually, he was able to secure permission with a top security clearance to take on the long-term undercover assignment that led them to this day.

As the public became increasingly skeptical of defense contractors, the Bush administration began moving away from hiring outsiders to do jobs that service members could complete. Thanks in part to Gable and the overall controversy around defense contractors in the Middle East, Gayton's government contracts all dried up. It became more difficult for them to access military bases even when they were providing security for private businesses and their access to junior enlisted troops became nearly nonexistent. Gayton Security went underground.

Meanwhile, Gable spent the next ten years of his deployments – a remaining product of retribution – working with JAGs to get the charges dropped against service members for crimes they didn't commit. In recent years, they were able to pull together modest amounts of compensation to help newly pardoned veterans get their lives in order.

His double life had been fulfilling, but it has also been a secret from the FBI for over a decade.

"Why should we believe anything you have to say?" asked the Chief.

Gable responded by pulling up the right sleeve of his undershirt to expose a tattoo of an Eagle, Globe and Anchor that covered most of his shoulder.

"You've seen my badge and heard my story," Gable said, "if you know anything about the United States Marine Corps, you know I took an oath to maintain an unparalleled commitment to honor and defend our nation. I earned the right to wear this emblem on my sleeve and I'm invoking that honor now."

The mayor looked over at McEvers.

"You were a Marine, what do you think?"

McEvers gave the mayor a nod.

"Well then Semper Fi," the chief responded. "My handshake is my bond."

Casey extended his hand and Gable shook it.

"So what now?" McEvers asked.

"Can someone tell me what happened to my phone?" Gable asked.

Gable's first call was to his supervisor with NCIS. He provided an update and relayed a number of other details as the St. Paul police listened in, conferring amongst each other. Gable ended his call.

"This is all going to move very fast," Gable said before turning to the chief, "Chief Casey, forgive me for not knowing too much the political scene here, but is it fair to say you're politically connected? You mentioned a meeting with the Governor earlier."

McEvers and the officers stifled mild laughter, and the chief smirked in response.

"I've been accused of worse," he said. Later Gable would learn the Chief Casey spent two terms in the Minnesota Senate and was retiring from the police soon. He was planning to run for governor.

"My next call is to Rafe Paxton," Gable said. "He's a congressman out in Illinois now, but before that he was a JAG I worked with on a number of investigations including this one. We're going to need him."

"I know Rafe Paxton," Chief Casey said with a laugh. "You should have led with that."

Gable made the call.

The Congressman answered the phone on the second ring.

"This is Rafe," he said.

"Do your friends call you asshole?" Gable responded.

"Welcome back, my man," Paxton answered, "give me a minute."

They listened to some shuffling around, then a return.

"I had a feeling you might be calling today," Paxton said.

"We will need a secure line for most of this conversation."

Gable listened to an audible pause and an exhale.

"Is this about what I think it's about?"

"It is, and the shit is pretty deep."

"I'm walking to my office now. How deep?" Paxton offered a friendly wave to a couple passersby as he walked down the steps of the Capitol facing the Washington Mall. He pivoted left and headed to his office in the Cannon House Office Building. There were shorter ways to his office, but he wanted a little time in the sun.

"I'm laying in a hospital bed in Saint Paul with a bunch of stitches in my head. I've got one FBI agent and a St. Paul cop both in surgery with multiple gunshot wounds. Byrd was the shooter."

Paxton took long strides to the Cannon House Office Building entrance. Flashed his ID to the Capitol policeman on duty and greeted him by name. He usually made time for small talk with the Capitol Police, but his uneasy smile and wave told them both he was in the middle of something big. The senior cop waved him past and he managed a "good to see you, Tom" as he breezed past.

His gingerly walk turned to a sprint up the marble stairs to his office. He was in his fifth term as a representative in the minority, but never seemed to fare well in the lottery for plush office space that took place after every election. He didn't care. He liked his office.

"How sure are you?" Paxton managed.

"I saw him, Rafe," Gable said. "My partner heard one of his boys call him by name. We chased two of his guys through a residential neighborhood and crossed a set of tracks on whatever they call their Metro. The station was nearby. If they have surveillance cameras, we'll be on tape."

"Hang on," he said.

Paxton breezed into his office. There was one constituent in the office who was originally there to meet with his staff. She was a gold star mom who also volunteered for the American Cancer Society. He put the phone on mute.

"Hey Pam," he said, and gave her a tight hug.

"Congressman!" she exclaimed. "I thought I was meeting with Jason."

"You are, but how long are you here?" He struggled to keep his cool.

"Oh, all afternoon, but everything okay?" she asked. "You seem out of breath."

"I'm great," he responded, "just dealing with a work thing." He shrugged and rolled his eyes.

"Oh, I'm sure you have your hands full these days," she responded.

He looked back at his staff assistant.

"Jackie, tell Jason that when he's done meeting with Pam, I would love to catch up and say hello. I need to make a call in my office on line seven."

Jackie nodded knowingly.

"Pam, I'm so sorry I have to be so brief right now," he said.

"You can do no wrong in my eyes, Congressman," she responded.

"If we can't connect while you're in town, let's grab coffee back home."

He smiled and shuffled into his office. For some Members of Congress, their deference was reserved for business executives and high donors. For Rafe's brand of politics, Pam was a high roller. He started out as a 30-something unknown Iraq veteran Democrat who knocked off a safe incumbent in a wave election. His district consisted of one large suburb and a string of small towns that screamed safe territory for the other party, but nobody on either side of the aisle was going to outwork Rafe Paxton. It was a swing district on paper, but safe territory for him because a quirky brand of throwback politics he brought to his job.

Jackie followed him into his office.

"I assume I can call you back at this number," he said.

"Yes," Gable responded.

Paxton hung up as Jackie dutifully handed another phone line to him and directed him to the key pad.

"I'll lock the door from the outside, Congressman," Jackie said.

"Thank you Jackie," he responded. "And Jackie?"

The nervous young brunette turned to look at him.

"It's Rafe," he said. "You're on the team. It's Rafe."

"Thank you, Rafe," she said.

Rafe Paxton dialed the number. Gable answered on the first ring.

"Okay, can I ask what you're investigating in Saint Paul?"

"Still figuring that one out, but it looks like a professional killer who targets sex offenders."

"How long have you been on this case?"

"About three days. Did you read about the guy who blew up his apartment in Alexandria?"

"I know more about it than I want to."

"Then my guess is that when I tell you one of the victims in this case is a man named Nicolay Belov, you're not going to be surprised."

Paxton leaned back in his chair and rubbed his eyes.

"Nope. How much do you know?"

Gable looked at his hospital gown, the IV sticking out of his arm and the entourage in his room hanging onto every word of his end of the conversation. He thought about the bullets ripping through Cavalera's chest and stomach. He thought about the exit wounds splattering blood all over the back of his crisp white dress shirt. He thought of the sound of Cavalera sucking and wheezing as he struggled to call out Byrd's name. He wasn't going to live. He was probably dead already.

"I know I'm in deep with this one, sir."

"You know Gunny, this would have been a lot easier if you would have called me last two years ago."

Gable didn't correct the Congressman about his current rank.

"Well, sir, the rats don't come out when the sun is shining."

"Okay, did you say you were in Saint Paul?"

"Yes, and I have the police chief here," Gable put his hand on the mouthpiece of his cell phone and whispered, "It's Kieran Casey, right?"

"Yes," the chief responded to a room full of cops who were now giggling at the idea of an agent not knowing the name of their larger-than-life police chief with political aspirations.

"Kieran Casey is in your hospital room?!" Paxton said in exasperation.

"Yeah, do you know him?"

Paxton laughed out loud.

"Maybe we're not completely fucked."

"Well, I need you to tell him who I am and that I'm not completely nuts," Gable responded. Meanwhile, Chief Casey waited anxiously for the phone like child waiting for a candy cane from Santa. Gable didn't understand politics.

"Put him on the phone," Paxton responded.

Gable handed the phone over to Casey and watched the two converse. They exchanged pleasantries, then quickly got to business. From Gable's perspective, Casey nodded, and occasionally acknowledged what Paxton was saying with an "uh-huh," or simply a nod. Gable watched as Casey turned to face the window, then slowly turned to face him again. Casey looked Gable in the eyes as he digested whatever Paxton was sharing with him. He handed the phone back to Gable.

"Gable?"

"I'm here."

"I will take care of things on my end. You go find that son of a bitch and keep your phone nearby."

"10-4."

Gable hung up the phone and looked up at Casey.

"What's your opinion of Rafe Paxton?" Casey asked.

"I'd take a bullet for him," Gable responded without hesitation.

"Huh," Casey marveled, "he said the same thing about you."

Casey turned to face the officers.

"Where'd McEvers go?"

"He's in the hall," one of the officers responded. "He took a call while you were on the phone."

McEvers walked back in on cue.

"There you are, McEvers," Casey said. "Agent Gable is officially one of us. Whatever he needs."

“We have our first request from the NCIS, chief,” McEvers responded. “They’ve asked us to arrest and detain Agent Gable’s supervisor as soon as her plane lands.”

Casey and McEvers looked at Gable in confusion.

“You were investigating your boss?” Casey asked.

Casey and the officers looked at McEvers.

“For the record, I’m not investigating any of you,” McEvers said.

Gable drank water from a plastic cup the nurse brought him earlier, and shook off the cobwebs he was still feeling from the painkillers. He proceeded to fill the crew in on their investigation, Cade Stuckley, Blake Sergeant and the string of unsolved murders they were chasing. As he was talking, a uniformed officer stepped in and whispered something to McEvers.

“We need to get back to Blake Sergeant’s house,” Gable said. “If we can figure out where they are going, we’ll find Byrd.”

“Agent Gable,” McEvers interrupted, “I think we might have a lead.”

McEvers nodded at the uniformed officer, who opened the door to Blake’s room. Doctor Scott Warner walked in sheepishly.

“I believe I have some information on two men who were probably involved in today’s shooting,” Warner said, “And I know where they’re going.”

Chapter 27

"Rise and shine, sleeping beauty," Blake said.

Cade Stuckley stretched and groaned. Even at 5 foot 7, it was tough for Cade to sleep comfortably in the back of a Mustang. His shoulder was throbbing and his back was stiff. He felt a strange tingling at the top of his cut that seemed to travel to his neck. Blake helped him out of the car and handed him a cup of coffee.

It was the early afternoon and the sun was shining down on them. Cade stood up and felt the stiffness of his back some more. He wanted to stretch his shoulders and arms, but everything just throbbed. They were in a hotel parking lot staring at a large river, from what Cade could tell. There was what looked like a bike trail along the water. On one end was the hotel and on the other were a handful of nondescript buildings and a pizza place. Cade noticed an open box from the same pizza joint on the hood of the car next to a couple bottles of water and soda.

"You need to take off your shirt," Blake said. "I need to change out your bandages and apply more ointment."
Cade responded dutifully as Blake went to work.

"I bought you some Advil," Blake said with a smirk as he applied the ointment, "or I should say you bought you Advil when you bought us lunch."

Melody was sitting on a bench adjacent to the walking trail staring at the water, eating her pizza and drinking a coke.

"Where are we?" Cade asked.

"Pierre, South Dakota."

Upon learning that police found Peterson's body, Blake decided to stay off major highways. He took 494 to Highway 212 in the Twin Cities and headed west, slowing down for the small towns, trying to maintain a low profile, to the extent that it was possible in a

Mustang. With the two of them officially on the run, his concerns about the congresswoman and her assistant heavy-hoofing all over the crime scene became an even bigger issue for Blake to worry about. They needed to keep moving.

"You shouldn't take my old painkillers again," Blake said. "Opioids are addictive and unpredictable. They cloud your mind. We dodged a bullet this morning but I need your head clear if we get into any more trouble."

"What are you talking about?" Cade said. "I might have been drunk and stoned, but I'm pretty sure I watched you singlehandedly take out three mafia enforcers."

"We got lucky," Blake responded. "She shot one of them," he added, giving a nod toward Melody.

Cade stared at her as she watched the current.

"How is she?"

"She's scared. She's pissed off that I won't let her smoke in the car."

"You're worried about cancer?" Cade laughed.

"I'm married to a nurse," Blake responded.

Cade didn't correct Blake. He learned a long time ago to let his friend talk about his wife and kids as if they were still alive. Blake's brain liked revisionist history. It was best to honor his quirks.

"What are we going to do with her?" Cade said, nodding Melody's way again.

"I don't know. She wasn't part of the plan and that's on me," Blake responded. "I wanted to drop her off at a bus stop somewhere. Give her some cash for her troubles and wish her the best. Or maybe drop her off in front of a police station. Still give her the cash, but ask her to wait a couple hours before she turns herself in. She'll get caught by someone, and I need to make sure we are long gone. The cops would let her live."

"Not a lot of good options," Cade demurred.

"We couldn't leave her behind in Saint Paul, especially now that we know we have a pack of mercenaries after us too. And they aren't above shooting cops."

"What are you talking about?"

"You were asleep," Blake said. "The news reported an officer involved shooting this morning in Saint Paul, just a few blocks from my place. A police officer and a federal law enforcement officer are both in critical condition."

"You think it's connected to us?"

"It has to be. I had two FBI agents waiting for me at work last night. Looking for you."

Cade's eyes widened.

"One of them talked about your apartment."

"Why the hell did you go to work?"

"To get more information. And we got it. By my count, we have your family, Gayton Security and the FBI after us. The first two want us dead. If the feds catch us, it's only a matter of time before we're behind bars."

"So we're fucked."

"We're still breathing," Blake corrected.

"Well, aren't you the little ray of sunshine."

"Listen," Blake handed Cade his shirt, "I'll always back your play, man. I trust you. But can we trust these cops in Marion? They weren't exactly shining examples of good law enforcement when I was living there."

"We don't have a choice," Cade responded. "But I feel better knowing if the shit gets deep, you're here to help shoot our way out of it."

Blake nodded in agreement and walked over to Melody. He stood next to her and scanned the parking lot above him. There were tourists walking into the hotel followed not too distantly by a business man on his cell phone. A biker was situated across the parking lot playing with his motorcycle. It looked like he might be trying to fix something on the fly.

"It's pretty," Melody said, breaking the silence.

Blake turned to face the river. They still had a couple hours of sunlight left, but the days were getting shorter. The river's current clapped and hissed as water flowed southeast.

"Do you know what river this is?" she asked.

"It's the Missouri River," he responded.

"Aren't we in South Dakota?"

"We are," Blake answered. "Its official start on paper is in Montana, but one of the original streams that feeds into it starts in Madison Lake up in Yellowstone."

"What are you, an encyclopedia?"

"My dad took me there when I was younger. The Missouri eventually joins up with the Mississippi River."

"Does that happen in Missouri?"

"Yeah, just outside St. Louis."

Melody exhaled.

"And where does the Mississippi end?"

"Gulf of Mexico."

"So the water here will eventually be in the ocean?"

"I guess you could say that."

"So I'm on the beach right now," she said with a smile.

"You probably won't find any seashells."

"If your escape plan works out, will you end up on a beach?" Blake smiled.

"You know I'm not going to talk to you about that. We still need to figure out what to do with you."

"I told you, I don't really know where to go. My mom's still pissed at me and I have no idea where my dad is. My sister thinks I'm a joke and if I show up at her front door, she's just going to spend the next hour telling me how right she is about me being a fuck-up."

"I've found my family and I get along best if we stick to Christmas cards as well."

"Do you get along with your family?"

"I don't know how to answer that," Blake responded. "I haven't seen my mom or sister in a couple of years. I don't know why I would need to. Everything we ever need to say to each other has already been said. There's nothing left to talk about."

"That seems very lonely."

"It's not," Blake said, "I need your help thinking about you. We have some people after us, and your life is in danger every second we're together. If we cut you loose, you would need to keep a low profile because if the guys who are after us catch you, it won't be pretty. Then there's the issue with the cops. We could drop you off and let you turn yourself in. I'm fine with you telling the truth."

"If I do that, I'll go to jail too."

"You were a hostage."

"I killed someone, too."

"And the murder weapon is in my car. That means it's your best interest that we escape. I just want a good head start before you say anything. We have enough problems."

Melody didn't respond. She was resolute.

"Tell me what you want to do, Melody. We're not keeping you prisoner. Eventually, we'll come to a juncture where there are three people and two seats. You're the third person."

"I have nowhere left to go. I don't give a shit about the life I left behind. I don't need money now. All my cash is in my bag. If you don't mind, I'd like to stay with you and Cade."

"You've seen how dangerous that can be. His family will catch up to us again."

"And you handled them."

"They weren't expecting a fight. They will next time."

"And you'll be ready," she said, "it's what you're good at."

Blake thought it over.

"Okay," he responded. "You can come with us for now. The only reason I'm good with this is because I know what's behind us, but you need to know this road has an end."

Chapter 28

Denise Towe sat resolute in a sterile interrogation room in the bowels of the St. Paul police station. She played the events of the last twenty-four hours through her mind over and over, trying to determine exactly what led her to the position she was presently in. Eight words ran through her mind over and over.

"Anthony Byrd. That's the guy who shot Beckett."

One day earlier, she was in New York City sitting in a command center investigating the murder of Nicolay Belov. The room was bustling with bureaucrats and agency heads like herself who were summoned to be part of a larger investigation of a high-profile murder. She was glad to finally be included in larger meetings such as this. Years ago, she was on the fast track to a plum senior assignment with the FBI and command center operations were the norm. Then she hit a dry spell. The FBI director was fired. His assistant was shown the door a few months later. The dry spell was over. She should be happy, but her mind kept coming back to the one thorn in her side that she could never fully comprehend – Steve Gable.

Looking around the room, she saw a lot of agency brass. State department, New York Homicide, other FBI agents, representatives from the Russian Embassy. Nobody was a household name in political circles, but they clearly had administration level advisors on their speed dial. The room also looked like the type of environment where secrets were not going to be kept. Their respective departments also hadn't found a damn thing with respect to the investigation until Jake Cavalera called with a lead. They had a name and address. They were two hours away from bringing in the first thing resembling a person of interest. She took a little hometown pride in her agents' investigative prowess.

That hometown pride gave way to anxiety as soon as Anthony Byrd called her.

She and Byrd met years ago as part of another joint service investigation. In that case, the DoD was involved as were a handful of defense contractors who were sitting in situation meetings for which they probably didn't have the appropriate security clearance. It was a different time. Between long hours and a natural rapport, their partnership eventually became romantic in nature. There was never going to be a future for them. She was married with a kid and he was a mercenary whose job required unpredictable hours and long stints in other parts of the world. That didn't stop them from willingly carrying on an intermittent affair for nearly fourteen years.

Byrd first reached out to her about Special Agent Steve Gable in 2005. Gable was a Marine sergeant asked to investigate the rape and murder of an Iraqi citizen. He became convinced that the two Marines accused of the crime were not the culprits, and he was working overtime to pin the crime on two of Byrd's employees. Towe heard of Gable as a holier-than-though Captain America-type who believed that every ounce of Marine's blood was worth its weight in gold. He was incapable of processing the notion that sometimes, people in uniform broke laws. It seemed like an odd thing to accuse an MP of, but she believed Byrd.

When he wasn't in Iraq, Gable was an FBI special agent stationed in northern Pennsylvania, not too far from his reserve unit. Because of his military connections and several years in law enforcement before he joined the FBI, Gable was incredibly connected in his region. He was also a guy whose character would be tough to question. When he began investigating Gayton Security as an FBI agent, Byrd asked Towe for help.

At that time, her star was rising with the Bureau, and she successfully hindered Gable's efforts. Byrd and his boss used their contacts at the time to arrange for Gable to partake in multiple consecutive deployments to the most dangerous parts of the Middle East. Instead of suffering under pressure, he thrived, securing multiple promotions. Byrd sent mercenaries to kill Gable in the Middle East. It didn't work.

Towe arranged to have Gable transferred to her unit so she could keep a closer eye on him and his extracurricular investigation of Gayton. She arranged for him to be partnered up with a team player who would keep her apprised of his every move. Instead, her team player became close friends with Gable. The multiple deployments were intended to throw him off his game and never allow him to catch his footing. That didn't work, either. He would return from deployment, solve a few crimes, then return to the Middle East.

When she finally found some leverage they could hold over Gable related to his family, Colonel Gayton himself gave Gable the ultimatum. He could back off his investigation, or the CIA would inform the Russians that Gable's father-in-law, an ex-KGB spy-turned-informant, was still alive. Gable's father-in-law was a high-profile target and without the witness protection provided by the United States, his whole family would be in danger.

Gable backed off, or at least that's what it looked like. She had overheard that he had made a practice during his deployments of overturning convictions in the Middle East if he decided in his own mind the service members were innocent. She would occasionally hear from Byrd of the DoD and American-owned businesses terminating relationships with defense contractors including Gayton with little explanation. The only correlation was that each agency had a current or former employee who was being accused of a crime overseas by a pissed off Marine Gunnery Sergeant who moonlighted as an FBI agent.

She also knew Gable had an old Marine buddy who got himself elected to Congress. That buddy, Rafe Paxton, made tormenting Gayton Security a personal hobby and there was little Byrd and Gayton could do about it. Like Gable, Paxton was a boy scout with nothing to hide.

Gable had never indicated to her that he knew about her relationship with Byrd, but as she worked with him longer, she became increasingly suspicious that he knew about the role she was playing in hindering his investigations. She suspected that he knew it was her who gave Gayton and Byrd the information on Gable's family. But he never made a move. He never made an accusation. He never made a threat. He continued about his business as an investigator. He was one of the best investigators she had ever seen. As time went on, she had wondered if bringing him to her unit was a mistake.

As Gayton lost defense contracts, Towe's rising star seemed to stall. There was a new president, political appointees, retirements, a suspicious director, and through the process, there were fewer senior members looking to her as the next executive. Her role didn't change. She wasn't brought into as many high-profile cases.

That changed after the last election. Gayton received a few new defense contracts in the last year. Private employers were hiring them again and they regained some office space on an Air Force base. A new president, new political appointees and a series of retirements translated into things looking up for Towe and Byrd.

They weren't collaborating as closely as before, but she knew that taking Byrd's calls brought with them the political fringe benefits that were the norm when they first met. When Byrd called asking about Cade Stuckley, she felt nauseous. She gave him the information he wanted. Four hours later, she was standing next to an irritated new special agent and Gable, professional as ever, but watching her like a predator. He looked like an owl perched on a branch, waiting for a rodent to come out into the open. She heard he had gotten divorced after the last deployment, but noticed he was still wearing his ring. She took it as a symbol of his one weakness.

Nevertheless, having Byrd encroaching on Gable's investigation felt too close for comfort. After Gable and Cavalera left for St. Paul, she was sick with wondering what Gable knew. Whether he suspected anything.

The calls from Byrd continued, and she gave him everything she had. Blake Sergeant was all she had. She envisioned Gable and Cavalera going about their work as Byrd sat with a squad of mercenaries waiting to pounce. Through the process, Byrd never told her who he was working for, and she knew better than to ask. She tried to focus on her command center responsibilities – sitting on her ass and waiting for the next update, which came Tuesday morning.

The chief of police from Saint Paul, Minnesota was patched through via Special Agent Cavalera's cell phone.

He informed her of a shootout in St. Paul, and both of her agents were down. He also had an officer down and an injured private citizen. Something about a burned hand. She remembered thinking he was pompous and self-righteous. Hours later, she joined a cadre of white men in black suits for a government flight to the Twin Cities. She was one of two token female investigators. The other female investigator, who was probably from the CIA, was younger and barely acknowledged Towe.

Towe arrived in the hospital and found Maxwell sitting anxiously in the lobby, typing away at his laptop.

"I wanted to thank you," she said. "Our team checked the hotel server because of your suggestion, and they found something called a pineapple."

Maxwell's eyes lit up.

"Then it's gotta be the same guys."

"You're right," she responded.

"Denise," Maxwell asked. "Is Cavalera going to be okay?"

"I don't know."

She immediately went to Cavalera's bedside. He was out of surgery. An artificial respirator pumped air into his lungs, inflating his bandaged chest cavity. The doctor was courteous but didn't offer a good prognosis.

"Call his family," the doctor suggested.

As she exited Cavalera's room, her entourage backed away from her and two uniformed cops placed her under arrest. She looked around in exasperation. Demanded an explanation.

"You're being detained at the request of the Navy Criminal Investigative Service, ma'am," the female cop said. "That's all I'm at liberty to say."

As they drove to the station, two cops rode in one vehicle, with the passenger holding her belongings in a large ziplock bag. One male cop, one female. The male cop, who looked like he might be of Indian decent, didn't speak. The female cop rode in the passenger seat. Towe's phone rang and she looked up. The female officer looked down at the caller ID, then back to her partner.

"Anthony Byrd," she said. "That's the guy who shot Beckett."

The male officer only nodded and clenched his jaw. They looked like they wanted to pull over to the side of the road and shoot her execution style, but resisted temptation. They pulled into the entrance for the detention area and walked her to an interrogation room without controversy.

She wanted to ask more questions, but based on those eight words spoken minutes earlier, she knew their undying loyalty was to

Sergeant Beckett, whoever he was. She took her seat, and the male officer finally spoke.

"One of our investigators will be with you shortly," he said with a trace of a Minnesotan accent. If his family was from India, they probably moved to Minnesota when he was very young.

She spent the next half hour waiting in silence, wondering how much the St. Paul police knew.

The door to the interrogation room opened, and in walked Steve Gable.

He was wearing a Saint Paul PD sweater over dress pants. There was a large bandage wrapped around his head and streaks of dried blood still on his face. He looked like hell.

"Please accept my apology for the casual nature of my attire," he said, "my dress shirt is covered in blood."

Towe glared at him.

"What's going on Steve?"

Gable responded by flashing his badge and identification, and her jaw dropped.

"My name is Special Agent Stephen Gable, Navy Criminal Investigative Service," he said. "We've been investigating you for a while now, and I would like to ask some questions about Anthony Byrd."

"You must be out of your fucking mind," she erupted. She attempted to stand, and her cuffed hand pulled her back down to her seat. "Special Agent Gable, I don't know what lies you have told to these local cops or the NCIS, but so help me God when this is all over, your self-righteous ass will be wearing hanD.C.uffs just like these . . ."

Gable twirled his right index finger in the air and looked back at the double-sided mirror behind him. Towe looked at him in confusion as an audible hiss from the room's speakers filled the air. She heard the recording of a phone ringing, followed by her answer.

"You shouldn't be calling me at this number," she heard herself.

"You worry too much," a man with a deep baritone voice responded. "It's a new day. This is a joint operation."

"Yes, but during our previous operations, you and Doug were in the command center."

"Yeah, but you and I don't need to worry about all that."

"What's that all about?" Gable asked, raising an eyebrow.

"This is not what you think," Towe interrupted, "and you have no authorization to wiretap . . ."

Gable slid a signed warrant across the desk in Towe's view. She didn't recognize the name of the judge.

"We turned your wiretap back on after I saw Cade Stuckley's apartment," Gable said. "Not the first time someone has interfered with an FBI investigation."

"Oh you try holding me on . . ."

Gable put his finger to his mouth and pointed to the speaker in the room.

"This is a good part," he interrupted.

"His name is Blake Sergeant," Towe heard a recording of her own voice say, "He's at work now in Minneapolis. My agents are going to talk to him."

She listened to the recording of her giving an unidentified man all the details of their investigation, just a moment after acknowledging that he was not officially part of their task force. She provided Sergeant's address, his background and an estimated time for when he returned home.

She heard the click of a phone, followed by the recording of another phone ring.

"What the hell is going on Denise?"

"I don't know, Anthony," she growled. "You tell me."

"Well, my boys are staring at a clusterfuck of a crime scene, and guess who is there now, a day late and a dollar short."

"Well maybe if Cade Stuckley didn't get the drop on your boys, we wouldn't be here."

"That's a hell of a thing for you to say – hang on."

They heard muffled conversation then Byrd returned to the line.

"I'll call you back."

Detective McEvers walked into the interrogation room as the recording played and introduced himself.

"You're being held as a suspect by the Saint Paul Police Department as part of an ongoing investigation an officer involved shooting," McEvers said. "The shooting and ensuing chase las left one civilian injured, one officer in critical condition and two fatalities."

"We found Alfred Love's body in a stolen van outside a local airport," Gable continued. "Love was a known associate of Anthony Byrd and an employee of Gayton Security. And Special Agent Jacob Cavalera died about 15 minutes ago."

Towe sighed heavily and put her face in her hands, which were still cuffed to the table.

"He was going to propose to his girlfriend in a couple of weeks," Gable said. "Did you know that?"

"I didn't know they were that serious."

"Oh, they were. They dated off and on. When his undercover gig finally ended, he called her again, hoping this new assignment would offer better hours and a more family friendly pace."

"The NCIS has graciously agreed to the city's request to keep you in custody as a suspect in a local homicide for the time being," McEvers added. "If the FBI wishes for a transfer in custody, they'll need to talk to my police chief."

Both men exchanged a smirk and a glance.

"Special Agent Towe," Gable said, "is there anyone else talking to Byrd or Doug Gayton?"

Towe shook her head, still in her hands.

"I don't know."

"Who is Gayton working for?"

"I don't know that either."

"You're going to divulge sensitive information about a federal investigation over an unsecured phone line, and you don't even know who is paying Gayton's meal ticket? Bullshit."

"It's a lot higher up on the food chain than you or I, Gable," Towe responded, "which is why I'm surprised you even got this wiretap."

"I want a name," Gable said, never raising his voice.

"This is a whole new world that you don't understand. I don't care what you think you know, you just picked a fight you won't win."

"Who is Gayton working for?"

"That's classified!" she screamed. "You don't get to know. You are the one who is interfering with a federal investigation of something way bigger than any of us! Get me out of these cuffs right fucking now!"

"I don't have authorization to do that," Gable said.

"Technically, he's right," McEvers added. "Did Officer Maloney read you your rights?"

"You are making a huge mistake."

"And you got one of my officers shot," McEvers shouted.

"This is bigger than my agent or your officer," Towe screamed back. "And if you don't uncuff me right now, both of you motherfuckers will be the ones cuffed to a table next time I see you! Traitors!"

Gable grabbed McEvers' arm and nodded.

"I'm going to try to ask my questions again," Gable said calmly, "is anyone else leaking information to Gayton? Who is Gayton working for?"

"I'm staring at a dead man," Towe responded.

Gable didn't flinch. He and McEvers stood up and walked to the door.

"How's your family, Steve?" she asked.

Gable paused.

"They've been safe for a while," he responded.

Gable and McEvers shut the door to the interrogation room.

"Did I just hear her threaten your family?"

"You did," Gable said. "She's rattled."

Officer Gupta met them in the hall.

"Agent Gable and Detective McEvers, you have a call in the sat-com room. The chief is in there waiting for you."

McEvers led the way to a large conference room with the shades pulled over the windows. They met the Casey who was staring at a plasma screen monitor at the end of the room engaged in conversation.

Congressman Rafe Paxton was on the screen, standing next to a shorter, slender African American woman with her hair pulled by in a tight bun. She wore a black business suit with a white blazer and was likely in her mid-fifties.

"Good afternoon, ma'am," Gable said to the woman on the screen.

"Agent Gable," Victoria Perez responded, "I am sorry to hear about Agent Cavalera."

Gable nodded, still processing the information he had also just learned moments ago.

"I didn't know him well," he responded, "but from what I could tell, he was a good agent. His family . . ."

"I'll take care of everything," she interrupted. "My counterpart on the West Coast knows his old SAIC well. Plus, the FBI has its hands full."

"Gable, are you okay?" Paxton asked.

"I'm fine," Gable said. "What do we know?"

"We know you kicked one hell of a hornet's nest," Paxton responded. Perez shot him a cold stare. "One heck of a hornet's nest."

"Language, Congressman," Gable corrected with a smirk. Paxton shook his head and continued.

"I don't want to get too much into it right now, but Nicolay Belov had some friends in high places in Washington, and so does our buddy Gayton."

"How high?" Gable asked.

"I think we both know the answer to that," Paxton replied.

The room sat silent for a second that felt like minutes.

"I think a couple of his buddies are waiting for us to give them a tour of the crime scene now," Casey finally said. "They look like politicians, but a couple of them have badges."

"Do I need to talk to them?" Gable asked.

"No, you're not an FBI agent," Perez responded. "We'll figure that out. Congressman, do you want to continue?"

"Gayton is in some trouble because we have military types blaming each other for him having an office on base. Pentagon brass is blaming the base commander and vice versa. It's a cluster. Gayton is not on base now and word on the street is it looks like he isn't coming back. Chief Casey, we're going to get a lot of federal pressure to turn Towe over to their custody. Are you and any political contacts you might have around town ready for a pissing match?"

"I'm ready, but you know it's only a matter of time before they can invoke a couple federal laws to tie my hands. How much time do you need?"

"A couple days?" Paxton responded, though it sounded more like a question.

"We'll do our best," Perez responded assertively.

"We can keep the suits occupied," Casey said. "I'll escort them myself."

Everyone in the room looked at Gable and McEvers.

"What do you need from us, boss?" Gable asked.

"Find Byrd," Perez responded. "There are strings that the Congressman and I will pull on our end."

"And when we catch him?" McEvers asked.

"He is a suspect in a St. Paul homicide investigation, Detective," Perez said. "Special Agent Gable is here to offer full cooperation and assistance with your investigation. Whatever you need."

"Thank you, ma'am," McEvers responded.

"And Gable," Paxton added, "your family is safe."

"Thank you," Gable responded.

"I've called in a couple favors," Paxton continued, "they're happy to help."

"Go find me a bad guy, Special Agent," Perez responded to Gable before raising her hand to her throat, signaling the Sailor likely sitting to her left to cut the feed.

Casey grabbed McEvers by the arm.

"We'll will resume your investigation at the crime scene and pass along any additional info we can find," Casey said to McEvers. "I want the two of you in Wyoming. Maloney and Gupta are coming."

"Maloney and Gupta?" McEvers asked.

"Well, I didn't stutter," the chief said. Both men paused and acknowledged an unsaid communication. Casey turned to face Gable and McEvers. "Gentlemen, I want to be clear. As far as we can tell, the feds are going to do everything they can to impede this investigation."

"Your old boss," Casey pointed his finger at Gable and continued, "or whatever she is, is going to be a free woman pretty soon. When you bring Byrd back, he might have a get out of jail free card, too. I'll bet the Russian in that entourage I'm getting ready to babysit has it in his pocket."

Gable and McEvers nodded.

Casey looked over his shoulder, leaned in closer to Gable and McEvers' personal space and lowered his voice.

"We don't have a death penalty in the State of Minnesota," he growled. "That motherfucker took one of ours down and killed one of yours. You shoot one East-sider, you just shot a family." McEvers and Gable looked at each other, then back at Chief Casey.

"We understand," McEvers said.

Casey exited the conference room leaving McEvers and Gable to confer. Before they could exit, Officer Maloney walked in with Vernon Maxwell following her. Maxwell was still in his wrinkled slacks and button up shirt under a tan sports jacket.

"Detective McEvers," Maloney called out.

"Mr. Maxwell has some new information that's pertinent to the case. Do you have a moment?"

Maloney shut the door behind her, and they all grabbed a seat. Maxwell opened his laptop and plugged in his password. The police detectives and Gable watched him intently as he attempted to gather his thoughts. Maxwell had just watched a young agent die, and the Special Agent in Charge of his old unit hauled off in handcuffs. He wanted with every fiber of his body to ask what the hell was going on, but four decades in government taught him that sometimes, you resist that temptation and do your job. He turned to face Gable, who was closest to his research.

"Agent Gable," he started, "my theory was correct. Cade Stuckley has been running a deathpool on the dark web." He paused and waited for the officers to process the information.

"Does everyone know what I mean by the dark web?"

Gable nodded, but caught a look of confusion in Maloney's eye before answering.

"Assume we don't, Vernon," Gable said.

"The dark web can be best described as the underbelly of the internet. It is a deep web that exists between Tor servers and their clients."

"Okay, now you have lost me," McEvers said.

Maxwell paused, scratched his chin, then tried again.

"A Tor server is a place on the internet where people can communicate with each other anonymously. You know the message boards at the bottom of newspaper articles, where people write stupid comments?"

Gable, McEvers and Maloney all three nodded.

"Well, that's not anonymous. If you write about how you want to kill the President, you're going to get a call from the Secret Service because that can be traced back to you. On a Tor server, that's not always the case. Users can communicate anonymously. Nobody sees it. You can write all kinds of bad shit, and no one can trace it back to you unless they hire someone like me. And I can't even find it half the time."

"Intelligence agencies, the military, law enforcement and others can use Tor servers to communicate with each other with a lower risk of their communications getting intercepted by another government. The dark web is a place where bad people use multiple Tor servers to do bad things. Hackers, identify theft, drug trafficking, sex trafficking, assassins, you name it. The Russian mob uses it. The Yakuza uses it. There's a lot of activity coming out of the Pacific Rim. You get the picture. Cade Stuckley was running a deathpool on the dark web."

"He had full profiles of different people convicted of sex crimes or accused of sex crimes, and people could vote on which one should be murdered. Then, the group would take bets on which of the top three vote-getters would die. I'll bet Cade and probably a partner – maybe this Blake Sergeant guy – would lure these guys to a place like a park or rest area where they could easily take them out. All of our guys are listed on the deathpool as wins, Agent Gable."

Gable nodded in amazement.

"And there are more," Maxwell said, "A lot more. I can find out exactly how many if I have a better place to work. We might be able to solve several cold cases, but here's the big thing. This Nicolay Belov, the Russian they just killed?"

"Belov was the initial murder victim that brought us to your crime scene in the first place," Gable said to McEvers. "Blake Sergeant, the guy whose apartment makes up half your crime scene, was the close friend to my person of interest. I think it's safe to say he's involved."

"Someone is pissed that he's dead, and that he died in an, uh, embarrassing manner," Maxwell said. "The Russians put a one-billion-ruble bounty on Cade Stuckley's head. That's about fifteen to twenty million dollars depending on the market rate."

"The Russians? Do you mean the Russian government?" McEvers asked.

"Supposedly it's the mob, but according to the web chatter, the lines are blurred," Maxwell responded.

"Who the hell was he?" Gable asked.

"Everything online just says he's a business man with lots of political connections, but if that were true, they probably wouldn't be talking about him on the dark web."

"And there wouldn't be a one-billion-ruble bounty on Cade Stuckley," Maloney added.

"Is Towe still in the interrogation room?" Gable asked. McEvers was already standing up to make his way to the room. Before he stopped, he looked at Maxwell.

"Is there anything else?" he asked.

"Nothing that can't wait," Maxwell responded. "You need to find this guy, if you can."

McEvers looked to Maloney, "Maxwell, here, is going to need somewhere to work, with security."

"Thank you," Maxwell responded.

"On it," Maloney responded.

McEvers and Gable walked into the interrogation room where Towe was still sitting.

"When were you going to tell us about the one-billion-ruble bounty for the man who killed Nickolay Belov?"

Towe's eyes widened in response. Gable and McEvers watched her intently.

"What do you think, Detective McEvers," Gable asked, "do you think she knew?"

McEvers took a seat.

"She looked surprised, but you know her better than I do." Gable pulled the opposite seat closer to him and sat in it, leaning back.

"Definitely surprised," Gable answered, "but is she surprised about a bounty, or surprised that we know about it?"

"Does she know because this investigation is much bigger than Beckett and . . ." McEvers looked to Gable.

"Cavalera?" Gable responded, finishing his new partner's sentence. "I don't know. If she knew, she didn't tell us."

"You know, her buddy Byrd said she wouldn't need to worry about 'all that.'"

"I've been thinking about that, too. I think they have been working together all along."

Towe looked down at the desk in front of her.

"She flew to New York to hang out with the high rollers, and sent Cavalera and I on a rabbit hunt," Gable said. "It was only my first day back, but it looked like a lot of our agents were on rabbit hunts, chasing down leads, but we weren't working together."

"That's strange," McEvers opined, "is it normal that you would look for different leads on the same case without working together?"

"Unusual," Gable responded, "but not unheard of. We know she was feeding Byrd details about our investigation. Were she and Byrd working with the whole command center or did they go rogue?"

"We should ask her friends. They're with the chief, now."

"You two have no damned clue," she growled.

"Chief Casey will ask them," McEvers responded, "after he tells them about our friend Towe here giving details of my crime scene to the mercenary who shot Sergeant Beckett. He's going to show some pictures of Beckett's kids on his phone. Mrs. Beckett texted them over."

Towe shook her head and clenched her jaw.

"Do they know you've been undermining the investigation?" McEvers asked Towe.

She didn't respond.

"I don't think it matters," Gable said. "Even if they don't, she's going to be the fall girl. Female agent, had to work hard to get promoted. Federal law enforcement is a largely male occupation. Look at us, we're both male. She had to work twice as hard to get promoted. She had to get some dirt under her fingernails."

"You don't know anything," she growled.

"I know my fingernails are clean."

"Go to hell!" she said, raising her voice.

"I also know that's not true. Special Agent Perez, my real SAIC, her fingernails are clean. She had to work her way up the chain just like you, but she did it through hard work and integrity. Imagine that."

"Fuck you."

"But not you. You made the hard call. You paid your dues, but we have evidence on you. Between those calls and the bounty, it looks like you undermined a federal investigation and Cavalera is dead. That's on you. And here's another thing. This is a good ole boys club. Joint operation. An operation that big would need someone real high in the chain of command signing off. My money is on the President, but he won't get his hands dirty. The good ole boys will keep their hands clean. And they'll let you take the fall, because the Saint Paul Police Department has plenty of evidence to put you away. Unless, of course, you want to answer our initial question."

"Are you and Byrd going rogue?" McEvers asked.'

"Or is this another case where a couple traitors who are running the country I have been serving for over twenty years is content with being Russia's bitch?"

Towe looked at Gable and didn't speak. Gable nodded.

"Russia's bitch," he affirmed.

Towe looked ahead and didn't speak.

"We're gonna find Byrd, Denise. You have some time to make a decision."

"Such the boy scout," she growled.

Gable brushed his fingernails against his sweater, then looked at them.

"I've been called worse," he responded, "it's never too late to start fighting for our country again."

Both investigators left the interrogation room.

"We need to get to Wyoming," Gable said.

"Come on, the team is waiting for us," McEvers responded.

Chapter 29

Frank Silvera, Cade Stuckley's stepfather, stood outside the storage unit that was still rented out to Blake Sergeant. He had already inspected the dead bodies of his three associates to include his nephew, Tony Silvera. Jerry Campanella followed nearby like a puppy, trying to relay his play-by-play of the sequence of events. He vacillated between fear and survivor's guilt, consistently second guessing his moves until Frank grew weary of his restlessness.

"Campanella," Frank said with irritation, "I need you lucid. We're gonna find these guys, and when we do, we will need to be ready. Can you do that for me?"

Campanella paused, composed himself and nodded in response.

An ice truck pulled up to the storage unit, which was the product of a favor Frank was calling in from a local associate. Frank had a rolodex of associates across the country, and many of whom owed him favors. That was the product of nearly 40 years in the trucking business, both legitimately and illegally.

His mother was a diesel mechanic in the fifties and his dad was a trucker. They worked for the same business Frank's sister and her wife owned on paper. As a boy, Frank always knew he would follow in his family's footsteps, but wasn't sure which parent's occupation interested him more.

When he was thirteen, Frank's father found himself stranded in a broken-down rig in a blizzard outside of Billings, Montana. His CB radio was down, and he waited for two days until the roads were opened again, and another truck driver found him. Upon returning, Frank's father lamented that he didn't have enough space in his cab to pack the tools he would have needed to fix the truck himself.

A designer at heart, Frank responded to this experience by drafting different designs for creating hidden compartments within a trailer. When he found a design he liked, he persuaded his parents to let him use an arc welder to take his vision from paper to the back of his father's cab. It later turned out his father was lying about the whole thing and in truth spent his disappearance in the trailer of a waitress he met in town. Nonetheless, Frank continued working on the project of designing and building compartments within cabs and storage units where a truck driver could store extra tools or equipment.

It was also during those years he became fast friends with the Carbone family. Angelo, the family patriarch and Frank's eventual father-in-law, spent many hours in the front office of the family business and the kids occasionally came by to hang out with Frank. Joseph and William Carbone, known back then as Joey and his kid brother Billy, were regular fixtures. Frank and Joey were the same age, and Billy was the precocious kid brother following the older boys around. Their sister Bette would occasionally join them as well, and Frank immediately fell in love with her. Unfortunately, the love was always a one-sided affair.

The Carbone boys were particularly impressed with Frank's storage compartment concept, and encouraged him to build similar hidden compartments on their cars where they could hide their dope. As he went into the trucking profession, Frank started using his extra component to run dope across the country. He met other dealers, made contacts and eventually developed a network across the continental United States where small time meth cooks could get their products on the larger market. Soon, he was making so much money that with the Carbones' help, he began funneling money through a couple of their front operations.

There were dry cleaners that never washed clothes, diners who seldom served patrons, a clothing store that once went three months without selling a single outfit and of course gentlemen's clubs. All the front operations ran on money brought in by the Carbones and Frank's trafficking operation. Frank even brought Billy on as *his* trusted lieutenant.

Frank managed to find a couple police departments willing to launder his cash while looking the other way as his operation continued. He didn't need the help. They needed the money, and their loyalty was a nice perk. If a high school dropout in Montana decided he was going to spend his days fried on meth made in California, chances are one of Frank's truckers brought the supply into town. One of Frank's bikers peddled the drugs to local dealers. One of the dealers sold the goods. Frank Silvera was making millions of dollars off rural America's drug addiction.

All through this time, he remained in love with Bette. He waited patiently for her courtship with an Army sergeant stationed at Fort Dix to run its course. He was there to console her when the sergeant, upon discovering her family's operation, used the court system to secure full custody of their son Cade and disappear to a small town in Northern Idaho. He dutifully agreed to keep an eye out for them and he eventually found their family.

He spied on the Stuckleys from afar and provided regular reports. When Gary Stuckley died unexpectedly, Frank was instrumental in helping the Carbone family swoop in and seize custody of Bette's seventeen-year-old son Cade.

He slept with his share of women trying to find some connection to supplant his childhood infatuation, but he always only had eyes for Bette Carbone. They eventually married, and shared a common bond. She was in love with a man who was never going to want to share a life with her. He was married to a woman who was never going to see him as a first choice.

Eventually their consolation partnership provided Frank with opportunities to build his empire while moving up the ranks within the Carbone family. He was effectively Angelo's third Carbone son and a trusted lieutenant. He also knew he was the most logical choice to take over the family business if Angelo ever chose to hang up his cleats.

Jerry Campanella promptly scurried over to the Explorer to help two more of Frank's other employees move the bodies of the three men Blake and Melody murdered to the ice truck. It was only a matter of time before the St. Paul police found the storage unit, and they needed to disappear.

Frank surveyed the blood on the floors of the Explorer, pulled out a pen and pad, wrote an address on a sheet, tore it out and handed it to Campanella.

"Take the rental to this address," he instructed. "They'll be expecting you. Give them the Explorer and switch it out for another vehicle. Drive all night if you have to. We know they're going west."

Frank walked around the ice truck to the cab and handed the ice truck driver another address along with similar instructions. He returned to the back of the cab and looked at his nephew Tony Silvera's body. He sighed deeply and lowered his head.

"Poor, poor Tony," he lamented to the October air.

Billy Carbone joined him at the back of the cab.

"This kid, Billy," Silvera continued, "I've been saying for years, nothing but trouble."

Carbone nodded.

"Just like his old man," Carbone offered.

"No," Frank countered, "worse. His old man was a short asshole, and he became a real asshole when he put on a badge. I told Cade's mother, we should just leave them be. The kid was a daddy's boy. When his dad passed away, he became something else. Asshole like his dad, but . . ."

"Thinks he's better than us, but he's one of us," Billy interjected.

"Whether he wants to admit it or not."

"Anyway, Frank, I've got the guy on the phone," Billy said, producing a burner phone.

"What's his name?"

"Skyler Roy."

"Skyler Roy?" Frank asked. "What the hell kind of redneck name is that?"

"I don't know, Sturgis redneck. He's a good mule. Does most his work on bike. Knows his area well."

"Does he have a mullet?"

"I don't know what you'd call that shit on his head."

"And he's got eyes on Stuckley?"

"That's what he says," Billy responded. "My guy says they match our description. Complete dumb luck."

"Maybe not complete dumb luck," Frank said with a smile.

"He just texted it to me. Take a look."

"All right, gimme the phone."

Silvera put on his reading glasses and stared at the screen on Billy's mobile device.

"Can you make it bigger?"

Billy took the phone back and zoomed in on an image of Cade Stuckley leaned up against a Mustang drinking a bottle of water. Off in the distance, Blake Sergeant was standing next to a bench staring at the Missouri River next to a gorgeous brunette who was seated. He couldn't get a good look at her, but Frank knew who she was.

"That's him. That's Cade. Where was this taken?"

"Pierre, South Dakota."

"They are headed west. All right, is Skyler – that's his name, right?"

"Yeah."

"Is he still on the phone?"

"Yeah."

"Well how the hell do I get him on the phone?"

Billy grabbed the mobile device back, took the phone off mute and handed it to Frank.

"All yours."

Skyler Roy fiddled with the hood of his bike in a hotel parking lot staring across the perimeter at Blake Sergeant, Cade Stuckley and Melody Slater. He knew Frank Silvera only by reputation, and the reputation was fairly cut and dry. Do your job, and you don't have anything to worry about.

Don't do your job, and you'll be fired if you're lucky.

Trafficking suited him well. He picked up meth, and delivered it to a network of dealers. He came by a few weeks later to collect or inspect. He wasn't asked to be an enforcer. If someone was short, he made one phone call. Most the dealers knew they had a good system, and there was always a market in small towns. It wasn't hard to stay one step ahead of the cops, and he had heard Frank even had a couple entire departments on the take.

"Hello Skyler?" The gravelly voice spoke into his ear.

"Yes, sir," he responded.

Sir, Frank chuckled. He was too young for the Vietnam draft and never felt that call to service other men his age occasionally spoke of. He did, however, like the sound of "sir."

"Did you take this picture?"

"I did," Skyler responded with a slight western drawl, not to be mistaken for southern. Skyler spoke like a character in a John Ford movie, not to be mistaken for a plantation owner in Mississippi.

"Are they still there?"

"They are, but they look to be leavin' soon," Skyler responded. "The shorter guy, uh, I think that's Cade."

"Yeah, that's right," Frank affirmed, "his buddy is the bigger guy."

"The short guy has something wrong with him. He's wearin' bandages of some sort. The big guy changed his bandages right here in the parkin' lot and put lotion on the cut, like a faggot. The big guy almost made me a couple times. He keeps scannin' the lot like he's checkin' to make sure nobody is following him."

"And Cade?"

"He ain't watchin' sheeit. Looks like he's in a lot of pain."

"And the girl?"

"Yeah that part's a little confusing. I don't think she's with them. Ah mean, she ain't a hostage, but she doesn't act like she wants to be there."

"Explain that to me, Skyler."

"When they pulled in, she just took her food and went to the river. Smoked and ate. The big guy changed the little guy's bandages, and they talked for a bit. The big guy then walked down, talked to her for a minute, and I guess he told her to get in the car."

"Do you think the big guy is running things?"

"It looks like the big guy is runnin' things but the little guy is in charge. If that makes sense."

Frank thought about that last observation for a moment.

"I think you're right, Skyler. Can you tell which way it looks like they're headed?"

"Ah'll know in a bit."

"Okay," Frank responded. "That's good. I think I know where they're going."

"Ah can track 'em."

"I'm sure you could. Listen, I want you to do that, but keep your distance, Skyler. Make sure they don't catch you following them. Do you understand what I'm asking you?"

"Ah can do it, sir. Ah've tracked people before."

"Okay Skyler, good work. Now be careful."

Frank hung up the phone and looked at Billy with a smile.

"Where we going?"

"I've got two guesses, and both are in the wild west. Get your shit kickers on. I'm driving."

Chapter 30

Anthony Byrd stared outside the cockpit of the charter jet as the plane touched down on a private landing strip.

"Where are we again?"

"Shenandoah Valley," the pilot responded.

"And why are we landing here as opposed to the air base?"

"This is where Colonel Gayton directed me. You'll have to ask him."

Byrd stared at the sea of peaks and valleys of the Blue Ridge Mountains. The leaves were well on their way to ushering in fall with color changes, but Byrd was in no mood for tourism.

"I intend to."

Byrd and the Gayton Security's remaining three mercenaries from the St. Paul mission stepped out onto the landing strip followed closely by the two pilots. Love's dried blood was still splattered on Kim's flannel button-up jacket and jeans. They had lost three men in less than 72 hours after nearly a decade with no casualties. This was supposed to be an easy job, but Gayton's crew was getting decimated. This time, it wasn't due to layoffs.

Gayton stood alone on the tarmac to greet his soldiers. Off in the distance behind him was the air traffic control tower, fueling station and a modest aircraft repair garage that looked like it specialized in hobby planes. A parking lot lay off in the distance near the air traffic control tower with several vehicles sitting dormant.

Byrd exercised a crisp salute and Gayton returned it.

"Sir?" Byrd said, only it was a question, not a statement.

"It's okay," Gayton said with a wave of a hand that quickly concluded with one finger to his lips. The international sign for *shut the fuck up.* "A little confusion with the base commander. We'll get it sorted out."

A squad of what looked like washed up soldiers emerged from the fueling station and began walking toward Gayton, Byrd and what was left of their team. Wisnewski was among them. There appeared to be 13 of them, and they looked like the military equivalent of a washed-up gothic emo cover band. All thirteen men had dyed their hair black intentionally, probably within the last 48 hours. The men, all men, appeared to be in their 30s or 40s. They had seen their share of cold nights on patrol, but those patrols hadn't happened for a while. Their skin tones were all soft, baring the evidence of uncounted hours under the glow of sterile incandescent light shining on cubicles. They had muscular builds, but not muscles indicative of brute strength. They had fitness club physiques. There was a difference.

They weren't marching in anything resembling a formation and didn't strike Byrd as men who could pull that off if ordered. Byrd had a pretty damn good idea of who they were, and he wanted nothing to do with them.

"What's this sir?"

"We've had a bad week, Tony," Gayton responded. "Client isn't happy."

Gayton wanted to tell Byrd more, but the soldiers were closing in on the conversation. Byrd sensed two things. Gayton was no longer in control. He wanted to tell Byrd more privately but wasn't going to be awarded the opportunity today.

Wisnewski and the soldiers were now among them. Their leader stepped in front and introduced himself. He wasn't a tall man. He was downright short. He was wearing combat boots which seemed to help him prop up to 5'5.

"First Sergeant Byrd," he said in a thick Russian accent, extending his hand.

Byrd shook it.

"Or should I say staff sergeant?" Great. A short Russian with a napoleon complex. He didn't appreciate the snide reference to his own self-inflated military credentials. The insult was meant to put him in his place or generate a response. Years of military bearing dictated his response which was no response. This little prick wasn't going to get under his skin. And that's what he was. A little Russian prick.

"And you are?"

"I am Viktor Namin, a business associate of your client."

Byrd didn't respond. They were being paid in rubles. He knew they were working for "the Russians," but neither he nor Gayton knew what that might really mean. On the surface, the money was coming from Nicolay Belov's employer. Byrd and Gayton knew well enough to know there was probably a mob connection and definitely a government connection. They were retained with the agreement to ask no questions. Kill Cade Stuckley and any of his associates. Split the one-billion-ruble reward that was now common knowledge among mobsters and mercenaries alike. Gayton and Byrd had the impression the Russians, whatever that meant, had little intention of paying the full reward. They wanted to cash in their own bounty but needed help.

"You came highly recommended by my associates," Namin continued. "Good contacts in American intelligence. Political clout. Able to squash bugs with few questions asked. Perhaps we were wrong?"

This was the second time Byrd was insulted about his failure to take down Cade Stuckley. He was getting tired of it. Towe never should have put that damned Marine Steve Gable on the investigation. His wife left him, and she sensed that he was broken. That was her specialty. Breaking men. She wanted to show off her tamed Rottweiler a bit. Have him do the investigative work and let them collect the bounty just to prove that she could. Byrd didn't see a broken man in St. Paul.

"Denise Towe was arrested by the Saint Paul police this afternoon as a person of interest in a local homicide investigation," Gayton said.

"She won't talk," Byrd said confidently, "and she'll be out in two days."

"That may be true," Gayton said, "but we don't have two days."

"Cade Stuckley is on the run and has help," Namin added. "If he gets out of the country, he has enough money to disappear forever. Have you heard from your source with the FBI?"

"Like the colonel said," Byrd sneered, "she isn't in a place where she can make calls right now."

"I see, another failure."

Byrd didn't respond.

"Well, I know something," Namin continued. "One of our business associates has a lead. After his operation became too lucrative for his internet company to serve as a believable front, Mr. Stuckley started working with an old cop in the state of Wyoming to move his money to an offshore account. He is planning to make a run for it, but he needs to make one last stop to do some business before skipping town."

Gayton and Byrd exchanged glances. Byrd wanted to punch the short man in his self-righteous nose. Since they were in the middle of the mountains, he didn't need to worry about a spectator thinking that he was striking a child.

"Would you like us to go to Wyoming? I would hate to disappoint you again," Byrd said, keeping his tone measured.

Gayton shot Byrd a cold stare. Namin looked amused.

"Are you getting angry, staff sergeant Byrd?" he responded. "Perhaps you would like to say something else?"

Byrd's temper was flaring up. He had lost three men in three days. Gayton knew that look.

"Gentlemen," Gayton intervened, "a schoolyard fight on the tarmac isn't going to do anything but waste our time. Our bird needs fuel and our pilots need a manifest. First Sergeant Byrd."
Byrd turned his attention to Gayton.

"He's a first sergeant in my operation," Gayton said to Namin before turning back to Byrd, "Mr. Namin and his associates are going to join you on your trip to Wyoming. Wisnewski is going too. You need reinforcements and they're going to need some help navigating a small rural town that probably isn't used to dealing with visitors. Is that going to be a problem?"

Byrd and Namin looked at each other.

"As long as the money is green, sir," Byrd responded.

"We look forward to working with each other," Namin added.

"Great," Gayton said skeptically. "I need to speak with your boss," he gestured toward Namin, "and get your source out of jail. I also need to handle this recent miscommunication regarding our office space."

"My employer can assist with your both matters," Namin offered.

"I'm counting on it," Gayton responded and looked back to Byrd. "Keep me posted. And Byrd."

"Yes, sir?"

"If any of you see Steve Gable, shoot that sonofabitch in the head."

"I shot him this morning," Byrd responded, confused. "He was bleeding like a stuck pig."

"Well he's alive," Gayton responded. "That cockroach is still alive."

As Gayton left, the soldiers began introducing themselves to each other.

"So why did you guys all dye your hair?" Wisnewski asked in his thick Wisconsin accent.

"Shut up, Wisnewski," Byrd growled.

Chapter 31

Blake Sergeant eased the passenger seat back, but not far enough to squeeze Melody Slater, who was going to sleep in the back seat. She opted to continue with them. It served them better to keep her nearby until they were out of country. It was also safer for her, so it seemed.

They had filled the gas tank and picked up some supplies before leaving Pierre. Cade rooted through the bag for snacks while questioning some of Blake's purchases. He found fruit, water, a couple protein bars and several items that looked out of place.

"Rope, tent stakes and baby oil?" Cade asked.

"They have a purpose," Blake responded. Cade didn't probe. He didn't want to know.

Blake wanted a couple hours of sleep and instructed Cade to wake him in Wyoming. Cade put the car in drive and headed toward Sturgis. Blake leaned back and his eyes were shut before the car was on the highway. He forgot to set aside a steno pad. Didn't need melatonin. He only needed an hour or two of rest.

Blake closed his eyes then opened them again. He was no longer in the Mustang. Cade wasn't driving. He was in a parking lot.

It was nighttime but probably a summer night. He could feel the warm air blowing against him in the darkness. Moths flew and flickered around the streetlights above him and he began surveying the area. He knew where he was. He was at the Alexandria campus of Northern Virginia Community College. He took a handful of night classes there while serving on active duty.

Upon leaving active duty, he took a job patrolling this campus several hundred times as a security officer while finishing his degree. He continued working there after transferring to the university up the street, and didn't leave until he left for the police academy. He knew the area well.

The parking lot led to the front entrance of the school. On the other side of the glass doors he would find the admissions office, the security office and a multitude of classrooms. There were still cars in the parking lot, but it wasn't full. Just by counting the cars, he knew it was probably a weeknight. After 9:00 but before 10:00. There were still a few night classes in session.

He took a deep breath and could smell the summer air. There was perfume off in the distance, and the faint smell of oil from the lot.

"Enjoying your trip down memory lane?"

The Harvester's voice called out from behind him. He wasn't surprised. She was wearing a white robe and the same sunglasses, though the sun had set hours ago. He realized he had still never seen her eyes.

"Had a lot of good times here," he responded.

"You went to college and worked as a campus cop," she said. "Most college kids think of frat parties when they think of good times."

They were now walking to the northwest corner of the parking ramp.

"I'm not most people," he said, "the nights were always quiet. Night school students aren't your average entitled youth. They're working people. Veterans. People who came here from other countries and were trying to make a better life for their families. Most of the times I needed to detain anyone, they were people who didn't go to the school. Why are we here?"

Blake looked up and noticed they were walking toward an old gray Honda Civic idling in the far northwest corner of the lot. The window was cracked and cigarette smoke was seeping out from the driver's seat.

"There are many types of harvesters, but they largely fall into two categories to reflect their clientele – good and evil. Angelic harvesters help guide people to the afterlife as they've passed on. I don't know too much about them, only when you hear about people 'going toward the light' as they're passing on, chances are they're looking at an angelic harvester.

"Then there's us. We come in two categories of our own. Protectors and punishers. I'm a protector. If I'm paying you a visit, you still have a chance to reject evil. Evil is a disease. It infects you and will permeate your entire being if you allow it. Most people don't even know they're being infected. Free will is the best cure for evil, but it's also the cause. You can change your path at any time, but it is not easy. Then there are punishers. Punishers harvest the souls that have already made a choice. Have you noticed anything different about yourself?"

"I had a premonition last night for the first time in years," Blake said. "I used to have them all the time as a child, but they only gave me fragmented, useless information. I didn't know what was true and what wasn't, and I was never given enough information to prevent a bad incident. This time was different. I saw exactly what was going to happen and I stopped it."

The harvester smiled.

"I noticed something else," Blake continued, "but I don't know if I was imagining it or . . ." he trailed off.

"You were faster when you disposed of the three intruders in Melody's apartment," she completed his thought.

"And I was stronger," Blake added. "I knew their next moves before they were going to make them in a way I haven't before. And . . ."

"Well, what?"

"I've never felt more alive than that moment in battle," he said. "I loved every second of it and I didn't feel an ounce of hesitation. I know I will struggle with it later, but all the internal conflict I've had over morality went out the door the moment I had my premonition. I wanted to go after the intruders. I needed them."

"That says a lot," the Harvester replied with a smile.

"One almost got the drop on me, but even now as I look back on it, I know I was never in danger."

"That says a lot too," the Harvester repeated, "but you still have much to learn."

They were within a few feet of the car at this point in the conversation.

"I want you to follow my lead," the Harvester said to Blake. "I want you to observe. Be seen and not heard. Clear your mind and allow your instincts to process anything that comes to it. Now focus on the gray sedan in front of us."

At first blush, the driver looked to be a white male in his early to mid-twenties waiting for his girlfriend to finish class. That wasn't unusual, particularly for younger couples who had one vehicle between the two of them. Perhaps he would pull closer to the front door when her class ended.

In an instant, Blake felt a flood of recognition cross his mind like a breeze. His mind was a house with lights that didn't work. That evening, a light turned on. He blinked, rubbed his eyes for a moment and focused again on the car, and found he knew a whole lot more about the driver. The man's name was Ethan Carpenter and he wasn't waiting for his girlfriend. There was a loaded .45 sitting on the passenger seat of the vehicle and he was there to settle a score.

Four years ago, Ethan was a sophomore at the university across town, working through a degree in business administration that was being paid for with a basketball scholarship. His team made the sweet sixteen in the NCAA tournament, and most of the starting lineup would be returning for another shot at the title. Ethan was the center. He was the big man, standing at a towering six foot eight and weighing close to 300 pounds, most of which was the product of many hours in the gym.

He looked like a giant in the civic, which was only meant to be his car for a couple short years until he made a run at the pros. He was big, strong, fast and coordinated. He would never be the best center in the NBA, but he might be good enough to earn a paycheck for a few seasons. He was okay with that.

Life was good. He had friends, talent and a solid support system. He was successful in nearly everything he tried. He wasn't used to hearing the word "no," often, which is probably why his encounter with Katie Martinez, the woman he was waiting for, remained a concept he was never able to fully process.

He met her at a frat party. They flirted. They danced. She felt uncomfortable. She said "no" and left. She had a boyfriend, she said. That didn't stop them from dancing, he replied. He followed, because nobody said no to him. He was on the team, bound for the NBA. She was playing hard to get. When his body said no in the gym or on the court, his mind said yes. Mind over matter. This wasn't different. No means maybe. Mind over matter. He raped her that night, or at least that's what she said.

It was a textbook rape and assault conviction. Because he had no priors and an army of character witnesses including parents, teammates, former coaches and even his priest, he was sentenced to five years in prison. He served nine months. The news media and victims' rights groups called the sentence offensive, but they didn't know anything. His basketball career was over. His scholarship was gone. He wasn't the family treasure anymore. He was an embarrassment. He was a registered sex offender living in his parents' basement. They didn't want him there, but reluctantly brought him back in. He was only welcome until his parole officer signed off on him living independently and he could get on his feet.

How was that going to happen? He had to wear an ankle bracelet everywhere he went. He needed to check in regularly with the state. He needed to notify prospective employers of his status as a registered sex offender. Where did he work? He was a janitor. He was supposed to be a hero.

Across the parking lot and in the school building, Katie Martinez was well on her way to competing her second semester at the community college since the incident, and would be twelve credits from graduating. She was already applying for admission to the nursing school at Georgetown. It would be expensive, but her grades were now high enough to make her eligible for scholarships. Plus, she had a story to tell. She was no longer afraid to tell it.

After the incident, she spent a week in the hospital. She spent another year in her mother's basement, paralyzed with fear and shame. She dropped out of school. She didn't eat. She didn't sleep. Her boyfriend left her, but her girlfriends didn't. Time and therapy helped her regain the pieces of herself that were recoverable. More therapy was helping her live with the pieces of herself that would be gone forever. The experience also solidified her original belief that she wanted to spend the rest of her life helping others and a career in nursing was her purpose.

The college welcomed her back with open arms. She had a part time job as a nursing assistant to augment her education. She still slept with the lights on, and was afraid to walk alone in the campus parking lot at night. That was okay. She had Darnell waiting outside her classroom. He was the campus security officer who escorted her to her car three nights a week. He was kind and brave. He knew her history but didn't pity or judge her. He called her courageous for coming back to school. Courageous. She had to admit that Darnell was the first guy she was starting to develop feelings for.

The Harvester walked up to the driver's side window and knocked gently.

Ethan jumped in his seat, and looked at her with a confused expression. He rolled cautiously the window down.

"Hello Ethan," she said. "When did you start smoking?"

"Do I know you?"

"No, but I know you're here because you're waiting for Katie Martinez."

Ethan Carpenter's eyes became as large as saucers.

"And I know why," the Harvester continued, "you came here to kill her. You've been watching her. She hasn't seen you, but she can tell you're nearby. Her anatomy and physiology class is scheduled to end at any time. Her car is parked across the lot, and you will be able to see her when she gets there. You will drive slowly across the lot, pull out that .45, roll down your window and fire. Your first shot will miss because your hands are shaking too much, but your second shot won't. You'll fire two more times and will hit her both times. You'll then turn your attention to the campus security guard next, but not before he's able to strike your forearm with his baton. He'll break the bone. Darnell's fast and strong. You'll drive off, nearly hitting two other students walking across the ramp. You'll rear end a vehicle on the way out, and make your escape, but not before clipping another pedestrian on the way out. She'll break her leg, but Katie will be dead."

Ethan sat silently and took the Harvester's story in.

"Who did you say you were?" he asked again.

"Think of me as a guardian angel."

"What the hell does that mean?"

"It means I know why you're here. I know what you plan to do, and I am asking you to reconsider."

He processed that idea, then stared at his pistol again. It made him feel resolute.

"She deserves to die."

"Why? Weren't you the one who raped her?"

"It wasn't like that. She said she liked it rough. It . . ."

He grasped for another excuse but knew this woman was seeing through every justification.

"We were both drunk. She wanted it. Then she changed her mind, and lied about what happened."

"Is that really what happened, or is that what you tell yourself?"

Ethan's face flushed with anger.

"Who the fuck was she anyway? My life is ruined."

"And hers isn't?"

"She cost me my scholarship. My career," he looked at the Harvester with red rings around his eyes. "Did you know that for the rest of my life, I need to disclose that I am a registered sex offender every single time I apply for a job. If I move to a new neighborhood, I need to register with the local police station. And anyone out there can look me up and see where I live. I'm treated like a monster." His chin wrinkled as he shuddered and thought about his life.

"I'm a janitor," he cried softly. "I was supposed to be in the NBA. My life is a prison."

"You can pick yourself up, Ethan," she responded. "You are still alive. You can still take one step at a time. Wake up each morning and treat it like a new day. They may not make the news, but this world is full of stories of redemption. You could be another one."

"How?" he asked.

"You can start by telling the truth. Drive back home. Call your parole officer tonight and come clean. Tomorrow, he is going to check the GPS tracker in that ankle bracelet you're wearing and he's going to see you've been coming here every other night. He's going to see you went to a gun show in Reston and he's going to find out you talked one of the vendors into selling you a weapon in the parking lot. Let him find all of that out from you, and tell him you're ready to put your life back together."

He stared at the front door of the campus. Students were beginning to trickle out.

As Ethan and the Harvester spoke, Blake noticed he could hear their thoughts. He knew their emotions. The Harvester wanted Ethan to leave. She wanted him to make the right choice, walk away and regain whatever goodness might remain of his soul – whatever that meant.

Ethan was sullen but resolute. He was convinced that Katie Martinez needed to die. Katie Martinez deserved to die. A small voice in the back of his head was urging him to reconsider, but he couldn't get over the notion that even if he came clean now, the consequences facing him for the rest of his life were still there. This was no life to live. He would shoot her, and while escaping, he would decide whether he would kill himself next. Those were the choices he was giving himself.

Blake knew that would never happen. He knew the Harvester would stop Ethan. He also felt his own biases shining through. He looked at Ethan and saw a soul whose light burned out years ago. He wanted Ethan to fail. He wanted Ethan to die. The Harvester looked at him out of the corner of her eye. She could hear his thought process.

"It's hard, you know," he said. "I've got to shoulder all this burden, and for what? One bad decision."

"Bad decisions have a way of giving everyone a burden of their own to carry."

"And what's her burden?" he shot back. "Looks to me like she's going to school. Laughing with friends every time she walks out of that building. She don't know shit about pain."

"Did you know she wouldn't leave her mother's basement for nearly a year? And when she did, she got hooked on antidepressants. Needed to go through treatment. Do you know how much courage it takes her just to leave the house each day? She needs a security escort to get to her car, and she needs sleeping pills to help her come down at night."

He thought about her comments, then his grimace turned to a smirk.

"You know, you say you're my guardian angel, but you sure do seem to care about her a whole lot."

Katie Martinez walked out the door with the security offer walking beside her. A radio was clipped to his shoulder and Ethan watched as he pressed the button and said something into the radio.

"I never said I was your guardian angel."

Carpenter looked at Katie Martinez then back at the Harvester.

"You mean your hers?" he asked indignantly. "That lying wetback bitch who has to come to a shitty community college because she's not smart enough to make it at a university?"

"She is studying to be a nurse," the Harvester responded calmly. "She will be an angel to more people than you will ever know. She'll save lives. She'll provide comfort to the dying in their last moments. She'll spend a lifetime caring for others with the type of compassion that we all would want in our most vulnerable moments. And you want to snuff out that light because of your own inability to take responsibility for your own actions. You need to drive away, Ethan. You need to drive away now."

"You fucking bitch," he growled.

He grabbed his pistol off the passenger seat and pointed it at the Harvester. Blake instinctively started to dive for the weapon, but the Harvester stuck out her arm and held him back. She removed her sunglasses with her other hand and stared at Carpenter.

She didn't have eyes. She only had a soft light like a cloudy sunrise where her eyeballs were supposed to be. Electrical currents pulsated from side to side creating brilliant flashes of light.

Carpenter instinctively squeezed the trigger, and a bullet fired out of the barrel of his pistol. The bullet soared about two feet then stopped in front of the Harvester, a foot away from making impact. It hovered helplessly in the air, struggling to fight its way toward her sternum. She seemingly stared at the bullet suspended in the air then watched it fall helplessly to the ground.

Carpenter squeezed the trigger again, but nothing happened.

She was now staring at him. The grip on the handgun began to heat up. Ethan felt it fuse to his hand. The pistol turned bright orange with heat, and his fingers began to sizzle. Blisters formed around the back of his fingers and gave way to open wounds. Droplets of skin began to melt off his hand like ice cream off a cone on a hot summer day.

Carpenter pulled the pistol back into the car and was planning to use his other hand to pry the weapon loose as the sharp burns of pain made their way to his brain like glass shards into bare skin. He screamed out. His right hand was fused to the pistol and his left hand was fused to the steering wheel of the car sizzling like steak and melting like ice. The steering wheel reached a red-hot temperature as clumps of skin melted off his hand on the wheel, exposing the bones of his fingers clinging for dear life.

The windows of the Civic rolled up by themselves as the cab of his car became an oven, roasting the skin off his body. Carpenter screamed helplessly in pain and horror as he was melted alive. His eyeballs stuck out like headlights as the skin melted off his face and fell in messy clumps on his previously white t-shirt under his jacket.

He stared at the Harvester in horror and screamed in agony as his lips peeled back and fell off his face, dripping off his chin in one long string.

His eyeballs exploded in their sockets leaving two fleshy craters. He was blinded and still cooking.

The car accelerated and careened across the parking lot as Carpenter screamed like a banshee. The car shot off the top level of the parking complex and crashed down on the ground below, bursting into flames as it hit the ground. His screaming finally stopped.

The Harvester slowly ambled to the scene of the crash and Blake followed as if he were in a trance. They arrived at the ledge and watched the flames jump out of the window as Ethan's skeleton still seemed to flail in the flames, his hand still stuck on the wheel.

A single burst of light shot out of the flaming car with a *ping* like a quarter hitting asphalt. The single burst shot up into the air, then turned into a solid object. It landed soundly in the Harvester's hand. She closed her fist around the object to catch it, then opened it back up. It was a coin, slightly larger than a silver dollar.

Blake watched the coin fly to the Harvester and instinctively scanned the parking lot for witnesses.

"Stop worrying," the Harvester said, "they can only see us when I want them to see us."

She held the coin out for Blake to observe it. There was nothing descriptive about the coin. It looked like it was composed of a bundle of twine braided to resemble a macramé. The coin, however, was slightly thicker than a quarter, and seemed to glisten with a dull orange glow.

"Here," she said, "take it."

Blake hefted it in his hand. It was heavier than it appeared, like a piece of steel. Silver wasn't like that. He lifted it to examine it and quickly concluded that one could not walk down the street with a roll of these coins in their pocket.

"It's the burden he's been carrying," the Harvester said. "The heaviness is from his burden. Some are heavier than others."

"What is it?" he asked.

"It's Ethan's soul."

"His soul?" Blake repeated back. He examined the coin again and immediately felt his mind filling with questions. *Do we all have coins for souls? Are we like the Merry-go-rounds at the zoo, just waiting for a child to extract a quarter from their parents?*

"You have lots of questions," she said, and started walking again, this time away from the wreckage below the parking ramp. "I can answer them all eventually, but we don't have much time now."

"Not every soul looks like a coin. This," she said as she took the coin back and held it up for Blake to see, "is what a soul looks like when we have lost."

She looked down in disappointment and continued walking.

"Everyone, regardless of dimension, is born inherently innocent. Some religions say inherently good, but innocent might be more appropriate. Think of lives, all lives on this planet, as a garden. A soul is supposed to shine, and every soul shines in its own unique fashion. Together, they create what we know as light. They create what we know to be the color of a sunrise, the color of day and even the color of night. Every soul has its unique glow, and together they make up a garden."

She paused and looked at the stars as students rushed from their cars and the school to what was now Ethan Carpenter's smoldering body.

"Evil is a parasite. It eats at the light that makes us all unique, that makes us all what we are. Who we are. And we are the victims, woefully outmatched by a disease that tries to eat away at our light. And when they're successful, this coin is what is left of our souls. This is all we become. We go on to do evil's bidding."

She held up the coin.

"You're either a sunrise, or something people toss into fountains to make a wish. Still beautiful in their own way, but a shadow of what they could have been."

"And we harvest the souls that are now coins?"

"As many as we can. We're woefully outnumbered here."

"And what happens to them?"

"That question will need to wait," she responded. "What you need to know is I wasn't lying about Katie Martinez."

They both looked to the campus doors to see another student walking Katie to the security office while Darnell the security guard ran to the wreckage speaking frantically into the radio clipped to his shoulder.

"She will save a lot of lives as a nurse. We need that kind of good in the world. Ethan Carpenter would have spent the rest of his life in a prison cell, acting as a glorified purse for this coin. He was never going to take responsibility for his choices. Because we are outnumbered, our duty as harvesters is to try to save as many Katie's as possible. If you are a protector, you instantly feel the gratification that I'm feeling now, thinking about all the light that young lady will bring into the world. If you're an angel of retribution . . ."

"All you do is kill," Blake said, then fought to hide a grin.

"Yes," she affirmed, "but you add some balance to the world. You become a subtle reminder for those in limbo, trying to fight for the light in their own souls. You become a reminder that even in today's fallen world, some are held accountable. Sometimes, it's okay to have a bogieman."

They reached the other side of the upper level of the parking ramp and stared out at the quiet night below them.

"How much do you know about the history behind your family's farm?" the Harvester asked.

"What do you mean?"

"I think you know."

Blake thought about the question for a moment. He had been sworn to secrecy on this particular matter, by orders of his father. When he left home, he tried to put those secrets behind him. He tried to put everything in his past behind him. He studied the Harvester.

"The land had been in the family for generations," he said. "But nobody wanted to live on it. I get that piece. It was haunted. My father always said we never had anything to worry about. Somehow, I always knew he was right."

"Was that it?" she asked.

"That was all he knew, or at least, that was all he was able to tell me. You seem to know something about it. Why don't you tell me?"

Now it was the Harvester's turn to be silent. She looked away for a moment.

"That's another topic that we can get into later."

"What if I don't want to be a harvester?" he asked.

"Oh, I think you do," she responded, "but we will have to reserve our conversation for another time. Cade is trying to wake you."

Blake's eyes opened and he was back in the Mustang, staring at a picnic table. He was at a rest stop and guessed they were likely just over the Wyoming border.

"What's a harvester?" Cade asked.

"A what?"

"A harvester," Cade repeated. "You were taking in your sleep. What's a harvester?"

Blake rubbed his eyes and stretched his arms.

"I'm not sure," he responded. "Bad dream. Where are we?"

"Just over the Wyoming border," Cade said, still staring at Blake with skepticism. "I'm feeling sick again. Need to tap out."

Blake drove the remainder of the trip with Melody riding shotgun and Cade sleeping in the back. She tested his geography skills every time they saw a stream or river, asking if it technically led to the ocean. For the most part, he had an easy time. Any tributary leading to the Green, the Colorado or the Missouri Rivers were fair game. The activity would grow more difficult as they continued to venture west where most of the streams led to the Great Salt Lake.

Chapter 32

Gable, McEvers, Gupta and Maloney arrived in Salt Lake City in time to catch the last few moments of a sunset over the Wasatch Mountains. Their flight was a charter jet, the product of a favor the pilot owed the chief. Their names were not on the manifest. They grabbed dinner in town and drove their rental truck to a chain motel on the main drag in Marion, Wyoming, arriving just after 10:00 PM.

Gable called A.K. for a suggestion and he didn't disappoint. He also promised to grab a drink with A.K. as soon as he was back in town. There was a lot to talk about.

"Be careful out there," A.K. said in his baritone voice. "The locals like to tell ghost stories. Some might be truer than we want to believe."

"Are you telling me you saw something?" Gable joked.
A.K. paused.

"Just be sure to call me when you're back, my friend."

The chain motel had a bar, and although it was a Monday night, there were still several locals nursing their suds and talking amongst each other. Gable noticed a burnt-out cowgirl well past her prime grinding up to a young roughneck, who didn't seem to mind the attention. He thought he overheard her say she found him attractive back when he was in middle school and she was still teaching. Some words shouldn't be spoken out loud.

Gable and his entourage agreed to unpack in their rooms and stroll back to the bar for a beer shortly before last call.

He used his hotel phone to call the direct line in a motel located in Dover, Delaware. He spoke to his wife briefly and comforted their kids. His father-in-law was there as well, but didn't speak on the phone. He was wiped from his flight and his head was throbbing. He was asking himself why in the hell he was still on the hunt when he should be in bed. Hearing their voices centered him.

He showered, changed clothes and headed to the hotel bar where he found his compatriots. By the time they were together, the cowgirl and her pupil-turned-boyfriend were long gone as were most the locals.

"How do we look?" McEvers said with exhausted manufactured exuberance.

"We look like a bunch of cops trying to blend in," Maloney responded. She looked to Gable first. "You look like you got in a fight with a windshield."

"It was a bullet," Gable responded.

"You're brown," she said, nodding her chin at Gupta.

"Locals won't like that."

"Hell, I don't like him," McEvers added, and the group laughed. Gupta only smiled.

"And I'm a woman," Maloney added, "don't even get me started on that one."

McEvers processed her observations and made a judgement call. He was tired and wanted a beer. They asked if there was a local brew, and the bartender directed him to a beer made just outside Park City, Utah. They each ordered the local drink and graded it against the Minnesota beers.

It was better than Grain Belt. Anything was better than Grain Belt. Almost as good as Summit. Not as good as Surly. Nothing was better than Surly.

Gable listened with interest, knowing that he would have preferred a Yuengling. It probably wasn't as good as Surly, but it didn't have to be. It was what he drank. This beer was okay.

A few more locals trickled out of the bar and the bartender ambled over to announce last call. The officers signaled for another round, and Gable turned to engage the bartender.

"You guys passing through?" the bartender asked. He spoke with a manufactured California surfer accent, and had the spiky bleached hair to augment the accent. He wore an old concert t-shirt under a black vest that was probably the uniform of the day, and made his way over to make conversation.

"You could say that," Gable answered. "Is it always this quiet?"

"Yeah, man," the bartender responded. "Summer is over and I haven't seen a lot of roughnecks around, so they're probably drillin' somewhere else. Fine by me. How long are you in town?"

"A couple days," Gable said. "We're looking for a couple guys who might be headed here."

"I'm guessing they're in trouble," he said with a mumbled laugh. Gable stared back at him inquisitively. The bartender stammered awkwardly then decided to own his comment.

"I'm sorry man," he said, "old habits die hard. My mental cop-o-meter used to come in pretty handy back in the day. Now I'm too old to do stupid shit."

Gable looked at him and guessed he might be in his early thirties at the most.

"So I heard y'all talking a little," the bartender said, "are those Minnesota accents?"

The St. Paul cops looked at each other, a little surprised any of them had a northern accent.

"He must be talking about the two of you," Gupta said.

"No man," the bartender responded, "all three of you. This guy is from the south or maybe the east coast. He has the military thing going, so it's hard to place it for sure."

"The military has its own accent?" Maloney asked. All four officers were intrigued.

"Oh yeah," he responded. "My brother had it when he was in. I get to hear all of 'em working here, a bar attached to a hotel. It's a hobby. I'm Blaze."

The cops introduced themselves and embarked on small talk involving the Twins and Vikings. Maloney wanted to talk about the Wild, but Blaze wasn't a hockey fan. Nobody outside Minnesota watches hockey.

***

Blake Sergeant, Cade Stuckley and Melody Slater pulled into Wyatt Shepard's driveway at roughly the same time Steve Gable and his crew were arriving at their hotel. Deputy Chief Shepard had been on the Marion police force for nearly three decades.

He had been telling himself he was going to retire for nearly ten years, but always found a reason to stay on. The truth was he was making too much money off his side business of laundering drug money through the department evidence locker. They had tens of thousands of dollars tied up in multiple investigations, some of which were years from being resolved. He also had a couple business colleagues around town who were happy to act as accomplices for a little extra cash.

He had recently moved onto helping clients such as Cade Stuckley invest money into offshore accounts. Cade was originally referred to Shepard through Frank Silvera. However, when Cade arranged for Blaine Crockett's murder, Shepard became Stuckley's friend for life. His step daughter Trista Daggett was Blaine Crockett's first rape victim.

Shepard was on the force when the rape occurred, but wasn't part of the investigation. He started dating Trista's mother a couple of years after the incident. Trista had fallen into a deep depression followed by alcoholism after the rape. Shepard helped her get clean, get back in school and eventually on the force after his predecessor retired. Shepard never liked his old chief.

Trista Daggett pulled up in a squad car as Blake, Cade and Melody made their way into Wyatt Shepard's rambler. Cade was well rested, and ready to do business. Melody was trying to gather her second wind and Blake was in need of a couple more hours of sleep.

Trista stood awkwardly like a child wearing a police outfit looking vulnerable, yet intent on introducing herself.

"Are you Blake?" she said awkwardly.

"Yes," he responded.

"You probably don't know me, but I remember your sister from high school," she responded. "And you killed Blaine Crockett, right?"

Blake shot a glance toward Cade.

"We're all familiar with the case," Shepard added, "you're amongst friends."

Blake didn't appreciate the public knowledge of all his deeds.

"Yes," he answered with hesitation.

Trista ran up and embraced him. He stammered, but held his ground and hugged her back. She cried into his shoulder thanking him over and over. He imagined that as a cop in a small town in Wyoming, she needed to keep a rough exterior, never showing weakness. If she was in uniform this late, that meant she had the night shift which meant small town drunks who had no problem taking a swing at a woman. Yet here she was crying into her shoulder. For a moment, he felt something other than confused remorse when he thought of Blaine Crockett.

He remembered looking at the picture leading up to the investigation, and thinking he knew the guy. He wrote it off as maybe hearing about Crockett on ESPN. All he knew about the guy was that he was on the Philadelphia Eagles practice squad for about five minutes, or maybe it was Cleveland. It wasn't until he was looking Crockett in the eye that he remembered him. There were no specific moments that came to mind. Just familiarity from a few fleeting moments. They probably saw each other around town shopping at Walmart.

He remembered how they shared a moment of mutual recognition. Blaine looked confused as he tried to place the man, while struggling with the context of their encounter. Blake raised his weapon and shot Crockett in the face. He remembered firing four more shots including one to the back of the head because the request was for a closed casket funeral.

"I can finally sleep again," Trista choked into Blake's shoulder. "I needed to drink myself to sleep for a while, then used pills after I sobered up. After we knew he was dead, I slept like a baby knowing he would never do it again. I still do."

She left as fast as she came, fixing her makeup in the squad car before disappearing into the night. A domestic abuse call came over the radio and she was on her way to provide backup to the first responders.

Blake went straight to bed. Cade handed Wyatt half of his cash to deposit and invest. They sat in Wyatt's living room as he sat at a small desk with his reading glasses hanging on the end of his nose, making sure the transaction went through. He then went about hiding Cade's accounts in case the FBI tried to freeze his assets.

"I called your pilot," Shepard said. "He can give you a lift, but you need to meet him up in Jackson. It's a busy time of year for him up there. He says he can fit you in, but it's gonna be one hell of a long flight."

"It's not that bad," Cade responded, trying to hide his own apprehension. "And I'm paying him more than he'll make flying ten yuppies around Yellowstone."

"Where are you going?"

"Nunavut, Canada."

Shepard looked at him with confusion.

"It's the northernmost province," Cade continued. "From there, we're hitching rides with a couple of cargo ships and will make our way south. We'll be in St. Kitts in a couple weeks. We'll need to buy swimsuits when we get there, because we'll be dressed like Eskimos." He laughed to himself, marveling that his getaway plan might come into fruition.

"I don't have winter clothes," Melody spoke up. Shepard looked at Cade with curiosity.

"We'll figure something out," Cade responded.

"There's a Walmart in town if you have time," Shepard offered. "On second thought, we're in Wyoming. No shortage of winter clothes. We'll get you taken care of. The fewer stops you make, the better."

"Thank you," she said with a smile.

"What about your other friend," Shepard asked, nodding at Sergeant. "Does he have winter clothes?"

"He better," Cade responded. "He said he packed 'em. He lives in Minnesota, so I know he's got some."

"I just can't believe he's sleeping in my house," Wyatt marveled. "I don't know how in the sam hill you got him here."

"He wasn't happy about it," Cade responded. "I don't think he has been back since before he joined the Marines."

"He probably hasn't," Wyatt agreed. "He probably never wanted to see this place again. That boy's dad was crazier than a bag of bedbugs."

***

Blaze the bartender and the cops spent ten minutes making casual conversation when Gable casually asked if there was a town called Muerto nearby.

"Oh yeah, man," Blaze answered. "Calling it a town would be generous. There's a trailer park out there and a few hobby farms.

Once you get further south there's a ranch, then you had the old Sergeant place, but I don't think anyone has lived there in years."

"Sergeant?" Gable interrupted, "as in Blake Sergeant?"

"Yeah," Blaze agreed. "He was a few years older than me. Sad fucking story with that family. A damned tragedy."

***

"Neal Sergeant was from California if I remember correct," Shepard said as he clicked away at his computer. "Came here in the service and was stationed at Hill Air Force Base out in Utah. Married a local girl and got a job with the Salt Lake PD. I knew a detective who worked with him in homicide and he was one of the best they ever had."

***

"The rumor was that he used to have premonitions," Blaze said, telling the agents the same story Wyatt was sharing with Cade and Melody. "He could supposedly walk onto a crime scene, and replay how the crime took place in his mind, just by standing in the room. He'd know where to find weapons, clues, evidence. You name it. Internal Affairs investigated him a couple times thinking he was planting evidence but he wasn't. In my opinion, it was probably damn good police work."

***

"The story was that the Mormon church wanted him to stop investigating a kidnapping, but he wouldn't let up. He found the girl and it turned out she was being held captive by a polygamist colony. He worked with the FBI to put a bunch of their asses in jail. Some of 'em are probably still there. The Mormons was afraid it would make them look bad so they kept trying to mess with the investigation. After he got the conviction, he retired and moved out to Muerto. Here's the weird part, the land he moved to had been in his family for generations and nobody even knew it belonged to anybody."

"He had all the right paperwork, land deeds. His family was even paying property taxes on the place but nobody ever even knew it was there. It was like they came out of nowhere. There was a little old cabin out there that nobody lived in for probably a hundred years. Neal moved in and fixed the place up."

***

"I went to middle school with Blake's sister. She was older too, but I remember seeing her in the halls. A couple of the regulars here remember Blake. Smart kid. Good football player, but didn't have a lot of friends. He moved here when he was a teenager. That's a tough time to be the new guy in school, especially in a small town."

"Most kids have formed their cliques, lifetime buddies and social habits. Hard for a new guy to break into that. Most the guys who remember him said he tried to fit in for about five minutes but it didn't take long for him to get to a place where he was pretty vocal about wanting to get the fuck out of town as soon as possible. Spent a lot of time looking at maps and trying to decide where he was going to move."

"Sounds like about half the Marines I've ever met," McEvers said. "Some join to serve. Others join for the benefits. Most are young men with no fear and a desire to do just about anything for a one-way ticket outta dodge."

"That was him," Blaze agreed. "Their dad took a job as a park ranger out in the Uintas and became a local hero. Same thing as when he was a cop. He could find a lost hiker, a missing boy scout or a missing child who wandered from their parents' camp."

***

"He could walk on the spot where they were last seen, or walk down the trail they were supposed to hike, and he could tell you exactly where they went," Shepard said. "I was on a search party with him once and seen it myself. We were looking for a local kid who wanted to hike to King's peak, over in Utah."

"He and I were paired up, and we were the ones who found him. We walked down this trail for a few miles and got to a fork. One trail went up the mountain. The other went into the primitive area. We stopped, looked around and he got real quiet. He stood there staring at the fork for what felt like five minutes. I'll never forget it."

"It almost looked like he was meditating or trying to listen to something off in the distance. I assumed the latter and gave him the benefit of the doubt because I couldn't hear a damn thing. He then just looks over at me and says, 'He went the wrong way. Got lost. He's about a few clicks up. If we go into the primitive area, we'll find him.'"

"'I radio it in, we follow the trail, and dammit if we don't find the kid six miles in, scared shitless and trying to find his way back. Sure enough, Sergeant was right. The kid took a wrong turn and spent two days hiking in circles. The newspaper did a big write up about the kid, the search party, and we were celebrated as heroes. It was a pretty cool thing to be a part of."

"I asked him later how he knew the kid made a wrong turn, and he just said, 'if you spend enough time in these woods, they speak to you.' It was a weird thing to say, but standing out there, I could understand what he meant. Still think he was crazy, but I respected whatever it was he had an ability to do."

"A year or two later, he calls me up and he's upset. You see, we had several women disappear over a few months off I-80, mostly up in Echo Canyon. That's over in Utah, west of here. Neal stops by the police station and says he knows what's been happening to the women. There's an auto junkyard about 20 miles past the Utah border. Real fucking eyesore. Owned by an old man named Horace Crane. Kind of a loopy fucker, but a good mechanic."

"Neal swears that Crane is snatching up the women and keeping them in his house. He's disposing of the cars to get rid of evidence, and he can't make himself stop. I ask him how he could possibly know that. He looks me in the eye and says, 'you know damned well how I know.' I tell him, 'there's no way I can turn around and kick down Horace Crane's door based on a hunch and demand to see the women he's kidnapped. Besides, that's in Utah. It's out of my jurisdiction. I ask him why he ain't in Utah and he says they already told him they drove by the house and didn't see anything. Told him the same thing I said."

"Anyway, I told his ass to give me some time to think. I was fixin' to suggest the two of us go check it out soon as I'm off duty, but never got to it. He said we didn't have time and stormed off, saying he needed to go home and take care of something."

"Later, we found out that he paid a visit to Horace Crane that night himself, and dammit if he weren't right about the whole thing. Horace Crane had twelve women in all, and he'd been keeping them in cages, torturing them. He caught Neal in a booby trap of some sort, and spent a couple days torturing him just like the girls."

"Somehow Neal got the drop on him and beat the living fuck out of him, but not before Crane used an oil funnel to pour strychnine down his throat. Sergeant freed one of the girls during the struggle and she called the police. Crane died on the way to the hospital, but we got there in time to save Neal. By the time we got there, the strychnine had left him catatonic."

"Five of those twelve women lived and are all probably still alive today. One still lives in Clearfield. The newspaper does a story on her every once in a while, but it's a sick and twisted tale.

***

"Neal lived for about another year or two, but was never the same," Blaze said. "They kept him in the state hospital for a while but spent his last few months living at home. He and his wife were technically separated at the time, but she came back home to care for the family after the accident. Blake quit football and came home every day to care for his dad."

"One night, the winter after he graduated high school, Blake needed to run to Salt Lake City and got stuck in town. A storm rolled in and shut the city down. Roads were closed. Blizzard conditions. It was the type of storm where you just stay inside if you wanna see your next birthday. Neal wasn't used to Blake being away, and everyone thinks he got it into his mind that his son was in danger and needed his help. He wandered out into the storm."

***

"We found his body in the Uintas. He had his boots on, but no coat, hat or gloves. He managed to walk eight miles through a blizzard before the elements got to him. He was one tough sonofabitch, and his death was a fucking tragedy."

Cade and Melody sat in shock listening to the story.

"He said his dad died a hero," Cade finally said, his voice cracking, "but never shared the story."

"Well, Blake joined the Marines a couple days after the funeral and I don't think he's been back since," Wyatt said solemnly.

"It was more like a couple weeks," Blake said, emerging from the spare bedroom. "I helped my mom move to an apartment in town and we shut down the cabin. And I came back a couple years later to help her move to New Mexico after my sister finished high school."

Melody leapt from her chair and grabbed Blake in an embrace that almost knocked him over. She cried into his shoulder, repeating over and over that she didn't know. He patted her back and patiently let the moment pass.

"Melody," he said, "it was a long time ago."

"Why didn't you ever tell me the whole story?" Cade asked, somewhat hurt.

"It was a long time ago, Cade," Blake responded. "I don't talk about it much."

"I'm sorry if I, uh," Wyatt trailed off.

"Don't worry about it," Blake responded.

"I thought you were sleeping," Cade said.

Blake plopped himself down in an empty seat on the couch.

"You were all too damn loud, telling old stories. Has he told you any ghost stories?"

***

"If you surf the internet, there are all kinds of stories about hauntings and ghost sightings, and most of them are bullshit," Blaze said, "but there is something down there. This is the wild west, so if someone can't explain something, or doesn't know what happened, they just make shit up. If they're in positions of authority, they tell you what they want you to know."

"Yeah, but that's everywhere," Gupta said. "Half our history books are filled with bullshit, and the other half are filled with the same bullshit from another perspective. But the other half is filled with good people trying to make the best of bad situations."

"Amen to that, my brutha," Blaze said, giving Gupta a high five.

"That's three halves," Maloney and McEvers said in unison.

"What are some of the ghost stories?" Gable asked. He was thinking the storytelling might help ensure this local bartender would be able to help them find out what they wanted to know. He also thought about A.K's warnings.

"Muerto is basically a ghost town, but if you travel south past the Utah border and into the mountains, you'll run into the remnants from an old farming community called Beacon. Back in the late 1800s, Beacon was a peaceful area where settlers could buy food and provisions on their way out West. There was supposedly an old inn and a couple of shops. I've never been down there, and the forest has basically swallowed everything. It's all national park land now. Couldn't settle it if you wanted to."

"Anyway, the townspeople and settlers were having some problems with the Indians down there robbing people, tormenting farmers. Then this old ex-civil war soldier came along and started butchering people for no reason. Indians, townspeople, settlers, anyone who crossed his path. Most of the old timers now think he just had a bad fucking case of PTSD. He staked out the land between Marion and Beacon and demanded that the people call it Muerto. He formed a small posse and they killed everyone they saw. The guy was just evil."

"Finally, some local farmers teamed up with a posse out of Provo and killed their whole group. The murders stopped, and the town of Beacon was left to survive and thrive, but that's not what happened. Eventually, everyone just left. Moved somewhere else in Utah, Wyoming, Arizona, you name it. They say the old soldier and his posse left the whole ground sour and crops didn't grow like they should. And they still ride around Muerto and Beacon, haunting anyone they see."

"The local kids who do go down there huntin' or fishin' don't usually come back with stories. Every now and then, someone might say they felt like someone was watching them, but I always feel like that in the woods. Most the teenagers won't drink down there, which is saying something because we're a small town where drugs and alcohol are big commodities."

"There's stories of an old Indian guy who will walk up to your camp and laugh as you realize that he's transparent. There are stories of an old Mexican who will guide you back to your trail if you're lost. There aren't a lot of people who talk about seeing an old soldier, but he's around."

"About ten years ago, some local kids I knew tried to break into the old Sergeants' cabin and claimed to see something that scared the hell out of them. They wrecked their damned truck because they were driving away so fast. That made the local paper. The journalist even wrote about the kids claiming they saw a ghost."

"Back in the sixties, a guy named Frankie Pace was hiking up there. Stopped to take a piss and realized he was urinating on an old tombstone. I'm not sure how you accidently piss on a grave but that was his story. Anyway, when he came back down from the mountain, all his hair was white and he was borderline catatonic.

"Worked as a handyman around town for the rest of his life. He was smart enough to carry on a basic conversation, but you probably wouldn't see him working for NASA. If you ever said anything about Beacon or Muerto or asked him about that day, he would have a panic attack. I seen it happen myself a couple years ago before he died. He was doing some work in the bar when a couple local guys brought it up."

"How did he die?" McEvers asked.

"Lung cancer. He smoked a pack a day. I used to visit him in the hospital. His death was slower, more painful and more real than any of the bullshit ghost stories you'll hear."

Blaze pointed to a cigarette vending machine across the bar.

"That motherfucker right there is the scariest damned thing in this town. I quit after Frankie died and can't believe how much better I feel. But as for the ghost stories, I hiked up there a couple times to check it out when I was younger, but never saw anything. I still won't go back because it wasn't what I saw. It was what I felt. The place is like a collecting ground for sorrow. If the story about the soldier is true, that's an example. What happened to the Sergeants is true, and it's a better example. All I know is when you're walking around up there, you get this feeling that something wants you to leave. Something wants to be left alone. There is an evil in the air and you need to get the hell away before it smells you."

"Once you get away from the Sergeants' old cabin, the nearby ravine and the creeks that flow through the area, you're cool. You can get drunk, get stoned, knock up your girlfriend and lie about how you're gonna be a good father and any of the other stupid shit that kids in small towns do. But if you get too close to Beacon, you're gonna wanna pack your shit and find another place to chill."

"And what do you think?" Gable asked. He was always good at getting people to talk.

"I don't know about the old soldier, but I remember the Sergeants," Blaze said solemnly. "I remember seeing Blake's sister Amy and how sad she always seemed. I remember seeing Blake around town, buying medical supplies, and he always seemed just as depressed. Ghosts can be scary, but it doesn't hold a candle to the real world we're livin' in."

"But I'm guessing you didn't come down here to arrest a ghost," Blaze said. "What brings you guys here?"

They looked at each other and Gable spoke. He talked about Byrd and said they would probably have people with them. Chances are they would be driving in newer model rental vehicles. He said that he and the cops were going to hang out for a couple of days in case his instincts are correct. He also asked Blaze to let him know immediately if he heard anything about Blake Sergeant being back in town. Blake was the link. Gable didn't mention Cade Stuckley.

Gable put their tab on his FBI card which was still working. He left a $500 tip on the tab, courtesy of Uncle Sam. McEvers raised an eyebrow, and Blake asked him if he had any idea how much money the CIA had given to a couple of fine gentlemen in Saudi Arabia in exchange for intel on Al Qaeda. Blaze was getting five Ben Franklins. He wasn't getting a new Lamborghini.

Chapter 33

Blake finally went back to sleep at 1:00 AM. The truth was he had been wanting to go back to bed ever since he woke up.

He wanted to talk to the Harvester again. He needed to know if his dreams were real. He wanted to understand what was happening to him. Why did killing feel like an addiction now? Why did it feel like a hunger? Before, he killed because he wanted to know about his family. Now it was different.

Something was growing inside of him. A darkness. A hunger. A need to kill. A need to harvest. He had intentionally been making choices through the last three days based on giving himself a chance to kill. This wasn't him. He was a cop. He was a protector. But now, all he wanted to do was punish. All he wanted to do was find people who hurt others and end their existence. This wasn't because of the pain he would save others from feeling, but for the pain he would cause. He craved it.

The dream came quickly.

He was just outside Marion, Wyoming, sitting in Charlie's Pizza, a local café on the edge of town. You could fill your tank, buy your liquor in the adjacent liquor store that Charlie also owned and rent a movie for the night, but Blake liked the pizza as a teenager. He looked around and was confused.

It was true that he had only come back to town a couple of times, but he still occasionally read the local newspaper online. He showed Nicole the story about a couple local kids crashing their car after thinking they saw a ghost near his old home.

Nicole knew everything about his past. They even drove through town once so he could give her the tour of the area. He remembered her saying she felt at home there, and felt a compelling need to share with her that his high school diploma was the academic equivalent of finishing the sixth grade in most other states. There was no way they were raising their kids there. Despite his innate hatred of the town for everything it had taken from him, he couldn't deny that he felt at ease when the two of them hiked around the old trails he and his family traversed.

She knew everything about him, and they both knew she was the cure for his past. She was the reason his own demons remained dormant for nearly a decade.

He also remembered trying to take her to Charlie's Pizza only to learn Charlie retired and the pizza place closed. Yet, here he was, and there Charlie was in the kitchen making pie in the back. He gave Charlie his order and wandered over to the jukebox. It was packed with songs from the mid '90s, right around the time he spent caring for his father and eventually left town permanently. This was also wrong. The original jukebox at Charlie's Pizza only had a handful of decent songs, and was broken down half the time. This one carried songs that Blake didn't hear until he was a young Marine traversing the globe.

Nonetheless, he slid a five into the dollar slot and plugged in a handful of songs. *Peppermint* by Drill Team was the first song to play, and he knew that *Stars* by Hum would be next. It wasn't one of the newer juke boxes where customers could order songs on their phones and pay extra to cut in line. This was an old school, first come-first served juke box.

As the mid 90's music chugged along, he watched as Madison Verley walked through the doors of the pizza joint. They went to high school together over two decades ago, but she still looked like the young brunette who sat next to him in History. The brunette who sometimes dyed her hair different colors and wore black clothes she purchased at the secondhand store, mixed in with t-shirts of her favorite bands.

She was from California like his father. She didn't fit in either, like him. They were the new kids in town. The high school cliques had formed and there wasn't room for them.

It didn't seem to matter that he sacked the other team's quarterback four times during the homecoming game. It didn't seem to matter that she could run three miles in 16 minutes, delivering medal after medal to a cross country team that wasn't used to winning anything. They were both from different cities and weren't part of the small-town plan. They occasionally bonded over their plight as two kids from different suburbs who were stuck in a small town with two radio stations – country and easy listening.

They were the only two kids in school who listened to The Clash, Joy Division, the Ass Ponies, the Meat Puppets, Dinosaur Jr., Lagwagon and No Use for a Name. They were the only kids who were unimpressed with Nirvana in the 90s because it seemed like they were trying too hard to be The Pixies. They were annoyed when their classmates discovered Pearl Jam, but remained undeterred from listening to Ten, Versus and later Vitalogy on countless occasions. No Code was still his favorite Pearl Jam album, but that came long after both had left town for bigger and better things.

If their lives were the set of a John Hughes movie, they would have been an inseparable duo capable of living out banal clichés with their existence. He would have probably pined for a cheerleader and she would have probably pined for him, but neither scenario reflected reality.

They were casual friends. They talked during class, and occasionally during lunch. If there was a school gathering of uncommon suspects, they would stand next to each other so neither one would need to stand alone. Both managed decent grades and made it to school on time, meaning neither one ever needed to know where to go for detention. Their lives weren't a John Hughes movie.

He worked up the courage to ask her out one day only to find out she still had a boyfriend in SoCal. He was still cordial and keenly aware of his dubious status as the clingy jock hoping she would break up. They mutually watched their respective parents' marriages deteriorate under the hopeless glow of a small town they hated with muted teenage ambivalence. They probably would have ended up together because she eventually did break up with the boyfriend.

However, by then, Blake had lost all interest in the nuances of teenage angst. He was riding the bus or his bike straight home every day immediately after school to care for his father. As she walked to his table, he tried to remember what ever happened to her. He seemed to remember that she split town just as fast as he did. Then it hit him. He remembered.

She sat next to him and took a sip of his soda.

"Well, hello Blake," she said. "You look like you've seen a ghost."

He only smiled. It only made sense that he was looking at a young woman who spent the last seconds of her life crashing into an unapologetic wall of rock in the Echo Canyon. This was unsettling.

"I see the afterlife is treating you well," he said, wondering where this dream was going.

Her brown doe-eyes peered upward as she listened to his music selection.

"Nice choice," she said as she took another sip of his drink. "Do you really still listen to CDs?"

"Are you going to order your own drink, or just mooch off mine?"

She took another drink.

"I'll let you know what I decide."

She stared at him for a moment and let out a knowing sigh.

"You hide your pain well," she said, "you always did." Blake didn't respond.

"I never knew what to say to you after your father . . ." she trailed off. "Everyone says they're sorry. Everyone said he was a hero, but nothing ever felt like the right thing to say."

"It's okay Madison, you were just a kid," he responded. "There was no right thing to say for a long time. And I am sorry about what happened to you."

"I guess we were both cursed."

"Well, for two morose Generation X children, doesn't it seem like a cursed existence was all we ever aspired to have?"

"All our heroes are dead, man," she said in her best impersonation of a sixties stoner.

"Were you alive long enough to know about millennials?" he asked.

"No," she said as she scrunched her nose, "but I know what they are," she said disapprovingly.

"Baby boomers hate 'em," Blake said. They both laughed.

"Mirrors can be offensive."

"Madison, do you know anything about what I'm supposed to be? About what I'm supposed to do?"

She nodded knowingly.

"I know I should have broken up with my boyfriend as soon as I got here. I know I wish I would have went on that date with you. Even if we didn't end up together, maybe I would have known what it was like to be treated with respect. Maybe I would have looked for that in other guys and I would still be alive. Maybe I wouldn't be stuck . . ."

She stopped herself abruptly as if her ghostly fate were an awful secret she wasn't supposed to tell.

Blake had a feeling she was probably confined to haunting the canyon where she died, in some sort of permanent limbo. He realized that he knew there was such a thing as ghosts confined to haunt places of tragedy. Perhaps another light in that house he called his mind was flickering on.

He had heard or read something about the ghost of Madison Verley, but they were in a small town. Bullshit ghost stories were a major commodity, though there might be some truth to this one.

"I don't know that being married to me would be considered a wise survival tactic."

Madison reached over and put her hand over Blake's on the table.

"Blake, there is so much about this world that you don't know yet," she said. "This is a terrible world. It wasn't just terrible for us. It's terrible for lots of people. You are going to learn a lot of things about yourself and the world around you and you're going to want to look away. Don't."

"Why not?"

"Because we need you. There is a battle between good and evil, and evil is winning. The darkness you feel inside you? The urges? Understand, that's an innate feeling to fight an evil that continues to take innocent people for no good reason. Evil took me."

Blake rested his forehead on his thumb and index finger.

"I don't know what to do," he said.

"Yes, you do. And you will."

"What side am I on?"

"I think we both know the answer to that."

Blake still wasn't sure, but he knew one thing. If his thirst from blood was a sickness, then he was sick. If it was a blessing, then he was blessed. Either way, he knew a fight was coming, and he was ready.

TUESDAY

Chapter 34

Skyler Roy polished off his third Belgian waffle in under twenty minutes. He kept making them one after another on self-serve waffle maker, and slapping them on the plate, save one moment when the child of another guest jumped in for the same culinary goodness. He'd never stayed at a Hampton Inn, but after this breakfast, he felt like a man on death row eating his pre-execution feast.

The hotel was the closest to the neighborhood where Cade Stuckley and his big friend were hanging out. There was no way to stake out the place without being made, and Mr. Silvera didn't think that would be necessary. He just wanted Skyler to observe and report. That meant staying up all night after a full day of riding.

Skyler carried a little concoction of meth laced with stimulants and household products for such occasions and smoked it when the group stopped at a rest stop. The stimulant worked like a charm, but made him hungry as hell after a few hours.

The hotel staff watched him suspiciously, and he knew what they were thinking. What the hell was a tweaker doing in their fine establishment that was owned by Paris Hilton's family? They catered to white collar men on business trips and soft-bellied families on vacation. Assholes like him usually stayed at one of the fleabag motels where the mice were big enough to chase the cats.

When they had money, they stayed at hotels that sold booze. Not the fucking Hampton Inn.

Yet here he was, eating their waffles and drinking their coffee. He tried the eggs but they tasted like rubber. So did the sausage but he ate a couple of links anyway. He didn't need to check out until noon, but knew he would go back to the room shortly to resume his spot in front of the window, watching one of the two streets their Mustang could pull out of.

His room was on the first level and two doors down from the fire escape. His bike was parked outside. There were only three directions the Mustang could go from where he was sitting and he would have plenty of time to tail them from a distance.

Mr. Silvera was just outside Casper and heading to town fast. He had been joined by a couple other guys who worked for him in roles similar to Skyler's. They were all excited about acting as the muscle for the boss.

He dipped the last of his waffle in the remaining drops of syrup on his plate and licked his fingers. It was time to go back to his room. Maybe he would make one more waffle. After all, if he were an inmate on death row, he'd wanna eat like a king before going out.

***

Gable and McEvers woke up early and headed to the cafeteria for a continental breakfast. Gupta and Maloney were grabbing a workout in the hotel's poor excuse for a gym and would be joining them shortly. Gable's head was still bothering him and he decided to place himself on light duty. McEvers hated treadmills. If he was going to run, it was going to be outside.

They were splitting a newspaper like an old married couple and enjoying a pot of coffee. McEvers noted with interest that their shootout in St. Paul was barely covered, but a former Congressman was murdered in his cabin "up North." That's the term Minnesotans use to refer to any community north of the Twin Cities. McEvers explained it, but found himself equally confused when Gable asked exactly when you knew you were "up North."

Gable also wondered if the dead Congressman was the high profile murder the rookie agent from Blake Sergeant's apartment was talking about when making an excuse for the lapse in surveillance.

Blaze the bartender walked into the diner quickly scanning the booths and seats. His coworkers waved at him and one waitress attempted to give him a hug, but he apologetically waved her off. He was a man on a mission.

Gable spotted him first and waved him over.

"I have to talk to you," he said as he speedwalked over to their table. McEvers made room in their booth and offered him a seat. Gable filled an empty coffee cup using the pot the waitress left them. Blaze nodded appreciatively and had a sip.

"You asked me to let you know if anything out of the ordinary happened in town last night, right?"

Both cops nodded.

"Last night, I made a couple calls to the other bartenders on the Monday shift. This might be something or nothing, but I think it's something." He took another sip of his coffee.

"There's another bar across town called the Rock & Rye. My boy J.R. works the Monday night shift. Last night, this whole group of guys walk in and they all sit down. Won't talk to anybody. All these motherfuckers had their hair dyed black and they looked like they were members of an emo band. You know emo, right?"

Blake hesitated and McEvers quickly described the music genre that was popular about a decade ago. He had a teenage daughter who was well versed in what was cool and what used to be cool.

"There's one guy who was probably from the same place as you," Blaze pointed at McEvers, "and he was the one ordering all the drinks. He had that awesome Minnesota accent, so they say."

McEvers shook his head.

"So Wade Barkley, a local guy, walks over and asks about their hair and one of those motherfuckers steps up on him, sticks a gun in Wade's face. Wade is an asshole. We make 'em by the dozen around here, but my boy tells me he wasn't doing anything wrong. So the Minnesota guy smooths everything out, apologizes for the trouble. J.R. tells him they need to pay for their drinks and get the fuck out or he's calling the police."

"The guys leave, and one of his other customers tells J.R. they were speaking Russian in the parking lot. Then a brother joins them, who looks just like the guy you told me about last night. He gets into it with one of the Russians about how they need to keep a low profile and walks them to the motel up the street."

"What motel?" Gable asks.

"Pink Flamingo," Blaze responds. "Piece of shit down the street, damn near next door to here. And they're driving in two black SUVs, just like you said."

"Did your friend J.R. call the cops?" McEvers asked.

"They did," Blaze said, "but the cops didn't do shit. I don't want to be disrespectful to your profession, because you seem like good people. Maybe things are different where you patrol, but our cops here fucking suck. Crystal meth is burning this city to the ground and they don't even pretend to give a shit in my opinion. Just poor white trash killing themselves and each other. They're good at handing out speeding tickets and DUIs, but you never see them doing shit when someone is really in trouble and last night was another example. The cop took a statement and left. Probably didn't even go to the Flamingo."

"Are their cars still there now?" Gable asked.

"They were five minutes ago," Blaze responded.

McEvers looked up at Gupta and Maloney who had joined them. "You two got a tracker?"

"I thought you would never ask," Gupta responded.

Gable and the cops piled into their rental and drove to the Pink Flamingo. They pulled into the parking lot of a gas station next door and observed the three black sport utility vehicles, about as inconspicuous as a clown at a funeral.

There were two guys with black hair next to the vehicles smoking cigarettes and keeping watch. Gable leaned back to ask if the team had a plan, only to see an empty back seat and two open doors.

Maloney was curled up behind a vehicle facing the trucks and Gupta was darting across the parking lot crouched down and watching the guards intently. Maloney scanned the parking lot and Gupta looked back at her. She nodded.

He darted again from car to car until he was crouched five feet away from the guards and the black trucks. He listened to their conversation as he slid a small device under the rear bumper of each vehicle.

He pressed a button under each device and a small red light responded, telling him they would not be able to go on any family outings without St. Paul's finest knowing their every move.

Thirty seconds later they were sitting in the car behind Gable and McEvers. Gable shook his hand in admiration.

"This motherfucker once rescued every single hostage during an attempted bank robbery while the gunmen were in the room talking to the negotiator," McEvers bragged. "By the time they noticed their hostages were gone, our S.W.A.T. team was busting through the bank lobby."

Gupta beamed with pride. Gable and the cops were back in business.

***

Blake Sergeant sat on Wyatt Shepard's back porch sipping a cup of black coffee staring at the view. It wasn't as strong as he would have liked, but did the trick. He checked his watch, which was still set to the central time zone. 11:00. He had been up for hours, and ran a few errands around town, making sure to return just as the others were beginning to arise.

He had slept three hours, but felt rested. He assumed it was adrenaline.

The back yard faced the Purple Sage Golf Course, but that wasn't the object of his deference.

"What are you looking at?" Melody asked, joining him with a mug carrying her own caffeine fix.

"Do you see that white house next to the club house?" he asked. "It has big pillars along the porch that look like marble from a distance."

"Yeah, I see it," she responded, hoping she was right. "Is it the one with a flower garden out front?"

"It is," Blake responded. "It's a battered women's shelter called Madison's House. I went to school with the girl it was named after."

He told her about Madison Verley. He talked about their mutual appreciation for the same bands and quickly switched subjects as Melody's eyes began to glaze over. He used her subconscious social cue to tell her about how Madison moved back to California after she graduated. The man she eventually married smacked her around and caused her to have a miscarriage. He talked about how she left their home in the middle of the night and tried to flee to her mother's house, which was located across the country.

He talked about how someone disconnected her brakes while she was inside a convenience store trying to get something to eat. He talked about how she crashed her car in the Echo Canyon and died almost immediately upon impact. Everyone in town knew her husband was the culprit, but without tangible evidence, he beat the charges. He was back in California these days, fixing cars by day and moonlighting as an aspiring musician by night.

Her mother raised the funds to open Madison's House, for local women who needed to escape abusive relationships. Blake drove his share of families to a home very similar to Madison's House as a cop in Virginia. He affirmed the women there were doing the Lord's work.

"Don't ever let a man slap you around, Melody," Blake said. "You deserve better than that."

Melody's eyes filled with tears and she tried to sip her coffee.

"Blake, there's a lot you don't know about me," she said. "I'm not the innocent person that you think I am."

Her hands started to shake and she put the cup down. She started reaching in her purse for something, probably her cigarettes. Blake watched her with curiosity.

The back door slid open and Melody froze. Cade poked his head out.

"We gotta roll," he said, then shut the door.

Shepard announced that the FBI put out a Be On the Lookout (BOLO) order for all three of them. He wasn't able to provide anymore assistance without putting him and his entire department in a very bad spot, and they weren't about to ask him to do that. They needed to leave town and leave now, drive straight to their getaway plane and head out to Canada.

He handed Cade three fake passports, the third being a rush job for Melody, using an old picture from her phone.

Fresh off her shift, Trista handed Melody a gym bag packed with winter clothes for Canada and a swimsuit for the Caribbean. She was along for a longer ride than anticipated.

They said their goodbyes and boarded the Mustang. Blake pulled out onto Wasatch Road, drove to the light at Harrison Avenue and turned left when the light was green. He took his time and drove the speed limit, making sure the biker pulling out of the Hampton Inn parking lot had plenty of time to stay close, but not too close.

Harrison snaked through town and became Front Street, then became 150. He drove past the state hospital where his father stayed briefly and he visited religiously.

As they were leaving town, Cade finally asked why they were going south.

"We're sightseeing, Cade," Blake said. "Plus, I want to get to know our friend behind us a little better."

Chapter 35

Blake progressively accelerated as the speed limit increased, keeping Skyler Roy at a safe distance. They drove past a creek where Marion kids used to drink and get high. A mile later, they saw a small trailer park and a sign welcoming them to Muerto, an unincorporated town with a population of 90. A few miles north of the Utah border, they turned left and headed east on a dirt road that didn't show up on maps.

The Mustang growled as Blake gassed up the increasingly steep hill, which would eventually plateau, then circle back down following the rugged mountainside. The road went on like that for another couple of miles and Blake picked up speed, hugging turns he used to blaze through as a teenager. The Mustang growled and climbed one last hill that plateaued like the one before, then turned a sharp corner.

Blake stopped the car and popped the trunk. He grabbed his M-16 off the top of the two bags with the scope and silencer attached, just as he left them the night before when everyone thought he was sleeping.

***

Skyler kept his distance from the Mustang and hoped his phone would still have a signal. They were in the middle of nowhere. He accelerated the hills with vigor, then would pause, waiting to see clouds of dust indicating that the Mustang was still moving.

One particular hill tested his motorcycle skills as he struggled to climb without making too much noise. He turned the corner of the hilltop with exhaustion when he looked up and saw something kneeling in the middle of the road. He felt the first bullet rip through his knee before he heard it, then watched his bike flip out from under him. It rolled off the side of the hill he had just climbed and began to tumble end over end down a desert mountain full of jagged rocks and rugged terrain. He was in the air now, twisting in the wind and knew when he came down it was going to hurt.

He laid on the ground in a daze when he felt something tugging at his arm. He looked up in a semi-conscious state of mind and saw the big guy rolling up his sleeve. The big guy had a syringe in between his teeth, and was using an elastic cord to form a tourniquet around Skyler's bicep. Skyler tried to open his mouth, but felt nauseous. The big guy found a vein he liked and injected something into his left forearm.

"Don't worry," the big guy said, "my wife's a nurse. I know what I'm doing. Sweet dreams."

Skyler felt darkness engulf him, and he was out.

***

Cade ran up behind Blake in a state of shock.

"Animal tranquilizer," Blake said. "He'll be out long enough."

"Long enough for what?" Cade asked.

"You'll see. Back the car up, we're putting Cletus in the trunk."

Blake drove the Mustang to the top of the hill, then unloaded Skyler's body. He carried it to an open spot in direct view of the sun. Cade looked down from where Blake was standing and noticed he had a full view of the entire mountainside below him.

"Melody," Blake said calmly, "drive the car for about two miles. It's going to head back down the hill. You will then take your first right. Take that road for about a half mile and you will come up on an old cabin that looks like nobody has paid any attention to it in years. Back into the driveway then stay in the car. There's food and water in the cooler in the back seat. I packed it last night. Whatever you do, don't leave. If you hear gunfire, don't leave. When the shooting stops, don't leave. Keep all the lights off. If we're not back tomorrow when the sun rises, you can leave. The cash is yours. I'm trusting you. Don't let me down."

"I won't," she said.

Cade looked at Blake with indignity. Blake rolled his eyes.

"We're coming back. It's time to get our hands dirty."

Blake ripped off Skyler's shirt and laid him on a slab of rock and sand. He put duct tape over black nylons to create a blind fold, then tied Skyler's hands and feet down, spreading him out and tying him to tent stakes, so he was facing the sun.

"As soon as I knew he was an albino, I wanted to do this," Blake said gleefully.

He then pulled out the baby oil and lathered a thick coat all over Skyler's bare skin.

"We're at about 8,000 feet above sea level. The sun is going to bake his ass," Blake giggled.

Cade was still dumbfounded and watching Blake in shock.

"What the fuck are you doing?"

"Give me a minute, and I'll let you know."

Blake finished tying Skyler off, grabbed the gym bag he unloaded from the Mustang and carried it down the hill to a jagged rock formation that looked like a fighting hole. Most of the formation was natural, but Cade could see it was reinforced with boulders that were probably moved there a hundred years ago. Layers of dirt caked the rocks and vegetation struggled to grow between the cracks between the manmade stones and the original weathered canvas.

"My dad and I found this years ago," Blake explained. "We're not sure who used it, but it was clearly a lookout point of some sort. Facing Marion."

Blake poked his rifle through different cracks within the makeshift fighting hole until he found a position he liked. He then set the rifle down propped up next to his chosen position. He tossed a bottle of water from the gym bag to Cade who still watched him in shock and confusion, then pulled out three boxes of 5.56-millimeter rounds. Next, he pulled out an old web belt like they used in the Marines and grabbed his magazine pouches. He liked his old gear. Old habits died hard.

"We're green on bullets," Blake said. "but we should still make sure every shot counts. My .45 and the pistols we lifted from the guys who attacked us in St. Paul are in the bag. You can take your pick."

Cade stared at Blake as he pulled the gym bag toward him. Blake looked back, inhaled deeply then exhaled.

"I think Cletus up there works for your family," he said, nodding his head toward Skyler, who was still unconscious, tied down and baking in the sun. "I've got his phone. He's been following us for a while. A lot of people have. FBI, Gayton Security and your family. That's just the people we know about. It's time to thin the herd."

"When did you first see him Blake, and when were you going to tell me?"

"I first saw him this morning, but I knew it was going to happen. I woke up early, gassed up the car and picked up some supplies. Bought the ammunition."

"Did you really know?"

"The stories your buddy told about my father," Blake said. "They're true. My dad used to call them reflections. He could walk into a room, think about something that happened in that spot in the past, then watch it play out in real time. That's how he found all those kids and lost hikers in the Uintas. He used it to solve crimes as a detective."

"We didn't advertise it, but rumors spread. When he had one of his reflections looking for that lost Boy Scout, that big mouth cop told damn near everybody."

"That big mouth cop is also saving our ass," Cade corrected.

Blake responded with a shrug.

"I've never had reflections, but I've had premonitions all my life," Blake continued. "Usually they were just fleeting moments, like déjà vu. I would never remember enough to get any useful information. Most of the time they were dreams and I would see fragments. I dreamed of my daughter once, almost five years before she was born. And I knew Nicole and I would end up married before we met. The first time I ever saw her, I knew who she was."

"I had a premonition of my dad getting hurt but that didn't come until he was already missing, and I had a premonition about his death, again, probably right around the time he was dying."

"Yeah, but you were caring for him every day, and you were away from town," Cade said. "That would have been completely understandable thing to worry about."

"Maybe," Blake said. "I knew about my premonitions and I knew about his reflections. After my family died, I started trying to force my mind to generate reflections like my dad used to. I was there the night my family died, but I still can't remember a damned thing. I can't see the face of the sonofabitch who shot me. Can't get my mind to open that door my father lived with. Reflections. My premonitions have gotten a lot stronger. I get enough information that I can do something with it. I can actually change the future with the information I'm given."

"I knew those guys who worked for your family were going to come by our house. I also knew the same guys who came to your apartment, the mercenaries, were right behind them. We got away. They ended up in a shootout with the cops."

"You predicted that we were going to initiate the getaway plan," Cade said in agreement, "I thought you were being paranoid at first, but it stuck with me. I was a lot more aware of my surroundings on Sunday and I stayed dry all day. That's unusual for me."

Blake thought about it. He remembered the conversation at the diner.

"That was one of the weaker premonitions," he said. "I knew something was going to happen, but didn't know what or when. I tried my best to warn you, but you're right. It probably sounded like paranoia. What I can tell you for sure, is I saw that fucking biker sitting in a hotel room eating a pancake or waffle or some shit, watching our car. He called someone to tell them our movements, then I saw him following us on his bike. I had that one while we were driving."

Cade didn't respond.

"Like I said, I don't get a ton of information, but I'm getting enough to work with these days. We've been running a long time and if we don't stop now and fight, we aren't going to make it to Jackson. Something is up there waiting for us and it's not good. If we strike now, that changes our future. It's time to fight."

Cade sat silently and stared at the ground in front of him. His shoulder was still sore.

"Why are you just telling me this now? In fact, why didn't you ever tell me about your father?"

"I didn't talk about my dad because that felt like a part of the past that should stay in the past. It was important that we kept our abilities quiet because people in this country do fucked up things when they don't understand shit. And people go completely nuts when someone can see a truth they don't want the world knowing. We lived with a lot of secrets, Cade. Just being here now has unlocked a lot of stuff I haven't thought about in years. I've been so focused on Nicole, Anni and my son, all of this just fell by the wayside."

"I'm sure there's a lot more about your past that Wyatt didn't know."

"There's a lot more. If your plan works, and we end up in the Caribbean, I'll tell you shit that will make your skin crawl. We'll drink half the rum on the island trying to understand the world around us."

"Did Nicole know?"

"Nicole knew everything and loved me anyway. She was fascinated by it."

Cade paused again, then reached into his coat and pulled out an envelope. He handed it to Blake.

"I meant to give this to you in Minnesota, but didn't get the chance," he said. "I don't want you to read it unless shit goes south and something happens to me."

"What is this, a love letter?" Blake said with a laugh.

"No man, it's your escape plan if I die," Cade said. "But don't read it now. Promise me you won't read it now."

"Okay, I promise."

They sat in the fighting hole for a moment.

"Why don't you want me to read it now?" Blake asked.

"Because I have shit too," Cade said. "We'll drink the other half of the rum on the island talking about my shit. If we make it out alive, I'm taking that letter back and burning it because some of that shit never needs to see the light of day."

Blake nodded.

"I can respect that," he said. "Maybe we will have a chance to exorcise some of those demons today."

Cade didn't respond for a moment. They just sat in the fighting hole watching the hills in front of them.

"I know Frank Silvera killed my dad," Cade finally said. "He did it because my mom wanted me to live with her in New Jersey. As long as my dad was breathing, that wasn't going to happen."

"I have a feeling you might get to take something else from him," Blake said. "I need to run down the hill and check up on Melody. If he wakes up, keep him tied up. Shoot his leg below the knee if he tries to get away, and see if you can get into his phone."

"You know where you're going?"

"Yeah," Blake responded, "she's in my old driveway."

"Is this place really haunted?"

Blake paused and thought about the question.

"Guess we will find out," he said as he ran down the hill out of sight.

I'll tell you shit that will make your skin crawl.

Cade looked around him. There were dark black clouds approaching from west. He thought about what Melody said back at the apartment, how Blake shot from wall to wall, killing their intruders. How he was smiling the whole time. Blake didn't give a shit about escaping. He wanted this fight.

They could have made it to Jackson. Blake was running around this mountain like a kid on Christmas morning, excited about the idea of a fight. He probably dreamed of killing bad guys on this hill as a child and here they were, on a mountain in the middle of nowhere like sitting ducks. The whole thing was pissing Cade off.

He turned his attention to the biker's phone. It was password protected with a four-digit pin. If he were back in his apartment, he had a program on his computer that could unscramble pin codes. The laptop was in the car.

He looked at the biker again. He was still sleeping with baby oil glistening on his bare chest and stomach. The first signs of pink skin were emerging from his pale white body. He had light blonde mullet, tattoos on his arms, a pale goatee and probably a case of meth mouth. If he unlocked the phone, there would likely be copious supplies of porn and Nickelback songs downloaded for his amusement.

What are the odds? Cade thought to himself. He typed in "6-9-6-9." The phone was open and he was free to learn everything he ever wanted to know about Skyler Roy but was afraid to ask.

"You have to be the dumbest human being on the face of this planet," Cade said to the dormant biker.

The first thing he saw was a text message from Frank Silvera.

Chapter 36

Viktor Namin sat at the small desk in his room at the Pink Flamingo, listening intently on the phone and jotting notes. His door was slightly ajar, and Byrd stood outside trying to eavesdrop.

"Uh huh," Namin said, or "da."

Namin had been in America for close to eight months, shortly after his employer began serious talks about acquiring Precision Energy, an American oil company with investments in defense contracting. Back in its day, Precision had a portfolio that was the envy of its contemporaries, but some bad public relations issues and a frosty relationship with the Obama administration hurt their earnings.

Their executives could have retired comfortably, but in their world, there was no such thing as too much power. By the time they had a friendlier administration to work with, their finances were in a place where a merger could prove more lucrative.

For Namin and his men, life in the corporate sector was very similar to life in the military. They provided routine security, conducted miscellaneous duties as assigned and most recently, spent painstaking months planning an operation only to have the plug pulled at the last moment. Now here he was, leading a manhunt that his team should have been tasked with initially.

The longer he was in America, the less he liked most of their citizens. The gentleman he was on the phone with now, however, seemed to be an exception.

He knew Byrd was behind him trying to listen in on the conversation and that amused him. In a matter of hours, he and his men were procuring better intel than the *mudak* standing in his doorway.

"Yes," he said into the receiver. "Spell the name for me please? M-u-e-r-t-o? Is that an unusual name?"

More silence.

"I see. This has been very helpful. Of course, and it was a pleasure speaking with you."

He hung up the phone and slid his chair back.

"Did we get anything?" Byrd asked.

"Maybe," Namin responded. He was lying.

"Should we pack up?"

"No, we should stand by. We shall leave shortly."

Byrd nodded skeptically and returned to his room where his men sat quietly passing the time playing hearts.

Outside their window, Gable, McEvers, Maloney and Gupta sat in their rental waiting for the mercenaries' next move. Gupta used his ninja skills to procure coffee and breakfast for the group, never drawing the attention of the Russian sentries parked by the vehicles.

***

Blake Sergeant found Melody parked in the Mustang in the driveway of his childhood home. The vegetation was overgrown and patchy around the house, the product of several draughts and a lack of attention. He had a cousin whom he had never met checking in on the place periodically. It looked like most of the attention was probably given to the home versus the grounds.

The car was backed up to the front of the padlocked driveway adjacent to the front porch. Melody was smoking outside the car, begrudgingly, and waved at him. He opened the trunk of the Mustang. He pulled out a backpack she hadn't seen before and slung it around his shoulder.

"I forgot to grab this one on the hill," he explained.

"So this was your childhood home?" she asked.

"For a few years. High school mostly."

"This place has some charm."

"It was a lot cleaner when I lived here."

She smiled.

"Where was your bedroom from here?"

"Around back. I had an awesome view."

"I'll bet you charmed a lot of girls into that room."

"I wasn't as exciting as you might have imagined," he said. "You make it sound like I could probably charm one more this afternoon."

"I think we both know that all you need to do is say the word."

Blake let the comment pass and pulled an old key out of his pocket.

"This key unlocks that padlock. There should be enough room to back the car in. If you hear gunshots, back in and stay put. I will come back. If you hear sirens, shut the garage door. If we're not back by tomorrow at dawn, I want you to leave. Turn right on the driveway, don't go back the way you came. This is a service road used by park rangers and it's not on any maps."

"Follow it and take your second left, about a mile up. You will then veer south for another twenty miles until you hit another dirt road. Turn right and follow that for another few miles. When it turns to pavement, you will know you're only a few miles from I-80. If you want to stay longer, you can. On any other day, you would be safe, but because I'm here, someone might know to come looking for me here. Do not leave the car."

"Blake," she said in the form of a question. "Is this place really haunted?"

"No," he lied. "There are plenty of bad people on earth for us to spend our energy worrying about."

This is a terrible world, he thought. Of all the dreams he had been experiencing in recent weeks, the last one was the one that kept coming back to him.

Melody approached Blake and touched his hand. She went in for a kiss and he pulled back. She stepped back.

"I'm sorry, I know you miss your wife, but it seems . . ."

"No I'm sorry," he said. "You're a beautiful girl and perhaps . . ."

Melody went in and pressed her lips on his and for a fraction of a second he didn't fight it. Blake pulled back and stared at her briefly with an expression of unnerved vulnerability.

"Just come back safely," she said

Blake only nodded as he grabbed his backpack. Their moment of contact opened a door in his mind. He looked into her eyes.

"What were you going to tell me before, back at the cop's house?"

It was Melody's turn to feel conflicted. She bit her lip and looked up and to the left. Blake spotted it and waited for a lie. She then looked down, then back at him.

"Remember back at your apartment when you asked who left the rear sliding door unlocked?"

Blake nodded, then held his finger up abruptly. He moved it to his lips. The international sign for *shut the fuck up.* He looked up and listened intently.

Melody watched him then cocked her head sideways trying to hear whatever it was that caught his attention. She heard birds and strange sounds coming from the forest. Blake looked down at his shoulder and nodded quietly to himself.

"Someone's coming," he whispered. "I've changed my mind. Unlock the padlock on the garage. If you can back in, do it now. We have a few minutes and you can tell me whatever you were going to tell me later."

With that, he disappeared, running back up the hill where he came from, thinking about their conversation.

He felt like he could hear every movement on the mountain, but he also felt something new. He knew he had blind spots. Lots of blind spots. He thought about Madison Verley's ghost. "*Blake, there is so much about this world that you don't know about yet,*" she said.

He inhaled deeply and raced up the hill. *You are going to learn a lot of things about yourself and the world around you and you're going to want to look away. Don't.*

Melody wanted to tell him something. He had been thinking about how fast those two thugs picked her lock back in her apartment. It was too fast. He thought about Melody shooting the third guy. Her hands were shaking. She was holding the weapon wrong, and yet she fired a perfect shot from about ten feet. There were several things about that morning that still didn't sit right with him.

Melody did as she was told and unlocked the padlock. She raised the garage door which creaked and hissed in response. The door clearly hadn't been opened in at least a year, though there were subtle signs of life in the darkened garage. The floor looked as if it had been swept in the recent past with a thin layer of dust from time caking the floor.

There were tools hanging on the back wall of a workstation. The door, the workstation and the sheet rocked walls looked like additions potentially made by his father. The garage had the feel of a newly finished project that didn't have the chance to benefit from years of use.

She backed the car in and pulled the garage door shut. The house gave her the creeps and her mind kept wanting to wander back to some of the ghost stories Wyatt Shepard told them last night.

She tried to imagine a young Blake Sergeant running around the garage possibly doing household chores. Her brother used to mow the lawn. Maybe he did the same. Unfortunately, her mind games didn't work. She didn't feel fear or horror in the house. Only sadness. She dug into the cooler and found several kinds of deli meat, cheese, bread and condiments. She made herself a sandwich, grabbed a can of diet soda and ate alone in the dusty garage. Alone and afraid.

***

Blake made it to the top of the hill in about fifteen minutes, and found Cade playing with Skyler Roy's phone. Cade turned to face Blake and tossed him the phone.

"He's working for Frank, and has been following us for a while," Cade said. "Frank knows we're here and is on his way up."

Blake started looking at the device for himself and found an application tracking his position.

"It looks like Frank has been using one of those lost child apps to keep track of this clown," Cade said from behind him. "I'll bet he uses this app to track most his drug mules."

"I was counting on that."

Blake peered out at the dirt road behind him and didn't see any cars kicking up dust. He could have sworn he heard a vehicle. He used to be able to hear them from miles away.

"Why are we out here?"

"I already told you that."

"Because you had a feeling, or a 'premonition?'"

Blake could hear Cade's voice rising.

"Keep it down," he said, nodding his head at their junkie prisoner.

"What is it that you think you know, Blake? What did you see?"

"You got something to say?"

"Yeah, I do. We have a plan. A good plan. It might not be perfect, and I see you clenching your jaw every time you hear something you don't like. But it's my plan and it's got us this far. We are a couple hours away from our flight. Are we hauling ass out there? No. We're out here like sitting ducks in the middle of fucking nowhere and you're running around this mountain like a lunatic. I think you're losing your mind, man. Talking in your sleep. Saying you're psychic and your dad was psychic. What the fuck dude?"

"That asshole over there made us," Blake growled, cutting him off, "and I think your step dad has a whole fleet of crank snorting tweakers all over the Wild West just like him looking for us. They have a network. I wanna know what the hell we're walking into. And by the way, your buddy down there is a dirty cop."

"He saved our asses," Cade shot back. "And he owes us because of what you did for his daughter. He appreciates that."

"He's also a dirty cop."

"And you're not a cop anymore, Blake. You haven't been in years. You've killed twenty-six people for money. You're not some holy roller who gets to walk on water. Your hands are just as fucking dirty as mine. You haven't given a shit about right and wrong for a while. All you want to do is fight. You're a hammer, Blake. And right now, everything looks like a nail."

Blake didn't respond.

"The fact that your pet redneck made us is all the more reason why we should bail on your desire for a shootout. We need to go and we need to go now."

Blake thought the notion over, then heard movement behind him. Skyler Roy began to wake up.

"First, we gather some intel," Blake said.

"Or we just shoot this fucker and leave!"

"Where am I," Skyler muttered. He groaned, paused, muttered some more, then started pulling on the tent stakes holding him down. A sharp pain in his knee shot up his leg and he began screaming.

"Easy there, Skyler," Blake said. "Scream one more time and I'll cut your throat."

Skyler paused, shuttered and struggled to see through his nylon and duct tape blind fold.

"Where am I," he stammered.

"I don't mean to be the bearer of bad news, but your leg is broken," Blake continued. "My bullet in your knee didn't help matters, and I think you have a sunburn."

Blake slapped Skyler's beet red stomach and listened to him shriek.

"You're fucking crazy," Cade whispered as he trudged away from Blake.

"Calm down," Blake said. "If you're lucky, you can spend tomorrow trying to heal up."

Blake looked up at the black clouds that were now above them. Light raindrops began to trickle around them. It was the midafternoon, but the clouds were sucking the light out of the day.

"In the meantime, that should feel refreshing."

"Where am I?" Skyler asked again.

"You're in deep shit."

"Is this Cade?"

"Close enough."

"You're the big guy."

"Who hired you?" Blake asked.

"Your mother."

Blake squeezed Skyler's leg below the kneecap where a disjointed bone was threatening to poke out of his skin. Skyler screamed in pain.

"I don't have time for this, Skyler. Next time you piss me off, I break your other knee. It's gonna be hard enough crawling off this mountain with one bad leg. Don't make it worse."

"How do you know my name?"

"Your wallet Skyler," Blake responded. "your wallet. Who are you working for?"

Skyler laid back, feeling defeated.

"Mr. Silvera."

"Is he on his way now?"

Cade walked back to the interrogation.

"We already know the answer to that question," he grumbled.

Blake looked back at Cade with disgust. This felt like amateur hour.

"Yes," Skyler answered seemingly undeterred. His hands were shaking.

"How does he know where you are?"

"GPS on my phone."

Blake wanted to know Skyler was going to tell him the truth under duress and he was. Skyler didn't know they were already looking at his phone. It was time to get some more substantial information.

"Your text message from Frank stated that he was in Casper at about 9:30 this morning. He should be here by now."

"He's meeting some guys in Rock Springs. I don't know how many. Man, I'll tell you anything you wanna know. I fucked up. I know I fucked up and I know you'll kill my ass without thinking twice."

Blake watched him with little surprise. He was an addict. He dressed tough, talked tough, but at the end of the day, all addicts were slaves to their vices. Once they're under any type of stress, they immediately want to feed their addiction. Nicotine. Alcohol. Meth. Didn't matter. Addiction made you weak, and this particular man had never been strong. He wanted a sniff, a smoke or an injection of whatever was in the knapsack in the bike that was halfway down the mountain they were standing on. His brain was also in a place where it would never be able to accurately solve problems. He was a junkie. There was no five-year plan. His life was lived one fix at a time.

"Are they on their way here now?"

"Yeah, man. And I don't think they wanna kill you."

"Why do you say that?"

"Because Mr. Silvera said he wants to see Cade alive. Mr. Carbone said if they wanted to kill Cade, they could have done that weeks ago. Ah think they wanna talk."

"Which Mr. Carbone is with them?" Blake asked.

"Billy, er, uh, he's Mr. Carbone to me but everyone else calls him Billy."

Blake walked back to Cade, who was visibly tense.

"My uncle," Cade said lowly. His left fist was clenched and his right hand was squeezing the grip of his pistol.

"You all right?" Blake said. "Keep squeezing that thing, you're gonna shoot your foot."

Skyler writhed in pain. His arms and legs were stretched out and tied down. Every time he tried to move, his left leg sent shockwaves across his body. He couldn't see. He couldn't look at his leg to see how badly it was messed up. Was it shot? Was it broken? Was it road rash? He felt like not knowing what was wrong with his leg made the pain worse.

The big guy said his leg was broken and he was shot. He didn't know. He remembered riding around the corner and seeing the big guy in the middle of the street kneeled and firing bullets at him. There was no time to react. He was in the air, then darkness.

Now, the big guy seemed calm but merciless. Cade, the little guy, seemed agitated. If he was smarter, he could think of a way to play them off each other. But, he wasn't that guy. He was never going to be that guy.

"Listen man," Skyler said, "you can kill me. You can torture me. You can do whatever man. All I know is Mr. Silvera put a fifty-thousand-dollar finder's fee out for anyone looking for Cade. Now all three of you have your faces all over CNN. Cops are after you. Ah spotted you takin' a piss at a Pizza Ranch. I called my guy and got a call from Mr. Carbone an hour later. Next thing I know I'm talkin' to Mr. Silvera who tells me to follow you. Observe and report, is what he said. I've been followin', observin' and reportin' since we were in Pierre. Ah don't know this place. If ah need to crawl to a hospital, my ass ain't gonna know where to go and ah'll probably die up here on this mountain. If that's even where we are. But someone else is gonna see you. There are a lot of people looking for you and someone else will find you. And they'll observin', reportin' and followin' too. That's all ah know man. Just let me go, man. Please let me go."

He carried on like that in a quiet moan asking again and again softly to be let go, promising to never sin again. He would crawl to a hospital. He would crawl to a church. The truth was he wanted to crawl back to his knapsack which was his hospital and church rolled into one.

The rain picked up into a steady downfall. Not a storm, but no longer a trickle. Lightning was cracking in the west and thunder was hissing in the distance, threatening to join them in a moment. The storm would be on top of them soon, and it was hovering their way like a slow-moving train.

Blake tuned out Skyler's overtures and listened to the sounds of the mountainside in the distance. Someone was coming.

"Watch him," Blake said to Cade who was still sulking and stewing.

Blake perched behind the rocks in their makeshift fighting hole and saw movement in the distance. He heard a low mechanical rumble. Motorcycles.

"They're coming," Blake said to Cade.

"Where?" Cade responded. He looked around him as if Frank was going to walk up the mountain. Blake pointed toward the sound off in the distance. The ground was too wet for their group to kick up dust, but Blake could hear the distinct rattle of an idling chopper. Probably four or five of them.

Frank had to climb up and descend one hill, and would be in a valley directly below their fighting hole before circling the next hill for another steep incline. They would be sitting ducks, but only if Blake and Cade seized the moment. It was a mountain side designed for an ambush.

Blake grabbed a set of binoculars out of his backpack and peered into them, hoping to get a better look. They were out of range from his view, but he would have plenty of chances to see them in the coming minutes. He knew it was Frank.

"Is it them?" Cade called out from behind.

"I think we both know the answer to that one."

They listened to the idling bikes off in the distance. The rain continued to fall and was threatening to pick up.

"It's your stepdad and uncle down there, Cade," Blake said, keeping his voice low. "They've already tried to kill us once, and they're back. We can run back down the hill and hide out in my old house. They'll drive right past or maybe just find this goofball." He nodded his head toward Skyler, who was ten feet away, tied up, still mumbling and getting rained on.

"We can still get away, but like he said, they've found us once and they have eyes everywhere. We take them out, or leave a sizable dent in their armor, that slows them down. Then we just need to worry about the FBI and Gayton Security and whoever else there might be."

The sound of the bikes grew closer and the rain was gradually picking up.

"What's it going to be, Cade? Fight or flight? And why do they still want you alive?"

"They want me alive because they can still make money off me," Cade responded immediately. "I built something successful, and they need me to make sure it continues. They want the website to continue. That's all it is. That is all it has ever been, and I will never get rid of them."

Blake saw the first two bikes pulling around the first visible stretch of dirt road from his vantage point. They would need to climb one hill, descend to the valley where he could attack.

"We've got about one minute."

"I'm thinking," Cade shot back.

Skyler's mumbling was barely audible now over the rain.

Blake saw two bikes, a navy-blue explorer and two more bikes behind the vehicle. He ducked down and motioned for Cade to do the same.

Skyler Roy's phone rang in Cade's pocket. The ring tone was the opening chords of some God-awful country song. Cade looked at the phone and saw Frank's name pop up in the caller ID. Blake looked at Cade.

Cade answered the phone.

***

Gable, McEvers, Maloney and Gupta saw the first signs of life coming outside the Pink Flamingo at around 3:00. The Russian mercenaries piled out of motel rooms looking like gothic rock stars on tour. One of them, a short man, was directing his men into their vehicles and giving out orders, inaudible from the cops' vantage point.

Not far behind them, Byrd emerged with four of his men, traveling with the Russians, but all body language sent signs of a tense relationship.

"That's Byrd," Gable pointed out, "and the Asian guy, you remember him?"

"Beckett and your guy chased him," McEvers whispered excitedly. "We're in business."

Byrd, Namin and the mercenaries turned right out of the hotel parking lot and headed toward Muerto, going the same way Blake, Cade and Melody traveled hours earlier.

The cops followed from behind, keeping a sizable distance and monitoring the tracking devices installed on all three vehicles. The men continued south past the road Blake used to bait Skyler Roy into an ambush and made a left turn on another dirt road a mile south. A metal gate reading "keep out" was opened and welcomed them to the private road.

The mercenaries drove four miles in, and parked their vehicles at a fork in the road. One street led back to Utah and the other headed up the mountain, ending abruptly about a kilometer downhill from where Blake and Cade were stationed. On the opposite side of the dead end was a wooded area that concealed a jagged ravine. Fifty feet below the ravine was a small meadow with the remnants of a series of fences where Neal Sergeant was growing cold weather grapes two decades before.

They parked their vehicles, put on rain jackets, grabbed their gear and began hiking up the hill where they would have a clear view of Cade and Blake.

McEvers, Gupta and Maloney exited their car and staged themselves behind the mercenaries' vehicles. Gable drove down the dirt road that led back to Utah looking for a hidden away place to park their vehicle. With the men on foot, the cops would need to hike in as well. They were all coincidentally wearing windbreakers to protect themselves from the rain, but picked up black ballcaps at the hotel souvenir store when Gupta spotted the storm that morning.

Gable ran back to the group from where he parked the car. They watched the mercenaries hike up a mountain. They knew where they were going, and were exercising tactical awareness. Three hundred meters behind, the cops plotted their next move.

"We're going to have a hell of a time taking on an Army in the mountains," McEvers observed.

"But it won't be as difficult if we can secure a tactical advantage," Gupta responded.

The cops and agent looked at each other, and without words, began creeping up behind the mercenaries, keeping distance but maintaining their visuals.

***

"Skyler, where the hell have you been?" Frank called into the phone. "I've been trying to call you for the last hour. Tell me what's going on."

There was no response on the other line. Billy Carbone looked at Frank with concern.

"Skyler," Frank said again, "are you there?"

"Did you kill my father?" It was Cade Stuckley.

"Cade?"

"Did you kill my father?" Cade repeated.

"Cade, where is Skyler?"

"I asked you a question."

The first two motorcycles emerged over the top of the hill Blake was watching, and began to make its way down. This was originally supposed to be a two-man job, but Cade hadn't been much of a help. *I should have kept Melody up here.* He thought.

Blake opened his spare backpack. He pulled out a rain jacket and quickly put it on over his already wet windbreaker and jeans. He threw another jacket to Cade who didn't notice.

The rain picked up. Skyler called for help, and tugged at his ropes. If the rain soaked the ground enough, he would be able to break free. If he had any upper body strength at all, he would have been free an hour ago.

Beneath the jacket, Blake pulled out the AT4 disposal rocket launcher that Cade admired in his garage a couple days earlier. His M-16 was staged in the fighting hole under a poncho. Cade's eyes grew in amazement as he saw Blake with his new toy. Blake began to prepare the weapon for fire and smiled at his friend.

"Cade, you are in a whole lot of trouble and we need to talk."

"Talk? Is that what Tony wanted to do as well when he broke into my partner's apartment?"

"Cade you've got it all wrong you dumb sonofabitch and you've …"

"Did you kill my father?!" Cade yelled. "Yes or no?!"

"You just killed my nephew you little sonofabitch and you have no fucking right to . . ."

"Did you kill my father?!"

Cade was in a rage. He looked at Blake, who was holding the AT4. The Explorer was driving down the mountain, flanked by motorbikes.

"I need an answer, Cade," Blake said, calm as an accountant eyeballing a tax deduction, but holding a rocket launcher. Cade looked up at him with rage in his eyes. "Fight or flight?"

The phone was still in Cade's ear.

Skyler had gotten one hand free and was pulling at the other. He grunted and cringed in pain with every move he made. His leg, the sunburn and the rain all intensified. Everything hurt. He heard screaming from downhill and yanked at his left hand.

"Where is Skyler?!" Frank yelled into the receiver, meeting Cade's rage.

"Right here, motherfucker!" Cade screamed back.

Cade raced up the hill.

Skyler freed his second hand and sat up. He pulled the blindfold from his eyes and looked downhill.

The short guy was yelling "motherfucker" into the phone with one hand and waving a pistol in the other.

"Aw, sheeit, man," Skyler groaned.

Cade fired twice. Two rounds blasted through Skyler's midsection, snapping his body back to the damp ground where he had just been laying.

Cade turned to face Blake and nodded. Blake positioned himself in his chosen break between the rocks in the fighting hole. He aimed the AT4 just ahead of where the Explorer was driving and fired.

***

Billy Carbone saw it first.

Frank was screaming into the receiver at Cade Stuckley, sick of his attitude, just like the day when he finally grew sick of Cade's father's attitude.

"We're gonna kill the motherfucker," Billy was growling behind the steering wheel. Sure, they had plans, but enough was enough.

Frank was asking Cade about Skyler when they heard gunshots off in the distance. It was tough to tell where the noise was coming from in the mountains, but those shots had to be in front of them. That's when he looked up and saw what looked like a missile.

The rocket made impact just below the front bumper of the explorer. Billy saw the hood fly open and felt the truck leave the ground, flying backwards. Billy jerked the steering wheel, but it did no good. The truck landed with a thud on the side of the road and began rolling end-over-end down the mountainside. The windows shattered and all Billy heard was his own ears ringing from the initial explosion.

***

Blake hadn't fired an AT4 in nearly 20 years and felt like his shot was a little rusty. He wanted to plant the rocket right in the cab of the Explorer so it could blow up between the driver and passenger. The alternative was marginally better. The truck flipped up on its hind wheels, then rolled down the mountain getting smashed by jagged boulders as it continued to tumble. The Explorer rolled about a hundred meters then fell off a ten foot drop off onto an embankment adjacent to a spring that eventually led to the Bear River.

The occupants probably wouldn't be dead, but they would be mangled. Blake quickly turned his attention to the four bikers, who were still shell-shocked by the crash.

Both bikers in the rear fell off their choppers in shock and the other two bikers were pulling their bikes to the side of the road as fast as they could to seek cover, but it was too late. Blake grabbed the M-16 with the scope still mounted and aimed in at the two bikers in the front. They had the better shot at getting cover.

His first shot missed, but his second round blasted through the meaty part of the biker's shoulder blade just above his collar bone. His next shot hit the man in the chest. The second biker dove to the ground behind a boulder on the side of the road, but he was a sitting duck from Blake's vantage point. He paid for the sin of poor concealment with three quick shots ripping through his back as he lay in the prone position.

The first biker in back had seen one too many westerns and figured out where Blake's shots were coming from. He stood in the middle of the road one hundred meters away, drew a sidearm and began shooting at the boulders about twenty yards below the fighting hole. Blake lined up his crosshairs and fired three times. He watched Rambo the biker fly back as blood splattered from his chin. He would likely still be alive but in an inordinate amount of pain.

Injured from his accident, the fourth biker was dragging himself to the side of the road. Blake almost felt bad about this one. Almost. The biker should have stuck to dealing meth. Blake shot this one in the head. Why make him suffer?

Cade was standing next to Blake after the firefight. He tried to run down the hill, but Blake grabbed his shoulder.

"There could be more," Blake said. "Let's hold our position."

Blake kept his sights on the bikers looking for signs of movement. From their vantage point, they could see movement coming from the Explorer. The vehicle landed on the driver's side, then mercilessly rolled upside down.

"Binoculars?" Cade asked and Blake pointed to them, sitting on the poncho next to Cade's unfired rifle.

Cade grabbed them and peered into the wreckage.

"They're alive," he said. "They're fucking alive."

Cade ran around the side of the fighting hole, this time, too quick for Blake to grab him. Blake yelled out, but Cade didn't listen. He was headed down the hill.

"Cade, that's a bad idea!" Blake yelled out. "I can take them out from here."

They had the perfect position, but Cade wasn't listening. Blake used his rifle sights to scope out the bikers once more, then the road, then the area around him. He didn't see anyone, but felt like they weren't alone on the mountain.

He knew they weren't alone.

***

Gable and McEvers dove for cover when they heard the first two gunshots. The rain had dampened the previously solid ground.

The mud softened their landing, but splashed onto their forearms as they took cover.

Gupta and Maloney knelt next to them in a small embankment. They watched intently as Byrd and the Russians did the same. Kim and Wisnewski ran to the back of the mercenaries' makeshift formation and scanned the premises behind them. Neither Gayton employee spotted Gable or the cops.

Both men scampered back to the front of the formation. The two Russians in the rear of the march made cursory glances behind them. When they heard what sounded like a rocket launcher, all heads went down.

The familiar pops from an M-16 followed in methodical shots. Someone was aiming and firing. Quickly.

"I think that's Sergeant or Stuckley," Gable whispered.

"Maybe both."

"We should stay down, let this play out," McEvers said. "Maybe a shootout could thin out the herd."

The mercenaries resumed their movement up the hill when they heard a pause in the gunshots. The M-16 was being fired from the other side of the hill the mercenaries were climbing. If the mercenaries stayed focused on what was ahead, Gable and the cops could take out a good chunk of their group from behind in the event of a shootout. Gupta unveiled the Winchester scout sniper rifle he had kept concealed in plastic covering. Maloney holstered her pistol and unveiled two hunting knives.

"You're bringing knives to a gunfight?" Gable asked.

"We brought these two for a reason," McEvers calmly responded.

"Tell you what," Maloney said to Gable, "if I look like I need to be rescued, you'll be the first to know."

She then turned her attention to Gupta.

"Don't you fucking shoot me."

Gupta smiled.

Maloney began low-crawling up the hill, though it almost looked like she was slithering, from rock to rock, with a hunting knife in each hand.

***

Wisnewski was serving as the point man alongside one of his new Russian friends. He heard the guy referred to as "Sergi."

Byrd and Namin were a few steps behind with Byrd keeping Kim close. Wisnewski was the best sniper in their group, but Kim was a less than distant second. Wisnewski and Sergi took their positions at the crest of the hill and the Russians and remaining mercenaries fanned out behind them, digging down in the mud and preparing for a final order.

Wisnewski and Sergi kept their rifles trained on the other side of the hill and waited for orders. Byrd and Namin crawled up to join them and take in the situation. Off to their right lay a biker whose legs looked to be tied to two stakes dug into the ground. His head was cocked to one side with a duct tape blindfold hanging around his neck. His arms lay flopped on either side of him, and two bullet wounds were plainly available on his midsection.

Byrd took one look. He was dead.

Slightly lower down the hill was what looked an old fighting hole probably carved out by a cowboy outlaw. Inside the fighting hole was a used AT4, two backpacks with various pieces of gear.

This was their targets' post where they took down what looked like another group of followers. Byrd remembered hearing one of the targets had connections to organized crime. Perhaps they were also pursuing the bounty.

He had a perfect view of the street below them where a fresh crater from a rocket launcher left a new dent. Four bikers flanked the crater and appeared to be dead or dying. They found the remnants of the shootout they overheard from the other side of the hill. Looked like Cade and his trusty partner got the drop on these poor bastards.

He saw Cade Stuckley walking down the street toward one of the bikers, making no effort to conceal himself.

"Kim," Byrd said without looking at him.

"Already on it boss," Kim replied. He had his rifle aimed at Cade Stuckley. "I have a shot."

Wisnewski settled in next to Kim and had his rifle in his shoulder scanning the mountain. The Russians had their rifles out but nobody was pointing their muzzles at anything.

"Where's the other one?" Byrd said.

"I see him," Wisnewski responded. "He's traversing down the hill, but maintaining cover. I don't have a shot yet."

"Stand by Kim," Byrd said. "Wait for Wisnewski."

Namin watched the mercenaries with amusement.

"Okay," Wisnewski said after a moment. "He's stopped, but I still don't have a shot. He's behind that big ass rock."

"Why don't you boys hold your fire," Namin said. "I want to watch this play out."

"We can end this now," Byrd growled.

"I said wait, comrade," Namin replied coldly.

"You're the client," Byrd responded, then gave the order to his men. "But I'm not your damn comrade."

Namin smiled and would have laughed out loud if circumstances allowed it.

"You don't like me much, do you, Byrd?"

Byrd faked a smile.

"The customer is always right."

"You don't like what I represent," Namin continued, "but the man signing my checks is the same man signing yours today." He lowered his voice to give effect to his next comment.

"Your hands are just as bloody as mine, comrade"

Byrd looked away.

"Kim, Wisnewski," he called out, "get down in that fighting hole and see if you can get a better shot. Might as well capitalize on the good cover."

Byrd turned to Namin.

"I recommend we keep our shooters positioned in their new spot. Your guys should form a perimeter just in case shit goes bad." Namin nodded in agreement and gave the order.

Gable and the cops remained about 15 meters behind, watching the Russians take their new positions. Once everyone was settled, they would crawl in and take the high ground. Tactical advantage.

***

Cade walked down the middle of the dirt road to the bikers in the rear of Frank Silvera's formation first.

Blake Sergeant sat crouched behind a boulder covering his partner and less than happy about giving up the higher ground. He scanned the hill behind him, but the rain was now pouring. It was the afternoon, but the October clouds were shielding out most of the sunlight. It looked like nightfall was a moment away. He didn't see anyone up there, but couldn't take the risk of exposing himself. He knew someone was behind them. He could feel it.

The first biker was dead. One of Blake's bullets blew through the man's bottom teeth and blasted through his spinal cord on its way back out his head. It was a perfect shot. The second guy also had a steady stream of blood and rain flowing down his face and getting caught up in his beard. He was unconsciously twitching. Cade put another bullet in his head for good measure.

"Cade," Blake whispered loudly. Cade only responded with an empty glare and walked to the second two bikers. The first man was wheezing loudly and struggling furiously to draw his sidearm holstered in his belt. Cade shot him in the forehead. The fourth biker was face down, still alive and muttering something under his breath. Cade walked in closer.

"My name is Special Agent Danny," he coughed, "Box with the DEA. I'm an undercover . . ."

Cade put a bullet in the back of his head.

"You were undercover," Cade growled.

He walked slowly to the edge of the dirt road and began traversing down the hill to where Frank Silvera's overturned Explorer landed.

***

"We need to kill him. We need to kill him and make it look like an accident, Frankie. Nobody needs to know." Billy Carbone'skull was cracked, and a broad stream of blood continued to run up his forehead, forming a puddle on the roof of the Explorer. Frank wheezed, breathed hard then looked at his brother-in-law, following the sound of his voice. They were both suspended by seatbelts and hanging upside down. Their faces were both smashed by airbags that probably saved their lives for the time being. Or at least Frank's.

Jerry Campanella's legs were in the back. As they were driving down the dirt road moments earlier, Campanella unbuckled his seatbelt and slid half of his body out the rear window of the vehicle, looking for the source of what sounded like gunshots. Seconds later, Blake Sergeant fired an AT4 at his vehicle.

The rocket flipped the Explorer on its roof just off the side of the dirt road, sending vehicle tumbling end-over-end down the mountain. Campanella instinctively tried to jump out of the vehicle, but his plan didn't work. Half of his body was still in the vehicle when the roof of the explorer first made impact. The explorer left pieces of Campanella splattered along the side of the mountain.

The Explorer tumbled down the hill, then fell ten feet from the final dropoff, landing on its side. The vehicle then slowly flopped on its roof. Inside the cab, the remaining fragments of Campanella's lifeless body laid on the roof of the cab.

Frank's left arm was likely broken from the airbag, but he was astonished to find he was still alive. That didn't change the fact that he felt like shit. He could taste blood and felt like he was going to throw up. His whole body felt like it was throbbing. He wasn't feeling pain, but more so an adrenaline-fused message from his brain telling him, *Listen Frank, you're not the spring chicken you used to be. Your body has sustained some damage. I need to break this news to you slowly . . .*

He could vaguely tell there was too much sunshine on the other side of the airbag. Most of the front of the car was gone. He turned his head toward Billy and quickly saw his partner in crime's delirium wasn't from an airbag. His legs were gone just below his knees and what was left was a pile of hamburger decorated with bone and shreds of denim that used to be his pants. His left arm was gone, too. Pieces of the dashboard panel were sticking out of his body. His right arm was still intact, but busted and mangled.

Frank stared at Billy and tried to force his head over to look at his own body. But when he turned his head, he just looked up. He didn't want to know. *It's bad Frank. It's bad.*

He heard footsteps from behind the vehicle.

"Wake up, Billy," Frank said. "We got trouble."

His mind was finally letting his body out of the fog he felt trapped in. He tried to unbuckle his seatbelt with his left hand, but it didn't respond. Something was wrong with his shoulder. He grabbed the door handle with his right hand, but nothing happened. The door was wedged shut, but the window was gone. The fog in his mind was back. He tried to think. He felt something smack his face, and saw stars again. He felt a pair of hands reach in under him and pop his seatbelt button.

His body fell forward, but didn't hit the roof of the car. Instead, he felt his stomach and legs wrapped around whomever reached across him to unbuckle his seatbelt. He heard someone yell "fuck."

Cade? He thought.

Cade drug his body out of the explorer and laid him out on the wet ground. The rain continued to fall. He tried to sit up, and flopped back on his back as pain shot through his entire body like glass shards. His back felt broken. His ribs were broken. His legs were numb, but he could feel his toes tingling. *That's a good sign, right?* He asked the voice in his head. *Your body's in shock, Frank. Just stay still.* Frank listened to the voice, although it wasn't like he had a choice. He breathed in and out and tried to assess the damage. He was hurt, but maybe it wasn't as bad as he initially thought. Maybe he just needed to wait for the shock from being whiplashed multiple times to subside.

Seconds later, Billy Carbone's body flopped next to him, minus two legs and one arm. He was no longer speaking in complete sentences. Only breathing heavily and mumbling,

"Oh fuck, Billy, what are we going to do?" Frank asked. Billy's eyes opened.

"We should have killed him Frank," he said lucidly. "Years ago."

"What the fuck is this, Frank?" Cade was back. "Look at me, you piece of shit!"

Frank tried to move but his body didn't respond.

"I don't think I can," he said helplessly.

Cade grabbed Frank and moved his whole body, and propped him up against the mangled explorer. Pain in the form of the heat of a thousand suns blasted through Frank's body as Cade moved him. Cade was rough, sitting him up like a bag of sand and dragging his legs under him. Frank screamed in pain, finally finding his voice.

He looked down and found his body was still intact. He could *feel* pain, which was good. That meant he wasn't paralyzed. He was banged up, and something was definitely wrong with his left shoulder. He looked Billy, who was in much worse shape, missing limbs and seemingly delirious.

Cade followed Frank's gaze and stared at Billy.

"Oh, that's just fucking gross," he said, then laughed.

"Hey Cade," Billy called out in barely a whisper.

Cade leaned forward, giving Billy his undivided attention.

"Fuck you, you little cocksucker!" Billy began laughing hysterically. "I never liked you. We should have killed you years ago, you little cunt."

And he laughed some more.

"Fuck me?" Cade asked. "Fuck me?!"

Cade walked over to Billy, and stuck the barrel of his pistol in his face.

"Say it again, asshole."

"Cade," Frank called out meekly. "Don't do it. Don't do it. We need to talk. Jesus, Cade."

Billy smiled at Cade with tears in his eyes.

"Don't do it Cade, Jesus!"

"Say it again," Cade growled.

Billy closed his eyes and smiled, quietly muttering what sounded like the Lord's Prayer to himself. Cade slapped him in the face and Billy opened his eyes.

Frank used his good arm to reach for his sidearm and only felt an empty holster. He exhaled helplessly. Billy ended his prayer and opened his eyes. His bloodshot eyes stared into Cade's and his blood soaked lips turned upwards to flash a gleeful smile. Teeth were missing and a stream of blood and snot flowed freely from his nostrils.

"Fuck you, you little prick," Billy said, then laughed again.

Cade squeezed the trigger, sending a bullet through Billy's right eye socket and out the back of his head.

Frank wept as the sound of the weapon echoed off the mountain.

"Oh, Billy," he cried. His right-hand man was dead.

"Now for you," Cade said, then he disappeared.

Blake followed Cade with the M-16 still in the ready position. He scanned the perimeter which only made him more anxious.

"Cade, we've given up the high ground," he said in a measured town as Cade carried a chainsaw toward Frank.

"We need to get back to high ground, we have limited . . ."

"Isn't this what you fucking wanted, you goddamned maniac?!" Cade yelled back, foaming at the mouth. "You wanted a fight? Now you've got it."

"I can't protect your ass when we have no visual on . . ."

"I fucking know!" Cade yelled. He stomped back over to Frank Silvera, who was weeping at the sight of his dead brother-in-law.

"Look what I found on my way down the mountain," Cade said, waving the chainsaw at Frank. "You just wanted to talk?! Since when do you bring a chainsaw to the conversation?"

Blake kept his rifle trained on the hill above him. He knew something was on the hill above him.

Frank inhaled, then exhaled deeply. He resigned himself to the fact that he was never making it off the mountain alive. He felt the rain pelting his face and breathed deeply again. Cade continued to scream in his face, and he only sighed in response.

"You're going to kill me, Cade," he finally said. "You've made that decision. There's nothing I can do about it."

Cade paused from his tirade and stared at Frank. His left eyelid trembled. Cade's eyelid always did that when he was in a rage, even when he was a sullen teenager.

"I wasn't going to kill you, Cade," Frank said. "We were never going to kill you. The Russians are after you. We were going to kill that sonofabitch standing next to you because he's fucking nuts, but never you."

Frank looked at Blake. His body was starting to come out of the fog of the wreck, but it was too late. He knew his fate was sealed.

"No offense son, but the shoe fits," Frank said to Blake.

Blake took his eye out of the sight of the rifle, looked at Frank.

"You're loyal as hell to this boy," he said. "More loyal than he deserves, but you're fucking crazy. Losing your family made you crazy."

Blake studied him for a moment. This was yet another moment he planned to discuss with Cade in depth if they made it out of their situation alive.

"Did you kill my father?" Cade asked.

"I wasn't going to kill you because we wanted to help you, son," Frank said.

"I'm not your fucking son!" Cade fired up the chainsaw and it started with the first pull of the choke. It was a brand-new chainsaw with that new tool smell still gleaming off it. "Did you kill my father?"

Frank didn't respond.

Cade fired up the chainsaw and brought it down toward Frank's leg.

"Yes! Jesus, yes!" Frank yelled.

Cade stopped.

"You knew that, Cade," Frank said exasperated. "You've always known that, and I've felt terrible about how that whole thing went down for twenty years now. I am sorry. After your mom got clean, she wanted to be in your life. She would have settled for visitation, but your old man wasn't having it. He moved back to Idaho where he knew damn well he was always going to get the benefit of the doubt in any custody battle. I came down to talk some damned sense into him and the son of a bitch broke my nose. Threatened my life. I was young and pissed off. So, when your uncle Billy cut his brake line, I didn't object. You know how young guys are. Then I thought about it, thought about it some more and said man, he's just a dad trying to protect his kid. Doesn't want his son getting into this type of life. Wants his kid to grow up and become an Idaho state trooper or a potato farmer. We thought you deserved better than that. And look at you, son, you did good, but you've never been happy.

"So we followed your old man and tried to stop him. Tried to warn him about his brakes. This was back when a few people had cell phones, but we weren't exactly exchanging numbers. We were trying to get him to stop, but your old man, he was a hothead. He saw us, got all pissed off, and tried to spin his car around or some shit. I don't know what he was trying to do, but he flipped the car. It went end over end and left him all busted up just like I am right now. He was dead. And god dammit Cade there's not a single fucking day I don't regret it.

"That's why I was never going to kill you. That's why when Wyatt Shepard told me you were coming to his place, I told him to tell you to stay the fuck there. Kill the crazy guy – sorry man – but keep Cade there. I don't know why the hell you're out here, but we were going to set up a real getaway plan where you could live a quiet anonymous life in Argentina, or Jamaica or wherever. Because I did this to you, and I am so sorry, Cade. I am so fucking sorry."

Frank Silvera began to weep, looking down at Billy's lifeless body.

"I was keeping it from your grandfather, and your uncle was helping because he always had my back. I don't know why your family wanted you back so bad. It was never gonna work. I told all of them. And I was right. You've been staring at us like a caged pitbull ever since we brought you back after your father's death. And you were right to feel that way. It wasn't supposed to go down like it did Cade. So, do what you gotta do son. I love you. I understand and I forgive you."

Frank hung his head down so he could wipe the tears from his eyes.

Cade didn't respond. He only stared at Frank expressionless.

Blake wasn't. He was scanning the hill above him with more intensity.

"Cade, that cop was asked to keep us at his house, and now we're here," he said. "We need to get to higher . . ."

Cade fired up the chainsaw and walked toward Frank Silvera. He revved up the engine and brought the blade down on his stepfather. Frank instinctively held up his good hand and the saw chewed through two fingers like a knife through melted butter. The blade came down on Frank's neck and splattered blood and skin all over the black Explorer. The saw jerked back a bit as it hit Frank's spinal cord. Cade yanked back as Frank's body twitched and convulsed. Cade laid into the throttle once more and cut through the bone. Frank Silvera's head flipped down and hung over his midsection as one flap of skin struggled to maintain structural stability. Cade used the saw to clip that last piece of loose skin and Silvera's head fell to the muddy ground next to his lifeless body.

"You're right," he said quietly, "you should have left us alone."

Cade looked at Blake, who stood with his rifle out of his shoulder.

"We gotta go," Blake said.

Cade's eyes widened, then they both heard a gunshot. Cade flew backwards and tripped over his uncle's body as the first seven millimeter round blasted through his shoulder. The second shot tore into his rib cage and took a meaty chunk of flesh and bone out of his back as he flew to the ground.

Blake pulled up his rifle and turned behind him, toward the sound of the noise. As Blake turned his head, something big and black crushed him in the face. It felt like a truck.

"Jesus, Mary and Joseph," Blake heard someone yell. It was a familiar voice.

He grabbed at his head where something hit him and felt an open wound just above his right eye socket. The skin was broken, but the bone probably wasn't. He would survive, though he was going to be covered in blood shortly. And it was going to hurt like hell for a while.

"Hoo, doggy," the voice called out in a howl, "he got the drop on you, crazyman! Mister talking in your sleep, crazyman."

Blake looked up and saw a big tall redneck in a state trooper uniform poking the business end of a winchester rifle in his face.

"Make a move, son," he said in a western accent. Not the kind you hear in a western, but the kind you hear from a man who's unemployed and living off his girlfriend's food stamps.

Blake fell backwards and rolled over intentionally, then crouched down with his knees under him. The redneck cop kicked his rifle away from him, but didn't yet see the hunting knife sheathed along his left leg. Blake faked a defeated roll to conceal the knife. His head hurt like hell, and he needed to plan his next move.

"Stop rolling," Griff called out. "I'm lookin' for a reason to fuck you up."

"You better watch out," Wyatt Shepard called out with a laugh. He held his rifle up using his left bicep and used his right hand to fish a hand-rolled cigarette out of his shirt pocket. "Ole Griff here was a linebacker for the BYU Cougars, back in the day."

Two other men followed Shepard and Griff out from the spot on the mountain where they had watched Cade attack Frank with a chainsaw. They didn't look like cops, not even by Wyoming standards. One man wore a weathered ten-gallon hat over a meaty face and a bushy silver mustache. The other man wore a ball cap, trucker's jacket and jeans. His face bore a red fleshy complexion that was only earned from years of heavy drinking. Shepard put his head down and lit his smoke with a zippo, trying to keep the rain from ruining his moment. He took a large drag and blew out a plume of smoke. The stench of marijuana filled the air.

"Fresh from the evidence locker," Shepard explained as he admired his joint, "I need this crime scene to smell like a drug deal gone bad."

The other men in his posse snickered as Shepard strutted confidently toward Cade.

"Jesus fucking Christ, look at this mess," Shepard howled. He walked around the vehicle looking at Campanella's mangled body, Billy's corpse and Frank Silvera's severed head. "I suppose we all got daddy issues of some sort, but some bitch, this is messy."

He looked at Cade Stuckley, who was reeling from his two new gunshot wounds, but still cognizant.

"Did you ever consider therapy? Forgiveness? Finding a way to let bygones be bygones? I heard Buddha has some good advice for that type of thing."

"Wyatt, what the fuck?" Cade gasped.

"Oh, now I'm the asshole?" Shepard yelled out. "You shoot a daggum rocket launcher at a man, then kill him with a chainsaw and I'm the asshole?"

Shepard took a deep drag from his joint and exhaled out his nostril over his circa 1983 mustache that was only still fashionable on the sex offender registry and in the great state of Wyoming.

"You know what I'm looking at?" he continued. "One billion rubles."

Chapter 37

Melody Slater sat in the dark garage, but occasionally fired up the engine to keep her warm. The garage was cold and dark. She was on her third cigarette. She didn't care anymore if Blake got mad at her for smoking in the car.

Outside her garage, it sounded like a warzone. Thunder and gunfire sent alternating audible shockwaves through her psyche like a cruel duet. She stared at her phone and the fourteen calls she ignored from Frank Silvera.

Frank met her in one of Angelo Carbone's clubs where she was a dancer. She had been on the circuit for nearly two years and it wasn't until a month before her eighteenth birthday when an eagle-eyed manager named Ruby Malloy spotted a discrepancy between her stated age and her driver's license.

She had been dancing since she dropped out of school her sophomore year. A more observant teacher would have noticed the telltale signs of dyslexia when she was young, but Melody was rotated through an educational system plagued by oversized classrooms like cattle. With a low self-esteem that was reinforced by years of academic underperformance, Melody learned two things about herself. Boys found her to be gorgeous and she was going to make a hell of a lot more money off her looks than her brains.

Within six months of dropping out, she was living in her own apartment. Within a year, she had squirreled away nearly ten thousand dollars in cash. When Ruby spotted Melody's real age, she didn't call Joey Carbone, the oldest of the Carbone boys. He was rough with the girls, and this one was just a couple months shy of her eighteenth birthday. Ruby called Joey's brother-in-law Frank Silvera, the level headed member of the Carbone-four. Joey was violent. Billy was stupid. Their sister Bette was crazy.

Guys like Joey and Billy were criminals because they were never going to be successful without breaking a few rules. Plus, it was the family business. Frank was a good boy, Ruby thought. His mom was a trucker and she raised him to be tough but compassionate. His love for Bette Carbone was what kept him coming to the trough. Frank helped Melody.

He gave her a job as his clerical assistant, whatever that meant, until she was eighteen, then returned her to an adult establishment. Joey never noticed. Frank continued to look after her from time to time mostly because she was a gorgeous young lady who would make them a ton of money if they could keep her semi-clean and single.

He was the closest thing she ever had to a father, but she was savvy enough to know that he viewed her as a commodity. Bette Silvera, who in private still considered herself Bette Stuckley, was the only woman Frank ever considered a human being.

Melody struggled with sobriety and Frank put her through treatment twice. After her second stint, he gave her a new life and a new purpose. He needed to keep her away from some bad influences. She was moving to Saint Paul. He had lined up a job for her at the King of Diamonds in Inver Grove Heights, but her real job was to keep an eye on her next-door neighbor, an ex-cop named Blake Sergeant.

Frank told Melody what he knew. Blake served with his stepson Cade in the Marines and was a cop. Family was murdered. He left the force and eventually became Cade's triggerman. The murder left him a little off, Frank said. He talked to himself. Talked in his sleep and had issues with memory. Cade told Frank once his friend seemed like he "had nothing to live for." It was Melody's job to keep an eye on him.

She did her job well in the two years as Blake's neighbor. She took copious notes of his activities and reported back to Frank. He was grief stricken just like Frank said. He barely seemed to notice her the first year they were neighbors. It wasn't until a guy she briefly dated decided to get violent with her. The violent boyfriend threw a dish across the house and smacked her in the face.

She heard a knock at the door, and was surprised to see Blake Sergeant standing there asking if there was a problem. Her boyfriend demanded that Blake mind his damn business or else. Three minutes later, his nose and jaw were broken. Blake was quietly dialing 9-1-1 and letting her boyfriend know he used to be a cop. He would ensure the guy spent some quality time behind bars if they ever saw each other again.

That's when Blake and Melody became friends. That was also when she began including fewer details about his day to day activities. She was always attracted to him, but in the last twenty-four hours, she found herself having feelings for Blake she didn't understand. She also knew they weren't mutual. Blake wasn't crazy, which is what Frank thought. He was haunted.

The gunshots paused for a moment. Lightning flashed and lit up the garage from the windows on the door, and that's when she first saw it. A shadow, or something that looked like a shadow. She peered into the darkness, squinting her eyes at the darkness in front of her. Something was moving, but what could it be? She couldn't tell. It looked like a man standing in front of her car.

She sat frozen in her seat, staring at the darkness in front of her. All of the lights were off. If lights were on, someone might know she was hiding in the garage.

Her instincts kept her rear end planted in the seat of the car. She took another drag from her smoke and flicked ash in an empty coffee cup from their road trip. Then she reached with her left hand and turned on the headlights. That's when she saw him.

His skin was pale white, almost blue and his hair was gray. His eyes were hollowed out. He wore blue winter overalls over a black flannel shirt. He stared at her with intensity.

The thing she saw moving was his arm, moving back and forth, back and forth, back and forth. His finger was extended and he was pointing at something.

She screamed out loud, then froze again, watching him glare at her and gnash his teeth, pointing with more intensity. She was staring at a ghost. A very real, honest to God ghost and he was pissed off.

He kind of looked like Blake. She followed the direction of his incessant pointing. It was a red, white and black sign that read "No Smoking."

"Okay! Okay!" She screamed. She exstinguished the cigarette in the coffee cup she was using as an ashtray, and he stopped pointing. He kept staring at her, though, with those hollow, bloodshot eyes.

"He doesn't like secondhand smoke," she heard a man say from her right. "It's weird. The man has been dead for nineteen years. It's not like he needs to worry about cancer. He was healthy when he was alive, provided you don't count the day he drank strychnine. He said he was forced to. I don't believe him."

The soldier leaned in closer, allowing a sliver of light from the garage window to help the car's dashboard lights show his face. His skin was course and leathery, the skin of a man who had spent an eternity outdoors under the sun.

"I've had the privilege of meeting his wife."

Melody turned in horror and threw herself against the driver seat door, shivering.

There was another man. No, it was a ghost. He wore an old tattered blue jacket like the guys from the wars in the history books she used to see as a child. But he had an old hat, shaped like a cowboy hat, but smaller. The brim was smaller and the whole hat was worn down without any of the pretentious nooks and crannies on the hats that country singers wore. His hat was old, and looked like it was used for what hats were supposed to be used for, keeping the sun out of his eyes. It looked gray, but was probably black when he bought it.

His hair was probably long, but it was tucked under his hat. She could see a few strands that managed to sneak out of the hat and over his left ear, the ear closest to her. He had a beard too, and sad eyes, but they weren't eyes at all.

When she looked closer for a moment, she realized they were like bodies of water attempting to shape themselves like eyeballs. It was a sad current, if that made sense.

"Melody," he said, "you haven't been incredibly honest with his son."

"Careful, man, your scaring her," a voice from the back seat commented.

She snapped her head behind her. There were two men in the back seat. One looked to be Hispanic. He studied her with curiosity. The other man was Native American, and he was bouncing up and down lightly in the seat of the Mustang.

"These seats are comfortable," he said to her.

They were ghosts, all of them. The man in front of the car had his hands on the hood of the Mustang. His glare was no longer hostile, but studious. The other three studied her as well.

"You're in danger if you leave, but you're welcome to stay with us for a while," the soldier said.

The door popped open behind her and she fell out of the car. The man in the coveralls walked around the car to meet her, and behind him was a plump older woman wearing a maid's dress. She had long curly hair that was pulled back using an old handkerchief. They approached her with curiosity.

She screamed again in horror and crawled to the garage door. They continued to follow her. Still on her hands and knees, she pulled the door open, then looked up. The Soldier was kneeling next to her.

"You shouldn't go out there," he said.

Melody screamed in response and rolled out from under the garage door.

The old soldier ghost that Deputy Chief Shepard told her about was real. He was a murderer, Shepard said. He was also scary. Shepard was right about that.

She also saw the Mexican and the Indian he spoke of. She didn't know who the other man and woman were, but she was not about to find out. She ran to the edge of the driveway, turned left and ran, never hearing the gunfire taking place in front of her.

The thunder was in a rage, but that didn't matter. Nothing mattered except getting as far away from those ghosts as her body would allow her.

Her legs pumped and pumped and pumped, heel to toe, one foot in front of the other. On any other day, her smoker's lungs would have let he know a couple hundred meters into her sprint that her running days were finite. Not tonight.

Tonight she ran and screamed, scared to death they were behind them. She didn't care about the rain. She didn't hear the hell in front of her. She kept thinking about those ghosts. Blake lied about the ghosts, she thought. *Why would he do that?*

***

"Keep your eyes on the targets, gentlemen," Byrd said as they watched the carnage below in horror.

Cade Stuckley was in a rage, dragging the bodies of the men out of the wrecked explorer, screaming and yelling throughout the process.

Byrd sat crouched behind his two shooters. Kim had Cade Stuckley in his crosshairs. Wisnewski had the big guy. Kim was crouched earnestly behind them acting as a backup.

Namin watched the operation with a thin-lipped smile, as his deputy, a brooding man named Kruznetsov, scampered from man to man on their perimeter, relaying orders. He never saw Natalie Maloney, who laid crouched in a muddy embankment a few meters behind the soldier on the left end of the perimeter. Nor did he see Gupta, whose rifle was aimed at the man on the right.

Cade Stuckley shot the guy with hamburger for legs in the head. And the other guy began crying.

"It is very nice of Mr. Stuckley to take care of a loyalty problem I was having," Namin said. "It doesn't absolve him of the trouble he has caused."

Byrd wanted Namin to stop talking, but knew he had to listen to it.

"Is he your better shooter?" Namin said, pointing to Wisnewski.

"Yeah," Byrd responded.

"Good. Because he's the one who killed Nicolay Belov," Namin said as he pointed to Blake Sergeant.

Byrd turned to look at him with surprise.

"Thought that was Stuckley."

"No, Stuckley runs their website. Him," Namin pointed to Blake a second time, who was watching Cade Stuckley with an expression of disgust that could be seen from the top of the mountain. "I saw him in the hotel that night wearing a suit. He walked right past me."

"You were on his security detail?" Byrd said, cracking a smile.

"On paper, yes."

"What does that mean?"

"Are you sure you want me to tell you why I was in New York City, comrade?"

Cade Stuckley fired up his chainsaw and brought it down on Frank Silvera's head.

The men watched as Wyatt Shepard got the drop on Blake and Cade. Shepard, wearing a camouflage poncho over his police uniform, was hooting and hollering in enthusiasm.

"What the fuck is this?" Byrd asked.

"Hold your fire," Namin said calmly. "The officer is with us."

***

"I trusted you," Cade groaned as he lay on the muddy embankment glaring at Shepard.

Lying a few yards away near the creek, Blake stared at the man they called Griff, who stared back. Blood poured down Blake's face, but he was undeterred. He was waiting for Griff to take his eye off the ball. He only needed a second.

"Oh, now you wanna talk to me about trust, do you?" Shepard called out. "Hell, I'm doing your ass a favor. When were you planning to tell your partner over there that you only have one getaway ticket up in Jackson? Had you figured that part out yet?"

Blake looked at Cade. They made eye contact and Cade looked down.

"Maybe you were just going to say, 'gee, Mr. Crazy Man, I'm sorry. I only got one ticket outta the country. You and that cute little brunette are on your own. Or maybe you were planning to cut his head off with a chainsaw too."

"What's he talking about Cade?" Blake asked.

Cade didn't answer.

"Oh yeah Crazy-man, Cade had some pretty nasty things to say about you," Shepard said. "He talked about how you talked in your sleep, saying crazy shit. The girl you were riding with was scared of you. He talked about how you had this whole bedroom with mugshots all over the walls and diaries with scribbled notes and shit."

Only he pronounced the word *shee-it.*

"How you drive around the country, step out of your car, blow people's heads off then lecture everyone around you about morality. I told him your old man was nuts, but he wasn't hearin' it. Anyway, it ain't my business, but I'll tell you what is. One billion rubles. Do you know how much that is?"

"Eighteen million dollars," Cade answered, "or seventeen depending on the currency rate."

Blake looked at Cade with amazement.

"Yeah, that's the bounty on your buddy's head, Crazy-man. It's the bounty on your head too. You were smart and careful when you killed Mr. Belov, but dipshit here bragged about it on his online deathpool. Called him a 'Russian kidfucker who thought he was above the law.'

"I know you think I owe you something on account of Blaine Crockett and all Cade, but it's eighteen million dollars. That's a lot of money."

"Sure is," Griff echoed.

Blake turned his eyes back to Griff and waited.

***

"You know," Namin said, "Mister sheriff down there is going to be entitled to a significant portion of the award."

"That's our money," Byrd said.

"Is it?" Namin asked with a bear toothed grin. He was probably in his thirties, but this was the first time Byrd noticed that his decayed teeth looked more like fangs.

That's when they heard a woman screaming.

***

Melody continued to run. She ran up the hill and rounded the corner. She thought she saw a wrecked bike and a man laying on the side of the road and paid it no attention. She kept running and screaming in the rain.

***

Shepard heard it too. He stopped talking and looked up.

Griff kept his rifle trained on Blake.

Shepard squinted into the late afternoon dark cloud cover and pouring showers. The rain was billowing into mountain in waves showering everything in its path. He squinted into the storm and saw her.

She was beautiful. She was wearing the gray windbreaker Blake bought that morning and jeans. her hair was pulled back into a ponytail, but he could see strands of loose hair pasted to her face by the rain.

"Bla-a-a-ake!" she called out. Over and over in terror.

Shepard threw his joint on the ground and smashed it out with his boot. He put the rifle in his shoulder and lined her up in his sights. He inhaled, then squeezed the trigger on the exhale.

***

"She is with them," Namin said.

Byrd nodded at Kim, and he aimed his rifle at her.

"Hold your fire," Namin said.

"So they can collect the award?!" Byrd responded.

He saw Shepard aiming at her as well, looking for a shot.

"Deputy Jackass can't make the shot," Byrd added. "You know it."

Namin studied the angle Shepard was at. The rain and wind smacked him in the face. He nodded at Byrd.

"Take the shot," Byrd said.

Kim giggled, like he always did before carrying out such an order then steadied his breath. He took his aim and fired.

***

McEvers was a father. He was a dad to two little girls before he was anything else. That was how he was wired. Gupta and Maloney knew it. He had been that way for years, ever since the first day he held his oldest daughter.

He, Gable, Gupta and Maloney arrived to the top of the mountain in time to watch Cade Stuckley execute the fourth of four bikers. The cop in him was sick of this bastard, and wanted to take him down.

That's why he was encouraged when he saw two local cops and some townsfolk creeping down the mountain as their rampage continued.

"Looks like we have a posse," he said into his mouthpiece. Gable, sitting right next to him, nodded and kept his rifle trained on Namin's back.

Gupta nodded as well in agreement seeing the same scenario and Maloney took their word for it. Crouched just feet away from the first of the Russians, she couldn't do much more.

"Let's keep our powder dry. If the gentlemen in front of us try to intervene, we'll light 'em up," McEvers said.

They winced in agony when Cade Stuckley attacked a man with a chainsaw and Sergeant stood behind doing nothing. They pumped their fists quietly when Shepard put two in Stuckley and his young partner smacked Blake Sergeant with the butt of his rifle.

One could write them up for excessive force, but nobody on the mountain was going to do that tonight. They had two other dudes with them who looked like local cowboys. The posse looked different, but they had all seen different before. Small towns were different.

The older cop was lecturing too much for McEvers' liking.

"Cuff him," Gupta said quietly.

Nobody disagreed.

"Cuff 'em goddammit," Gupta repeated.

"I don't think they plan on arresting them," Gable said quietly. The cops kept their sights trained on the Russians and mercenaries. They were doing nothing to intervene.

"I don't think they're on our side," McEvers added.

Then came the screaming.

Then came the girl. She was unarmed. She was scared. She was running and screaming at the top of her lungs and she was screaming for Blake.

The sheriff pointed his rifle at her.

"He's gonna shoot her," McEvers said to himself out loud. "Don't do it," he pleaded quietly.

The sheriff fired.

Chapter 38

They felt like bee stings.

Melody ran. Her lungs begged her to quit, but her legs and brain were dead set against it. All she could think about was the ghosts.

The man who looked like Blake. The creepy soldier with the leathery face. The laughing Indian and the silent Mexican. Then there was the old woman behind them.

It was all so horrible.

Something cracked against the rocks next to her. She instinctively looked toward the direction of the sound, then felt the first bee sting. She was stung by a bee once, as a child. She remembered crying herself to sleep in her mother's lap. The next day, she remembered thinking about the pain, but wondering if the fear of a bug perhaps enhanced it.

The sting hit her in the side. She was startled, but undeterred. She was running. The second hit her chest. It felt like something bit her with the strength of a baseball, but it felt like a bee.

Her chest felt tight, but she willed herself to keep running.

The third bullet went through her windpipe and ripped her breath from her lungs. This one knocked her down. She tried to catch her breath but couldn't. Her throat filled with fluid. She tried to cough but only gargled. She couldn't breathe.

She fell to her hands and knees and started choking. Those weren't bee stings.

She wasn't afraid of the ghosts anymore. As she heaved and choked, she realized sitting in a garage with the undead was the safest place on the mountain.

I tried to warn you, she heard the soldier say. He was kneeling next to her. She could feel his presence. *Stay calm my dear.*

She was going to die on that mountain.

She heard the sheriff yelling. She heard another man scream. Then more gunshots. She gurgled again, fighting for a breath that wasn't going to come. Intuitively she knew it, but it's hard to tell a body to stop fighting for life even when the mind knows the party is over.

She felt a warm hand on her back, and knew it was one of the ghosts – the soldier. The hand felt warm and soothing.

Such a sweet girl, he said without saying a word. She could hear him in her mind and wasn't afraid. *This isn't the first-time innocent blood has been shed on this mountain, and you were innocent my dear. You were innocent.*

A single tear rolled down her cheek and although her body heaved and choked in anguish, her mind was at peace.

She felt something else punch her in the back, then through the side of her neck. The last punch felt like a light switch turning her off.

The soldier stood and stared down the mountain. He could see the cop. He could see into his soul.

His eyes turned from water to flames. He stepped to the edge of the road.

This is my curse, he said. In one movement, he leapt down the mountain.

***

Wyatt Shepard knew he missed as soon as he squeezed the trigger. He pulled up. The bullet might hit the rocks near her if she was lucky, but it was a miss.

"Sheeit," he said under his breath.

He quickly regrouped and brought his sights back to the girl when he heard gunshots from the mountain.

"Hey!" He yelled.

They were quick shots, consistent with a trained shooter's breath, and every round sent downrange was a hit. She ran through the first shot, but the second one slowed her down. The third shot dropped her to her hands and knees.

"Hey, God dammit!"

Shepard aimed his rifle at the girl, who was on her hands and knees panting, struggling to catch her breath. As soon as she was in his sights, he squeezed the trigger, sending a seven-millimeter round through her throat.

He saw her head jump. He saw blood spray out the back of her neck, and he watched as her head fell stupidly to the side, taking her body with it in clumsy fashion.

He killed her. That piece of the reward was his.

"We had a deal. We had a fucking deal!"

He continued walking toward the mountain yelling.

***

"No!" McEvers said loudly.

He was always a father.

They felt the same tense moment the mercenaries were feeling at that very moment. The mercenaries knew they weren't alone. The cops knew the mercenaries knew they weren't alone.

McEvers fired three shots into Kim's back, smashing him into the rock wall.

Byrd and Namin ducked for cover as Gable fired at them. Gable's first round hit the rock. His second round blew through Namin's left shoulder blade, flipping him on his back.

Maloney pounced on her first target, both knives drawn, plunging them both into the neck of the Russian she had been perched behind. She yanked one blade forward and the other toward her. Blood poured onto her right hand as she went in for another laceration to finish the job.

Gupta fired two rounds into the back of the head of the Russian on the opposite end of the perimeter.

Their first volley was enough to let the Russians and Gayton Security know they were in for a fight.

***

Blake and Griff remained locked in eye contact, with the muzzle of Griff's AR-15 in Blake's face. Blake didn't flinch when he heard the screaming.

He didn't flinch when he recognized Melody's voice. He didn't flinch when he realized Melody was calling his name. He and Griff remained locked on each other like a serpent staring at a mongoose.

He heard Wyatt miss, and mutter to himself and he heard the other shots.

Blake bit his lip, knowing what was happening. He felt rage. Griff's eyes widened.

He heard Wyatt yelling about a deal, then he heard more shots.

Griff glanced toward the commotion out of the corner of his eye.

Whatever he saw was enough to compel his eyes to widen. His sideway glance turned to a stare.

Blake reared his leg back and mule-kicked Griff's leg just above his ankle. It wasn't a move of grace, but of brute force, designed for one purpose. His heal crashed through Griff's leg like he was stomping a branch from a tree. Griff's tibia and fibula snapped and he screamed in pain.

Blake wasn't going to have time to reach for his weapon. Not with three other men nearby with rifles.

He darted for the creek, and jumped in.

He heard gunshots behind him, and thought he heard a bullet impact the mud next to him as he dove for cover.

He pulled himself to the side of the creek with only his head above water. He flushed his body flat against the weathering from the current and grabbed the roots above him for leverage.

The rain had turned the quiet creek into a raging river. Rapids raced over his shoulders. He waited for gunshots to follow him and didn't hear any. That didn't make sense.

He unsheathed his knife with his right hand. He pressed his boots to the inner wall of the river. He was ready to strike.

Melody Slater was dead. Cade was planning to fuck him over all along.

Everybody on the mountain was going to die tonight.

***

Wisnewski jumped when he heard the gunfire behind him and squeezed the trigger. He had the perfect shot. As he squeezed the trigger, his target kicked the younger cop. The cop spun, and Wisnewski's bullet caught the cop in the stomach, sending the man to his back, screaming in agony.

"Ah shucks," he yelled, then aimed again. Sergeant was diving for the creek. This was it.

Wisnewski aimed, then his shot was blocked again, this time it was a woman.

His first thought was *She is hot!*

The second thought was, *what the heck?!*

It was the Harvester. She was in a white robe with her arms extended. She was coming up the hill. Not walking. Not crawling. She was gliding. There was a ball of fire in her right hand and she was swinging it at the muzzle of Wisnewski's rifle. He was frozen.

"Not today!"

The rifle turned a magnificent orange, then gleamed with a light that was as bright as the sun. Wisnewski let go, screaming. Both of his hands felt like they were on fire and so did his right cheek, just below his eye. He fell back gripping his face in pain.

The Russian Maloney was sneaking up on next turned and fired his weapon at her. His partner knelt back to back from him, firing at Gupta to end the systematic takedown of their perimeter. Maloney ducked, sheathed her knives and drew both of her pistols in one smooth motion.

As she prepared to pounce, another Russian jumped behind the embankment with her and squeezed his trigger.

This is it, she thought, then it wasn't. The bullet hung suspended in air a foot from her face. Rain was falling on it. She reached her hand up and tapped the bullet. It fell harmlessly to the ground.

The Russian gunman was staring at something behind her and stood in horror. She fired two shots from each pistol and watched him fall back. She rolled to another crevice in the mountain she spotted earlier, and turned to look at where she was. The Russian mercenary she shot was distracted by something behind her. Now she saw what he was looking at.

***

"My reward, dammit!" Wyatt yelled.

He fired another bullet into Cade Stuckley for emphasis. Cade screamed out in pain, then stared up into the sky in amazement.

The Soldier landed on both feet behind Wyatt.

"You should spend more time listening to the ghost stories you tell."

He snatched Wyatt's rifle out of his hand and threw it into the creek.

He turned to face the two ranchers that acted as Wyatt's security detachment.

"You gentlemen have a choice. If you run now, I'll only turn your hair white. Stay and fight, I will cut you down and take your souls."

The younger cowboy didn't buy it. He drew his weapon.

The Soldier's eyes turned to fire and he raced to the cowboy who was midway through a drawing ritual he perfected on the shooting range. He never finished.

With one swoop, the Soldier brandished a blade of fire and severed the man's arm. As he screamed and backed away in shock, the Soldier cut him again, this time bringing his blade down diagonal across the man's body from right shoulder to left hip. The cowboy fell to the ground in two piles of flaming meat.

In the backdrop, the Soldier saw Blake Sergeant diving into the creek after kicking the leg out from the other dirty cop. Blake peaked up from the creek and his eyes met the Soldier. Though he felt the man's presence many times in his youth, this was the first time he ever saw him.

A coin popped up from the dead cowboy's body and landed in the Soldier's outstretched hand. He tipped his hat to Blake and gave him a wink.

The solider turned his attention to the second rancher who stood in shock, staring at what had just transpired.

The Soldier pointed at him with a flaming right index finger.

"This is your last chance to fuck off."

The old cowboy gave a nod, threw down his rifle and ran like hell up the mountain where he came from. As he sprinted, his greying mustache and hair underneath his ten-gallon hat turned a glorious shade of white.

***

Griff writhed in pain as unapologetic showers of rain poured over him. His leg was busted and his midsection burned in pain where he had taken a bullet.

He looked to his right to see some old cowboy set his friend Skeet on fire, or at least that's what he thought he saw. The whole world was going to hell before his eyes. Another round of gunshots erupted near him, and he crawled for cover. As he was moving, he realized he was crawling toward the creek.

That's where the crazy man slithered, Griff thought. *Just like a snake.*

"I'm gonna kill you, motherfucker," Griff growled every time he advanced his body closer to the creek in agonizing pain. The cadence helped him as he dragged his broken leg toward Sergeant using his one good shoulder.

***

The Soldier walked toward Wyatt with unhinged focus.

Wyatt drew his sidearm and fired at the Soldier. The bullets whizzed past him.

"Wyatt, you know I'm a ghost, right?"

He grabbed the deputy chief and shoved him to the ground.

"I want you to watch this," the Soldier said as he turned Wyatt's head to the creek where his trooper Officer Griff Abbott was crawling toward the water. Blake Sergeant sat crouched in in the creek bed. The river current thrashed against his body, but he didn't budge. He was watching Griff's every move.

From his vantage point, Wyatt could see Griff had no idea what he was crawling into.

"Griff!" Wyatt yelled out, and Griff looked his way.

Blake pounced. He grabbed Griff Abbott by the back collar of his jacket and spun him around. Griff swung his good arm around, holding the pistol, and tried to aim at Blake. This was his one shot, but his movement only added momentum toward the direction Blake wanted him to go.

He landed on his back and raised his pistol for a second attempt.

Sergeant was standing on a foothold on the side of the creek, and he brought his dagger down. He stabbed Griff two inches below his navel, but above his genitals, and pulled the knife toward him, fileting the cop like he was cleaning a fish. Lightning struck, and creating a silhouette of Blake Sergeant as he brutally stabbed Shepard's young protégé, a second time. All Wyatt could do was watch.

As he brought the knife down for a third time, Blake slid back into the water and allowed his own body's momentum to rip the knife across Griff's midsection.

Griff's good arm flailed about stupidly dropping the pistol as he screamed. Blake pulled him closer to the creek. Blake sheathed his knife, then stuck his fist into Griff's open wound. Blake grabbed a fistful of Griff's intestines. He ripped up and listened to Griff scream in agony. He showed the young deputy his own entrails and yanked them upward again for effect.

"BYU Sucks!" Blake yelled as he dove back into the current with Griff's entrails grasped tightly in his right hand.

He disappeared into the water as Griff lay on his back, continuing to scream in agony. As he writhed on the ground, the slick grassland gave way underneath him. The creek's current picked up, and Griff's body slid into the water. He screamed until the rainwater filled his lungs and swept his body away.

This was the second time Wyatt distracted Griff in less than a moment and both instances had dire consequences.

"I think you pissed him off," the Soldier said into Wyatt's ear, "and he's coming for you."

Wyatt began to weep helplessly.

"He doesn't get you," the Soldier continued. "Your soul belongs to me."

The Soldier simply touched Wyatt's shoulder. Wyatt's entire body locked up in a seizure like trance. His spine arched and he wheezed as every ounce of oxygen left his body. His blood began to boil internally. Vessels started bursting, creating red, then black striations on his face like small spider webs. His eyeballs exploded in their sockets and his body went limp as the Soldier's touch sucked the life out of him.

Wyatt's body collapsed, falling to the ground like a deflated balloon. A coin popped out of Shepard's back and the Soldier caught it.

This is our curse.

Blake climbed out of the creek downstream from where he dispatched Officer Griff Abbott. He saw the gunfight taking place at the top of the mountain, but he was beyond thinking about tactics. He was after Cade Stuckley.

As he pulled himself up, the Soldier offered him a helping hand.

"I know you want to talk to your old partner," the Soldier said, "but we still have some work to do."

The both looked to the top of the mountain where gunshots continued to echo into the darkness. Blake knew in an instant there were men on top of the mountain who intended to do evil. He didn't know who they were. He didn't need to. All he could think about was Melody. Someone up there shot her. That was all he needed to know.

Blake looked back to the Soldier and another man who was walking up to join them. It was the ghost of Neal Sergeant and he was holding two daggers.

"Dad?" Blake asked.

"There will be time for this as well," the Soldier instructed. "You two are the welcoming committee. I will be sending you the party guests."

"Let's harvest," Neal Sergeant said in the same strained, raspy voice he bared in his last year on earth.

In an instance, Blake was back in the enthusiastic, wicked mindset where he found the most comfort these days. *Killing is the only thing I've ever been good at.*

Like two animals, they darted out of sight and waited at the bottom of the mountain.

Chapter 39

McEvers, Gable and Gupta continued to exchange fire with the Byrd and his men as well as the Russians. Maloney and Gupta successfully dispatched three when the fighting started, and Maloney was making her way back to their side.

McEvers took out the Asian male shortly after he shot the young lady running down the street. Gable clipped the short Russian who appeared to be in charge of their operation while aiming for Byrd.

One of Byrd's men appeared to have accidentally deployed an illumination grenade, burning himself in the process. That's what it looked like from their vantage point. He fell to the ground screaming, but had since grown silent. Gable could have sworn he saw a woman in a white dress approaching that individual, but his mind wasn't accepting what his eyes witnessed. No time to process now. They were in battle.

Four dead. One likely dead. Two injured. That left nine who could still potentially shoot back.

The Russians on the left side of their perimeter were making their way up the hill slowly amid cover fire. Gupta and McEvers alternated occasional shots, but their ammunition was finite. They were also still outnumbered two to one.

"We need to come up with something if we wanna get out of this jam alive," Gupta said.

"Guys," Maloney said, joining their side, "I saw something."

"So did I," Gable said, thinking about the woman. The words left his mouth before he could take them back.

"Right now we got bigger problems," McEvers said as he fired another shot, but the Russian mercenary he aimed at was already behind the rock he was using for cover.

"You missed, man," McEvers heard a voice behind him he didn't recognize and turned slowly. He saw a Native American man wearing leather leggings and a buckskin shirt under what looked like a breechcloth jacket. The clothing didn't look like anything that anyone from any tribe had worn casually for decades, maybe longer. His skin was dark and leathery, and his eyes were a deep unnatural green that seemed to brighten up as he flashed a creepy smile. "Were you aiming for the rock?"

"Holy shit, that's a ghost," Maloney yelled. "That's a ghost." She kicked herself up against Gable's side

"Yeah and I just saved your ass back there," said another ghost. This one was Hispanic wearing a leather jacket with leather streamers hanging off the shoulders. "You're safe."

They all four stared for a moment in awe, when another stream of gunfire interrupted their moment, smacking the boulders they were hiding behind. Gable rolled over and returned fire at the Russians.

"I don't feel safe," Gable groaned as he reloaded.

"We're up, Moki," the Hispanic ghost said, and they both leapt effortlessly over the boulders Gable and the cops were hiding behind.

Kruznetsov saw them first, as he was getting ready to send a fresh round of bullets toward whomever was shooting at them.

The Hispanic ghost and the Native American they called Moki walked toward them. As they progressed, the brunette with the glowing white dress who Gable saw a moment before joined them and began approaching the remaining mercenaries.

The Russian they called Sergi began firing first. The three ghosts continued walking undeterred.

Gable, Gupta and McEvers looked at each other, shrugged and provided cover fire behind the ghosts, making sure not to hit them.

Kruznetsov yelled out an order in Russian and his comrades began firing at the ghosts. Byrd and the remaining mercenaries looked at him with confusion. Kruznetsov huffed angrily and rolled his eyes.

"Kill the Village People," he yelled at Byrd.

"Did he say Village People?" Moki asked the Hispanic ghost, who smiled as they approached. Moki increased his stride and approached Kruznetsov, ignoring the flurry of bullets being fired through him. Not at him. Not into him. Through him.

Moki smacked Kruznetsov's rifle out of his hand with a swat, and lifted him by his throat.

"Village people?" he yelled with anger. "That's racist, man."

Moki threw Kruznetsov into the air. His body flew twenty feet into the storm, then down the hill. He soared over the fighting hole, over the dirt road and made impact on the hill near where the Explorer had tumbled end over end. He bounced on impact and rolled helplessly down the hill. Kruznetsov brought his arms and legs together in a crouched position as he started rolling in hopes of preventing any broken limbs. He felt the wind get knocked from his lungs, but had been through worse. He needed to stop his fall.

He tumbled off the hill, down the ten-foot drop, and landed next to the explorer. He didn't have time to think. Just fall. He rolled on his stomach and struggled to catch his breath. Between the Indian throwing him and the last drop off, he had two ten-to-twenty foot falls within seconds of each other.

He heard something flash past him. He thought he saw movement out of the corner of his eye. He turned and looked, but didn't see anything. Another man dropped off the embankment and landed about ten feet away from him.

"Olav," he said curtly, the combination of a yell and a whisper.

Olav groaned and rolled to his stomach, then groaned again.

"Olav!" Kruznetsov said again.

Another man landed behind him, the man they called Sergi. Olav finally looked up and saw Kruznetsov holding up his closed fist, their patrol signal for freeze.

They heard something dart past them again.

"Who the hell are you guys?" Kruznetsov heard someone yell.

He looked over and saw Cade Stuckley laying helplessly on his back looking at him.

Then they heard a swoop, a slash and another swoop. Kruznetsov looked back at Olav, who was still on his hands and knees. His tongue was sticking out and his face was shaking as he fought for air. His throat had been slashed.

Another man flew off the ledge. This man bounced off the wrecked Explorer. His head smacked the rear axle and cracked open as his body bounced onto the ground. He was dead on impact.

A loud cheer came from the top of the mountain.

Kruznetsov heard the sound again.

Swoop. Slash. Swoop.

He turned.

Sergi was screaming, only it came out sounding like a soft whistle. His throat was sliced from ear-to-ear. He heard a swoop behind him and he dove forward on his knees and elbows. He winced from a sharp pain in his side, or maybe it was his back. He turned around to look for the source of the sound and saw nothing.

He heard another swoop and looked back, this time long enough to see the big guy, the one they called Blake, dart to the other side of the wrecked Explorer. Only he wasn't running. He was galloping, pouncing, it appeared, and he was fast.

Knowing Blake was probably on the other side of the Explorer, Kruznetsov came up to a kneeling position with his boot on the ground and his other knee still down, and reached for his side arm, keeping his eye on the car. He heard a swoop behind him and went back down to his knees and elbows.

He felt something knick the back of his scalp and rolled over. He didn't see who came behind him, but it couldn't be Blake. Blake was behind the car.

He rolled over twice and fished out his pistol. He pointed at the wrecked car.

There's two of them, he thought.

Another man fell from the ridge and crashed to the ground. It was one of the Americans.

Kruznetsov jumped to his knees and was rising to his feet, and his first instinct was to run to the American. He realized the man was hurt badly. *Bait,* he thought.

Blake swooped out from behind the Explorer. He looked up. Kruznetsov aimed his pistol.

Swoop.

Two blades went into his neck, one from the left and the other from the right.

He watched Blake Sergeant slice the American's throat and look up at him with a smile.

Gotcha.

That idea about a decoy was a good one. He felt a jerking motion, then darkness.

Kruznetsov didn't get the chance to hear Blake Sergeant say the word, "cool," as his head fell from his body and bounced in the mud.

Coins popped up from the assailants' corpses. Blake and his father promptly caught them in midair.

***

Moki and the Hispanic ghost, Hector, and the Harvester systematically threw each of the Russians off the mountain plunging to their deaths at the hands of Blake and the ghost of his father, who the ghosts referred to as Strychnine.

Gable, McEvers, Gupta and Maloney realized early into the process that the ghosts did not require suppressing fire. They witnessed the systematic takedown of their opponents with jaws dropped.

"How exactly am I supposed to put this in a police report?" McEvers said. Gable thought of A.K.'s report and Cavalera's reaction. That felt like a long time ago.

Byrd and Namin remained on the mountain, each nursing gunshot wounds courtesy of Gable and McEvers. They were each still holding weapons, but making no attempt to fire at the ghosts. They were prisoners of war.

"I can't believe he said Village People," Moki groaned as they stood over the Russian and the mercenary. "Did he say Sitting

Bull? Geronimo? Crazy Horse? No. Fucking Village People. That's racist as hell, man."

"Shut up Moki," Hector said.

"You wouldn't be dismissing my civil rights if he insulted your Mexican ass," Moki said. "If he said Ricky Martin or some shit, I'd have your back. I hope Strychnine killed his ass."

"He did," the Soldier said as he joined them from behind. "Cut his head off."

Moki responded with a smile and a raised fist.

"Stupid ass Russian," Moki continued. "I'm glad Rocky kicked Ivan Drago's ass."

"That's enough," the Soldier and Hector said simultaneously. Moki smiled. He loved getting under their skin.

"Go to hell!" Namin yelled as he raised his weapon. Surrendering didn't agree with him.

The Soldier raised his hand and pointed at Namin, whose hand snapped to his side. The soldier pointed to the ground and Namin dropped to his knees.

"You've got a lot of anger in you," the Soldier said.

Namin glared up at him.

"I am only kneeling because of your dark magic," he snarled. "Well then by all means," the Soldier held up his hands, and released Namin.

Moki and Hector smiled. The Harvester shook her head.

Namin stood up on his own. His shoulder throbbed, but his other arm felt fine.

"What now, tough guy?" the Soldier asked.

Namin gave the Soldier the same smirk he had been giving Byrd for the past twenty-four hours. He took a step back, then threw a sucker punch, connecting with the Soldier's jaw. The Soldier didn't budge. He only looked at Namin with an expressionless stare.

Namin's hand felt cold. He raised his fist and watched as his skin turned dark navy blue. He opened his hand in horror and watched helplessly as the dark blue spread up his arm. It felt like a horde of ants eating away at his flesh. He began to scream as the dark blue complexion spread up his shoulder, his neck and his face. His spine buckled and he fell backward, hitting the ground unceremoniously.

His arms and legs twitched upward uncontrollably up and down, up and down as if he were marching in place on the ground. He arched his back again and let out a gargled wheeze as his eyeballs exploded, and he was gone. A coin popped out of his chest and into the Soldier's hand. The coin was blackened as if it were dipped in tar.

"Wow," the Soldier said, "haven't seen a soul this tarnished in a long time."

He nodded at Hector, who walked behind Byrd. Anthony Byrd was still on his hands and knees, bleeding and watching Namin's deceased body continue to wither away before his eyes. Hector grabbed Byrd by the scruff of his neck and threw him in front of the cops.

"I believe you have a score to settle with this one," the Soldier said.

"That is correct, sir," Gable said.

"He took one of yours," the Soldier said to Gable. He then looked at McEvers, Maloney and Gupta. "Your partner is going to live."

They stared at him with amazement.

"He can't leave the mountain alive, Agent Gable," the Soldier said. "When you're finished, you are going to get back in your car and return to your respective jurisdictions. Do we have an understanding?"

"We also have some unfinished business with Blake Sergeant and Cade Stuckley if they're still alive."

"No," the Harvester interjected, "you don't."

Gable looked at the two ghosts and at the carnage around them. The rain was finally dying down to a mild shower. He could faintly hear sirens in the background.

"I hope this isn't going to be a problem," the Soldier said.

"No problem," McEvers interjected. "No problem at all, gentlemen."

"Good," the Soldier said.

Hector, Moki and the Harvester were all three standing at the crest of the hill looking down at the creek and the pile of bodies that Blake Sergeant, Cade Stuckley and Strychnine dispatched.

The Soldier looked over his shoulder.

"Remember, he doesn't leave the hill alive."

They all nodded in acknowledgement.

"Semper Fi," the Soldier said.

The four apparitions then leapt off the mountain, headed for the creek.

The cops turned their attention to Byrd, who was pointing a pistol at them. He squeezed the trigger, and the bullet jammed.

He stared at his sidearm in confusion, then looked up just in time to see Steve Gable's fist. Gable's first punch shattered Byrd's nose. He followed with an uppercut that smashed Byrd's teeth together with a clatter. Byrd stumbled backward with stars in his eyes as Gable closed in, punching him in the right temple.

Byrd fell to the muddy ground and coughed in pain. He rolled over, holding up his right hand, and begged Gable to stop. Every punch Gable threw felt like a stone club bashing him in the head.

The beating stop, and Byrd looked up to see Gable standing over him with his weapon drawn.

"That was for every day one of my Marines spent behind bars because of your bullshit," Gable growled, and fired one round between Byrd's eyes. "That was for Cavalera."

A coin popped out of Byrd's lifeless body and fell down the mountain.

Gable stood, surveying the wreckage around him. McEvers walked up behind him.

"Next time you decide to get in a pissing match with four killer ghosts," he said, "don't."

Gable smiled and listened to the officers' laughter.

"Let's get the hell out of here," Gupta said.

They walked down the opposite side of the hill to where Gable hid their vehicle, glad to be alive.

***

Blake Sergeant embraced his father tightly and they stayed that way for a moment. They stared at each other, taking in the reunion.

"There is so much I want to say, and so much I want to know," Blake said.

"There will be a time," Strychnine responded.

The police sirens were getting louder.

"Are those cops?" Cade called out. He was still laying on the ground surrounded by puddles of mud.

Blake and Strychnine walked from the creek that was still overflowing to where Cade was still lying next to the overturned Explorer.

"You've got to get me out of here," Cade said. He tried to prop himself up and fell back down to his back. "There's still time."

Blake looked at his father who didn't respond.

"Is it true?" Blake asked. "Were you planning to fuck me over?"

"No," Cade groaned. "Wyatt didn't know shit. He was trying to divide us."

Cade coughed and winced again.

"You haven't been straight with me, Stuckley," Blake responded. "You haven't been straight with me about a lot of shit. As soon as I said I had a premonition about Jackson, you flipped out. What is it you're so afraid about me learning?"

"I can explain everything, Blake. If you can get me out of here, we can make this work. We've made a lot of money, and now we can split it two ways."

"Now?" Blake asked.

"Just help me up, man, we've gotta go. You had your fight, and I'm all busted up . . ."

"He can't leave the mountain," the Soldier called out from behind.

Blake turned to face him. The Soldier was flanked by Hector, Moki, Strychnine and the Harvester.

"Look, he's an asshole," Blake said. "He's a lying motherfucker, but he's also a friend."

"This isn't a debate," the Soldier responded, cutting him off. "And you're not a Harvester, yet."

Blake looked to the Harvester, who nodded in agreement. Blake thought about reaching for his dagger, but knew he wouldn't be able to do anything to change the outcome. Cade was going to sell him out. Instead, he was the one who was going to have to walk away.

"Look at you, all grown up," the Soldier said and his men agreed. His brow furrowed and his eyes narrowed. "But you've still got a lot to learn. You also have work to do."

He walked to where Cade was laying.

"You're still only seeing what you wanna see with this one," he said. Cade looked up cautiously. Strychnine glared at him then back at Blake. He shook his head side to side with a look of disgust on his face. He then looked back to the Soldier.

Blake nodded. He understood. He didn't have all the facts, but he understood.

"I'm also going to need those souls in your pocket," the Soldier said.

Blake looked down, fished out two coins and held them out. Hector produced a small leather knapsack and Blake dropped them in.

"Blake?" Cade called out quietly.

Blake looked at Cade.

"I'm sorry," he said. "There's nothing I can do."

The sirens were getting louder. The Harvester joined Blake's side.

"We have to go," she said.

Strychnine stepped forward and gave his son another hug.

"You're doing the right thing," he said into Blake's ear.

"Blake, where are you going?" Cade called out.

Blake and the Harvester began walking along the stream, away from the group. The sirens were a moment away.

"They won't see us," she said before Blake could ask about picking up their stride.

"Blake, you can't leave me here," Cade called out as the Soldier and his men closed in on him. "Blake, we are partners goddammit. I can explain everything."

Strychnine walked toward Cade with his fists clenched.

"I think we all know that's bullshit," the Soldier said to Cade, "and his old man hates it when you lie to him."

Cade was undeterred.

"Blake!" he yelled out. "Blake!"

"He's going to know the truth soon," Strychnine said. "He'll know everything."

"Wanna do the honors?" the Soldier asked Strychnine, then handed him a dagger.

"Blake, God dammit," Cade screamed out.

Blake and the Harvester kept walking away. He heard Cade's screaming, and then he didn't. He only heard the "ping" sound that a coin made when it popped out of the body of a dead man. Cade Stuckley was dead.

"Amelia," the Soldier called out.

The Harvester looked back, only this time, she no longer had two seas of fire where her eyes should have been. She had big brown eyes. They looked like the eyes of a child.

"Yes?" she asked. A tear was forming under her right eye.

"Don't be a stranger," the Soldier said. His eyes were soft and brown as well. They were full of life. "There's always a seat at the table for you."

"I won't," she said, "and I know."

As they continued to walk, Blake looked at her with curiosity. The eyes of fire were back, and she was putting on her sunglasses.

"I take it they're harvesters, too?"

"Yes," she responded.

"But they can't leave the mountain?"

"That's correct," she responded. "They're ghost harvesters and this mountain is cursed. You gave them the souls you captured not just because you're not a harvester yet, but because that's etiquette."

"How is it cursed?"

"Remember how I mentioned the balance between good and evil?"

Blake nodded.

"A lot of unspeakable evil has transpired on this mountain. When that happens, a bubble is formed and souls are trapped, unable to move onto the afterlife. Good souls. Evil souls. The Harvesters collect the evil souls, which is what happened today. They'll never be able to collect enough to restore balance in their bubble because they're trapped, just like everyone else. If you would have died, you would have been trapped too."

Blake thought of his father.

"How do you break the curse?"

"By restoring balance," the harvester said as she stopped walking. Blake stopped with her.

The first squad car arrived on the scene and the others were rolling in as well.

"You have to go," she said and she touched his shoulder. In an instance, Blake was standing in front of his old garage. The door was open and the Mustang was backed in.

Chapter 40

Blake Sergeant sat in the driver's seat of the Mustang thumbing through his old CD booklet looking for an album to listen to. He didn't want to hear the news. He wanted to clear his mind. He fished out *The Fury of Our Maker's Hand* by Devildriver.

He found the keys on the ground next to the garage door where Melody dropped them the moment she found herself face to face with the Soldier. He knew about the ghosts. They never bothered him.

His encounters were feelings. A warning of danger. An occasional prank. That was probably Moki. The most prominent feeling, however, was a feeling that he was welcome.

He could still hear the sirens wailing in the distance, but knew he wouldn't be bothered. The police would be canvasing the bloodbath left in his wake for a decent amount of time. He realized at that moment that for the first time in a while, he didn't know where to go or what to do.

He felt a presence next to him and looked to the passenger seat.

It was Melody.

Her mouth was turned downward, and he could see the bullet wounds on her chest and her neck. Her skin still had its color, but that would subside. As time went on, her appearance would change. Her wounds would only be seen when she wanted them to be seen but would otherwise only be viewed as prominent scars. She had an expression of sadness and resolution. She knew about her curse.

"You should have stayed in the damn car like I asked you to," he said. "I hope you don't take it personal that I'm not afraid of ghosts."

He stared ahead at the light shower outside the garage door. The blanket of clouds was beginning to break, revealing a darkened sky. Blake knew he needed to leave, but wasn't sure where he needed to go. He looked at Melody's ghost.

"You were working for Cade's family," he said. Not a question, but a comment.

She closed her eyes and nodded solemnly.

"Back at your apartment, I was amazed at how fast they guys picked your lock. They were so damn good at picking locks, but they went to the wrong door? That made no sense. They had a key."

She continued looking at him with the same solemn blank stare.

"They walked into your place with nothing to hide, like they owned the joint. They didn't have weapons drawn. They didn't look like they had anything to fear. The one guy looked right at me as he shut the door. I thought they were just sloppy and undisciplined, but that wasn't the case. They were unprepared.

"And the guy who snuck into my place? That's where you had me fooled. He was breaking in. He was looking for a fight. You did look scared, but you were playing Cade. And about Cade. He was a drinker. He was a big drinker, and even he would have been able to stand alcohol and painkillers. It's a stupid mix, but those were expired pain meds. You drugged his ass. Frank didn't want him dead, so you drugged him.

"As for the blonde little shit who followed us on his bike, that might have been dumb luck, but I doubt it. Frank knew exactly which highway we were traveling down. He knew which direction we were headed, and all he needed to do was tell his guys to stay alert. I'll bet if I opened up this phone, I would see text messages telling him where we were going."

She nodded her head back and forth, the international sign for *no*.

She looked down. He followed her gaze and saw her purse. "I promise I'm not trying to get fresh with you," he said as he reached down for her purse, "though last I recall you weren't completely opposed to that."

That mustered a small smile on her face.

He pulled out her New Jersey driver's license and looked at it for a moment. He then saw her cell phone, and pressed the button. Fourteen missed calls from Frank Silvera. He slid the key to the right. The phone asked for a pass code.

"I don't suppose you want to give me your passcode?"

She held up her fingers to spell out 1-2-3-4.

"Really?" he asked, and typed in the code.

He read through a string of text messages where she gave updates to Frank Silvera on their whereabouts. The updates were intermittent. She probably typed them with excruciating patience, but she was diligent. He occasionally pumped her for information she didn't have.

At one point, she texted and asked him if he knew that the Yellowstone River was connected to the Missouri River, which eventually led to the Mississippi which eventually led to the Gulf of Mexico. Blake remembered their discussion on the same subject, and read where Frank scolded her for sending irreverent messages.

He read her final message, sent that morning, telling Frank she thought they were headed for Mexico. He looked at Melody.

"You lied to him this morning," he said. She only stared at him, with pain in her eyes wishing she could tell him what was on her mind.

The next fourteen text messages were from Frank urging her to run away, escape their group and do it as soon as possible. He warned that her life was in danger, then demanded a response to his multiple messages.

As Blake read through the phone trying to decipher what Melody wanted to tell him, he noticed a pale finger reach across his body. She pointed at his jacket. He looked at her, and she pointed again with insistence.

Blake remembered the letter. He fished the envelope out of his inner pocket that Cade gave him. Blake held it up to her with an inquisitive expression. She nodded. He could hear more vehicles and sirens above him. The cops would be canvasing soon. He started the car.

"I have one more question," Blake said. "When you shot the guy on your porch, were you aiming for me?"

She looked at him and initially nodded in the affirmative, then the negative. She paused for a bit and shrugged her shoulders.

"You didn't know," he said. "You didn't know what you were doing."

She only stared at him in sadness.

"I'm sorry Melody," he said. "I wish things would have been different. You're welcome to ride in the car until the curse prohibits you from going further."

She nodded.

They pulled out of the garage and Blake locked the door. He refastened the padlock, knowing it would stay that way until the cousin he had met once returned to look after the property.

He returned to the car, and didn't notice the commotion through the kitchen window of his old home. Hector and Moki were sitting at the dinner table across from Strychnine. Moki gave Strychnine a playful punch to the shoulder and they laughed amongst each other. The woman Melody saw earlier walked up behind the men and filled their glasses with more wine while the Soldier cooked in the kitchen. A child ran across the room chasing a bouncing ball.

Strychnine stood from the table and walked to the window. He watched his son leave the house and smiled. He knew they would see each other again, and tried to hold back his own sorrow for only having a moment together. The woman came up behind him and put her hand on his shoulder. Hector joined him from the other side doing the same. Soon they were all watching out the window. The Harvester joined the group as well, only to them she was Amelia.

"You done good, Strychnine," the Soldier said clasping his shoulder.

"You should be damn proud," Hector added.

Strychnine beamed with pride.

Blake and Melody rolled through the service road without headlights. He knew where to turn and where to slow down from memory. The road was bogged down with puddles and potholes, but he studiously maneuvered the Mustang. Perhaps later he might get a carwash. They were at the intersection between the service road and the paved road that led to I-80 when Melody suddenly stirred, like a dog finding the end of her leash.

Blake pulled over to the side of the road and surveyed the area. They were twenty miles from the crime scene. He had a moment. He turned on the dome light in the car and pulled up Cade’s letter.

Chapter 41

Blake,

If you're reading this, that means everything went to shit. I'm probably dead. The escape plan didn't work. Or maybe you didn't follow instructions. Either way, I'm writing this letter for two reasons. You need to know the escape plan in case I die.

There's not much hope for you if I'm not around. That's the long and short of it. We're supposed to take a plane from Marion to Nunavut. That's a province in Canada where I'll meet another contact who will hook us up. We've got a guy who runs a shipping operation. He's a regular on the website. He says Nunavut is the best place for us to hitch a ride on one of his rigs and he can have us over to the Caribbean in a few days. It's out of the way, but the guy tells me this is the best way to do it. We've gotta take his word for it. Don't have any other options. But none of that matters if I'm dead. No Stuckley, no escape plan. I'm sorry man.

"Thanks for wasting my time, Cade."

That brings me to the other reason I am writing this letter. I know losing your family changed you. It's hard to see, man. You're not the same man you used to be. I don't know how to explain it, but I think we both know it's true. You talk to yourself. You don't talk to anyone else. The closest thing you have to human interaction is me, and we don't talk much. We haven't talked much in a while.

One night, I was having a couple beers at a place downtown when I hear these ex-frat boys talking a bunch of shit at the table next to me. I hear one of them start bragging about how he and his girl, Savanah, took care of this racist cop that wrote her up on a bullshit DWI, and I start listening.

I buy the guys a couple drinks and start probing the guy. I tell him that you wrote me up too, and even dropped your name. He told me the whole thing. It turns out Savanah Martin is his girlfriend. Savanah Martin is the lawyer who you pulled over. Her boyfriend's name is Trond Petersen. He's not from the Middle East. His family is Norwegian. He's six-two, I'm guessing about two hundred pounds. He's got blonde hair and blue eyes. He claims he used a disguise.

Anyway, I'm sorry I didn't share this with you when I found out about it. I wanted to, but I always knew the only way my getaway plan would ever work is if I had the best damned triggerman money can buy watching my back. I love you, buddy. And I'm sorry for everything.

Cade

Trond Petersen's address was written at the bottom of the letter, but Blake didn't need it. It was Savanah Martin's address. Same luxury townhome located in Dupont Circle. He read the letter twice, then three times, then four. He looked at Melody's ghost, who was still in the front seat.

"You know that ninety percent of what's in this letter is bullshit, right?" he said to her.

Melody gave him a smirk. The kind that young adults made when they snapped pictures of themselves and posted them on the internet. What were those called? Selfies? He smiled back.

Blake studied the highway and looked back at Cade's letter. He thought about Cade's last moments on earth, and what the Soldier said to him. *You're still only seeing what you wanna see with this one.*

"I have to pay Savanah a visit if I want the truth," Blake said.

Melody nodded and disappeared. When Blake pulled the Mustang off the side of the road and began driving to the freeway entrance, he saw Melody again on the side of the road waving at him. Next to her stood Madison Verley's ghost, watching him intently.

He heard more sirens off in the distance, probably headed in from Utah. He had no doubt they would need an army to clean up the crime scene in his wake.

Chapter 42

He was lucid. The Mustang chewed up asphalt as he tore across the country only stopping for gas. He stuck to small towns for most of his stops where paying cash wasn't unusual and outsiders were barely noticed. He wasn't tired. He was focused.

He could be on Savanah Martin's doorstep in thirty hours if he didn't sleep. That was a distinct possibility.

The Harvester's words crossed his mind. She was the first one to make the observation. *We often see only what we want to see in life.*

He thought of Madison again. What did she say?

You are going to learn a lot of things about yourself and the world around you and you're going to want to look away. Don't.

"Okay, Madison," he said to himself.

For years, he had nothing but time. He played the events of the worse night of his life over and over in his head. He began focusing on what he could remember instead of what he couldn't. He had spent the better part of two days viewing the details he could remember as annoyances, easily glossed over and barely examined. When trying to remember his dreams, he focused on, the fruitlessly lamented, what he didn't see.

The freeway sign announced that he was 100 miles west of Rock Springs, but he wasn't reading signs. He was watching the road. His mind was somewhere else.

He was back in his squad car, parked at the Eisenhower Metro Station. It was dark outside. He had been on the prowl for drunk drivers who decided they couldn't handle Duke Street. He saw a train stop at the station and decided to stay nearby while the passengers walked back to their cars. There would be a parade of

office workers, janitors, nurses and a couple night school students walking to the station from a nearby college. People living their lives. He wanted to make sure they were free to do so safely.
His cell phone vibrated and he looked at the caller-ID. It was Cade Stuckley. He was on duty and would call back later. *We'll come back to that,* Blake thought.

A call came over the radio. House fire off Huntington. They called out the address. It was his home.

Blake took the call. He cranked the sirens and flew across the highway at breakneck speed. He ran into his home past a wall of flames inside the living room. He wouldn't be able to use the front door on the way out. He found his wife Nicole and daughter Annabelle – Anni for short – both in Anni's room. Both had gunshot wounds to their chests. Nicole had two more bullet holes in the middle of her baby bump. Their son was due in two months.

Blake forced himself to look at the details this time instead of wincing and avoiding sickness. If he needed to pull over to throw up, he would.

He carried Anni out first, rushing her to the basement and out the back door. He whispered into her ear that everything was going to be okay, but he knew it wouldn't. There was no "happily ever after" in this fairy tale. She muttered something, but "Daddy" was all he caught. He looked at the blood from her exit wound on his hand and it looked black, not crimson. That wasn't good.

He rushed back and grabbed Nicole. As he carried her down the stairs, she was almost lifeless though he told himself he felt a pulse. He wondered if he should have carried her first.

As he was laying Nicole on the grass next to Anni, he felt a bullet graze his left shoulder and it flipped him on his back. He took cover behind a large oak tree in their back yard. He spotted the shooter. 5'7 maybe 5'8, about 200 pounds, knit cap, Middle Easter decent, mustache. Portly. Two more shots fired. Sergeant took cover and drew his weapon.

Now go back, Blake. Look again. Are you sure he was from the Middle East?

He pressed his first mental pause button. The guy's skin was dark. He had a mustache, but his facial features didn't look like those of an African American male. Could he have had Caucasian features?

You don't know. You barely saw him. You saw his height. You barely saw his frame. You wanted to believe he was from the Middle East, but was he? It made sense. A reporter writes a hit piece about you being a racist cop and someone came to your house to settle a score. Isn't that how it went down?

Keep watching. What did you see? What didn't you see?

He radioed for backup and heard sirens in the background. The shooter was nestled behind a makeshift garden in their back yard. They settled for a smaller house because of the relatively large back yard. The shooter fired another shot Blake's way and he instinctively took over.

"Drop your weapon!" Blake yelled, but they knew that wasn't happening. Blake fired another round, trying to draw the shooter out. the shooter responded by firing at Nicole's body. The bullet smacked the soil a few feet from where she lay dying.

Blake screamed in response and fired two more shots, charging into the open to defend his family. He was exposed. The shooter fired twice and the first shot missed. The second ricocheted off a tree branch and his Blake in the head.

He saw the familiar flash in his mental slideshow.

He's in his car running the liscense plate on a Prius, calling it into his radio, "Virginia YLC 68 . . ." He can't get a good look at the last number.

The flash appeared again, taking him to another moment in his past.

He's standing outside the vehicle of a man he just pulled over. Looking at his driver's license. African American. 25-years-old. Something isn't adding up.

There was another flash, but this time he knew where he was.

He's in uniform, walking toward the desk sergeant. He has something to say, but he's struggling to find the right words. He knew this was related to the guy in the Prius.

The next flash presented itself and he knew where he was again. It was the same day he was walking toward the desk sergeant. He is sitting in a conference room in the police station. Not an interrogation room, but one of the rooms they use for team meetings. He's in uniform. Detective Bob Hamilton is sitting with him. Hamilton is investigating Nicole, Anni and his unborn son's murders. Hamilton places his hand on Blake's knee.

"I have a hard time remembering things," Blake tells the detective.

The words hung in his mind.

But what about Cade?

They drifted apart after leaving active duty, and Cade never liked that.

When they did get together, Cade always wanted to hear about Blake's exploits as a cop, and Blake was usually reluctant to share details. However, when there were other cops around, Blake opened up.

He and his cop buddies laughed about the drug dealer whose girlfriend called to file a complaint against a junkie who owed them money. They hooted and howled over a young, petulant and intoxicated lawyer Blake pulled over for a DUI. After she gave him a very thorough legal argument for why she didn't need to take a sobriety test, she closed her argument with the comment, "besides, I'm too drunk." That particular surveillance video was incredibly popular in the break room.

Their distance only broadened when Anni was born. Kids are hell on a social life. When they got together, all Blake every talked about was sleepless nights, his daughter and coming to terms with the fact that he was a father. He talked about trying to become a little handier around the house to avoid paying for expensive repairmen. He talked about how life as a homeowner and father was forcing him to learn how to do shit that he never thought he would need to know. He talked about wishing his mother would visit them in Virginia more often. He talked about wanting to be a better man. He talked about how he and Nicole went to church on Sundays. None of it was shit Cade could relate to and they both knew it.

When Blake shared that he and Nicole were going to have another baby, Cade knew the fissure between them would eventually become a canyon. Calls were already sporadic and seldom returned. They went from living life on the same page to living lives in different libraries. Cade was getting increasingly clingy and Blake didn't have the time to deal with clingy. He was busy building a dollhouse for Anni. After that, he needed to replace the faucet in the upstairs bathroom. Maybe he would paint it too.

That was why Blake had no problem declining Cade's call on that November night. *I'll call him back,* Blake thought. He knew that probably wasn't true.

Blake allowed his mind to wander to the first "what if" in his nightmare.

Had they been on the phone, what if Blake would have missed hearing that his house was on fire? He wouldn't have been the first officer to arrive. Someone else would have rushed into the burning house and found his family gunned down. Someone else would have called for backup. Someone else wouldn't have known about the back door in the basement. Someone else would have tried to exit out the front. Or they wouldn't have entered at all.

But it was Blake who arrived. It was his family. It was his home. It was his bathroom with the leaky faucet. It was his daughter's dollhouse that would never get played with. It was his wife who laid unconscious, pregnant with the son he would never meet. Blake didn't wait for backup. He knew his house had a back door. He walked right into an ambush.

Blake was in a medically induced coma for six weeks. His family and in-laws were left to making heart-wrenching decisions while he laid unconscious. The human brain is a remarkable thing. Doctors told his family they didn't know when or if he would wake up. They held his wife, daughter and unborn son's funerals. Everybody came. They buried his family in Minnesota.

He didn't have a will or any type of advance care directive. Because of that, his mother and sister had to guess what he would have wanted. They opted to remove his feeding tube and pull the plug but his heart kept beating.

His brain was bruised badly. It had forgotten basic functions, but it was repairing itself albeit slowly. He remembered how to breathe. Then he remembered how to wake up. The neurologist called it a medical miracle, but the truth was he woke up angry. As soon as he remembered what brought him down, he was determined to get back up.

In six months, he had defied what statistics said he could do. He could walk, run, drive, read, eat, drink, fire a weapon. He went to the gym and his mind pushed his body to the brink several times over, but the truth was there was a dent in his armor. Memory.

He couldn't remember the face of the man who killed his family, but that wasn't all.

He was pumping gas in Cheyenne when it came back to him. *I couldn't remember.*

In the first days, he forgot colors. He forgot words. He forgot names. He forgot how to talk, how to eat, what cold felt like and he forgot that his family was dead. He relived that moment several times.

His mind grew stronger, but it was not the same as it once was. Blake Sergeant the cop, husband and loving father might have went into a medically-induced coma, but somebody else woke up. His family was buried in the Midwest. His house was burned to rubble.

He tried to get his old life back. During his recovery, a local public defender who always seemed to be representing people Blake arrested approached Blake and the police force about suing the publication that wrote a hit piece on him. They sued the law firm that employed Savanah Martin as well. There was no case because there was no proof of a connection between the hit piece and his family's murder, but that wasn't the objective. The lawyers who worked with Blake on both sides of the law wanted to send a message and the court of public opinion was a pretty good venue. It worked.

The newspaper parent company and the law firm each settled quickly. The lawyers took modest cuts, but the majority of the check went to Blake. The insurance covered expenses associated with his house and he worked with a local realtor to sell the lot. It sold within hours. Blake didn't remember a thing about the settlement. He only remembered cashing the check.

The journalist who wrote the hit piece committed suicide two years later. The article about her death used more ink retelling the story of Blake's family. Her life, in summary, was characterized as a disappointment.

He came back to the police force on limited duty and probably could have kept a position in that capacity, but he wanted to be back in a squad car. Once he cleared all waivers, he went to work.

His first three weeks were uneventful, but as he settled into a routine, his brain had other plans.

He was in his squad car running the license plate on a Prius, calling it into his radio, "Virginia YLC 68 . . ." He can't get a good look at the last number. That wasn't true. The number was a "7." He stared at the number. He couldn't remember it. He couldn't remember how to say it. He couldn't remember what it meant.

A door within his mind opened. He remembered and was ready to see what he originally didn't want to look at. The man's name was Abdul Awad. Blake followed him around town for almost fifteen minutes. Scared the hell out of the poor guy. He gave Awad's name to Detective Hamilton who quickly found out there was no connection.

Hamilton also found out about Mr. Awad's rough afternoon of having a squad car follow him around town inexplicably.

That same day, Hamilton was approached by the internal affairs officer who was investigating a similar complaint. Officer Sergeant pulled over 25-year-old Eddie Green, a grad student at George Washington University who was running errands around town.

Green might have been going five miles over the speed limit when he was pulled over. He handed the officer his license, registration and proof of insurance. The officer stood awkwardly holding the documents in front of him, saying the words "something isn't adding up" over and over.

The experience was quite distressing for Green to watch. When he asked the officer if he was okay, the officer snapped out of his trance and looked at Green as if he had no idea why they were both standing there looking at one another. He handed Green his documents back and asked him to have a good day.

When Eddie returned home, he spent some time surfing the web and recognized Blake Sergeant from the recent news coverage.

Blake Sergeant was sitting in the locker room before his next shift when he realized he had a problem. He couldn't speak. The words were there. He knew what he wanted to say. He wanted to scream out, and prove to himself and the world that it was wrong. He *could* remember how to do this, but the words weren't there.

His mouth and vocal chords were foreign tools that his mind didn't know how to use. He was paralyzed. When he first arrived, the desk sergeant asked him to stop by Detective Hamilton's office before going out on duty. While getting dressed in the locker room, he overheard two other officers he didn't know talking about seeing a lot of traffic in and out of Hamilton's office. The IA guy, the chief. Something was up and they didn't know what. All one guy heard was Hamilton say, "let me talk to him first."

Blake knew it was about him and that's when he discovered his problem. He remembered walking up to the desk sergeant, trying to figure out how to tell him that he had forgotten how to speak. They were twenty feet away from each other, but the walk felt much longer. The sergeant nodded at him and directed him down the hallway.

"Blake," Hamilton said in the conference room surrounded by the chief, the internal affairs officer and a handful of other senior officers he thought he would spend the rest of his career working alongside. "You have more heart than any cop in this building, but your brain has been damaged. It's time."

He remembered realizing he hadn't just lost his family, but his career. His purpose. That sonofabitch took everything from him. Even his mind. He handed his badge to Hamilton. There was nothing left to say or do. He was offered a goodbye party, but wanted nothing of it. All he wanted to do was put a gun in his mouth.

His mom wanted him to move closer to her in New Mexico. She said they had specialists there with expertise in that sort of thing. All he could think about was an old television show with a meth dealer that he used to watch. That was filmed in New Mexico. No. He didn't want that.

He wanted to be next to the only people who ever really understood him. He wanted to move to the only people who mattered to him. He moved to St. Paul, five miles up the street from the cemetery where his family was buried. Between the settlement and his disability payment, he had enough money to manage, but he didn't know how long that would last.

He found a cheap apartment in St. Paul where nobody in their right mind would want to live and he checked on the rent. Three hundred dollars a month, minimum one-year lease. He signed on for three years and handed the landlord a $4,000 check. Three years of rent plus a security deposit. He figured if they ever found him dead inside, the extra pay could compensate for the mess.

He ran to the gravesite every morning and sat at their headstones. Sometimes he talked. Sometimes he listened. Most of the time he wished it was him. After a while, he ran back to his home. At that point in time, he wasn't trying to solve anything. He watched television, but he couldn't name one show he paid attention to. He surfed the internet, reading anything he could find about anything at all. He memorized every tributary that led to the Mississippi.

Mostly he just waited for that moment that the last ounce of will in his mind and body that wanted to live would shut the fuck up. He kept his revolver in his lap waiting for the moment. As soon as the will was gone, he would be too. He was low. He was broken.

One morning after his visit to the cemetery, he heard a knock at his door. It was Cade Stuckley. He had a twelve pack of beer.

"I was nowhere near the neighborhood, and wanted to see if you had any interest in getting shitfaced in the middle of the day."

That was the first of several consecutive days of drinking irresponsibly and living on Chinese takeout. Eventually, they decided to embark upon a booze-filled road trip to the beach. They would drive until they were sick of driving. Then they would drink. Then they would drive some more.

They ended up in Key West and spent another week drinking and sleeping on the beach. It was the happiest Blake had been in quite some time. That was when Cade first floated the idea of Blake being a professional hitman. Cade informed him that things were going quite well for him financially, but web development wasn't his only source of income.

He handed Blake a manila envelope. Blake opened it up and found a picture of Tommy Montoya, the first man he would eventually kill.

Looking back, Blake realized something. They were together nearly a month, drinking beer and catching up, but more was going on. Cade was studying Blake, trying to decide if he were up for the job.

■■■

Cade realized a couple of things. Blake's brain was healing. He could perform normal functions such as driving or paying his bills. A piece of Blake was coming back. He also noticed that is friend still had memory lapses.

Had Blake never been shot, there is no way in hell he would have agreed to kill Tommy Montoya. No man in his right mind would have. Blake wasn't in his right mind. He suffered from a traumatic brain injury. He lost his family, his home and his job. He lost himself. He was suicidal. He was depressed, and he was still angry.

He took the job. He studied Cade's plan, and he executed it. He might have memory issues, but the tactical skills he learned as a Marine and as a cop were still intact. After years in law enforcement, he knew what clues cops looked for on crime scenes and knew how to leave a murder scene without any clues. As a cop, he lamented how easy it was for thugs to land firearms, and as a criminal, he used the Second Amendment to his advantage.

On the night of Tommy's murder, he discovered something else. He dreamed about the night Nicole, Anni and the baby died. He remembered more about that night than he had been able to recall in the past year. Murder unlocked a door in his mind.

There were several times that Blake would say he was done killing, but all Cade had to do was politely wait and hand him the next assignment. Blake's brain was wired differently. Once Cade figured out the algorithm, he was all set to make money and continue making money.

He told Cade about the dreams once and Cade chose to never bring it up. He didn't have to.

Blake wasn't Cade's partner in crime. He was Cade's pet. A brain damaged triggerman who killed without hesitation and spent his nights clinging to the idea that he might get a glimpse of the face of the man who killed his family.

That's why Frank and Wyatt called him crazy.

Blake stepped on the gas.

■■■

THURSDAY

Chapter 43

Savanah Martin and Trond Petersen were having a terrible week.

They were four days into a much-needed vacation featuring white sands, an ocean breeze and lots of cocktails when they got the call nobody wants to get. Their firm was on the cusp of the greatest client opportunity in years and they needed to cut their vacation short.

Their client, Precision Energy, was technically not their client on paper. No contracts had been signed. No invoices had been processed, but there was about to be a major acquisition and the firm's partner in charge of this effort wanted all the work completed in advance.

Savanah and Trond spent weeks drafting the appropriate paperwork along with several other legal documents that did not need to appear on any server until the time was appropriate. Because of that, everything was located on three laptops and a flash drive. Two of the laptops were in Savanah and Trond's possession. The flash drive was in their apartment.

As a celebration, Jim Peterson, their partner in charge, told the two of them to take a long weekend. Book a vacation. Leave town for a few days. He wrote them a check from the company to help foot the bill. He was that kind of boss.

Unfortunately, Peterson was found dead in his northern Minnesota cabin. It sounded like an attempted robbery and was under investigation. In the meantime, the show had to go on. Their vacation ended early.

With the paperwork completed, and their partner gone, they had one job – stay close to the phone and await further guidance from the client. Once they received the call they were waiting for, Precision Energy would officially become a client. The documents on their laptops would be public.

They spent the day at the firm waiting for the call. They used the time to review and update their materials. They drew up the first invoice for the new client. They completed tasks that could have waited until after the vacation, but there they were – by the phone. The call never came.

Still devastated by cutting their vacation short, they decided to forward the office phone to their cell phones and go out for dinner and a drink. One drink turned into three, which turned into six. Now they were staggering into their townhome in need of showers, sleep and maybe some drunk sex if Trond was lucky.

Trond was fumbling for his keys when he noticed the door was unlocked. *That's weird*, he thought. *I always lock the door.*

He opened the door and looked closely at the locking mechanism scanning for any type of striations.

Their door opened to expose a narrow hallway. The kitchen was on the immediate left and the living room was further down the hall past the closet on the right. They kept the couch flush with the wall at the opposite end of the hallway, but Trond couldn't see the outside arm of the couch.

"Oh hurry up, slowpoke," Savanah said from behind, "I'm ready for bed."

Trond obliged and stepped aside. He kept a nine millimeter in his handbag fastened to a holster that was built in. He reached into his bag and unsnapped the leather fastener that kept the weapon from sliding out.

Savanah pushed past him, walked into the kitchen and pulled out an opened bottle of wine. Trond pulled out his weapon and crept to the end of the hallway. He spun around the corner and pointed his weapon. The couch was moved two feet over. He heard something behind him but it was already too late.

Blake swung his arm down like a hammer with the handle of the knife pointed at Trond's head, connecting at the base of his skull. Trond gasped loudly and went down like a bag of rocks, hitting his forehead on the base of the couch.

"Trond?" Savanah said from the kitchen. She stepped out of the kitchen and stuck her head out into the hallway. She didn't have time to react. All she saw was a closed fist, then fireworks as her whole body flew off the ground and her head smacked the opposite side of the doorframe on her way down.

Her face was bruised and her nose bled onto the tile floor. It looked expensive. Blake walked back to the living room and punched Trond again in the temple as he struggled to pull himself up and reach for his weapon.

"Rise and shine," Blake said.

Trond and Savanah began to awaken from the fog of unconsciousness. Somebody was spraying something on them. Was it water? Urine? No. It was lighter fluid.

They both sprung awake in fear and found Blake Sergeant standing facing them.

"Good morning, sunshine," he said.

Trond attempted to lunge from his seat and Blake kicked him in the forehead with the base of his foot.

"Sit the fuck down," he said. "Next time you get up, I'll shoot your right kneecap and slice your left Achilles tendon. We can watch you try to walk and you can tell us which one hurts more."

Blake looked at Savanah.

"Normally I don't hit women, but given the circumstances, I think we can both agree that chivalry no longer applies to you."

They weren't tied up. Their phones were sitting on the coffee table in front of them. They saw the two laptops and the flash drive removed from their bags and stacked neatly on the bookshelf on the other end of the room.

How long has he been watching us? Savanah thought.

"I saw the luggage in your bedroom," Blake said. "Going somewhere? Or are you just coming back?"

They stared at him silently. Trond finally spoke.

"I always knew you would come," he said. He was exhausted. His head was throbbing.

Blake set his handgun on the coffee table in front of them, never letting his eyes leave Trond's. He marveled at the couple. They were beautiful people. Blonde hair. Blue eyes. Perfect teeth. For years, Blake was on the prowl for a paunchy man from the Middle East with a molester's mustache. Trond was so white he was the treasurer at his alma mater's chapter of the College Republicans. He was so white, his mother had an umlaut in her maiden name. He was so white his girlfriend wrote a thesis paper in college researching where Native Americans originally immigrated from, and whether there were any legal means for deporting them. She was so white her father called the dean after the professor gave her a failing grade and bought her a degree.

Trond was the guy from that night. Blake recognized him. Blake grabbed his .45 with the silencer already installed.

"My nose hurts," Savanah said, sitting to Trond's right.

"Yeah," Blake said unsympathetically, "I'll bet my daughter's chest hurt after your boyfriend shot her. Is that true, Trond? Did you shoot her?"

Trond looked down and to the right. He breathed deeply.

"Like I said, I always knew you would come."

He was resigned to the inevitability of his own death.

"Well, Trond Petersen, I need to hear you say it. Did you kill my wife and daughter?"

"I shot your daughter," he said in a monotone voice.

"And Nicole?"

"Cade Stuckley shot her."

Blake straightened up. He felt his breath leave his chest. He backed up and steadied himself using their plasma screen for balance. He thought about the expression of disgust on his father's face as Cade begged Blake for help. Trond looked at his pistol. Blake's expression of surprise turned to a lucid glare and his .45 steadied in his hand. Trond slumped in his seat.

"You heard him," Savanah called out. "Your little boyfriend Cade shot your wife twice. Once in the chest and once in the stomach."

"Four times," Blake corrected.

"Savanah don't," Trond tried to intervene but Savanah wasn't going to be silent today.

"It was all your friend's idea," she said. "After I saw your little award, I talked Melinda Bryan into digging up some dirt on you and she found the disproportionately high number of minorities you arrested. She always wanted to be my friend, so I shouldn't have been surprised when her reporting turned out to be a little biased."

"Bullshit," Blake corrected. "The article was bullshit."

"Whatever," Savanah said sullenly. "So that article was going to end everybody's careers and that's when Cade stopped by our place. He manages our firm's website. That's how Trond knew him. He knew you from the Marines, and he explained his whole idea. He knew you were a natural at hiking, camping and police stuff and he always thought you would be the perfect hitman for his business. He would lure in sex offenders and you would shoot them. People could take bets on it."

"We thought it sounded like a great idea," Trond said with gasp. "The problem was you would never go for it."

"Not with your wife in the picture," Savanah continued. "He said she changed you. So he talked Trond into coming with him to kill your wife and daughter. He said you would be devastated. He said they were your whole life. Once they were out of the picture, he could bring you back into the fold. He said he couldn't do the job alone. He also told me what you were going to do, so I talked Trond into it."

"I was just the triggerman, like you," Trond added.

"Come again?"

"Oh, don't pretend you don't know," she scoffed. "He told me about how you still had the video of the night you pulled me over."

Blake stopped and thought about it.

"You mean, the one where you incriminated yourself?"

"No!" she yelled. "The one where you made me look like a fool. He told me how you and your cop buddies used to listen to it in your breakroom and thought it was the funniest thing ever. He also told me about how one of your little cop buddies was looking into getting it sent to one of those stupid reality TV shows. Something called 'World's Dumbest Criminals?' Did it ever occur to you how that might affect my career, as if you hadn't caused enough damage? What else was I supposed to do?"

"The plan worked," Trond said, ignoring his girlfriend. "After Savanah was taken off the partner track, you know, because of the article, we were short on money. She is, you know, used to a certain quality of life and when, you know, the firm let her go after the settlement with you, you know."

"If you say 'you know' one more time, I'm shooting you in the nuts."

"I'm sorry," Trond said. "I'm really scared and I feel like shit for everything that happened."

Blake studied him for a moment, the man he hunted for three years. Trond wasn't a vindictive, evil mastermind. That would be his girlfriend. Trond was an idiot and a follower who was in love. Blake always had a feeling Savanah Martin was involved and he had every intention of putting a bullet in her head as soon as he could ID the killer. He thought about crashing down their door and interrogating them like he was doing today. He felt like if she lied to him about the killer or pointed him in the wrong direction, there wouldn't be a second chance.

Hamilton questioned her. She and Trond had an alibi and plenty of witnesses. They were at a costume party. She was Miss America and he was Mitt Romney. *Mitt Romney has dark hair. How much effort did Hamilton really put into investigating these two clowns?*

He also remembered that they lawyered up. Blake cursed his own mind. He should have started with Savanah Martin. His mind was still a house with lots of darkened rooms at the time. Today's interrogation was something he should have done years ago. Nevertheless, he was here now. Everything was clear. His mind was working better than it had in years.

Blake had seen his share of guys just like Trond Petersen as a cop, usually sitting in the back of his squad car. Not bad kids. Guilty kids. Stupid kids who were never taught right from wrong. Kids whose parents either needed to work two jobs to put food on the table and didn't have the emotional wherewithal to provide a moral foundation. Kids whose parents suffered from alcoholism or drug addiction, trying to self-medicate using substances to treat some unknown mental illness. In the wake of poverty, kids often didn't have a chance. They were easily manipulated by people who were evil. They were tricked into doing stupid and terrible things and they often paid the consequences.

He felt some pity, but pity had its limits. Trond didn't strike Blake as an incredibly smart guy, but he had more opportunities than most of the guys from Blake's past. He was an attorney with a nice townhome in one of Washington's premier neighborhoods. He worked for what seemed like a reputable firm. Yet, he still allowed himself to commit an unspeakable crime. Blake considered whether he might settle for marching Trond into a local police station to make a confession.

"Was Cade with you when you shot me?"

"I don't think I shot you. We were both shooting at you. Cade tried to shoot a branch hoping it would fall on you. I read that a bullet ricocheted off a tree and hit you, so I guess that's what happened."

The suburban dad in Blake rolled his eyes. He had pruned that tree several times over. One bullet wasn't going to remove a branch. A chainsaw like the one Cade used to kill his stepdad would have been a better option.

"We thought you were going to die and that we made a mistake, you know . . ."

Trond stopped and his eyes widened.

"Keep talking," Blake said. He had fished out FBI Agent Steve Gable's business card from his back pocket. He was surprised he still had it and the rain hadn't ruined it.

"Then you started going through rehab and stuff. You tried to be a cop again and were brain damaged. You were unpredictable.

Cade went to see you in Minnesota and the rest was history. That was when the money started rolling in."

"What money?"

"We had a deal," Savanah said. "If Cade got you to do your job, we got a commission every time there was a payout. And we needed it because I took a pretty substantial pay cut after I lost my job thanks to you. I was thankful that Jim hired me, but it was less than what I was making."

She went on pining about her career, her life on the partner track and how she and Trond were eventually going to relocate back to Tennessee where she would run for Congress. She kept coming back to how her arrest and the incriminating video could derail everything she had worked for. Blake wondered whether the only thing worse for this couple than death was going to jail and losing their reputation.

Savanah continued talking. Blake observed them and tried to think about how he could get a confession out of them. They were terrible criminals, but they were also lawyers. This confession was coerced. Her nose was broken and Trond probably had a cracked skull. Blake could see his dilated pupils from a distance. If they continued this fight in a courtroom, they would have the advantage. It would be his word against theirs. The justice he wanted would never be attainable. Not today. Not ever. They were trust fund babies with a legal armada. He was an ex-cop with brain damage.

He started to slide Gable's card back into his pocket.

The cell phone on the coffee table rang and Blake picked it up. There was a number, and it looked international. It was a 007 area code, but Blake wasn't looking at the number. Blake was looking at the field where the name was supposed to appear, but it only showed the name of a city. Moscow.

"I'll never be able to run for Senate now," he heard her saying off in the distance.

He was looking at the phone and the city triggered a premonition. He saw the phone, the two laptops and the flash drive behind him. He looked back at them in shock.

Trond was now sitting upright, looking at Blake's visible distraction. He was in a daze.

Savanah was still filling the room with banter about her career.

Blake looked down in confusion. Closed his eyes.

Moments ago, Trond thought his number was up. Now there was a window. Trond lunged for the handgun. He grabbed it. He racked it. He pointed it up. He squeezed the trigger.

You are going to learn a lot of things about yourself and the world around you and you're going to want to look away. Don't.

Blake snapped out of his trance and kicked Trond's hand as the gun went off.

The round blasted through Savanah's eye socket. She flew back onto the couch. She wasn't dead. She began panting like a wounded animal, making an unnatural guttural sound.

Blake grabbed his .45 and fired six rounds into Trond's chest. Then, he thought about the lighter fluid on their bodies and marveled at how they did not catch fire.

Trond's fell back on the couch, wheezing for breath. Blake took the pistol out of his hand, flipped the weapon on safe and pocketed it.

He walked to the ashtray he saw by their balcony door earlier where a pack of cigarettes and a zippo lighter lay dormant. He wondered if they liked to smoke cigarettes together like the two politicians in the old Netflix series that he and Nicole watched a couple times.

He knelt next to Trond.

"You aren't like me," Blake said.

He grabbed the lighter fluid and sprayed a fresh splash into Savanah's gaping eye socket. She panted and managed a muffled squeal in response.

"Remember that night I pulled you over?" he asked. She was beyond understanding him. He didn't care. "You should have called a cab."

He threw the lit zippo at her face and watched her eye socket catch fire. The beautiful couple went up in flames wheezing and panting in pain as fire melted the skin from their faces. They looked like two Arian candles melting on a five-thousand-dollar couch.

Blake walked out of their classy townhome in a daze. Had he spent another moment in the room, he would have seen two coins pop out of the bodies of Savanah and Trond and land unceremoniously on the ground.

He stopped at the end of their porch and looked at the metal fence panels bordering their front lawn. He squatted down and placed the flash drive on the lower bar of the fence which bordered a red brick retaining wall. It was inconspicuous unless someone were looking for it. He set the two laptops behind the retaining wall.

The flames were beginning to spread from the couch, but there wasn't anyone around to see them. It was the middle of the night, an hour after the bars closed.

Blake slowly walked to the Mustang parked three blocks over. He would have taken the Metro had it still been open. The Dupont Circle stop was only a block away. The secret to a clean getaway was acting as if you weren't escaping from anything.

The truth was he was doing nothing to remain tactical. He had a hunting knife strapped to his right hip that undoubtedly carried the DNA from several victims. He was still carrying his .45 with a silencer attached to the end. Trond's nine-millimeter was tucked in his waistband behind him. Trond's phone was still in his front pocket. He marveled at the notion that the only time Trond tried anything to defend himself was when a client called.

In all fairness, Blake hit him pretty hard in the head. Twice.

He sat in the car for a moment, then forgave himself for not doing this sooner. Losing Nicole, Anni and their son left him in a dark place emotionally. The bullet added physical limitations to his ability to reason. He wasn't going to spend another moment regretting it. Everything played out like it did for a reason.

He made his way down Massachusetts to 395 South and drove. There was a small motel off Route 1 that accepted cash and didn't ask too many questions. He didn't need to plan his next move tonight. He just needed sleep.

Chapter 44

Around the time Blake Sergeant was driving to the motel, Steve Gable was ambling to his home office. He spent five hours trying unsuccessfully to stop spinning. There were intermittent periods of sleep, but mostly he wanted to lay near his wife. He wanted to intercept the kids if they wandered in the room and he wanted to put them to bed. It felt good to be dad again.

He powered up the computer in his office and pulled up his written report of the events that transpired since Friday morning. He read the report for accuracy while ruminating on the last twenty-four hours.

After the "Muerto Massacre," that was the term a local newspaper used to describe their shootout, Gable and the St. Paul cops rode down the mountain in inconspicuous fashion. They dutifully pulled to the side of the road as streams of squad cars, ambulances and fire trucks screamed down the highway. They heard a chopper above head, and Gupta successfully identified it as a medivac helicopter.

They wondered who on earth could have possibly lived. Gable speculated that it might have been Cade Stuckley. He was shot a few times but he wasn't dead the last time they saw him.

They drove the rental car to Salt Lake, turned it in and boarded their complimentary charter flight back home. They were still soaking wet from the gunfight, but opted against explaining their circumstances at the rental car lot.

"Everybody is soaking today," the friendly but tired cashier observed as she took their keys.

They spent the flight sharing tangential paranormal experiences from their respective pasts, but nothing compared to what they witnessed earlier that night. Everyone agreed without hesitation.

When the plane landed, Chief Casey met them on the tarmac. It was two in the morning, but he was there to welcome his team. They gathered the cops' weapons and other relevant belongings. Each officer was instructed to return to the locker room as soon as possible, shower and toss their clothes in the trash immediately.

Gable got a different set of instructions.

"Your ride is over there," he said.

A young officer stood posted next to black sedan.

"He's gonna drive you to the airport. There's a firehouse on the way you can shower and change at. Your luggage from your original trip is in the back of the car. If you have a change of clothes in there, you have something to wear. What you're wearing now goes in the trash."

The chief handed him his boarding pass and shook his hand. His flight left in three hours.

"I know I'll see you in a few days," he said. "A little birdie told me that you will be spending a lot of time on this investigation."

That was news to Gable. He and the cops said their goodbyes then got on the road.

Gable arrived in Washington, D.C. to find a young NCIS agent waiting for him outside his gate. The agent suggested that Gable purchase breakfast because they had a long drive. Gable grabbed coffee and a muffin.

When the agent headed toward the Woodrow Wilson Bridge, Gable looked at him with confusion.

"Where are we going?"

"Fort Meade."

They drove to a nondescript building on the Army base, arriving just in time for rush hour.

"What are we doing here?" Gable asked, looking out the window.

Fort Meade was home to the National Security Agency. Government agents and civilians pretended like they didn't know of the Army base's most prominent resident, but people knew. If reputation wasn't enough of a giveaway, the randomly placed satellites around the base that service members cynically pretended not to notice served as evidence.

Gable followed the agent into the sterile lobby of the nondescript government building.

"Daddy!"

He heard the familiar shriek of Gideon Godwin Gable as the young boy sprinting across the main lobby and lunging at his father. Gable had enough time to brace his back for the impact as his son jumped without hesitation into his father's arms. Gable hugged him tight.

Gideon was ten-years-old. He was at that age where his body was growing to that of a young man with the innocent, loving mind of a child. One day he would need to navigate those awful years of hormones, mood swings and middle school, but today wasn't that day. Today he was the hyperactive son excited to see his dad.

Behind Gideon came Belinda, sprinting with all her might. At seven, she was still little and easy to absorb. Steve hugged both his kids and marveled at how much they had grown. He had been gone too damned long. He had missed too much time, and with Anthony Byrd dead and rotting on a mountain in Wyoming, he was ready to hang up his spurs as a Marine.

Rachel came around the corner and embraced her husband, planting an unapologetic kiss. He took it all in. Gable towered over the short brunette who had surrendered her wild side for motherhood, but still donned a couple tattoos underneath her motherly outfit.

"Can we stop pretending we're divorced now?"

"You got it," he said as he kissed her back.

At the back corner of the lobby, Rafe Paxton and Victoria Perez marveled at the reunion.

"I never get tired of watching that," the congressman said. "I'm serious. It's the real reason I never miss it when a unit in my district returns from deployment."

"His wife is gorgeous," Perez said. "How does she end up with *that*?"

She nodded her head at Gable for effect.

"Marines," Anton Osborn said from behind them with a laugh. He spoke with a deep baritone voice and a thick Russian accent. "They charm the hearts away from even the smartest of women. It's the eighth wonder of the world."

Osborn stepped into the lobby. Although he was at least six inches shorter than Gable, the barrel-chested man commanded the presence of every room he seemingly stepped in.

Gable strolled across the lobby and hugged his father-in-law. He always wondered how the man managed to be a spy with the charisma his presence demanded.

"How are you all?" he said to Osborn.

"I am well, my son," he said. "Your family has been very hospitable, and the kids have taken quite well to farm life."

"And your daughter?" Gable asked as Rachel cuddled up under his arm.

"Maybe your parents could plant a crop that grows shoes or shopping malls," he said with a chuckle.

"I am doing just fine," she bantered back.

Anton Osborn's eyes turned serious.

"I think the Russians might hate you more than me today, special agent."

Gable took the comment in.

"We should get started," Perez said as she motioned for Gable to join her in a conference room down the hall. "You'll have some more time with your family as soon as we are finished."

"Thank you," Gable responded.

They stepped into the room full of suits. Functioning on zero sleep and wearing a dress shirt still wrinkled from a suitcase and a plane ride, Steve didn't feel ready for a meeting. Two of the men in the room were United States senators. Gable recognized them both. The Democratic senator spent a career in the Coast Guard and the Republican served in the Navy. He had seen them on the news and generally liked what they had to say about the military, as well as what they often left unsaid.

He knew they were senior officials. He also recognized the older white man in a black suit from the St. Paul police station. He was the CIA guy who Mayor Casey distracted with a tour of the city the previous day. Not too far behind him was the young female agent he also remembered from that day. They were cordial.

They approached Gable, and the man extended his hand.

"Special Agent Gable, I'm Agent Marcell Hadderly with the CIA," he said.

Gable shook his hand.

"I'm Agent West," the young woman said, shaking his hand. "Nice to meet you both," he said, wondering whether he might be on the verge of being reprimanded.

"We appreciated the tour you arranged of Saint Paul, Special Agent," Hadderly said in a dry tone.

"The mayor up there is quite a character," Gable said.

Perez and Paxton joined their conversation from behind the CIA agents, both giving Gable reassuring head nods.

"We're on the same side," Hadderly said. "Towe is still behind bars, but she won't be there long."

Gable nodded.

"She should be. Agent Calavera is dead because of her," he replied.

"Welcome to the resistance," the agent responded and he shook Gable's hand again.

One Marine major general, a Navy admiral and an Army lieutenant general joined them in the room, and the guests took their seats. Each of the men and women in the room carried with them a level of tension as if they were taking a great risk being in that room.

Hadderly sat at the head of the table next to both senators. Congressman Paxton took the empty seat by his side. The General looked at Gable and gave him a nod. Gable, less than twenty-four hours removed from a shootout that involved ghosts, tried to think of what the hell he was going to say to this room of dignitaries. He hoped he wasn't asked.

"Before we get started," Hadderly said to the room, "I want to be clear. By participating in today's discussion, a sitting commander-in-chief, if he felt so inclined, could prosecute anyone in this room for treason or possibly U.S. Code Section 2385, advocating to overthrow a government. That would be patently false and recklessly irresponsible, but I think you all know it's a true risk. For the men in uniform, I don't have to remind you of those consequences. If anyone here wishes to leave the room, now is the time."

Gable's jaw dropped. He looked at Perez and Paxton, who both nodded.

A lieutenant began passing folders out to the attendees and Gable waited for his copy.

"Agent Gable," Hadderly said, "I know this is the first time you've met some of us but many of us are familiar with your work. A more updated report from this crime scene investigation will be here soon."

Gable opened the envelope and saw what looked like a preliminary report from an investigation of the shootout in Wyoming. There were photographs of the Russians with their names underneath. Gable took a moment to examine Viktor Namin. He read through the specifics of the report and, not surprisingly, the investigator who typed the original memo could not make sense of what transpired.

Gable looked to see if there were any early signs of evidence of his involvement, but part of him knew such evidence wouldn't be found. He had a mental image of their unpoliced shell casings sinking into the ground of that cursed mountain.

"Does this mountain look familiar to you?" Agent Hadderly asked.

They were testing Gable. He was done playing games.

"Yes," he said.

"Is there anything you want to share with the group?" Hadderly asked.

Gable flipped to the page with Viktor Namin's picture.

"I think this guy was in charge," Gable said, holding up the picture. "That's what it looked like on the mountain. That's why I shot him first. There was a lot that happened on that mountain that I am going to spend the rest of my life trying to make sense of and I will tell you everything I witnessed. You have my word. I would just like to know one thing first before we get started. Who were these Russian guys with the black hair and what did they have to do with Gayton security?"

The men looked at each other, and the Senator who served in the Navy chose to respond.

"That's a fair question, and I will honor your word and answer it," he said. He looked around the room and the other attendees gave him the deference he sought. The other attendees simply nodded. "Early last year, shortly after the election, Aresneft, an energy conglomerate owned in part by the Russian government and private investors, opened new offices in northern Virginia to explore expanding into North American market. They brought in analysts, lobbyists and other business types to begin meeting with American companies and exploring what an expansion looked like. That part wasn't a surprise. I don't think anyone here denies that the Russians helped this president get elected."

"What was surprising was that among the men and women who relocated to the Washington area on work visas were thirteen men who our intelligence agencies flagged as individuals whom in their view deserved a little more scrutiny. The White House stonewalled multiple efforts to investigate these men further and determine whether we wanted them in this country.

"They all had checkered backgrounds that deserved additional scrutiny and a number of my colleagues and I advocated for that through the appropriate internal channels. We were shut down again and again despite multiple overtures and accused of creating a hostile working environment for businesses. Agent Hadderly, with whom we have worked before, conducted some research anyway. This was done without the knowledge of the President."

"The thirteen men we flagged as potential threats to national security," Hadderly said. "Their bodies were found at the mountain described in your crime scene."

"So who are they?" Gable asked.

"We think they might have been a terrorist cell," Hadderly responded. "We also believe that Aresneft intentionally flew them in and housed them as they trained for an attack of some sort."

"What sort?"

"We don't know, but our intel suggests these men were the same individuals who orchestrated a bombing in Iraq that led to an increase in security around different oil refineries. The private security was provided by Aresneft. We saw a very similar incident occur in Kazakhstan a few years ago."

"They're committing terrorist attacks to generate business for their oil company," Paxton added. "It's all about money."

"Jiminy Christmas," Gable said.

"It gets better," Paxton said.

"We don't know this for sure, but we believe the President has a financial relationship with Aresneft," Hadderly said. "We also know that Aresneft has been in talks with Precision Energy in recent weeks, but we don't know details. It sounds like either a merger or an acquisition. And the President has some business dealings with Precision Energy as well."

"Nikolay Belov was a senior executive with Aresneft, and he was in the country on business travel. We think he might have also been in town to activate the Russian terrorist cell we spoke of. Someone killed him before he could do it."

"Blake Sergeant," Gable said.

"Yes," the senator responded. "The man you've been hunting. Somehow he has been a step ahead of our entire investigation."

"He killed most of those Russians as well," Gable added. "In pretty gruesome fashion."

"He's either a clairvoyant hero or a mass murderer," the Senator responded. "We would like to know what you know. Start from the beginning and tell us everything."

Paxton slid a cup of black coffee in front of Steve Gable.

"Very well," Gable said, taking a sip of the coffee. "You're gonna think I'm crazy, but I'll put my hand on a bible and swear if you need me to. Everything I'm about to say is what I saw. I also plan to include all details in my final report."

Chapter 45

The senator was right about the attack. On Thursday night, right around the time Nikolay Belov was scheduled for a night of companionship with a teenage girl he met on the internet, twelve Russian mercenaries were at Viktor Namin's home with a makeup artist. She was using a combination of oils and foundations to darken all of their complexions. She was striving to make them look like Arabic men.

They had dyed their hair black and Viktor Namin did the same in solidarity even though he was in New York, tasked with carrying out Belov's orders. Once their makeovers were completed, the Russians would fan out to different Metro stations around the Washington area and wait Namin's call.

When Belov's flight left American airspace on a 6:00 AM flight departing from the JFK airport to Moscow, Viktor Namin would make one phone call activating their cell.

They would each be traveling with large pieces of luggage on rollers. They would board their respective trains and head to the busiest Metro stations in the Washington area. They were instructed to deploy the large cyanide bombs on trains during the peak of rush hour, then exit.

Each man would leave his respective station and travel to one of several getaway vehicles strategically placed in overnight parking ramps around town. They would drive to a rendezvous point in northern Maryland and be out of the country on a charter jet around the time surveillance footage of them conducting their attack was released to the public.

Hundreds would die. Thousands would suffer debilitating injuries requiring hospitalization. Working people, service members, kids on field trips, congressional staffers, nurses, doctors, teachers. They would smell the scent of almonds, then quickly become overpowered by cyanide poisoning.

The American people would see Arabic men on surveillance footage. A video from ISIS taking credit for the attack would be released to the media. The video was a fake, but it didn't matter. The American public would be quickly overpowered by fear. People would see what they wanted to see.

Aresneft was acquiring Precision Energy. Lobbyist Jim Peterson and his two crack associates pre-drafted all of the legal paperwork for a quick acquisition. That acquisition would not make headlines. Peterson and his aides were to leave the Washington area over the weekend to avoid injury, but deploy the necessary paperwork upon hearing from Nikolay Belov.

The attack would prompt the president to launch a full-scale attack on Iraq in search of ISIS. Precision Energy would receive a no-bid contract for a sophisticated upgrade in antiterrorism security equipment for public transportation services across the country. Thousands more would die in the impending war. Collateral damage of mass carpet bombs.

Americans would be fooled and Russian skeptics would be silenced, but the international community would immediately smell a rat. It would be unclear who fired the first nuclear weapon at the United States, but North Korea was the second country to strike.

Nobody would be able to figure out where North Korea received a nuke. Nobody would be alive to lead the investigation.

Tortured by the notion that his legacy would be defined by the inception of a nuclear war, the President lost his mind. Once he was safely aboard Air Force One with the pilot trying fruitlessly to fly away from the destruction of an attack, he gave his last order to launch preemptive nuclear strikes on every country whom he felt might have been involved. Germany, North Korea, China and France were just a few of the initial targets. Everyone except Russia. In his mind, this was bravery. In truth, he was an unhinged lunatic suffering a nervous breakdown with unchecked access to a nuclear arsenal.

The attack would result in over one hundred million deaths around in the United States alone. Total fatalities around the world would exceed two billion in the first week. By the time all the missiles had exploded and the ensuing radiation from the attacks spread, it would have been the end of humanity. Evil would have won.

Chapter 46

The attack didn't happen. Blake Sergeant killed the mastermind of the attack, Nikolay Belov, before he could leave American airspace. The bodies of the thirteen men who comprised the Russian terrorist cell were being scraped off a mountain in Wyoming. Their souls were destined for indefinite purgatory.

Jim Peterson was never able to execute the paperwork needed for Aresneft to acquire Precision Energy. Neither were Savanah Martin or Trond Petersen. Blake Sergeant killed all three of them.

It was fall. Days were getting shorter and soon blankets of snow would be falling around the country. People would be making holiday plans, spending time with families and creating new memories. Kids would open presents. Families would reunite for celebratory dinners and the Hallmark channel would run an endless supply of holiday-themed romantic comedies featuring actors who were famous in the eighties.

Empty nesters would go on cruises, and as the holiday season ended, countless Americans would say to one another that they work too hard. The kids are growing up too fast. They would be right on both counts. They would book vacations they probably couldn't afford and travel across the country to places like Yellowstone, Disney World and the Grand Canyon, creating memories.

They would continue to go to work, school, church and social gatherings around town. There was a lot to love about the planet and a lot to be thankful for. Blake Sergeant ensured that people could continue to remain thankful. Divine intervention and a brain-damaged killer handed down Old Testament style punishments to a handful of greedy and evil people whose actions would have caused the deaths of many. It was a miracle. A flawed, dirt-under-the-fingernails miracle.

Blake sat stunned in his Mustang staring at a red light on Massachusetts Avenue. The light turned green, but he didn't move until another motorist startled him with the honk of a horn.

He drove to a motel of his choosing off Route 1. The manager accepted cash and paid no attention when Blake used the fake identity created by Wyatt Shepard.

He ordered Chinese takeout at a small shop adjacent to the hotel and ate quietly in his room, still trying to mentally process his last premonition that would never come true. He finished his meal, then took the remains to a trash can next to an ice box on the motel complex. Then he made the phone call he had intended to make back at Trond and Savanah's townhome.

It was five in the morning, but he called anyway.

"Hello?" a groggy Steve Gable said into the receiver of his cell phone as he stared at his computer.

"Special Agent Gable?"

"Speaking."

"This is Blake Sergeant."

Chills ran down Gable's spine. He was awake.

"I wasn't honest with you when we last spoke last week," Sergeant continued.

"Blake, you're in a lot of trouble."

"Story of my life."

"Blake, I need you to come in."

"That's not happening. If your guys find me, I will not resist arrest. But I think we both know you've been one step behind all week."

"Blake, that's not a good decision . . ."

"I haven't made a lot of good decisions lately. I'll manage. You're going to get a call that Savanah Martin and Trond Petersen have been murdered."

"Was it you?"

"Yes," Blake said. "I left you something. There's a flash drive and two laptops in the front of the row house along their fence."

"Blake, we know the Russians were part of a terrorist cell."

Blake paused.

"That's why I need you to come in. I need to know what you know. I need to know how you know."

"If you know about the terrorist cell, then the laptops and flash drive will give you enough evidence to begin building a case."

"How did you know?"

"I think we both saw some things on that mountain in Muerto that we will never fully understand."

"How did you know?" Gable asked again.

"Goodbye, Steve."

Gable tried to call him back but the phone went straight to voicemail.

He was set to call again when the phone rag in his hand. It was Hadderly.

"We've got a lead," Hadderly said. "A motel manager in Alexandria just reported that he thinks a guy who looks just like Blake Sergeant checked into his motel. We're on the way now."

***

Blake took a hot shower for what felt like hours. As the water beat against his weary body, he finally broke down, weeping in the bathtub. He was completely overcome by the grief of his family, by the weight of the pain that he had carried for so long. He was overcome by the guilt he had been carrying for all the lives he had ended over the last three years only to find his own best friend was the man he had been looking for all along. He wept because of all the lives he saved. He wept because he had been confronted with a notion that contradicted everything he had believed about everything he was.

His wrongs *did* make a right. It wasn't supposed to work like that. His murders *did* end a cycle of evil. His mind was exhausted. He needed sleep. He thumbed through his bag and spotted the daily devotional book given to him by a pastor in Northern Minnesota.

He turned on the television set and viewed the date, then turned it off again. He opened the book and read it, then read it again. The passage beckoned him to stop carrying the burdens of his life on his back, and give it to God. There were two scriptures referenced in the devotional and he read them both.

The second scripture was from the Book of Proverbs Chapter 19 Verse 21:

The Human mind may devise many plans,
But it is the purpose of the Lord that will be established.

***

Steve Gable and Marcell Hadderly met two uniformed officers at the front entrance of the motel, on the opposite side of where the owner said Blake Sergeant was sleeping.

Gable relayed Blake's message, then reminded Hadderly this was the same man who fired a rocket launcher at a vehicle and brutally murdered several individuals with a knife shortly thereafter.

They were joined by four more cops as well as Detective Bob Hamilton. Sergeant Harris also pulled into the parking lot because Gable thought having a few friendly faces nearby might help their case. The officers huddled and drew up a plan for engagement.

***

"God," Blake said, as he knelt beside his bed, "I know we haven't spoken much. Please forgive me for my sins. I know I don't deserve it, but I am sorry. Please forgive me for loving my greatest sin. I am sorry for what I have become. I don't know whether a harvester is working for you or for the devil. All I know is I'm laying my burdens down before you. I'm asking you to help me. Help me find the way. Help me know what to do. I don't know what to do."

***

Four uniformed cops staged themselves outside the window at the rear of the motel and four more joined Gable, Hadderly, Harris and Hamilton in front. They drew their weapons and crept slowly to the door of Blake's room.

***

Blake continued to pray, asking God over and over for forgiveness and guidance. When he looked up, he saw four black coins sitting on the nightstand near the bible he read from.

He stood, refastened his towel around his waist and examined the coins. He knew who they represented, and holding them in his hand only confirmed it. Nickolay Belov, Jim Peterson, Savanah Martin and Trond Petersen. They were probably all good people at one point in their lives, but somewhere down the line, evil got to them.

The room was silent. In the background, he could hear traffic from the highway, but it was distant.

The silence was broken by the alarm on his cell phone, which was still sitting on the counter in the bathroom. *Wake Up Boo* by The Boo Radleys filled room and the bathroom acoustics pushed the sound out to the motel bedroom. It was the song that Nicole Sergeant tormented Blake with on many mornings during their marriage, and the same song he kept as his alarm in order to torture himself. Blake couldn't remember why he would have set the alarm. No, he was certain he never set the alarm. Nevertheless, the song played on, beckoning him to come to the restroom.

There were footsteps outside his room, but he paid them no mind. He followed the music into the restroom. The mirror was still covered with steam from condensation, but Blake closed the door anyway. He wanted privacy.

He heard someone knocking on his door, but it sounded distant. It sounded like it was from another world.

He set the coins on the sink. He wiped the mirror with his hand and looked at his reflection in the mirror. His eye was still blackened and swollen shut from Griff's rifle. The swelling was grotesque, and he guessed that maybe the motel clerk was watching him closer than he initially imagined.

He stared at himself. He looked himself in the eyes intently. He touched the mirror and left his hand on the glass never losing eye contact with himself.

"Blake Sergeant! Open up!" he heard from a distance. He ignored them.

He continued to stare.

The mirror turned to liquid and his hand sunk into the glass as if he dipped it in a silver pond.

The reflection stared back at him and smiled.

He saw the Harvester in the distance of the reflection. Or was her name Amelia? He saw Nicole and Anni waving to him in the reflection. There was a small boy next to them. He knew they were on the other side of the reflection.

He heard a kick on the motel door and a hinge break.

The silver sea of a mirror came alive and wrapped itself around his arm. It felt like he was being sucked into a pool. Like a current, the silver reflective mirror sucked his whole body in through the reflection leaving only his towel on the damp bathroom floor. The four coins followed him through the glass, splashing as they entered. The mirror became still again as the currents from Blake's entrance subsided.

Gable pulled the bathroom door open and the officers jammed their weapons into an empty room they watched their suspect walk into seconds before.

They cleared the room, then cleared it again. There was a small window in the bathroom that Blake would have never been able to climb through. Had he tried, the two officers waiting outside would have apprehended him.

Gable looked behind the door, helplessly into the empty shower stall. Hamilton stood over Blake Sergeant's clothes, which were folded on his bed, then back up at Gable. They smelled like lighter fluid. There were blood stains on the shirt, ostensibly his from his head wound.

"These clothes match the manager's description of what he was wearing," Hadderly said.

Gable got on his hands and knees and examined the floor, looking for a hidden cellar he knew he wouldn't find. Hamilton joined him in the bathroom and poked at the plaster ceiling.

Wake Up Boo continued to play in the background, blaring from Blake's cell phone, which was still on the bathroom counter. The cops were too stunned to pay the music any mind.

He had vanished into thin air right in front of them. Gable stared at the towel on the bathroom floor then back up at Hadderly and Hamilton. Nobody spoke. They all reached the same conclusion. He had nowhere to go. They all watched him walk into the bathroom wearing nothing but a towel. They had him cornered and he disappeared.

Blake Sergeant watched Gable, Hamilton and a man he didn't know from the other side of the glass. He could have reached out and grabbed one of them if he wanted to. They stood a few feet away from each other and a dimension apart at the same time.

Blake could hear voices behind him. He could hear his future calling. He turned around to face his destiny. The Triggerman became a Harvester.

Made in the
USA
Monee, IL